11649878

ADVANCE PRAISE FOR

"*Sir Callie and the Champions of Helston* is **fierce,** transmuting beloved classic fairy-tale elements with the fiery conviction that every person deserves an authentic expression of self. **Symes-Smith has forged a razor-sharp story of bravery, emotional resilience, deep honor, and adventure!**"

> —Ash Van Otterloo, author of CATTYWAMPUS
> and A TOUCH OF RUCKUS

"This **warm hug of a book** is a love letter to classic fantasy novels and a joyous celebration of found families, finding your place, and making your way in the world on your terms (and with your chosen pronouns). It's **thoughtful, inclusive, and an absolute joy.**"

> —Jamie Pacton, author of THE LIFE AND (MEDIEVAL)
> TIMES OF KIT SWEETLY and LUCKY GIRL

"A groundbreaking, magical story about fighting for who you are, Symes-Smith's debut paves the way for nonbinary characters to shine in their own adventures. **Callie is a character every middle-grade reader deserves to have on their shelves.**"

> —Nicole Melleby, author of HURRICANE SEASON, IN THE
> ROLE OF BRIE HUTCHENS . . . , and HOW TO BECOME
> A PLANET

"A nuanced exploration of identity rarely seen in tales about brave knights and fearsome dragons. Symes-Smith has created a **groundbreaking story with engaging, unforgettable characters,** whose personal journeys will mean the world to so many young readers."

> —A. J. Sass, author of ANA ON THE EDGE and ELLEN
> OUTSIDE THE LINES

"A debut that balances lush prose with all-too-relatable characters. . . . **Sir Callie is the hero I needed while growing up,** and I am so grateful this story exists for kids today."

> —H. E. Edgmon, author of THE WITCH KING

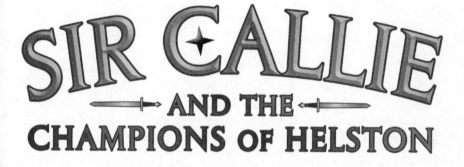

SIR CALLIE

→✦ AND THE ✦←
CHAMPIONS OF HELSTON

✦ **ESME SYMES-SMITH** ✦

LR LABYRINTH ROAD | NEW YORK

Text copyright © 2022 by Esme Symes-Smith
Jacket art copyright © 2022 by Kate Sheridan
Map art copyright © 2022 by Kate Sheridan

All rights reserved. Published in the United States by Labyrinth Road, an imprint of Random House Children's Books, a division of Penguin Random House LLC, New York.

Labyrinth Road and the colophon are trademarks of Penguin Random House LLC.

Visit us on the Web! rhcbooks.com

Educators and librarians, for a variety of teaching tools, visit us at RHTeachersLibrarians.com

Library of Congress Cataloging-in-Publication Data
Name: Symes-Smith, Esme, author.
Title: Sir Callie and the champions of Helston / Esme Symes-Smith.
Description: New York: Labyrinth Road, [2022]. | Series: Sir Callie; 1 | Audience: Ages 8–12. | Summary: Trapped in a rigid hierarchy where girls learn magic and boys train as knights, twelve-year-old nonbinary Callie, who dreams of becoming a knight, and their new friends find themselves embedded in an ancient war, but in order to defeat the threats outside the kingdom, they must first defeat the bigotry within.
Identifiers: LCCN 2022009881 (print) | LCCN 2022009882 (ebook) | ISBN 978-0-593-48577-4 (trade) | ISBN 978-0-593-48578-1 (lib. bdg.) | ISBN 978-0-593-48579-8 (ebook)
Subjects: LCSH: Gender-nonconforming people—Juvenile fiction. | Knights and knighthood—Juvenile fiction. | Father and child—Juvenile fiction. | Magic—Juvenile fiction. | Dragons—Juvenile fiction. | Friendship—Juvenile fiction. | CYAC: Gender identity—Fiction. | Knights and knighthood—Fiction. | Father and child—Fiction. | Magic—Fiction. | Dragons—Fiction. | Friendship—Fiction. | Fantasy. | LCGFT: Fantasy fiction. | Novels.
Classification: LCC PZ7.1.S995 Si 2022 (print) | LCC PZ7.1.S995 (ebook) | DDC [Fic]—dc23

The text of this book is set in 12-point Macklin.
Interior design by Ken Crossland

Printed in the United States of America
10 9 8 7 6 5 4 3 2 1
First Edition

For Christine:
My best friend,
my wife,
my champion

AUTHOR'S NOTE

Dearest Readers—

This is a story about magic and fantasy. It is equally a tale of bigotry and bias, and within these pages you will witness kids fighting the very real battles that kids are forced to fight every day in our world. The enemies Callie and their friends face are not just dragons and witches but queerphobia, child abuse, and the generational trauma that comes from a society determined to suppress the very elements that make us shine the brightest.

Names and gender identity are used as a source of power for our queer kids but also wielded as a weapon against them by those wishing intimate harm. I can promise you light and triumph for our champions, but the paths they must travel are dark and winding, long and complicated. It is my intention to arm you with the best tools to travel alongside them unharmed, but if you are afraid and your own wounds run too deep, then please set aside this book until you are ready. Callie will still be here for you when you are.

Every person and every character's path through the darkness is different, and I hope the stories of these journeys will help you find your own. Know that you are not alone, no matter who tries to make you believe otherwise.

If you need extra help, here are some resources for you:

Trans Lifeline: translifeline.org

Childhelp: childhelphotline.org

The Trevor Project, confidential helpline for LGBTQIA+
    Youth: thetrevorproject.org

You are loved and you are enough, exactly as you are.

—Esme Symes-Smith

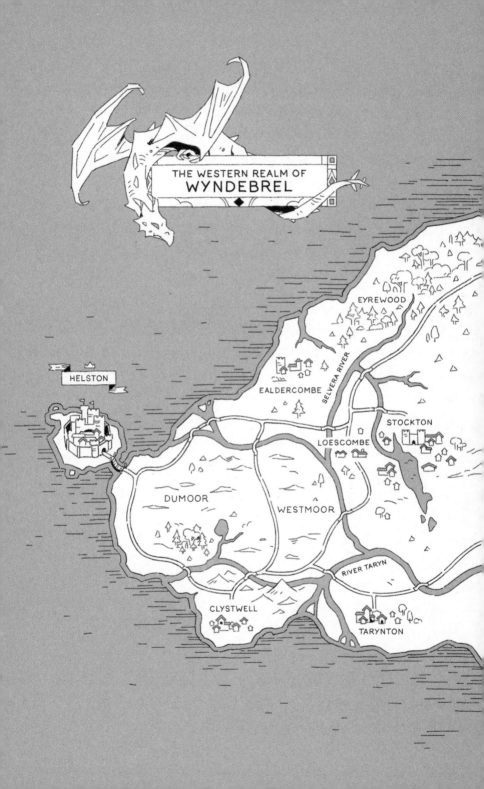

PROLOGUE

Clystwell

*C*alliden.

The name that is allegedly mine doesn't fit me anymore. If it ever did. It's all sharp corners and broken pieces from where Mama tried to jam it into me. It rips me apart from the inside out.

Bundled onto my bedroom's windowsill, I can't hear much of what my parents are talking about—arguing about—downstairs, but the shape of my name and all its accusations seeps right up through the floorboards. A list of transgressions that has grown every day from the moment Papa rode out to Helston to the moment he rode back home.

Not girl enough. Not good enough. Not trying hard enough.

It's been three months of just me and Mama, and while it's never good when Papa's gone, it's never been this bad before.

We're unfixable, she and I. Neither of us is ever going to

change for the other. Not willingly. I'm never going to fit the shape of the daughter she thinks I should be, and she's never going to see me as anything else.

And if it comes to a fight, the grown-ups always win.

I pull my legs up and rest my chin on my knees.

Outside, wind ripples across the river's surface, shattering the moon's reflection. Clystwell, my home, is beautiful. Everyone says so. Tucked in the dip of the valley, surrounded by hills, we are protected. It's a haven. A little piece of paradise.

I want to get out.

I *need* to get out before I give up and give in—losing the battle and myself.

I'm tired, and it scares me. In the darkest moments, I think maybe it would be easier to surrender and just let myself be crushed into the shape of Calliden. Sit still and be quiet. Swap my dreams for Mama's. They're more possible, anyway. It would be nice not to be on the fast road to failure.

Because girls don't get to be knights. Even girls who aren't girls. That's all anyone sees when they look at me, so apparently that's all that matters. It doesn't matter what I am on the inside to anyone but me and Papa, and an ally who's here maybe two weeks out of ten is hardly an ally at all.

Usually Papa's homecoming is the best time ever. It marks a break from Mama's ruthless campaign and reminds me of who I really am and what the world can be, even if it's only temporary. He treats me like a kid, like myself, and we go out riding and fishing, and he shows me how to fight, and doesn't force me into dresses, and doesn't care if my hair is a mess. Usually, waiting for Papa to come home keeps me going all the way through his absence.

It doesn't feel like that this time.

I'm too tired to fight anymore.

I'm too tired to hope that anything will make a difference.

The voices downstairs get louder, and I close my eyes.

"You *need* to tell her!" Mama shouts. "You are ruining her by indulging her. She is out of control, and I am at the end of my patience!"

Papa doesn't shout. He never shouts. I wish he would, just once. I wish he would shout for me and fight for me. He's the king's champion, the best knight in the realm. Legendary. He's faced dragons and led whole armies into victory, but this is a fight even he can't win.

The stairs creak beneath the weight of Papa's boots. He never got the chance to change after he arrived before Mama demanded her conversation.

I squeeze my knees and turn my face toward the window as the lock clicks back. I don't want him to tell me that I need to get along with Mama and compromise with her and that we have to learn to live with each other. I don't want to hear the tiredness in his voice, knowing that I caused it.

I wish I could jump out the window, saddle up my horse, Flo, and ride away as far and as fast as I can.

"Hey, kiddo." Papa slips in and sits on the floor beside the window. He's tall enough that his head's the same height as mine, even from the floor.

"Hey." I don't look at him. I know what he's going to say, and I don't want to hear it.

"It's really not getting better, huh?"

I shake my head.

Papa sighs, and I want to cry.

"Sorry," I mumble. "I dunno—"

I stop when Papa looks at me, all wide-eyed and miserable. His dirty-blond hair is dirty for real from road dust, and there's hair on his chin where usually there's none. That means he's been out in the field.

"Hey," he says, "you have *nothing* to apologize for. Nothing at all."

My lip wobbles. "Doesn't feel like that."

"Yeah. . . . What're we going to do about this?"

I can't work out whether he's really asking or fake asking, and I just shrug, because what is there *to* do? I know what I want, but it hurts to want something knowing you'll never get it. Besides, anything Papa starts now will just fall away once he leaves again. So what's the point?

"Callie?"

My name—my real name—breaks me. No one calls me that. Mama won't let them. It's like my real self leaves with Papa, and I'm left with barely anything until he comes home. My chest tightens so hard I can't breathe. I just want to let go and stop being disappointed and sad.

Papa's arms wrap around me and squeeze. "I'm sorry, kiddo. I'm so sorry. We're gonna fix this. *I'm* gonna fix this."

I snuffle into his tunic. Luckily it's dirty from the journey anyway, so tears and snot won't make that much difference. "How?"

"We're getting out of here. You and me."

"Huh?" I pull back and wipe my face. "We're going to Helston?" Helston—the royal capital—is the setting of all my biggest dreams.

But Papa shakes his head, expression hard. "No. I'm done with Helston. The only important thing is here—you. I'm not going back. It's time we lived our own lives, Callie. On our terms only. What do you say?"

My mouth doesn't move and my words don't work. It feels like a biscuit is being dangled in front of me, and I'm scared to reach out or even want it, certain it'll be snatched away with a cruel laugh.

"Nicholas!" Mama's voice pierces through the door, and we both wince together.

"Up to you," Papa whispers. "Stay or go?"

I look around at my room, at the dresser with the brush that tears at my tangles and the ribbons that don't suit me, at my wardrobe full of clothes made for someone else and the dolls it takes all my imagination to pretend are knights.

This is Calliden's room, Calliden's home.

There is nothing of me here.

"I want to go."

CHAPTER ONE

Eyrewood, Two Years Later

"*Hiyah!*"

I lunge at the offending tree, swinging the too-big sword with both hands. The tree hasn't really done anything to deserve such abuse, but everyone else is asleep, so it's the only dueling partner I'm gonna find at this hour of the morning. Neal's sword is nearly as long as I am tall, and so heavy every blow makes me sweat, but it's the best I can do for the foreseeable future.

It doesn't count as stealing if I return it before Neal's awake. Right?

I sink deep into my favorite dreams, imagining myself in Helston colors—all clean scarlet and gold—striking out at classmates dressed up the same instead of stuck in dirt colors, fencing a tree. Two years and miles away from Clystwell, it feels a little more possible. At least I'm with people who want to help me, who see my potential and let me chase my dreams.

Eyrewood life is about as different from Clystwell as it's possible to be; we live in a clearing in the middle of the thick forest of hazel trees, a mismatched muddle of people who have somehow found each other and made a home. There's Josh, a man the size of a mountain with dark skin and flowers in his long hair. He's the self-appointed cook, and quite frankly it's lucky we're not all dead. Faolan's the youngest apart from me, with a copper complexion warm as the evening sun, and so weedy he looks like a breeze could knock him right over. He doesn't have magic in his fingers, but he's got a way with animals that calms even the most nervous rabbit. Rowena's pale like me and Papa, and just as likely to burn in the sun, and once upon a time everyone thought she was a boy. Don't know how anyone could've got that so wrong, looking at her now, but I guess it's the same way people call me "girl." Then there's Pasco the pirate, who got sick of the sea but longs for real sunshine and decent food, and promises to take me to his homeland one day.

Most important of all is Neal. Sun-blessed, even in the deepest winter, he's the one who found me and Papa wandering homeless after fleeing Clystwell. He's the one who welcomed us in and gave us a home, who can grow flowers in the palm of his hand and fight with a sword just as well as Papa, who tells me every day that I'm more than enough exactly as I am. Who loves me and Papa without condition.

8

"Family are the people who love you," he told me once. "Exactly as you are, regardless of blood and bond."

And home is the place where those people are, even if it's a cluster of tents around a campfire. I wouldn't swap it for anything.

Well, maybe one thing.

I strike a chunk of bark off the tree and stumble back, sweating. I've got great stamina, but Neal's sword takes it right out of me. There's a reason why people learn with practice weapons and gradually grow up into full-sized ones. I don't have that luxury. If I hadn't started with grown-up weapons, I'd never have started at all.

I prop Neal's sword against the abused tree and stand back, wiping sweat from my forehead with a satisfying flourish. It's only early spring, and the air is chilled pretty much anytime before midday, so sweating means I'm doing something right.

I'm about to go at it again when I feel thunder in my feet.

Thunder means horses, and horses mean—

New sun catches on gold the moment before the rider thunders through the trees and into the clearing where our camp's set up.

Gold and scarlet, and a flash of tempered steel.

My pulse spikes in a heady clash of dread and desire.

Helston.

So Papa's retired the same way I'm his squire—in all ways except the ones that actually matter. Even though he hasn't been to court in years and gave up his title of king's champion after the king disappeared, Helston still has the right to call him to duty and take him away from me. It doesn't matter how far we go or how well we hide, Helston can always find us.

By rights I should hate them. They're the reason I was left alone with Mama so much, and they're the gatekeepers locking me out of my dreams. But I want it so bad. I want to wear that uniform, and get all polished up and learn all the rules, and be part of something glorious. I want the same access to the same chances any boy gets, no questions asked.

I want to be a knight.

The enormous black horse pulls up so close, his hot breath whuffling through my hair. He's dressed up just like his master in the bright scarlet and gold of the palace, and he fixes me with the same disinterested eye.

I draw myself up tall and salute just the way Papa taught me, posture perfect. Maybe this is my moment. Maybe the Helston messenger will be so impressed, he'll invite me to ride back with him because obviously my potential is wasted here, and he'll personally make sure that my name gets added to the list of pages, and—

The messenger's lip curls. "I have an urgent message for Sir Nicholas. Please fetch someone who can deliver it directly to him."

The beginning of a very specific and way-too-familiar feeling starts in the bottom of my gut.

I keep my chin up and my demeanor pleasant. "I can take it," I tell the messenger confidently, reaching up for the letter.

It stays in the messenger's hand.

The uncomfortable feeling winds its way up into my throat as his eyes sweep over me, taking me in, disregarding everything that makes me *me*. So much for this being my moment.

"Don't mess with me, *girl*. This is royal correspondence of the highest consequence. To stand in the way of its delivery is nothing less than treason—"

"I'm not a girl—I'm Sir Nick's squire," I say, trying *not* to show how much I want to knock him off his stupid horse with Neal's sword. I'm a rubbish liar, even just with my face. "I can take it to him."

The horse shifts restlessly with a jingle of gold tack, reading his master's mood. I'm not worried. That sword looks like it's never seen a day's use in its life.

"I won't tell you again—"

"Hey." A hand falls onto my rigid shoulder and squeezes. "Everything all right here?" Neal grins easily down at me, but I can read his expression better than anyone's, and he knows what's going on. He salutes cheerily up at the messenger. "I'm Captain Neal—how can I help?"

The messenger turns his contempt onto Neal. "Captain,

is it? You're as much a captain as that girl is a squire. I don't know what kind of farce is being played out here, but I don't have time for it."

Neal tilts his head with a pleasant frown. "Girl? You're talking about this one here? This is Sir Nick's squire. You've misinterpreted. No worries, happens all the time. We'll just take the letter and an apology for Callie and call it quits with no hard feelings, okay?"

Neal might as well have asked for the souls of the messenger's entire extended family from the look we're getting. It's delicious. The uncomfortable knot untwists a little and I fold my arms, waiting for the apology I know I'm not going to get.

Finally, through gritted teeth, the messenger asks, "Where is Sir Nicholas?"

"Sleeping," says Neal. "You were probably anxious, assuming that loud growl was one of the wolves that have a particular taste for horse, but don't worry—just the king's champion, hero of Helston. I can wake him if you want, but I'd rather take on a pack of wolves if I were you."

I bite my lip against a laugh. Papa's the least scary person in the whole world, despite sounding like a bear when he sleeps. Thankfully, the messenger doesn't know that.

"See the response is delivered by your fastest bird." He shoves the letter at Neal and pulls his horse roughly around, kicking it straight into a thundering gallop in the opposite direction.

Once he's out of sight, Neal exhales a tight breath and

squeezes my shoulder. "Well, that was a fun start to the day. You okay, kiddo?" Now that the messenger's gone, the easy act drops away and Neal looks down at me all sorry and concerned. He knows what it's like to be seen as something you're not, no matter how hard you try to appear otherwise. It's not like I'm not used to it. And it's not like that makes it easier.

I shrug and lie. "Doesn't matter. You saw him off. Thanks, Neal."

He ruffles my hair, ruining my ponytail. "Always. Though, as a sign of gratitude, mind if I have my sword back?"

I pass it guiltily back to him, and he cleans off the last remnants of tree guts as we head toward the tent he shares with Papa. Early morning is slipping into reasonable morning, and the first of the camp's company is starting to stir. Josh steps out of his tent and stretches, waving when he sees us.

"Ready for your cooking lesson, Callie?" he calls.

Josh's cooking lessons are more like muddling through and making mistakes together, 'cause we're both *terrible*. And usually I'm totally up for that, but I'm more interested in the fancy envelope with Papa's name on the front.

"How about you fix breakfast and I'll do lunch?" I yell back, and he gives me a double thumbs-up and a toothy grin.

Neal winces. "Between the two of you, I feel there must be some kind of murder conspiracy going on."

"Hey!" I strike out with an elbow. "We've only temporarily incapacitated our victims. No one's *died*."

"Yet."

"Yet," I concede.

"You know . . ." Neal catches me around the shoulders and hustles me to his side. "If you ever did just happen to poison someone, there's a handy-dandy trick that *might* just save them."

I groan. "Neal . . ."

"Magic isn't just sitting around doing nothing. It can be very useful."

"Yeah, I know."

"It could save a life, Callie—"

"I *know*, Neal. Leave me alone." It comes out harsher than I really meant, but I can't help it. There's something about these kinds of conversations that sends me all the way backward to my old life with Mama, and I don't want to feel that way with Neal. "Sorry," I mumble at my feet so I don't have to look at the hurt on his face. "I just don't see why I need it. No other knights have magic."

"Don't you think that's their disadvantage?" Neal asks gently.

My shrug goes right up to my ears. "I'm not a girl. I wasn't supposed to have magic anyway." At least I can say that out loud now, here. At least I've learned how to put those feelings into words after a lifetime of feeling *wrong*. "I just want to be the same as everyone else."

"I know, kiddo." Neal kisses the top of my head. "But you're not. You're you. And, personally, I think that's even better."

I stick my tongue out and he laughs, pulling me along the rest of the way to wake Papa up.

Neal doesn't get it, though. He made the choice to leave and be different. I didn't. I never got the chance to try to be normal.

Being me isn't an advantage.

Papa does *not* do mornings. He's not really a wolf like Neal told the messenger, more like a dog who's slept too long in the sun. Just kind of useless for a long time.

He looks up and smiles wearily at us as we duck into the tent. It's ten times bigger than mine, basically a canvas house. It's not just the living space and bedroom Papa and Neal share, it's where all the important meetings take place, where all the complicated conversations happen. It's filled to bursting with an enormous table, all Papa's weapons he's not willing to risk keeping in the communal armory, and Neal's flowers. It doesn't help that Papa doesn't have a tidy bone in his body. Neal's captain of the camp, but picking up after Papa would be a full-time job if we didn't tag team. Papa might be a legendary hero, but he's also a total disaster.

He raises an eyebrow. "You causing trouble again, kid?"

"Dunno why you'd say that."

I beeline straight for the space on the bench next to Papa and a breakfast he hasn't touched yet. It's just bread and cheese, nothing like the substantial breakfasts Josh fixes, but it's the only thing Papa will consider touching this early. The plate's set in the middle of the huge map spread out like a tablecloth, and I'm super careful not to nudge any of the markers that mean "trouble." We're not any kind of official force, but we keep a keen eye on the goings-on around here, swapping our skills for food and anything else we might need. It suits us well. I get good practice out of it, though it's rarely anything bigger than bandits and packs of wolves looking for a long-needed meal. Not exactly the epic deeds I dream of.

The cheese is hard and the bread is harder, but that's fine. We get new when we finish the old. That's Neal's one big rule. He doesn't yell at me for sneaking in and stealing his sword, but wasting food is a heinous crime. Lucky I'm not picky. I draw the line at coffee, though. That stuff's *nasty*.

"Message from Helston," Neal murmurs, sitting on Papa's other side and sharing the coffee.

I try to focus on the food and counting the markers, and *not* on my dads' faces as they read. I especially try not to think about the last time a letter arrived with that same scarlet seal or the fear on Papa's face the moment before he rode away and disappeared for four weeks and six days. Or how when he came back, he was different. He wouldn't speak to anyone but Neal for a whole week. Not even me. He just held me like what he'd been through was too terrible to put into words, and when he got better, it was as if nothing had happened at all, and I was too scared to ask the question.

I wonder if this'll be like that.

I steal a peek over Papa's elbow. It's not very subtle, but we don't keep secrets from each other. Instead of moving away to keep it private, Papa puts an arm around me and tugs me closer so I can share the letter with him and Neal.

The handwriting is spiky and slanted, like the author scratched the letters into the parchment with a blade.

Sir Nicholas,

Though you have made it clear you want nothing more to do with court life since the loss of His Majesty, King Richard, it is with regret that I must inform you of the declining potential of our young crown prince and make a plea for your assistance.

It has been a difficult two years, as I'm sure you can understand. Prince Will does not come as naturally to leadership or the combat arts, or anything else required of a king, as his brother and father did. As chancellor, I have been careful to pick the best, most capable trainers at our disposal, but all, so far, have failed.

It would be less of an issue—His Highness is twelve years old and far from being of age—however, tensions across the bridge are growing at an alarming rate, and Helston is in

dire need of a ruler. While Prince Will is far
from the ideal candidate, he is, at present, the
only candidate, and I cannot in good conscience
consider displacing him without exhausting
every resource possible.

I consider you our last resource and
Prince Will's best and final chance. His
Majesty's twentieth jubilee tournament is fast
approaching, and the council has decided that
the six weeks leading up to it will give His
Highness ample chance to become proficient
enough to prove in front of the court that he is
capable of filling his role.

Please do not underestimate the gravity of
the situation. A kingdom without a king is dire
enough, but war is approaching whether we are
ready or not, and it is my responsibility to make
sure we are. It is your responsibility too, and I
expect you to do your duty.

Sincerely,
Lord Chancellor Peran
of Helston

"So," says Neal softly. "Peran made chancellor. Good
for him."

Papa gives a low chuckle. "He's worked hard for it. Though

I'm not sure these circumstances are exactly what he imagined. I wouldn't want to be in his shoes right now. That's a lot of responsibility, even for someone like him." He rubs the back of his neck with a sigh. "If he's asking for help, it's serious. I . . . have to go."

"But *six weeks*, Nick. That's a long time to be away, and you did promise that the last time would *be* the last time."

I can feel both their eyes on me, but I'm still staring at the letter.

That's a whole lot of words, but only one matters: *tournament, tournament, tournament, TOURNAMENT!* And I can see myself right there, surrounded by a rainbow of banners and a cheering crowd, victorious. The champion.

"Callie." Papa's hand settles on the top of my head, and I look up to see both my dads looking at me with equal worry. "I promised you I wouldn't leave again, and I meant it. I'm not going to go without your blessing, kiddo, but I need you to understand the importance of what I'm being asked to do. I know six weeks is a long time—"

I grin, then laugh at their confused expressions. "It's fine!"

"It . . . is?"

"Yeah!" I throw my arms out wide, knocking the crumbs of breakfast across the map. "Because I'm going with you!"

CHAPTER TWO

Papa and Neal stare, stunned and silent, and I take full advantage before they can tell me no. I'm so sure about this, I'm going to burst.

I push on, talking a hundred miles a moment. "Look, it makes sense, doesn't it? And you always promised you'd take me to Helston one day, so why not now?"

Papa winces. "I didn't *exactly* mean like this—"

"But this is even better," I insist. "I'm basically your squire anyway, and it's not like you'd even remember to eat without me or Neal. *Plus* it's a chance for me to learn in the proper place, even if I'm a few years late. Double plus it's just six weeks, and then I can fight in the tournament, and when I win, they'll *have* to let me in to train properly. 'Cause the champion gets a prize, right? They get to choose anything at all. So if I win, I can choose a fair chance at my shield." The plan's so perfect, it fills me up, and I don't get why they're still looking at me like that.

I'm about to tip over into disappointment, and I don't know how I'm going to keep from crying, 'cause it's not like I can tell Papa don't go and help this kid just because I don't want to be left on my own.

A broad smile starts to spread across Papa's face, and my heart flips in excitement for the yes, but then Neal says, "I don't think that's a good idea, kiddo," and my heart lands on its face with a crash.

"Why not?"

He tries to swap a look with Papa, like they're supposed to be on the same page with this, but whatever "this" is, Papa's not getting it.

Neal hesitates with a sigh. "Helston's not . . . I know you think it's a magical place where all your dreams will come true, but it's not. Not for everyone. Helston is—"

"Helston is what *you* make of it," says Papa gently, laying a hand on my shoulder and squeezing. "And I think this is the perfect opportunity. You can tag along as my squire, try it out, and if it doesn't suit you, no problem."

"It will! It's my *destiny!*"

Papa laughs. "Then it's set. You and me, kid, we're off to Helston!"

I shriek and throw myself at him, kissing his scruffy cheek over and over and over.

"Thank you thank you *thank you!*"

My head is an explosion of tiny rainbow flags and flashing armor and thundering horses, and me right in the middle, a part of it, unquestionably accepted, even as the lines between Neal's eyes get deeper and deeper.

"You don't need to worry about me," I tell him from Papa's side. "I can beat anyone who gives me trouble."

Neal's mouth twists, then finally breaks into a reluctant smile. "I never doubted it for a second."

"Does that mean I can go?"

"You think I'm going to be the one to stop you from chasing your dreams?"

Neal's blessing, as hesitant as it is, is the final touch that makes everything real.

I'm going. I'm *really* going! I used to spend every hour of every day that Papa was home begging him to take me next time he left for court. "One day," he'd always say, though Mama was quick to remind me it wouldn't be as a knight in training. Girls went to Helston too, to learn how to be ladies, how to sit still and be quiet and make pretty, useless things with their magic. I'm not delicate, no amount of training's ever going to make me delicate, and my magic knows it. What little I have. I wish I didn't have any. As far as I'm concerned, it's the only thing holding me back from my dreams.

Knights don't have magic. Period.

Sure, most people think boys don't have magic, but that's

not true—Neal's proof enough of that, but he's not a knight. Once upon a time he was a page in Helston, but he told me it didn't fit him right and he left.

Knights *don't* have magic.

I'm vaguely aware of Neal murmuring something to Papa, who nods; then Neal disappears into their private sleeping area and returns with a long, slender package wrapped in oilskin and twine.

"We had this made for your thirteenth birthday," says Neal, holding it out to me. Papa stands with his arm around Neal's waist, wearing the biggest grin I've ever seen. "It's early, but a real squire should never be without their own."

My heart thunders as I take it. From the shape and the weight, it *has* to be what I think it is, but what if it isn't?

"Plus," says Papa casually, "it'll mean you don't have to keep stealing Neal's."

I rip the parcel apart.

My name, stamped in copper, glints. *Callie.* The leather scabbard is dark and sleek and new. Made just for me.

I chew my lip, my eyes burning even though it's not hay fever season yet.

Papa smirks. "You gonna draw it or leave it wrapped up?"

"I'll spoil it," I whisper. "It's too nice." I wear dirt-colored clothes even when they're clean, which they never are; my hair hasn't seen a proper brush since we arrived two years ago, even though Papa taught himself how to braid my hair on his warhorse Bayna's tail; and the river I bathe in isn't exactly the cleanest. This sword is brand-shiny-new, and I'm going to ruin it just by looking at it.

"She's going to be your partner for a long time yet," says Neal. "You should meet her properly."

I look up from the scabbard. "She?"

"Her name is Satin."

"Satin . . ." She sings when I draw her, the hilt so smooth it's almost soft. My own hazel eyes stare back at me in her polished steel, unmarred save for her name etched deep into the blade. So clear I can count my freckles. "She's beautiful."

"Sharp as anything too," says Papa. "That's a real blade there, Callie. Only strike when you mean it."

"Yessir." Glittering and deadly. I can't stop staring, can't believe she's really mine. I take up the stance I've been practicing, feet shoulder's width apart, and test Satin's balance. It's perfect. She sits in my hand like she's part of me. Like she's *always* been part of me.

"You keep practicing that magic too, Callie," says Neal in his best impression of a stern captain. "Just because I won't be there to bully you into lessons—"

"Wait, what?" All the good feelings drop away in a heartbeat. "But you're coming too, right?" He has to be! We're a family! Family stays together.

"Someone's got to stay and make sure this lot don't burn the camp to the ground." He says it lightly, but there's more to it than that. I glare at him until he sighs. "I'm sorry, kiddo. I'm sorry I won't be there to watch your greatest triumphs, but me and Helston . . . we don't get on so well."

"'Cause you left? But it's not like you left on bad terms, right? They'd let you back. I'm sure of it!" I'm trying not to beg, but it's hard. We're family, me and Papa and Neal. Leaving him behind is as hard as the thought of Papa riding off without me. I don't want to be without *either* of my dads.

Neal hugs me close, careful to avoid getting stabbed in the gut by Satin. "It's six weeks, and I'll be waiting to hear all about it. Six weeks isn't so long."

"Yeah, it'll whiz by." Papa joins us, and we all end up in a bundle together. Me, my dads, and my sword. The best kind of family.

"Hey, Callie?" says Neal lightly as Papa ducks out of the tent to send a bird down to Helston with our reply. "Will you help me with my garden real quick? Say goodbye to the flowers so they don't miss you too much. That kind of thing could really mess with their growth. Abandonment issues and all that."

"Yeah. Course."

It's not about the flowers, though.

Neal's garden, tucked in a little clearing away from the rest of the camp, is where we go to talk about Big Things. It's where he asked me if it was okay if he and Papa got together. It's where I admitted that I don't just not *feel* like a girl, but I'm not a girl altogether. I told him here in the garden before I told anyone else. Even Papa.

It's half vegetable patch to feed the camp, and half flower garden to feed Neal's love of creating beautiful things. It's wild and wonderful, and the vines bend toward us, brushing our cheeks in welcome. I giggle, carefully extracting myself from a plant made of sticky tendrils and delicate purple blossoms, and settle on the soft ground with my knees pulled up. Neal says that magic is a living, breathing thing, no different to people and animals and plants. Magic needs fresh air and real light to be its best. Most of the time, that sounds like fanciful nonsense, but here it's impossible not to believe it.

Neal sits cross-legged beside me, hands resting in his lap, brow knotted.

"What's up?" I ask.

"I know I'm not your dad—" Neal starts softly, not really looking at me.

"Yeah, you are!" I interrupt, because he is, in all the ways that matter anyway. Neal's been more a parent in two years than Mama was in ten. Even before he and Papa got together, he always made it super clear he loved me and had my back no matter what. I've never had a moment's doubt that Neal is on my side.

He laughs and kisses the top of my head. "And I'm always going to worry about you, Callie. That's part of the deal. What's your dad told you about Helston?"

"Oh, everything." The only good parts about Papa spending months away from home at the palace were all the stories he'd bring back with him, like all the epic ballads and fairy tales but *real*. And *my* dad was the hero of all of them! He was the king's best friend and champion, and the greatest knight in the whole realm. I do *not* think about the way the messenger looked at me, or the fact that Helston took Papa away from me for months at a time. Only the good stuff matters.

"I know you have big dreams," says Neal. "And I don't doubt for a single moment you will accomplish them. I just . . . Your dad's experience was his own, and I don't want you going into this expecting the same." He winces, pushing fingers through oak-brown hair. "I hope that it's as good. I hope so more than anything, but . . ." He plucks a bud from the vine twining curiously around us and holds it carefully in his palm. We both watch it unfold into a beautiful flower, the color of amethysts and more delicate than a butterfly's wing. "I told you that I left, but I didn't tell you why." He takes my hand and tips the flower into it. It's warm with magic.

"They don't like different down in Helston," he continues. "And if you're seen to be something unusual, they will do anything they can to drive you out. I need you to understand that. Your dad, he fit right in—by Helston standards—and he was rewarded for it. People like me and you . . . we don't get that pass."

I nod silently. The living pulse of Neal's flower thuds softly in my palm. Boys don't have magic. That's the rule. Girls have it 'cause they're not supposed to be able to get their strength any other way. A girl without magic is weird. A boy with it is different.

That's not real life, though. This camp and all the people in it are proof that the rule is wrong. Papa might fit in the best in places like Helston, but he's the odd one out here. Mama always made me believe that I'd never fit in anywhere as I am, but being here with Neal and the others proved that wasn't true.

I guess I hoped it wouldn't be true elsewhere too.

I curl my fingers around the flower and hold it against my chest. "So—what? You're saying I shouldn't go?"

"I'm saying that you should go into battle fully armed."

"Isn't that why you gave me Satin?"

Neal chuckles. "Not all battles can be fought with swords, Callie—remember that. And not all enemies want you dead."

I can't imagine any like that. I try to picture the biggest, scariest monster possible, with a million teeth and claws the size of long swords. But even those kinds of beasts are living and breathing and can be struck down with a sharp blade. No big deal.

"I'll be fine." It feels true. Strong as a promise. "And it's only six weeks. If it doesn't go so well, I'll just come home."

But if all goes as planned, I'll be staying there to train properly. Away from Neal and the camp, maybe away from Papa too. My throat closes up and I nudge Neal in the ribs with my elbow. "Wish you were coming."

"I wish that too," Neal admits. "I'd give anything to watch you prove yourself in front of all those—" He stops himself quickly with a cough and gives a sheepish grin. "Don't think I'd be very welcome back, though. Anyway, you think this place would stay standing for one moment if there was no one to keep Josh from burning it to the ground?"

I laugh. "Fair enough."

"Now, go." Neal nudges me up. "If your dad's left to his own devices, you'll have a full armory of swords and no clothes. It's your job to keep that man functioning, Squire Callie."

I pick myself up and salute. "Yes, sir, Captain Neal, sir!"

The amount of stuff we have to do versus the time we have to do it is *intimidating*, given we're heading out first thing tomorrow morning, but Papa and I make a game of it. Anything's fun if you turn it into a competition, even laundry.

Who can pack up their clothes fastest? Me.

Who can squeeze everything into the fewest bags possible? Papa (though I'm pretty sure Neal helped him).

Who can get their fanciest tunic the cleanest? Well, we both lose that one, though technically victory should've been mine seeing as Papa sabotaged me first by elbowing me into the river. It's okay, though—I got him back, and it's going to take more than river water and elbow grease to make our tunics look pretty again. Maybe they'll have soap at the palace.

The whole time, Papa tells me stories about Helston: all the adventures he had with the king back when they were pages together, and all the trouble they got into.

"If Richard had been anyone else, we would've both been turned out over the bridge," says Papa with a laugh. "It's not what you know, kiddo—it's who you know."

I try to return the laugh, but Papa's words mingle with Neal's and make a hole in the bottom of my stomach. *They don't like different in Helston.*

Papa nudges me in the ribs. "Hey, what's that face for? Not having second thoughts, are you? We're committed now."

I grimace, trying to organize my feelings into words. I smooth out my soaking tunic across a wide, flat stone, hoping the sun beating down will be enough to dry it out in time.

Papa lays out his own tunic and sits by me, shoulders bumping. "Did Neal talk to you about Helston?"

I nod. "Don't be mad at him."

"Not mad, definitely not mad. I understand why he felt he had to tell you. But, Callie, listen—Neal's experience was his own, just like mine was mine. And guess what: Yours will be exactly your own, whatever you make of it." He grins. "*I* think you're gonna have the best time of your life."

I smile back, the knot of worry a little looser than before. I don't care about having the best time—I just don't want to have the worst time.

I want *that* to stay far, far behind me.

Papa ruffles my hair, pulling it out of my braid. "You and

me, we're gonna be okay," he says, low and serious. "We've been through our own wars and we've come out the other side. We can do this, Callie. Right?"

He puts out his fist, knuckles all worn and weathered, the ghost of his wedding ring still pale and visible. Proof he and I can get through anything.

I bump my fist to his. "Definitely!"

At night, we celebrate.

The moon is high in a clear sky speckled with stars. I lean against Papa as he braids my hair, coarse fingers deftly weaving Neal's delicate flowers through the way Rowena taught him. I hated anyone touching my hair in Clystwell, tugged and tied into part of a costume that didn't fit. But here, among people who see me, my hair's just part of me whether it's bundled up messy and out of the way or done up fancy.

Josh passes around bowls of a stew Pasco *definitely* helped with, since it's actually edible, and between the warmth of the food and the heat of the fire, I have trouble staying awake.

But I don't want to miss a single second of this moment. I want to commit it all to the very front of my memory and hold on to it through my adventures. Home. Family. Faolan playing a tune that's haunting and happy all at once, and Neal's lilting voice carrying clear over the top of everything else.

The song takes shape in the air, glittering magic mingling with the spitting embers and transforming the ballad into prancing pictures. I can admire magical talent in other people; it's beautiful and elegant, and I wish I could want it for myself. But for me it was never fun or pretty—it was just one more thing for Mama to berate me about. What little I had locked itself away years ago.

I'm too clumsy to make pretty things.

I nestle up to Papa and doze in and out in front of the blazing bonfire, the chatter of men and the clear sound of Neal's singing lulling me to sleep. He weaves his magic through smoke, conjuring pictures in the air as real as anything, and I don't understand how anyone could think magic is a bad thing.

I'm not worried. Like Papa said, my time at Helston will be whatever I make of it, and my goal is clear set in my mind. Helston might not like different, but I don't need Helston to like me. I'll have Papa and Satin, and Neal waiting at home.

Six weeks.

I can handle *anything* for six weeks.

Fire-maned horses paw the sparking air while bright, ghostly knights charge right through the flames, and Neal winks at me as his voice rises. "And there on the sand, between sea and land, is Callie, the champion of Helston."

CHAPTER THREE

The ride is two days long, which means setting out at ridiculous o'clock the next morning after a way-too-late night. It takes all my efforts and Neal's combined to wrangle Papa out of bed and get him standing and into his saddle. It's going to be fun managing on my own for six weeks.

"You make sure he eats breakfast *before* ten," says Neal, securing the last of our bags to our horses. "Else he'll be useless for the rest of the day."

"Yeah, I know."

"And bully him into keeping his quarters clean; otherwise he'll be miserable and it'll be all his own fault."

"I *know*, Neal."

"And you—" He gives me a significant look, and I grimace in expectation of the usual order to "practice your magic." But that's not what I get. Neal tips my chin up. "You stay yourself, okay?"

I open my mouth to say "Obviously," but my throat closes up before I can get the sound out.

"Hey." Neal pulls me into a tight hug. "No tears. This isn't goodbye, just 'see you later.'"

"Six weeks," I mumble into his chest. Forty-two days. One thousand and eight hours . . . "I wish you were coming with us."

"You making my squire cry again?" says Papa, as teasing as he can get while still more than half-asleep. His hair is a bird's-nest disaster, and he wobbles on his feet. If he stays on his horse, it'll be some kind of miracle. "Ready, kiddo?"

No.

"Yup."

"And you remember what I told you?" Neal asks anxiously. "As soon as you get to Loescombe, find the coast. It'll take a day longer, but do *not* go through Dumoor."

"I know, love." Papa kisses the knot of worry between Neal's eyes. "I have ridden to Helston a thousand times."

"Not from here—"

"You worry too much."

"And you don't worry enough. You're not just looking after yourself this time, Nick."

"You talking about this one?" Papa hustles me to his side with a grin. "I thought they were supposed to be looking after *me*!"

But Neal's face stays dead serious. "I'm not joking, and you can't afford to underestimate her. I won't lose you both."

A sharp warning sparks in my head. "What's wrong with Dumoor? And who's 'her'?"

Papa waggles his fingers in my face. "The wicked witch of the moors, who sends her dragons to prey on straying children—"

"*Nick.*"

"Okay, all right." He surrenders with his hands up. "I'll be serious. And we'll be fine. I'll write when we arrive, and I promise we won't die. Does that satisfy you?"

It is quite clear by the look on Neal's face that it doesn't. But he sighs and kisses Papa anyway. "I suppose it has to be enough. I love you. Both of you. Look after each other. And if you need me—"

"We'll be home before you know it," says Papa. "How much trouble do you think we can get into in six weeks?"

Flo follows Bayna by herself, and I keep looking back as long as I can until Neal and the camp and home disappear into the trees and the forest breaks onto the road.

"Just you and me, kid," Papa calls back to me. "Ready for an adventure?"

I settle forward, holding tight to Flo's reins. I've never been readier!

We ride and rest, ride and rest, and the road fades into vast moorland, marked only by huge rocks called tors that look like small mountains growing up out of the grass and speckling the moors with castle-sized shadows. We don't pass a single person, watched only by circling kestrels and curious glittering eyes hidden in the heather.

The setting sun sends dancing shadows across the hills.

If it was me alone, I'd lose my way in a heartbeat, but somehow Papa knows how to keep going south without getting turned around in a circle.

"The landscape remembers," he says when I ask how. "There is memory in every rock, every stubby blade of grass. If you ask for help, you will find it." He points across Bayna's neck at the biggest rock we've passed. As tall as a castle and ten times older. "She's been sitting there for thousands of years. Think of everything she's seen and everything she knows. They work together, the tors, to guide us across the moors."

I wonder if they've ever seen anyone like me before.

"Loescombe is a couple of hours that way," says Papa, pointing south. "It's out of our way, but we'd probably manage to find a bed. It is a clear night, though, so if you're up to camping—"

"We've been camping for two years," I say. "I think we can survive one more night. Though didn't Neal say we should find the coast once we get to Loescombe?"

"Neal worries too much," says Papa, urging Bayna on. "I've been through Dumoor a thousand times. You have to keep your guard up. And I don't know about you, but I just want to get to Helston. We can cut a day out of the journey if we go straight through."

Makes sense to me.

The line splitting the moors is subtle and obvious all in one breath. The grass is the same color, the trees are the same kind, but the air shifts like we just went up a mountain, turning all cold and thin. I pull my cloak tight and try not to regret not insisting we get to Loescombe.

A real bed sounds pretty good right about now.

Finally, Papa stops us in the middle of a circle made of seven standing stones and dismounts.

"We're not sleeping here, are we?"

"Yup," he says, already untying his blanket.

I don't move to join him on the ground. It's not like I'm expecting an inn with a soft bed and warm water, but we could at least take shelter beneath, well, a shelter and not just stop out in the open.

Papa reads my face easy as anything. "Trust me," he says. "This is the safest place to rest. These stones are imbued with ancient magic to protect wanderers from the moor's night-dangers. Nothing can get us in here."

"I'm not scared," I say immediately. I've faced my fair share of beasts and fought more battles than most grown-ups. I'd still rather take my chances and sleep somewhere protected from the weather with Satin at my side than linger in the very place Neal specifically warned us away from.

But Papa's as immovable as the stones. "If anything

happens to you before we even arrive at Helston, Neal will track me down and murder me," he says flatly. "We'll be fine."

I dismount with a grumble.

Mist rolls in and settles around us like a shroud. We huddle together beneath our cloaks, hunching over a fire that feels nothing short of a miracle. At least we have food and the promise of a warm bed tomorrow. The dream of it's almost enough to let me forget that we're out in the open surrounded by who-knows-what.

Doesn't help that the wind sounds like someone crying in the distance.

Papa glances at my pale face and chuckles as he passes me a cup of sort-of-warm soup. "Told you there was a witch who steals wayward kids."

I glare at him. "No there isn't."

"Yeah, there is. Dead serious. She collects the lost souls of those who've been cast away from Helston and turned out onto the moors. The traitors, the treasonous." He nudges me with his shoulder, smirking. "The bad kids who don't eat their vegetables. The worst of the worst."

I squirm. "I'm not the one who won't eat vegetables. You should be more worried than me. How'd you get away with it?"

Papa shrugs innocently, sipping soup. "Charm and wit. Helped that I was best friends with the future king."

I try to picture myself like that, charming and witty, and running around with royalty. It's a smudgy picture. "D'you know what he's like, the prince you're going to go teach? Is he like Prince Jowan?" My memory of the older prince gets fuzzier and fuzzier, but I remember the warmth of his laugh and feeling *safe* as myself for the first time at Clystwell the few times he visited as Papa's squire.

He sparred with me like I was just another boy, teaching me exactly the same, not going easy on me because he assumed I was weaker.

It was Prince Jowan who really made me believe there could be a place for someone like me at Helston. I hope his brother's like that.

But Papa says, almost apologetically, "They are as unalike as brothers can be. Jowan was born to be a hero, and Will, he's different."

My skin prickles. *They don't like different....* "How so?"

Papa hesitates like he doesn't want to tell me. "He's a . . . quiet kid."

"Is that bad?" It's not usually "quiet" that makes grownups unhappy. Usually they want kids to be quiet, to sit still and be good. I don't get why "quiet" would be a problem.

"Not bad," says Papa. "Just complicated." He sets his soup down with a sigh that sounds like it hurts. "I should've gone sooner," he mutters. "I should've been there to help him."

"Why?" I mumble around the lip of my bowl. "Not your problem."

"Doesn't work like that, kid. I didn't just fail my duty as a knight; I failed as a friend. And that's inexcusable."

I swallow a huff. I don't like the idea of my dad failing in anything. I especially don't like that Papa's blaming himself for stuff that's not even his fault. He didn't kill Jowan, and he didn't make the king disappear.

"Callie, do you remember when I had to leave last year?"

"Of course I do."

"Well, they summoned me because the king had gone missing and there was no one else with any chance of finding him."

I sit up. "What do you mean, gone missing?"

"I mean exactly that," says Papa. "He took Jowan's death very hard. Everyone did, but Richard . . . he couldn't cope. One day he just walked out of Helston and disappeared. They sent me to look for him, believing I knew him best and would have the best hope of bringing him home."

"But you couldn't?"

"But I couldn't," says Papa softly. "And because I failed, Helston lost a king and a boy lost his father. I need to put things right best I can."

"D'you think you'll be able to help him?" I ask.

"I hope so. I have six weeks to make a king out of him—that's enough time, right?"

"I believe in you."

Papa laughs. "Then it must be true."

Bundled up in as many layers as possible, we lie down beneath the open sky, stars spotting the night. I'm still watching them long after Papa starts snoring. It'd seemed pointless to pack a tent just for one night, but imagine being lost out here for days. Weeks even. A wandering soul. Is that really what they do to people they don't like at Helston?

Is that what happened to the king?

I shiver and curl up tighter to Papa. The thought of being sent away from your home and everyone you loved is even worse than the thought of being left behind. If a witch or a dragon came up to me, I reckon I'd go with them.

I dream of Clystwell. I'm running, away from my bedroom and my home, leaping over the river and the fence. Except then I get turned around and I'm back at the front door. I try again, faster this time, and I end up in my bedroom, in front of my mirror, staring at myself.

I don't look like me.

Mama's hands curl over my shoulders, and she leans down to murmur one word in my ear: *Calliden.*

I try to open my mouth, to tell her like I've told her a million times before, *That's not my name.*

And like a million times before, she doesn't hear me.

Sharp fingers tangle in my hair, tugging it into order, tying it too tight.

You cannot escape yourself. No matter where you go or

who you pretend to be. Her lips are ice-cold on my cheek. *You will always be my daughter.*

The noise of my own snarl jars me awake. I'm sweating and cold, and my head hurts so bad I can't stand it. I haven't dreamed of Clystwell since we set up life in Eyrewood, since I found a new definition of "home."

Papa's snoring is as loud and deep as a storm, not even close to being disturbed by my nightmare. There's no point trying to go back to sleep until I'm properly calm again, and I don't want to be completely exhausted when we ride into the capital tomorrow. I grab Satin, light a flame in my palm, and go for a walk.

I don't go far. Apart from anything else, my magic is barely good enough to keep the flame lit, and the light hardly reaches a couple of feet in front of me. I do *not* want to get lost out here. I'm not about to let myself become one of those wandering souls.

It was just a dream, I tell myself over and over. Just a dream. No one's called me Calliden in years, and just like in Eyrewood, everyone's going to know me as Callie in Helston. Callie the squire. Callie the not-a-girl. Maybe I should've cut my hair off before we left. I've thought about it a bunch of times just to make it easier for people to not make the mistake of calling me a girl. But I like my hair, and I like it long. Anyway, plenty of boys have long hair. It shouldn't make a difference.

A lot of things shouldn't make a difference that do, a

voice whispers in the back of my mind. Except it's not *my* voice. Not *my* thought. It's like someone's snuck into my ear and taken a seat in my skull. I thump the side of my head, hoping it'll dislodge whatever it is.

It doesn't matter how you dress and act, the voice continues, unfazed. *People see what they want to see. And no one in Helston will ever see you as anything but a girl.*

"You don't know that," I growl, even though I have no idea who or what I'm talking to. Whatever this voice is, they might as well be speaking from deep inside my darkest thoughts. "And if you think I'm gonna get scared away that easily—"

Foolish child, the voice murmurs almost fondly. It circles me, and I twist to follow it with my inadequate flame. *They will eat you alive and spit you out. Go home.*

Now I know for sure it's not me. I dig my heels into the soft ground and brace hard, one hand on the sword at my side, and command the darkness, "Show yourself."

The chuckle is soft and insidious. *I do not wish to scare you.*

"Only a coward hides in the darkness, and I'm not afraid of cowards."

As you wish.

The air shifts as though beneath the beat of wings, and the ground shudders, nearly knocking me over.

I'm not afraid. If I tell myself enough, it'll become true. I'm not afraid!

I don't believe you, the voice sings, and my flame snuffs out.

The darkness lasts only a moment, though, and when it breaks, I wish it hadn't.

My throat locks up tight.

I've never seen a dragon outside my imagination before, and the ones in Papa's stories . . . they're not like this.

Dancing flames circle the curling horns on their head, like some kind of halo. Their teeth are the size of Papa's broadsword and twice as sharp, and their eyes are a sun-bright yellow both painful to look at and impossible to turn away from.

The dragon grins.

You don't know much for someone so certain, they muse with a cocked head.

"I know enough," I try to retort, though my voice is little more than a croak. "I know that nothing you say will sway me. I'm going to Helston. And I don't know why you care enough to try to stop me. Who are you, anyway? The witch of the moors?"

The dragon's smile stretches wide, and when they speak, their voice doesn't come out of their mouth. *I'm flattered you think so. No, but I am a friend. Of hers and yours, even if you do not yet know it. Would you like to meet her, little knight? There is a place for you with us that there will never be in Helston.*

I open my mouth to tell them no way, but the words catch in the back of my throat. Suddenly I can't think as straight as I could, my certain path turning crooked with a doubt I'm not used to.

That's right, says the dragon. *Let's get you out of the darkness, shall we?*

One hooked claw snags in my belt, tugging me forward two stumbling steps. And it's enough to snap me back to myself.

"Get off me!" I draw Satin and swing with a bellow. *"Papa!"* My blade hits air.

There is no dragon. No claw reeling me in, no yellow eyes twisting my head. Just me.

And a low growl that splits into ten.

I've dealt with creatures a million times before, with others *and* on my own. They're rampant up near Eyrewood, especially in the colder months when the only way to find a good meal is by raiding the farms. Even village kids get trained on how to beat back wolves. This is basic stuff.

A growl turns into a snarl, and claws rip into my arm before I can even see anything. I grit my teeth against a yelp. It burns like fire, but I've had worse. They're hungry, Neal says. That's all. And hunger makes people do desperate things. Even creatures.

Green eyes flash in the darkness, and we circle each other. Satin stays steady in my hands despite the blood oozing warm down my arm.

This isn't the way it usually goes. They're not usually assessing like this creature, like it's trying to take a measure of me and decide something. I don't like *anyone* looking at me like that.

It's my turn to snarl, and I lunge, plunging Satin deep into the beast's soft body. Doesn't matter how sharp something's teeth are—flesh and bone are all the same.

The creature whines, high-pitched and ear-achingly loud, and the sound hurts worse than my injury. I struggle to focus, to keep my senses in check and my guard up, because that wasn't a mortal wound, and a hurt creature is a dangerous creature, and this fight is not over.

"Callie!"

I wheel to see Papa sprinting toward me, his own sword raised and ready, and relief comes in a flood. There's no way we can lose together.

But he doesn't make it the whole way before another beast flies out of the darkness with a snarling shriek, and Papa goes barreling over.

Fear and fury collide in my blood, and I throw myself fully into the fight, Satin swinging, hacking at fur and feathers; standing over Papa as he staggers back to his feet.

By the time he's up, we're surrounded. Not just the two creatures who attacked us already, but four, five, *six*, pairs of eyes and six deep growls advancing painfully slowly.

"You all right, kid?" Papa whispers, warm at my side.

"Yeah," I whisper back. "I think so. You?"

"I'm okay." He holds on to me tightly, eyes darting and

ready for the next attack. "Let's survive this, okay? Else Neal'll have my head."

Neal being cross feels very insignificant right now, especially when the beasts strike all together in a barrage of teeth and claws clashing against our steel.

I don't even know what I'm swinging at, only that I'm not going to stop until I'm dead or they're dead, and hopefully it's the latter.

But the weird thing is they don't even seem to be going for me. Not properly, anyway. Not like they're targeting Papa.

A huge wolflike thing circles me with bared teeth and familiar yellow eyes, its growl as deep as thunder and twice as dangerous.

"Prove yourself, little knight," says the dragon through the wolf's mouth.

"Gladly!" But Satin is heavy in my hands. Too heavy. Her point starts to drop. The wolf smiles.

"Callie!" Papa's yell breaks through whatever spell has fallen, and I swerve sideways as he lunges between us.

The wolf doesn't stand a chance against Papa's sword. Its snarl turns to a howl, which fades to a whimper, which dies into silence as the others flee into the night.

All my energy rushes out of me in a wave, and Papa catches me. I let him hold me up.

"Did we . . . did we kill it?" I ask. "Did we kill the dragon?"

"Dragon?" The fear in Papa's voice is contagious, and the look on his face is even worse when he turns me by the shoulders. "Callie, what dragon?"

For the worst moment, I doubt myself. Maybe I imagined it. Maybe it was some weird magical fever dream. But no. That dragon was as real as I am.

"They were here," I tell Papa, forcing my voice to stay strong. "Before the wolves. I think they brought the wolves. They talked to me."

Papa's fingers pinch through the sturdy leather of my tunic. "And said what?"

"They said . . ." My mouth's dry as dust, and no amount of swallowing helps. "They said there's a place for me here that there'll never be in Helston."

Papa hisses a curse and lets go of my shoulders. "Dragons lie, Callie. That's the first lesson you need to learn. They're the shepherds of the moors. They'll say anything to draw you in. Got it?"

I make myself nod and I try to believe him. Except the dragon's words were too much like Neal's to completely throw aside.

"But we killed it, right?" I ask, nodding at the fallen wolf. "It changed into that beast and we . . ." But my voice tapers off when Papa shakes his head grimly.

"Slaying a dragon is not so easy, kiddo. They are the trickiest beings in this world, made up of shadows and illusions. This poor thing"—he nudges the wolf with his boot, sending

the great head lolling back, its glassy eye staring into mine—
"this was a regular wolf once. You see, Callie? This is what
happens when a dragon catches you. It twists you up and
turns you into a weapon. Come, look."

He crouches down, fingers searching the pelt, and parts
the thick gray hair.

"What is it?" I whisper.

"Look closer."

I try, kneeling next to him and searching with my fingers
when my eyes refuse to cooperate.

"D'you feel it?" Papa asks.

"Yeah . . ." It's raised, the way big scratches are. But it's not
just one welt—it's a shape, etched deep into the skin.

"That's the Witch's Kiss, Callie." Papa's voice is low and
deadly serious. "Learn it. Memorize it."

"What is it?"

"It's the mark given to all who serve the witch of the
moors. This is how she controls her servants."

"Who is she?" I ask, the dragon's words still ringing loud
in my head.

But Papa shakes his head and rises. "Not here, kiddo.
You've already been targeted. We need to get to Helston
before they try again. I'm not letting them put that mark
on you."

I shiver. Neither am I.

We ride for hours, and it's excruciating to have to take it steady when it feels like there are eyes on us in every shadow. But exhausting our horses will only make the journey last longer, and it's not worth it. No matter the itchy feeling on the back of my neck.

Papa's stayed on edge too; he's switched from my easygoing disaster-dad into Sir Nicholas, the king's champion and hero of Helston—dead serious and on high alert, with one hand never leaving his sword. I remember watching for that difference when I was little, because it meant he was about to leave. It was weird, and kind of scary, like he was a totally different person. I guess he had to be, to command armies and train troops. I guess that's the one they're expecting to train this prince.

I've hardly seen this one since we left Clystwell, though. Even when Papa's teaching, whether it's kids or grown-ups, he's easygoing and gentle, just like with me. I don't think this side of him is comfortable anymore.

Only when the barren countryside breaks onto a high coastline do his shoulders relax as his hand leaves his sword, and I can breathe easier too. I'm 99 percent sure it's just wishful thinking, but it feels like this place has never been touched by dragons or cursed wolves.

The fresh, salty sea air *tastes* so good. I don't remember the last time I saw the ocean.

Boats bob lazily in the water as fishermen cast their glittering nets. Shrieking kids splash across the shore while their mothers shuck clams and mussels and oysters into buckets, tossing aside the pearly shells. Tiny brightly painted houses are nestled in the cliffs and hills above us, perched stubbornly on the edge of the land, like there's nothing in the world that could topple them. The only creatures out here are flocks of opportunistic seagulls and clouds of starlings making waves in the sky.

"There it is!" Papa calls back above the salt-filled breeze. "We made it, Callie!"

I shield my eyes and squint into the sun, made brighter by the sea. Through a nest of hills, on the line of the horizon, there's the faintest point of the tallest tower, like a church's spire.

"That's the palace?"

"That's the palace," says Papa with a grin, like the fight last night never happened. "That's Helston."

The closer we get, the more jittery my nerves and the worse I sweat. I'm pretty sure by the time we actually arrive, I'm not going to be much more than a puddle of salt water. I think it's excitement? But also bone-tiredness and nerves and a whole bunch of other stuff I don't have names for.

At least whatever awaits us in Helston won't have sharp teeth and yellow eyes.

Hopefully.

We pick our way along the cliff, halfway between moors and sea. I can't take my eyes off the water, the ripples nearly hypnotizing me out of the saddle. I want to climb down the cliff and dive in right now, digging my toes deep into damp sand and ducking my head beneath the surf.

The horizon is definitely a little bit cursed, like the farther we ride, the farther away it stays, until suddenly we're there on top of it, staring at Helston from the opposite cliff, with a huge crack of churning sea separating us.

Papa jumps off Bayna and leads her by the reins down a narrow path made of sand and gravel.

I don't like what's waiting for me when we stop.

"Best defenses in the country," says Papa proudly.

"Yeah, 'cause no one's gonna want to cross that."

It's a bridge, though "bridge" is a very generous term for something that's basically a bunch of sticks set across the ravine. It's narrow as the path and ten times more rickety, and there's no *chance*—

"Only way in, kiddo, unless you want to trek back to camp."

It's tempting. I'd almost rather take my chances with the beasts and the witch than with a bridge that looks like it hasn't been maintained for as long as the castle's been standing.

The bridge from the mainland to Helston is barely the width of a reasonably sized horse and almost certainly not strong enough to hold one, let alone two, plus our stuff.

I glare at Papa. "You're joking," I tell him flatly. "It's not funny."

"Come on—where's your sense of adventure?"

52

"On solid ground."

"It's solid. It's safe."

"I thought we didn't lie to each other?"

Papa rolls his eyes and starts off across the bridge. It creaks, sounding just like a taunting cackle. And it's not like I don't trust him or like I'm scared of heights or the sea or anything, but the whole mixture of it all just makes me sick. Everything is loud, from the roar of the sea mocking us below to the snap of royal flags flying high on either end of the bridge. So loud I can't even think beyond the steady beat of *I don't wanna I don't wanna I really really* really *don't wanna*. . . .

And then something zips through my whole body and I freeze with a squeak, squeezing my eyes tight shut and waiting to hit frozen sea.

"Callie, come on."

"What was that?"

"*Halt!*" a sharp voice barks, accompanied by running footsteps and, when I finally crack my eyes open, there are half a dozen arrows pointed right at me from the Helston side of the bridge.

Well, that's a nice welcome, especially after nearly being eaten alive. I feel like potentially being shot and eaten should've been included among Neal's warnings!

"Stop! That's my kid! What're you *doing*?"

The man in charge, dressed in the rich regalia of the King's Guard, bows to Papa. "Forgive us, Sir Nicholas. This is standard protocol for strangers."

Papa does *not* forgive. "They are *my* kid, Captain Adan, and *I* am the king's champion. We are no strangers. And I do not recall that threatening the lives of *children* was ever part of Queen Ewella's defense. Who gave these orders?"

Captain Adan looks uneasily at his men, then makes a gesture and they lower their bows. "With respect, Sir Nicholas, it's been a long while since you were at court. Things have changed, and defenses have been tightened by order of Lord Chancellor Peran on Her Majesty's behalf—"

"You think a *kid* poses any kind of a threat?"

"It isn't personal, Nick," says Adan softly. "We're not taking any chances these days. Please, let us do our job."

"Fine. But raise your arrows to my kid again and it won't be newcomers you need to worry about."

The captain grimaces, then turns to me and beckons me forward. I don't know if I want to make the rest of the journey if this is the way it's going to be. But Papa's on one side of the bridge and there're beasts on the other, so five guesses which one I pick.

"State your business here in Helston," Captain Adan orders as I reluctantly dismount to allow a soldier to pat Flo down.

"I'm . . . Sir Nick's squire." I hate how unsure of myself I sound when yesterday I was 100 percent certain of who I am and what I want.

The captain's eyebrow twitches, and I try hard not to imagine punching him in the face.

54

Papa steps forward. "Callie's my kid and will be acting as my squire while we're here."

"Mm-*hmm*. And how old is she?"

"*They*," says Papa pointedly, "are twelve, and more proficient than most squires about to be knighted. Are we done? If not, I'm sure Her Majesty will be interested in knowing the details of what's holding us up, given I know for a fact that those wards are a direct line to her and she knows we're here."

"Nick, I'm not trying to make trouble for you—"

"Then let us pass," Papa says firmly. "We've had a cursed trip and just want to get in and settled. Please let the chancellor know we're on our way."

Papa mounts back up without waiting for confirmation, and I follow suit, thankful to be back on Flo.

Adan looks doubtfully between us, and I make myself look steadily back and show I'm not afraid. I'm *not*. I'm not sure how I feel. Then he waves us on and I can breathe again.

"I'm sorry," Papa tells me as we plod on, following the path around the hill. "This is not what Helston is supposed to be. I've never seen anything like this. I don't know what they're thinking. We'll be having words, don't worry."

But from everything Neal told me, this is exactly what Helston is. Disappointment is lead in my stomach.

As soon as we round the bend, though, it's a whole different world. Papa's Helston, not Neal's. There're no beasts, no soldiers, no suspicious glances, just flags and celebration. Like this is what it was all protecting. It's jarring, like jumping from a cold river into a hot bath. For every smile, I think of the arrows being pointed at me. For every wave in our direction, I picture the soldiers' cold glares. I feel like a hero and an enemy all in one breath.

And I have no idea what people see when they look at me.

I lean low and run my fingers through Flo's mane.

I'm not scared.

Helston is tiny—I'd always imagined it huge, the center of the world, but it's just a little town set on its own hill in the middle of the sea. Its one street winds up between houses and shops and tiny businesses.

It's small but packed tight; a whole city crammed into a village. Everything is right here: workshops with salt-worn swinging signs, an already-crowded tavern with music coming from the open door, and a marketplace with stalls lining the streets, selling everything from bread to clothes to tools.

No one would ever need to leave.

I stare, trying to absorb every inch, every moment, and more people than I've ever seen in one place. They all stare back. Papa's relaxed, unbothered by the attention. I force my own back straighter, keeping my chin up and my face (hopefully) smooth of nerves. I have as much right to be here as anyone else.

I belong. *I belong.*

CHAPTER FOUR

The little town flows seamlessly into the palace grounds, like the huge castle is just another house, except this one is made out of shining silver stone and every window is rainbow-paned. It's as big as the rest of the town put together, not even including the sprawling outbuildings.

I follow Papa in a circle around a tall fountain spraying sun-speckled water, and finally we stop in front of a pair of enormous wooden doors at the top of a flight of granite steps. A family of four—man, woman, and two kids—stands at the top, waiting for us.

Some families are a mismatched muddle of people, others are a uniform set. This one is very much the latter. Everything about them is careful and considered, from the cut of the woman's dress to the placement of the pale blue ribbon in the girl's dark hair. Papa and I are pale in a pink sort of way, a *warm* sort of way. This family is white like a chilled winter's morning.

The boy wears Helston colors—scarlet and gold—and his tunic looks brand-new, free of creases or dirt, with a bright pin that marks him an official page: two snarling dogs rearing up on either side of a tower topped with a crown. Jealousy pricks like a volley of arrows, knowing what I would do for a chance to wear that pin and that he gets to just by virtue of being a boy.

But it's the man who commands the atmosphere, and beneath his bottomless blue eyes, I squirm.

I have never felt so out of place, and that's saying something.

The lady descends as Papa dismounts. "Welcome home, Nicholas. You have been missed."

Papa bows and kisses the offered hand. "Anita, it's been too long."

"And whose fault is that?" The man joins his wife, and the kids—a boy and girl of identical height and with identical features—follow behind like shadows. "I'm afraid you will find Helston changed from the last time you were here."

"Yeah, about that." Papa's trying to keep things light, but I can hear the annoyance sharp in his voice. "What're those new protocols about, Peran? Your men nearly had my kid's eye out. Bit extreme, don't you think?"

I focus on dismounting as all their eyes fix on me with cool interest, and I can't shake the worry about what they see me as. It feels like I left all my certainty and stubborn-ness with Neal. I wish I could go back and get them.

Lord Chancellor Peran flashes a smile that looks like he practiced it in front of the mirror this morning and still didn't have time to get it right. He is the human version of his handwriting—all sharp and fastidious, from the lack of crumples in his burgundy velvet tunic to the neat crop of his dark hair and beard to the too-bright blue eyes that dig into my skull and see into my mind.

"Helston is in a fragile position," he says smoothly. "The wards are designed to detect and alert us to potential magi-cal attacks. I'm sure you'll agree that we cannot afford to be anything less than cautious in that regard."

I snort, halfway through dismounting.

"Does something amuse you, my lady?"

It takes a long second before I realize that was addressed to me. Great. So I guess it doesn't matter how I present my-self. I guess the dragon was right.

I take a deep breath and make myself face the chancellor. One eyebrow has twitched up, and his mouth is set in a thin, disapproving line.

He already hates me.

Double great.

I shrug. "It's just pretty funny that you think my magic could be dangerous when I can hardly cast a flame."

"Don't worry, child," says Lady Anita, missing the point completely. "Here you will learn the control and discipline necessary to harness your innate powers and use them appropriately."

"Nah, I'm good, thanks—"

But it's like I don't exist at all.

Lady Anita gestures back, and the girl steps forward, her features as sharp as her father's, her expression as bland as her brother's. "My daughter, Elowen, will guide you. You are equal in age, so I'm sure you have a lot in common," she lies with a perfectly straight face. "She will show you to your room and make certain you have everything you need. Then, when you are ready, she will introduce you to Her Majesty and the Queen's Daughters."

"How many kids does the queen have?"

Lady Anita laughs, and I squirm, feeling all too much like there's a joke being made at my expense that I don't get.

"The Queen's Daughters are the girls of Helston," she explains so gently that it's impossible not to feel patronized. "Beneath Her Majesty's tutelage, they learn everything needed to be a lady of the court, such as etiquette and magic, and—"

I try to control my grimace. I do a bad job.

"That sounds great, and thanks, but I'm good."

"Lady Calliden," says Lord Peran, "no one is suggesting you are not good—"

That name. That name in that voice, all clipped with frustration, punches something deep inside me. My fists ball.

"My name is Callie—"

"All right, kiddo." Papa puts his arm around me and

squeezes my shoulder until my anger loosens enough for me to control it. To Lord Peran and Lady Anita, he says, "Thank you, truly, for the hospitality, but we've got things worked out already. Callie will be serving me as my squire while we're here, and we'll be staying together."

Lord Peran chuckles. "No, I don't think so."

Papa's grip on my shoulder hardens. "Excuse me?"

"You can understand, surely, Nicholas, why that would be inappropriate." There's something in the chancellor's voice, in his sleek enunciation edged with the subtlest bite, that catches me in the throat, like he's daring Papa to challenge him. "A girl's place is with *girls*."

"I'm not a girl—"

"Don't be ridiculous," he snaps, and I freeze up tight.

Behind him, Elowen and her brother exchange glances.

I hate that they're here, watching this. Watching me. Making their own wrong assessment. I don't want to be seen, not by anyone. Not like this.

"Forgive me," Lord Peran murmurs with a slight bow. "Pressure is mounting and time is not on our side. Nicholas, I need to brief you before your introduction to His Highness. My son will attend to the horses, and Elowen will ensure that your daughter is well taken care of." He puts out a guiding arm. "Shall we?"

It is not a question so much as a command, but Papa still falters.

"Look, Peran, I think there's been a miscommunication—"

"There has been *no* communication, Nicholas," Lord Peran says sharply. "That is the issue. You are here to do your duty to the Crown. Everything else can and *will* wait."

I hold my breath, waiting for Papa to argue that that's not how it works, to fight for me.

But he deflates and nods, and my heart hits the bottom of my stomach.

Satin is a comforting weight on my hip as I feel myself losing my grounding. She is confirmation of who I am and what I am here to accomplish. I raise my chin and glare at Lord Peran.

"My name is Callie, and I'm not a girl. I am here as Papa's squire, and I want to train as a knight."

Lady Anita covers a smile with a hand. I'm pretty certain it's not in my favor.

Lord Peran doesn't acknowledge me, just snaps his fingers—"Edwyn"—bringing the boy forward to take Flo's reins.

Elowen moves too and takes my hand. Hers is soft, her fingers delicate and free of calluses. And I bet anything she's noticing all the differences on mine too. My face *burns*, even when the only thing she says is "I picked the best room for you. Come with me."

I start to shake my head. I don't want to go with her, and I don't want to see it. I'm not supposed to be there, mixed in with all the girls and their pretty, delicate things. One look at me should be enough to prove that.

But Papa gives me a little nudge. "Go with her, Callie."

I wheel on him. "No! I want to stay with *you*! You said—"

"*Callie.*" This time Papa's voice is stern enough to make me stop. That means it's serious. Edwyn takes advantage and grabs the reins out of my hands, and I'm too heartsick to fight.

"And the sword, Lady Calliden," says Lord Peran.

My hand goes automatically to Satin's smooth hilt. "She stays with me."

Lady Anita smiles down at me. "The Queen's Quarters is the most protected in the palace. You have no need to defend yourself while you are here. Do not fear."

"I'm not afraid." But that's not true. Every muscle in my body is bunched, coiled. There is an instinctive warning in every thud of my heart, beating hard through my blood as my fingers find the buckle at my waist.

"I'll take her," Papa tells me gently. "Don't worry—you know I'll look after her."

I've had her just a few days, but the loss of her weight makes me feel like I'm a leaf on the water, a feather in the air—cast off and floating away. Untethered. Even with Papa—the person I trust most in the world—she looks wrong in his hands. As small and useless as a kid's toy.

Edwyn leads Bayna and Flo away. Lord Peran takes my dad away. My sword goes with them.

I don't even have my name.

"Come," says Elowen. "Let me show you around. You'll feel at home in no time."

That's what I'm afraid of.

CHAPTER FIVE

The palace is like a city, somehow feeling bigger than the town itself, though not like any of the cities *I* know, filled with sweat and dirt and broken things. The only thing sweaty and dirty and imperfect here is me. I hate it. I should be outside with Papa, or brushing Flo down at the stables. I might not be exactly like the other pages, but I'd fit in way better out there than in here.

Inside, I stick out as if I had wings and a horn on my head, and the deeper into the palace Elowen leads me, the more of an awkward potato I become.

Elowen navigates with the practiced expertise of a sea captain, dipping us left and right, sweeping through narrow stone corridors and wide wooden halls and more doors than I could ever hope to keep track of. Her best trick is weaving us deftly through the clamor of *people*, easy as if we were ghosts. If it was me on my own, I'd be bumping into most of them and probably breaking something expensive.

There's a lot of expensive to break. Which I guess makes sense for a royal palace. The walls are covered in tapestries and paintings, and ornate vase-looking things perch on plinths just asking to be knocked over. Even the floors are too pretty to step on, every tile gleaming like it's new.

Along the way, my guide gives me a history lesson that sounds like she's given it word for word a hundred times, and I can't make myself care enough to listen. I doubt she's particularly thrilled to be stuck with me either, and it's clearly out of duty rather than desire. She's obviously well skilled in this task, but I doubt she's ever been landed with anyone like me before.

"I hope you won't be too unhappy with us."

"Huh?" I break out of my miserable trance to look at her.

The only emotion on her face is in her eyes. Where the rest of her is cool and neutral, her eyes are bright and expressive, and I find myself falling headlong into them. *Sorry,* they say. *For what happened back there.*

"Mother prepped us on your circumstances when Father received the bird telling us you were coming," she says. "I'm sure it'll take some adjustment after living in a tent."

My face flares at the thought of people knowing things about me I haven't told them myself. "How does *she* know anything about us?"

"I'm afraid she didn't give me her sources," says Elowen apologetically. "Are they false?"

I shrug right up to my ears. "Dunno. Guess it depends on what else she says. I'm no girl, that's for sure. And my name's *Callie*, not Calliden. Got it?"

I brace myself for the inevitable "Well, what *are* you then?" as Elowen assesses me carefully. People who ask like they want to know never do. It's like they're trying to catch you in a lie or prove you wrong, like they obviously know you better than you could ever know yourself.

But it never comes. She just dips her head and says, "As you wish."

Not having the fight you're ready for is like swallowing a sneeze. Discomfiting.

She starts up her brisk walk again, and I trot to keep up. No easy feat when her legs are basically twice as long as mine.

"Does that mean I can go?"

She glances back. "Go where?"

"To wherever Papa's gone. If this is girls only—"

"No," says Elowen. "If Father says you're to be here, you're to be here."

"Why does he get to decide?" I demand, prickly as a gorse bush. "He's not my dad *or* the king. He's just a chancellor, and I dunno what one of them even is."

If someone had come after my dad like that, I'd have decked them, but Elowen doesn't react. She just pauses before a pair of double doors made of deep, rich wood and carved with a crest bearing a deer standing firm and looking back at us. Challenging anyone who dares come too close.

"This is the Queen's Crest," Elowen explains. "On the other side of these doors, she's in charge." She makes an elegant motion with her right hand, and there's the faintest sparkle of magic before the lock clicks back and the hinges swing silently open.

"But in the rest of Helston, Father has authority." She steps aside to let me through first. "Until a new king is crowned, at least. He decides who stays and who goes. Be cautious."

I don't tell her that cautious is not in my nature.

"I'll teach you the key later," says Elowen. "It's perfectly simple, even if you only have a little magic. It's designed to ensure that only girls may be permitted into the Queen's Quarters without invitation."

I roll my eyes. "Because boys don't have magic, I guess." *And people like me don't exist at all.*

There's a long pause before Elowen says, "Precisely."

I gnaw my lip. It's amazing how I've never felt less like a girl *and* less like a boy all in the same moment.

And by amazing, I mean awful.

For the longest time, gender felt like being crammed into a pair of shoes I'd never fit into in the first place. Except I didn't get to pick a new pair. I didn't even get to try on a different pair just in case. Day after day, I wore the same small shoes, and I kept growing. And the more I grew, the less I fit.

It was Neal who suggested I take off the shoes completely,

and it felt so *good*. Like I was breathing for the first time in my life. Everyone helped me—Papa too. Rowena had been through it all before, and it was so *neat* to meet someone like me, even if the shoes were different. She'd been born into boy shoes, but girl shoes fit her best. I tried on boy shoes for a few days, walking around and wiggling my toes. And they were more comfortable, but they still didn't fit.

I wasn't a she, and I wasn't a he, I was just . . . Callie. Eventually, I put on "they," and I haven't taken those shoes off since.

Now it feels like they've been ripped off and my feet have been crammed back into the girl shoes I thought I'd buried.

It hurts.

Elowen wasn't lying when she said she'd picked the best room for me. It has a great view through enormous windows, and all the light a person could possibly want in a room they only use to sleep in. The bed is vast, the frame and posts the same dark wood as the double doors, and hung with thick purple-blue curtains tied with silver tassels. There are fresh flowers in a vase on the desk by the window. Bright yellow. Perfect. Beautiful.

I miss my tent.

I sling down my pack and perch on the bed.

Elowen lingers in the doorway, mouth parted as though halfway through a question.

"What?" I ask.

"I was just curious what you were planning to wear to your audience with Her Majesty."

"I hadn't really done any planning. These are my best clothes." I make a vague gesture at myself, fully aware of the dirt and the sweat and the smell. "Not good enough?"

I glimpse the first twitch of a smile before Elowen hides it behind her fingers. "Would you allow me to make some small adjustments?"

"What kind of adjustments?"

"I believe I have several gowns that would suit you—"

"You're at least six feet taller than me!"

Elowen just wiggles her fingers, sending little stars sparking into the air, and disappears into the corridor with a last "Clean up. I'll be back shortly."

I kick off my boots and peel off my tunic. Behind a painted screen depicting a fair maiden with flowing golden hair stroking the nose of a silver unicorn in a meadow of daisies, there's a tub as big as a pond. I could fit my whole self in there if I wanted to. I don't. The water is *freezing*. I draw back with a hiss of disappointment. It's not like I'm not used to cold water. I don't remember the last time I had a hot bath. If cold water is all I have, I'd rather huddle under a makeshift shower or find a sunny spot in a stream.

Mama and the servants could heat all the water in Clystwell with a wave of their hands, and Neal makes sure we always have enough hot water for cooking. But even if I wanted to, even if I tried my hardest, my flame would barely be enough to heat one cup of tea.

They're assuming I'm magical enough, that I'm girl enough, and it doesn't matter what I say or what I do: Helston's inhabitants are not going to change their minds.

Fine.

I splash my face and my body and scrub away the worst of the grime; then I dress quickly in the first tunic I pull out of my bag.

I can't wait around for someone else to fix my problems for me. This is all upside down, and it's up to me to set it right. I don't care if Lord Peran's angry—he's not in charge of me, no matter what Elowen says. I need to find Papa and set this right.

Better to ask forgiveness than permission.

I tug my boots on and stomp out the way I came.

CHAPTER SIX

O r I *try* to go back the way I came.

Easier said than done.

I keep going forward, but it's not long before I realize most of the corners look the same and I'm pretty sure we turned way before this and I'm probably somehow going in entirely the wrong direction. Elowen was telling the truth when she said there aren't any boys allowed in the Queen's Quarters. I don't pass a single person who even *might* be a boy, and every single lady, every single girl, stares at me as I stomp past in my not-a-dress.

My face burns, but I determinedly do not look at anyone. Just keep moving onward, forward, focusing on my goal.

Find Papa and find Satin and set things *right*. I don't belong here, and five minutes is long enough to be certain. I need to find the people like me. Or at least *more* like me. Papa will understand once I can explain it. I'm not a girl, if there was ever even a doubt about that. I don't belong among them.

They don't like different down in Helston.

I didn't take Neal seriously when he gave me the warning. Far as I could tell, they don't like different anywhere. Why should Helston be any different? But it is. I can feel it. If there's anyone like me, they're hiding it well.

I break through a smaller door than the one Elowen magicked open, but as soon as I'm on the other side, the air shifts and I know I'm out of the Queen's Quarters. I'll take that one little triumph. My shoulders relax and I walk a little taller, actually looking at the faces I pass. They stare less out here, and I can breathe a little more freely. The pace is more urgent; everyone is on their way somewhere or in the middle of something, whether it's conversation or a task. No one has time to look at me, and I make the most of it.

I've never seen so many people in one place. I always thought the camp was busy, even claustrophobic, when all the kids from the nearby village came up to train and doubled our numbers, but that's nothing compared to the palace. It's like a city inside, and I'm just one among a million. Nothing special at all. Invisible. Almost like I don't exist.

Be quiet, be still, be unassuming, undemanding, don't take up more space than you're permitted, says the voice in the back of my head that sounds like Mama's.

I break into a run, pelting through the crowded corridors and shoving where I have to, gasping for fresh air.

I have no idea where I'm going, and I've never been this lost. All I can do is search for anything remotely familiar and beeline for it. There're no tents, and the horses are busy and working. None of the soldiers have any attention to spare for one lost kid, and the only other people outside are—

My heart leaps. Kids! Boys! Pages, spilling out of a silver-brick building like a broken bag of beads, all dressed up like they're ready to go hitting things with sticks. They pass around me without notice or effort, like I'm one of them who just happens to have stopped here.

Only one catches my eye, and my stomach leaps in relief. Elowen's brother.

"Hey!" I yell, waving with both arms. "Edwyn!"

But he ignores me.

Not just ignores me but rolls his eyes like he'd rather die than be seen with me.

Fine. I roll my eyes back at him, even though he can't see it. Like I need him to be my savior anyway.

I wander inside, drifting into a cavernous hall filled with long tables and benches. You could fit our whole camp in here, plus some. Fresh silence rings like an echo, until one set of hurrying footsteps breaks the quiet.

The last boy left behind. His black tunic is the same color as the hair curtaining his pale face, tilted all the way down to concentrate on the ground, and he would crash straight into me if I didn't step aside at the last moment.

"Hey." I pull my friendliest smile, which I'm pretty sure is just a really toothy grimace.

The boy doesn't even look up. "Pardon me."

"No, wait—" I grab his sleeve without thinking. Dark eyes flash with fear, but instead of pulling free, of fighting me, the boy freezes up. I let go and put my hands up. "I'm really sorry, but can you—"

"I—I have to go."

"Well, can I come with you? I'm new and I'm really lost. I'm trying to find a knight. Sir Nicholas. Do you have any idea where he'd be if he just arrived?"

The boy holds on to his arm like I've burned him, and all my hope of allyship or friendship or whatever seeps out of me in a sigh. I've hecked up with Elowen and I've hecked up with this kid. Two out of two. Great job, Callie.

"You're . . . looking for Sir Nicholas?" His voice is wispy, barely making a dent in the quiet.

"Yeah!" Mine, on the other hand, booms on every syllable. "He's my— I'm his squire. D'you know where he'll be?"

One moment of hesitation more, then the boy nods. "I'm going that way. Follow me."

Thank you thank you *thank you!*

⊰⊱

The world is a little smaller and a little more manageable with a guide. The boy walks briskly and undistractedly, and I glean what little I can from his back. His tunic and shirt are so crisp and clean they look brand-new, the fabrics rich and delicate. This kid is certainly nobility. He's a little taller than me, but most people are. I thought Elowen's hair was dark, but his is bottomless black, cut and kept neat in a way that mine never is. He is here out of duty rather than desire, going through the motions because he has to and resenting every moment. As out of place here as I am in the Queen's Quarters. It's funny how opposites can be so familiar.

The path dips down a hill, getting steeper and steeper until I'm *dreading* the walk back up to the palace. Poor Flo. Poor Bayna. After all those days of walking, and we made them end with a trek up a mountain. Papa and I owe them a *big* thank-you.

Finally the tiny path breaks out into a huge courtyard. Lush grass and green bushes give way to dirt and brick, and the smell of horse hits. I grin. This is exactly where I'm supposed to be.

The boy pauses and looks both ways for oncoming traffic, then dashes across the courtyard for the building on the other side. I take my own time. The pack of pages who passed me earlier are congregated in the near distance, all bunched around a tall man who looks like he's trying to conduct them. The boy keeps his face angled away from the class, like he's

75

specifically avoiding them. He doesn't seem like the type to skip class. And he *certainly* can't afford to skip training, all scrawny like that.

"Hey, if you tell me the rest of the way, I can find it for myself."

"It's fine. I . . . train separately."

He disappears into the darkened warmth of the biggest stable I've ever seen. It's like a palace itself, full of movement and life—hostlers wrangling the enormous tack, boys shoveling hay and hauling feedbags, and so many horses!

Giant heads swing to watch me, ears twitching curiously. They're so beautiful, and so well cared for. I feel a little bit better for letting Flo go with a stranger. They clearly love their horses here. Their eyes are bright, their coats sleek and shiny. Every feedbag is full or being filled, and the boy takes his own time with them too. He greets each one like a familiar friend, with a whistle or a scritch between the eyes, and sometimes a snack from a secret pocket. Even the horses who didn't come to stare at me swing around to greet the boy and claim their treat.

I fall back and breathe in the smell of horses. Animals have always been easier than people. They've never seen me as anything but *me*, whatever that is. They don't care if you're not magical enough, or you're good at things you shouldn't be and rubbish at the things you should. As long as you treat them right, in their eyes, you are perfect.

By the looks of things, the boy feels the same way.

He stops by a stall and whistles a soft tune, holding out his palm flat.

A long copper-colored nose dips and sniffs the offered hand, and I *think* I recognize that nose. . . .

A smile breaks out on the boy's face. "Hello," he murmurs, running his palm up the horse's nose. "What's your name?"

"Flo!"

She whickers in welcome, pawing the ground, happy to see me. The boy stands aside, and I touch my nose to hers. "I'm so sorry for letting them take you," I breathe. "I'm glad you're being looked after." Reluctantly, I have to admit that Edwyn or whoever he passed her over to has done a great job settling her in and cleaning her up.

Flo huffs in my face and I giggle. "I'll take that as forgiveness."

"She's yours?" The boy takes half a step closer and looks wistfully up into Flo's big brown eyes. "She's beautiful."

"Yup," I say proudly. "If you've got any sugar, you'll be her best friend forever."

A treat is immediately produced and offered up with a solemn bow.

Flo inhales it and thumps the ground for more. A demand that is met without hesitation.

I shake my head. "Absolutely shameless. No manners at all." I don't want to talk about whose fault *that* is.

The boy laughs softly, running his fingers through Flo's mane. "She knows she can get away with it."

"Yeah. . . ." But I'm only half listening. The boy's hands are a mess of bruised knuckles and angry calluses. Even on the field, away from anyone with magical healing, there're balms and salves for those kinds of injuries. This is the *palace*. There's no way there isn't the means to deal with those wounds.

"Your Highness."

I startle like I'm about to be caught with my hand on the biscuit plate. I didn't know I was around royalty. Far as I can tell, it's just me, a bunch of stable people, and this boy.

This boy whose eyes have gone wide and guilty, who snaps to attention as Papa and Lord Peran approach.

So this is the hopeless prince.

Papa's eyesbrows go way up when he sees me, and Lord Peran looks like he's about to bust an artery, but I'm too interested in this kid to worry about either of them.

In fifteen minutes, he's been three different people—the quiet boy, frightened of being late; the one who's happier around horses, who carries sugar in his pockets; and now this one, the prince with dull eyes and perfect posture, who looks away as the grown-ups bow to him.

"Your Highness," says Lord Peran stiffly, "may I present Sir Nicholas of Clystwell, the king's champion and your new trainer. Sir Nicholas, Crown Prince Will."

Papa cocks his head and grins. "You remember me, kid? I know it's been a while. You were about *that* high last time

I saw you." He pinches his thumb and forefinger together and winks.

The prince doesn't get the joke. He bows quickly, a twitchy motion that reminds me of a small bird. "Forgive me, I—I don't recall—"

"Just teasing, Your Highness." Papa smiles warmly. "I am very much looking forward to working with you. Your father and I were pages together, back in the day, and your brother was my squire. I know you're cut from the same cloth."

Prince Will says nothing, just stands there, stone-still and beet red. It's like he's hardly here at all. If I hadn't seen him with Flo, I'd have guessed he was the rudest, most stand-offish kid in the whole of Helston. But that's not it. Twenty minutes and I *know* that's not it.

He's scared. Of Papa.

How can *anyone*—let alone a prince—be scared of Papa?

"Lady Calliden." The name is bad enough, but on Lord Peran's tongue it stings like a poison bite. I grit my teeth and ignore him. That name isn't me and hasn't been in forever.

The prince turns to me with huge eyes. "Lady? But I thought you were— You're a . . . a *girl*?"

"No, I'm not—"

Straw crunches as Lord Peran steps in. "Lady Calliden, return to the appropriate quarters immediately and see you do not leave them again."

"That's enough, Peran," Papa growls. And, more gently,

to me, "You shouldn't be here, kiddo. Go on back—we'll talk later, I promise."

I plant myself solidly in front of him and glare. "No, now. *Please*. You said I'd stay with you. That was the deal. You said I'd be your squire."

Papa sighs like he's just squeezed a whole week into half a day. "Callie—"

"I want to help!"

"Callie." He sets his hands firmly on my shoulders. "I need you to hold on a little while longer, okay? Your mission is to be patient and wait. And you can help by not causing trouble." Papa's voice stays low, but it still catches me in the throat. Yelling doesn't always mean raising your voice. He softens and touches my chin. "I'm sorry, kiddo, truly. But think of it like an adventure. I know you can beat dragons and rescue princesses no problem, but can you survive wearing a dress for a couple of days?" He winks. "Sounds like this is gonna be your greatest challenge yet. You up for it?"

No. "I guess."

"C'mon." He nudges my arm with a huge fist. "Be assertive!"

"Yes, Sir Nick, sir!"

Papa laughs and ruffles my hair. "Much better. All right, Your Highness, what about you? Ready to defeat some invisible monsters? I hear they've grown pretty wild out in that training yard."

That's Papa's usual go-to method of coaxing little kids into warming up and showing off where their skills lie—shoving wooden swords into their hands and sending them out to do battle with imaginary creatures.

The prince remains locked in place, wide-eyed and confused, gaze darting doubtfully to the chancellor.

Lord Peran steps up to Papa, close enough to murmur, "We have discussed the prince's training regimen, Nicholas. This is not—"

Papa waves him off with a dismissive "Yes, yes, I know. But that's tomorrow. We need to get comfortable with each other first. Right, kiddo?"

Prince Will looks like he's never been called "kiddo" in his life, and Papa uses the astonishment to his advantage, steering the prince toward the training grounds on the other side of the stables.

Leaving me alone with Lord Peran.

I catch Flo's eye, and her ears twitch meaningfully.

Yeah, I know.

I start out the way I came, hoping to be gone while Lord Peran's eyes are still on Papa and the prince.

No such luck.

"A word of warning, girl."

I force myself to face him, dragging my feet. "I'm going back to the ladies. Isn't that what you want?"

There's no signal, not even a flicker of one feature before the chancellor comes at me and grabs my arm, locking me in. I don't get scared easy, especially not by men who think they're everything just because they're men, but Lord Peran scares me. There's no anger in his grip or on his face, just placid confidence that he has every right to do what he wants, like no one's ever suggested otherwise.

"Know your place," he murmurs. "And stay there. Your little knight fantasy ends now. Do you understand?"

My head is spinning from pain and panic, and I'm pretty sure I'd say just about anything to make him let go. "I understand."

Neal was right, I think dizzily, sprinting back up the hill to the palace. Not all enemies want you dead.

CHAPTER
SEVEN

M agic sparkles in Elowen's fingers as she weaves it through the hem of one of her dresses, adjusting it to fit me. "Stand still or you'll get burned."

"I'm trying."

"Try harder."

I breathe deeply and make every single muscle obey as Elowen works carefully on my hem. I feel jittery and unsettled after my confrontation with Lord Peran, and the ghost of his grip won't leave my arm. He won't get out of my head and he has no right to be there and I *hate* it.

Elowen pauses in her work. "If you're nervous about meeting Her Majesty, don't be."

"Nah, it's not that." Every place the dress touches itches. It's not the dress, made of lovely silky material, the same color as my favorite tunic. I don't think it would matter how talented and careful Elowen is as a seamstress—it's me who doesn't fit.

"Hey . . . I didn't get you in trouble with your dad, did I?"

"Of course not," she says a bit too lightly. "You're back where you're supposed to be now. That's all that matters."

"He seemed really angry. . . ."

Elowen extinguishes the magic from her fingers and rises, brushing the creases from her own dress. "Father's under a lot of pressure. The whole weight of the kingdom is on his shoulders, and when pieces don't move the way they're supposed to . . ." She forces a smile. "The best thing is to stay away until he burns out. That's my approach, anyway, and it works well enough. And it isn't as though you need to have anything to do with him. Just—"

"Stay where I'm supposed to."

Elowen dips her head. "Precisely. Perfect."

It feels just about as far from perfect as possible.

Finally, Elowen steps back and assesses me with an expert's critical eye. "Move around for me." She puts her arms out in demonstration. I copy, slipping into my normal stretches. It's weird, having loose material flapping around my legs. Not bad, just . . . different. "Good?" asks Elowen.

"As good as it can be, I guess. How do I look?"

"Would you like to see for yourself?"

I pull a face. "Not really—" But Elowen's already dragging me over to the mirror.

I brace myself, flooded with memories of all the hours I spent in front of Mama's mirror, watching her turning me into a poor likeness of the daughter she wanted. I always walked away not looking anything like myself.

But when I look at the face reflected back, it's still me. Still Callie. Just dressed up a bit different. And not looking half-bad.

Hazel-green eyes widen in the glass. *"Oh..."*

At my shoulder, Elowen smiles. "Good 'oh'?"

"Yeah..."

Bunched sleeves smooth out and roll midway down my arms at Elowen's silent command, and fine copper threads weave a subtle pattern into the sleeves, along the neckline, down the front, and out over the skirt. I catch my eye in the mirror and flush. I look *good.* Maybe this isn't as bad as I thought it would be. I don't know how, but Elowen's done what Mama never could and made me look like myself in a dress. That's powerful magic! Neal says magic's a manifestation of inner peace, and I can definitely see that in Elowen. She is calm and focused, and more in tune with her magic than I can ever hope to be. She trusts it and, in return, it obeys her.

I whistle, impressed. "That's real magic, right there."

Her laugh chimes, and she gives a bright grin. "I'll take that as a compliment."

I like that laugh, I realize. I want to hear it again.

"So—what do I need to know about the queen?" I bundle my hair up into its usual tail. Ideally I'd fix a nice braid, but I'm useless at doing my own hair. "Anything weird I definitely shouldn't bring up? Anything weirder that I should? If she's anything like her kid, I wouldn't mind being prepped."

Elowen's eyes go wide. "You met Prince Will?"

"Yeah, we crossed paths. Didn't know who he was until your dad turned up, though. Wasn't what I was expecting from a prince. Not that I was really expecting anything."

I laugh to fill Elowen's silence, but it doesn't go far. The lightness we achieved is gone like it was never there, and her face turns quickly back to neutral.

"Don't mention him to Her Majesty," she says. "Don't mention Prince Jowan or the king. Or anything, really. We have to be very careful with her."

I frown through an experimental lunge, testing the reach of my skirts. "She doesn't want to talk about her family?" I guess I get being delicate, but shutting off the subject completely sounds a bit extreme. Especially when one of her kids is right here.

"She's grieving," Elowen explains softly. "We don't talk about anything that might risk upsetting her. Father says we have to give her the space to rest and heal. She'll come around in her own time, but if we push her too hard, she might—"

"You think she'd disappear like the king did?"

Elowen neither confirms nor denies, but the press of her lips says enough.

I shiver in my dress, thinking about the prince with the sugar cubes and how I would feel if Papa just walked away one day and never looked back. At least I would have Neal. If his mum can't stand to even talk about him, who does the prince have?

Lord Peran's face flashes in my head, and I wince.

If I were Prince Will, I'd be worse than struggling.

—✦—

Elowen leads me through the halls of the Queen's Quarters. I don't know what to expect. I guess a Throne Room, a stately greeting, a formal introduction. Something quiet and serene, befitting a grieving monarch.

I definitely do *not* expect screaming.

Elowen winces. "You get used to the noise eventually." And pushes the door open.

The screaming gets louder and closer and promptly attaches itself to my middle. A round face with a gap between its two front teeth grins up at me.

"Hi," I tell the face.

The little kid shrieks in delight.

And once one comes, the rest follow like a swarm of bees, buzzing and excited and a little bit scary. Thankfully, they're not all as small as the shrieking one. Ages seem to range from way younger to nearly grown up.

"Is it true?" a pale girl with bright blond hair breathes, practically clutching the front of my dress. "Did you really live among soldiers? Were you the only girl among *hundreds* of men?"

"Well, I'm not really—"

A tall teenager with a startlingly orange dress and the kind of complexion that looks like she'll burn if she so much looks at a candle elbows forward. "Is it true you live in a forest and haven't ever been in a real building before?"

"Don't be absurd," a dark girl with glittering blue earrings snaps before I can respond. "Everyone knows Sir Nicholas left court two years ago."

The questions come like a barrage of arrows, so fast they don't even give me a chance to answer. I search wildly for Elowen, my one familiar anchor, but every staring face is a stranger's, and I don't even have the chance to speak for myself.

"Lady Calliden, welcome." A low, musical voice sends the girls scattering, leaving me face to face with a woman who can only be Queen Ewella. Even apart from the delicate gold crown nestled in crow-black hair, she looks exactly like Prince Will, from her deep brown eyes to her fragile smile to the ghosts following her around. She wears all black too, apart from little bits of silver stitching on the dress that sweeps the ground. But her presence is *huge*, like she could command a room with one finger.

I *love* her.

She certainly doesn't seem like she needs to be protected from, well, everything.

I stumble through a messy half bow, half curtsy and a mumbled "Thanks . . . Your Majesty. And it's Callie. If you don't mind."

"Why would I mind?" She lifts my face, long fingers cool on my cheeks, and her gaze sweeps over me like sunlight on the sea, her smile just as warm. "You are certainly Nick's daughter.

I'm so glad you're finally with us. I hope you will find your time here valuable. Helston has much to offer any young person."

My chest fills with hope, and I shoot my shot, straight and true. "I will! And it definitely does and, Your Majesty, I'm sorry for wandering off and causing trouble, but I wondered if I'd be allowed to spend time in the training grounds too? With your permission, of course. My horse is down there, you see, and I met Prince Will, and I think I can help—"

Her hands fall from my face like they're suddenly too heavy to hold. "You met my son?"

"Yeah." I falter, Elowen's warning ringing too late in my head. "I reckon I can help Papa help him if I'm allowed to."

But the queen turns with a sound that might be a sigh or might be the swish of her long skirts around her ankles. "I am tired," she tells no one in particular. "I think I will rest awhile."

She leaves with soft murmurs to some of the girls. A few drift after her. Most wander away into adjacent rooms.

An elbow digs into my ribs.

"Ow, Elowen!"

She glares at me. "I told you not to talk about him. I told you she is grieving."

"Prince Will isn't dead."

But by the look she gives me, I feel like he might as well be.

CHAPTER
EIGHT

It takes me twenty-four hours to realize the Queen's Daughters do *everything* together. Behind the magically protected door, it's like a tiny kingdom within a kingdom, like a family, like the camp. The girls train just as diligently, filling the air with magic that tickles my nose and makes me squirm. Neal would love it. He'd be dragging me from craft to craft, telling me to "Look, Callie!" and pointing at the living tunes rising from the Piano Room, the paintings that move on the page, the dolls that breathe just as deeply as I do. And I would hate every second, stuck in the middle of all the confirmation that I'm not what I'm supposed to be.

The closest I've found so far is embroidery. I stab the material, pretending the needle is a tiny spear and the red thread is the blood of my enemies. It's like a miniature version of our drills. *Up down two three . . .*

"You're not obligated to stay with me, you know." Elowen's

fingers move deftly, stitching delicate white flowers with egg-yolk-orange middles throughout a thread orchard. The picture she's crafting is so intricate; I feel like I could get lost inside if I peered closely. "I know for a fact there's a raging debate going on about who's going to be your best friend. You have other options."

"What does that me— *Ow!*" I stick my thumb in my mouth before the oozing blood smears on Elowen's dress, but she quickly takes my hand and inspects the wound (which feels way bigger than a needle prick). One brush of her magic, and it's gone like it was never there at all.

I nod, impressed. "Wow."

Elowen goes back to her sewing. "Not really."

"Yes, really. That was amazing!" It takes all of my focus *and* all of my magic just to ease the ache of a bruise, which half the time isn't worth it anyway. Elowen fixed me up like it was nothing.

She shrugs. "It isn't as though I reattached a limb."

"But I bet you could. Easy as anything."

Her chin dips to hide a smile. "Maybe one day."

"You learn this stuff here? Among all—" I wave a hand, from our stitching to the music patterns. "They actually teach you how to do useful stuff too?"

"A little," says Elowen. "I can teach you, if you'd like—"

"No." My defenses spark before I can get ahold of them. "I told you, I don't have much magic and I don't need it. Not everyone needs it, and I didn't come here to learn to be a lady. I came here to prove myself good enough to try for my shield. I don't need you or anyone here trying to tell me I should give all that up and learn how to sit still and be quiet and be invisible and—"

"Is that what you think magic is?" Elowen asks with a head tilt that's way more knowing than I'm comfortable with. "Is that why you're scared of it?"

"I'm not *scared!*" My burning face betrays me, and I turn away from her with a hiss.

I don't want to go backward.

I don't want to feel like I used to feel at home, at Clystwell, with Mama.

I've grown up and into myself now, and . . . and I'm scared of losing that all over again.

I don't want to be here.

"Just because it's enough for all of you to just sit here and look pretty and make pretty, useless things, doesn't mean that's enough for everyone! Just because you all want to pretend you're being useful when really you're just waiting for permission to be seen, doesn't mean *I* have to be invisible too!" I'm on my feet and my hands are fists and my sewing is on the floor, and heads have turned to stare.

I hate myself for throwing all their kindness back in their faces.

But I can't stop.

"Just because I don't want to be good at this stuff, doesn't make me less than any of you! It's not my fault I got stuck in here! I never said I belonged. I never said I wanted to try. I know who I am and I know what I'm good at, so stop trying to make me into something else!"

By the time I'm done, my whole body has tightened up like a bowstring about to snap. I catch my breath and brace myself for Elowen to shout back, or get up and leave, or order me out of her sight or—

"Forgive me."

"Huh?"

"Forgive me," Elowen repeats. "It wasn't my intention to make you feel like I want you to be something you're not. I'm sorry I did."

I comb the words for sarcasm and cool acid, but there's nothing in them but truth. She really means it.

I deflate, my own anger melting into embarrassment. "Me too. I'm sorry. For yelling and saying you're pretending to be useful. I didn't mean that and I shouldn't've said it. I'm just . . . no good at this stuff. *Any* of this stuff."

Elowen raises an eyebrow, a smile twitching on her lips. "You mean the Queen's Daughters?"

They're gone now, all the staring girls. They scattered like I scared them off. Elowen's the only one who stayed. I hunch down, elbows on knees, face burning.

"I'm sorry you're stuck with me."

Elowen laughs. "I've certainly been stuck with worse."

I snort. "Yeah, right."

"Oh, but it's true. Father always makes me look after the

daughters of visitors. And there have certainly been some . . . difficult ones. You're actually one of the best. Comparatively. Most have their own goals. They want to get close to Her Majesty and secure a position at court. Once I've introduced them, my part is over."

"Yeah, well . . ." I scratch my head awkwardly. "I'm not used to people who aren't, like, a hundred years older than me. This is all totally new for me too. And everyone's super nice, just maybe . . ."

"A bit grabby?"

I burst out laughing. "A bit grabby. That's it. Though, I mean, I'm sure you have more important things to do than babysit me, so if you need to go and do them, I can get along on my own, no problem."

She arches an eyebrow. "After the trouble you got into last time? I don't think so. But if you'd like, maybe after lunch we can go out and get some fresh air, and—"

I perk up. "Have an adventure? Yes, please!"

"Within reason," she adds quickly, like she can see the flash of swords in my imagination.

"Nothing your dad wouldn't like, right?"

She laughs. "That doesn't leave us with much, I'm afraid."

"What about horses? Are ladies allowed to ride horses?"

Elowen's face turns wistful. "I've never ridden, though I've always wanted to."

"Seriously, never?"

"Seriously, never. Some of the other girls do, but Father

says there's no point in me learning when it's not as though I'm ever going to go anywhere."

I roll my eyes. "Your dad seems like a lot of fun."

"Fun isn't a prerequisite for lord chancellor, unfortunately."

"Lucky we're not lord chancellor, then!"

It's as much an adventure for Elowen as it is for me. Even though she's lived here her whole life, she's never been on a horse.

"It was hard enough persuading Father to let me take lessons with Her Majesty," she admits as I saddle Flo. "He wanted me to stay in our apartment and learn from Mother, but I managed to persuade him."

I can't imagine Lord Peran being persuaded to do *anything*.

"What's she like, your mum?" I ask, mounting the horse and helping Elowen up behind me.

She's quiet until she's settled, and even then it takes a moment. "Mother is . . . She's like Father. She's comfortable in the order of things and doesn't believe there's any need for change."

There's a tiny pinch of pain in Elowen's voice that I'd never've noticed if I didn't know how that feels.

"They mean well," she continues softly. "Both of them. I

know they do. And I know it's wrong to be thankful that I don't have to spend much time with them, but—"

"I get it."

Her arms go tight around my waist. "Really?"

"Course. You don't get to pick your family. Not the regular kind, anyway. It's kinda inevitable that not everyone can totally get on with everyone else." The statement is painfully clunky. It's a pep talk I'm more used to getting than giving, and I'm nowhere near as eloquent as Neal.

Elowen stays silent for a long while, and as I nudge Flo to a trot, I'm increasingly certain that my helpful words are less inspiring and more like rocks chucked into the middle of a muddy pond.

Then, nearly lost on the breeze, she whispers, "You're right."

"Yeah?"

"Yes." And "Thank you."

I'm glad she can't see how hard my face burns. "Dunno there's anything to thank me for, but sure."

We ride out at a steady trot, Elowen holding tight to my waist and directing us to all her favorite places around Helston, from the highest spot on the hill with the best view out to the moors in the east to the tiniest of beaches concealed beneath a curving cliff.

"I haven't had anyone to go adventuring with in years," Elowen tells me, like she's a whole lot older than twelve.

"Usually as soon as I introduce newcomers to the others . . . well, let's just say I'm rarely someone's primary choice of companion."

Which makes zero sense to me at all. "How come?" I ask, hopping off Flo and helping Elowen down. "I mean, the others are fine, I guess, but you're . . . I dunno, different?"

Elowen grimaces. "Thank you."

"Not in a bad way—"

"I know I'm different," she says a little stiffly. "I don't spend all my time in the Queen's Quarters, as the others do. I don't know how to"—she blushes—"have fun and just *relax*. Sometimes it feels as though there was a lesson everyone else attended on how to be friends, and I missed it. I can be friendly when it's my duty, but it's not real. It's not *comfortable*. I like the others well enough, and I believe they like me too, but I know I'm too serious and there's nothing I can do about that."

"I don't think you're too serious," I blurt. "I think you're friendly. And I get it. 'Cause me too. I feel like I missed that lesson too. So maybe . . . I dunno, maybe we can figure it out our own way. Together. If you want to. Be friends, I mean. We can be different together."

Her eyes have gone wide, and there're bright pink spots in her cheeks. She stares at me, brows dipped into an almost-frown, and I feel like I just got shoved off a cliff I've only just found a steady footing on.

From all I know and have learned about the way Helston thinks about "different," I more than half expect Elowen to huff and flounce off, all offended.

"Hey, look," I start. "I'm sorry, I—"

"Don't be. You're right."

I gnaw my lip. It's impossible to tell if she's angry or not. That's what I like best about Eyrewood—everyone there says what they mean and means what they say. No games. No complications. No weird tones that make my gut twist. The world is full of enough scary things, Neal says. It's a waste of time being afraid of your friends.

Except I don't even know if Elowen *is* my friend.

"May I ask you something?" she says, wandering across the hill's peak with her skirts swaying in the breeze.

I drop Flo's reins to let her graze alone and trot after Elowen. "Sure."

"Why do you want to be a knight?"

I shrug, shoving my hands into my skirt's pockets. "Just always have, really." Literally, I can't remember a single moment when I didn't know exactly what I wanted. "In the beginning, it just seemed so cool. I'd watch my dad ride home, all dressed up after long adventures, and I wanted that too. I definitely wanted it more than sitting at home being bored like my mum wanted." I blow out a breath, like I'm expelling the thought of her. "Now . . . I dunno. It's different. Bigger. I know how it is, to feel like there's no one on your side. I don't want anyone else to feel like that. I figure, becoming a knight,

I can do something about it. No one should be helpless." I kick at a stone, sending it bouncing down the hill and over the cliff.

"What about you?" I ask when Elowen sinks into thoughtful silence. "What do you want to do?"

"The same," she responds, her voice soft but strong all at once. "I have nothing to prove, but I want to be able to protect the people I love." She looks at me, and her eyes sparkle in the sunshine. "You're right—no one should be helpless. We must draw our power from wherever we can."

"And where do you draw yours from?"

Elowen smiles, and it's different from the neutral smile when she's being a host, or the easy grin when she's relaxed. This one is sharp as a knife. A snap of her fingers, and sparks fly. They're not the soft orange glow of fire but a bright white so sharp it hurts to look at, even for a moment.

"There are many in Helston who would not be happy if they knew girls could learn to use their magic for anything other than quiet, pretty things. As far as anyone else is concerned, we're learning to control it and suppress it so it doesn't cause trouble. But that doesn't mean it can't. Wielded the right way, magic can be just as effective as a sword."

She closes her fist around the sparks, extinguishing them like they were never there, and laughs at my expression. "Just because I choose not to use it, doesn't mean I don't have it."

"Why don't you use it? You should! Think how much you could do if you trained in combat too—"

"Magic is worthless in Helston, apart from the few healers permitted to practice," says Elowen. "Even if I could win this war single-handedly, it wouldn't matter. Father says magic is a vessel for corruption. That it's unknowable and uncontrollable power that should be quashed. That anyone who has it is innately untrustworthy."

The top of the hill gives us a full view of the crevasse separating Helston from the mainland and the bridge stretching thin across it. The structure looks so fragile from here. It gives no hint at all that it's the Crown's main defense, or of what would happen if an enemy ever tried to breach it.

I shiver at the memory of all those arrows pointing at me, summoned by the threat of what little magic runs in my blood.

"He only lets me attend lessons with the Queen's Daughters because Her Majesty promised to teach me how to control my magic," Elowen continues, linking her arm through mine. "She convinced him it was better to learn how to use it than to try to suppress it and risk it exploding. If it was anyone other than the queen, he would've won the argument. Any sign that I was doing something more than learning how to be quiet and invisible, and it would be over. I would be stuck inside our apartments with Mother. It's not worth the risk."

"You don't get on with your mum?" Now that's something I can relate to.

But Elowen goes tight-lipped, offering only a curt "It's complicated."

Also relatable. I'd rather hack off my left arm with a blunt sword than dig into my feelings about Mama.

"What about your brother? Is he older or younger?"

"Five minutes younger," says Elowen with a faint smirk. "We're twins. It's not exciting," she adds when she catches my expression. "I promise. He feels similarly to me, though he has less opportunity to find time away from our parents. Father is very . . . invested in Edwyn."

I make a sympathetic noise, but it's hard to feel any kind of sorry for someone literally living out my dream. "Hey, if he wants to swap with me, tell him I'd be more than happy. Even if it means spending time with your dad."

Elowen catches my eye, then bursts out laughing. "I'll be sure to pass along the message."

"You ever think about leaving?"

"Leaving Helston?" Elowen stares at me like I've suggested jumping into the sea and swimming away here and now. Then she turns with a shake of her head and a hard frown. "No. Never. It's . . . safe here. I know what's on the other side of the bridge. We're protected from all of that."

And what about all of this? I don't ask. For most people, if it's a choice between struggling with parents who don't get you and dealing with dragons, it's an easy one.

Give me dragons any day.

We arrive at the stables way later than we should. The ride back blew out the seriousness of the conversation we'd ended up in, and Elowen is flushed and bright-eyed, and we're already plotting our next adventure by the time we dismount.

"We should make this a regular thing," I say as I unsaddle Flo and brush her down while Elowen feeds her oats from her palm. "Maybe we can make a whole day of it and take a picnic or something. I'll teach you properly so you can ride solo, and we can race and—"

Someone yelps from the courtyard at the other end of the stables, followed by a bark that sets my teeth on edge: "Pick it up."

"Callie." I'm already moving toward the commotion when Elowen tugs on my sleeve. "Don't. We should go back. Leave them to it."

"To what?"

Another cry, sharper this time, and hitched with tears. "Stop—"

"Training," Elowen whispers.

"*Again*, Your Highness," Lord Peran commands.

I stare at her. Okay, sure, this is my second day in Helston and I'm not going to even try to pretend I know all the weird ins and outs of how they do things here, but I'm not stupid.

Whatever it is I'm hearing, that's *not* training.

And the fear in Elowen's eyes confirms it.

No one who steps out into a training yard is under any delusion that they won't come away without scrapes and bruises. That's part of the deal. You don't learn without making mistakes and falling down. But there is a big difference between teaching and bullying, and I can spot that difference a mile off.

I pull free and run.

CHAPTER NINE

The courtyard is bathed in gold. The late-afternoon sun flashes off the polished wood of two blades: one pointing toward the ground, the other pointing straight at the prince's throat.

The prince.

The lump in his throat flickers, tears bright in dazed eyes. The sword in his hand is useless and forgotten. He's bleeding. Not a whole lot, not a mortal wound, but enough that it should've forced a pause in a training session. His knuckles are swollen and bruised, and I doubt he could lift his sword even if he wanted to. Sweat stains his tunic, his black hair plastered to his face.

"Again," Lord Peran calls, his voice hard and unyielding. He stands at the side of the courtyard, arms crossed, with Papa next to him. Papa with his face turned away. Papa not saying or doing anything.

The prince's assailant moves on command. It's Elowen's brother. Edwyn.

Unlike the prince, he looks as though he just stepped onto the field, with no signs of fatigue at all. His face is set as hard as his father's—blank and cruel—as he strikes.

Prince Will throws up his damaged hands with a cry, sword clattering to the ground.

If the blow were to land, it would crack a bone for sure, and my whole body braces for that crack. Except it doesn't land.

It's like Edwyn's sword has been frozen mid arc, stayed by an invisible hand.

A magical hand.

My breath catches in my throat. *He's magical.*

"Your Highness!"

The prince flinches with his whole body, and the magic drops as fast it rose. "I'm s-sorry," he gasps, turning to Lord Peran with a stammer in his voice. "I didn't mean to—" It peters out beneath Lord Peran's thunderous silence. Even Edwyn looks like he wants to run as Lord Peran strides toward them. He grabs the prince by the wrist with one hand and snatches the fallen sword up with the other, forcing it into the prince's bruised fingers.

"You will *learn,* Your Highness." And sharply to Edwyn, "Again. Go."

"Stop!" I move before I have a chance to think, getting myself between the boy and the blade before they can make contact. The sword cracks my wrist, and my eyes smart with

pain, but I grit my teeth and bear it. I don't care. This isn't right.

"Why are you letting them do this?" I demand of Papa with a snarl as he sprints over to us to stand by Lord Peran, who looks like he wants to turn Edwyn onto me.

I say bring it. Any would-be knight who thinks it's okay to attack someone weaker than they are deserves what they get. "Stand aside, girl," he snaps at me. "This doesn't concern you."

But I'm done taking orders from someone who just keeps proving they don't deserve the respect they command.

I glare back at the chancellor and hold my ground. "He told you to stop," I growl. "So *stop*."

Papa reaches for me. "Callie—"

"No!" I sidestep his touch. "You know this isn't right!"

He looks exhausted. Defeated after only being here a couple of days. He won't even look at me when he says, "It's complicated, kiddo."

"No, it's not. It's perfectly simple. You're bullying him. All of you. I don't care what you call it. It's not training. It's not *fair.* Just because he's magical—"

"A boy with magic cannot be king." Lord Peran doesn't shout. He doesn't need to. His voice fills every bit of space around us like thunder. "Return to your quarters, Lady Calliden, and be thankful your punishment is not worse."

Papa reaches for me. "I'll walk you back, Callie. C'mon."

"I said no!"

Lord Peran makes a hissing sound through his teeth. "You ought to have brought her to Helston earlier, Nicholas. The girl is out of control."

Fire blazes through me, hot and furious. I grab the sword from the prince's slack grip and turn it on the others. It's way lighter than Satin, and the edge is blunt as anything, but I know where to hit to hurt and I'm not afraid to do it.

Behind the chancellor, Papa hides a smile as he catches my eye.

I adjust my grip.

A knight's first duty is to the Crown, magic or not. I will not fail in my duty.

Edwyn falters, looking uncertainly between me and his father. I smack his blade none too lightly. "You're not afraid to attack him but you're afraid to attack me?"

His expression hardens. "I don't hit *girls*."

"I keep telling you lot"—I smack his sword again, getting dangerously close to his knuckles—"I am not a girl, and you are no knight. A knight's duty is to defend the defenseless, to protect the weak. Not take advantage and wield their power over someone who cannot fight for themselves. You should know that. If you don't, you're not being taught how to be a knight, you're being taught how to be a bully." I let the tip of my sword drop just a fraction. "You know this isn't right," I say softly, for him only. "You're training to be a knight. Knights *help* those being bullied. Do the right thing and apologize to the prince."

Edwyn's eyes—the same shape and color as Elowen's—flick up briefly to the prince lingering at my back, and I almost think I've gotten through and he's going to do it.

Then Lord Peran shifts. It's tiny, barely a movement, but it's enough to redirect Edwyn's attention, and he bares his teeth in a snarl. "As if a *girl* knows anything about what it means to be a knight. Put that sword down before you get hurt."

"Hurt? By *you*?" I laugh. "Only cowards attack people smaller than them, and I'm not afraid of cowards."

"Are you not going to do anything about her?" Lord Peran demands of Papa. "She has had ample warning. My son will not go easy on her simply because she's a girl."

Papa winks at me. "Oh, Callie knows exactly what they're doing."

I swell with Papa's faith and grin. I sure do!

And I'll show Peran and Edwyn what *girl* means.

We lunge at the same time and meet each other in a clash of wood that rings through my arm. I smile grimly. It feels good to be moving again.

One two, one two.

We keep time even as we both try to break each other's rhythm. Edwyn's good. So am I. In different circumstances, this might've been fun, we could've made a game of it. But I will get the prince's apology, even if I have to pry it from Edwyn's lips.

We might be equally matched in strength and skill, but I

have one underestimated advantage: I'm not tired. I haven't gone through a punishing day of training. I know what they feel like—all muscle aches and bruises, and feeling so satisfyingly tired, all you can do is eat and sleep. I know that feeling, and I know what time it hits.

Right about now, as day dips into evening.

Edwyn fights it just as hard as he fights me, rejecting the exhaustion and how much heavier his sword gets moment by moment. I watch his frustration at the betrayal of his body as he stumbles. Just a tiny motion, but enough to know I've already won. He knows it too. Sweat beads on his forehead as I chip away at him like stone. I can go for hours if I have to. Edwyn's got minutes left at most. His dad should've known that.

"What are you, anyway?" Edwyn pants, pressing as hard as he can against my blade. "Are you a freak in a dress or a freak with a sword?"

"Both," I snarl back. "And proud of it."

He shoves me, like there's something scary and contagious about me, and backs off.

"Does that mean you yield?" I make sure my voice carries all the way to Papa and Peran, so they know without any doubt that I've won.

Edwyn hisses in disgust. "Like you deserve that satisfaction."

"Then apologize to your prince. I won. Fair and square. Those were the conditions. You lost, so apologize."

Edwyn looks behind me to Will, and his anger shifts into hatred. He spits in the dirt, right at the prince's feet. "I don't answer to girls, and I *don't* apologize to princesses."

The venom in his voice catches me hard in the throat.

My head pounds and I hardly see him walking away through the thick haze of anger. This *stupid* dress is too hot and too bunched up, and no one is moving and no one is saying anything, and he's just going to walk away and get away with it, and it's not *right!*

A yell rips from my chest. I drop the sword and hurl myself at his back.

We skid across the dirt in a tangle of flailing fists, and it's impossible to tell when the pain is me landing a blow or him, and I don't care either way. My lip splits with a sting, half a moment before arms close around my waist and haul me up and back. I struggle, twisting with a snarl, but Captain Adan's expression is as hard as his grip. He's not letting me go any time soon.

"Enough, Lady Calliden," Lord Peran snaps, striding over with Papa two steps behind. And, to Edwyn, "Up."

Edwyn scrabbles to obey, wincing. He is covered in dirt and blood, and his face burns with furious humiliation. I guess that's the next best thing to an apology.

The prince shrinks back, arms wrapped around his body as Lord Peran bears down on us. Even Edwyn's anger has simmered down to something small beneath his father's fury.

Not that Lord Peran has any right to be mad when this was *his* fault in the first place.

I open my mouth to say so, but Papa steps quickly in. "Let's go, kiddo. I'll take you back."

"No," Lord Peran bites. "Your first duty is to His Highness. You will remain at his side." He snaps his fingers at my guard. "Get the girl out of my sight and keep her contained until further notice."

Papa shakes his head. "Hold on, Peran. You do not give orders concerning my kid."

What little patience the chancellor ever had is gone. "You have been absent from court for too long, Nicholas. You have forgotten how it works around here. Your daughter is a guest of the Crown, and as such, she is beholden to *me*."

They glare at each other. They're nose to nose in height, but Papa's bigger. "My kid comes first, *always*. And that is the end of it, Peran. C'mon, Callie."

He steers me away from Lord Peran and Edwyn and the prince, arm secure around my shoulders.

CHAPTER
TEN

"I shouldn't've let you do that," Papa murmurs, dabbing my lip with a cool, damp cloth.

I wince at the sting. Now that the rush of the fight's worn off, I can feel every blow Edwyn landed. He was good. *Really* good. I wouldn't mind fighting him again in better circumstances. "I'd have done it anyway."

He chuckles. "I know."

Sitting on my bed, Papa wipes the blood from my mouth and nose and keeps the cool cloth pressed to my eye to ward away the worst of a bruise. I don't mind war wounds, but it's nice to be looked after a bit. Especially after all that. It's not even the fight that's bothering me. It's not even Lord Peran and Edwyn.

"Did you know the prince is magical?"

The cloth pauses. "Yeah," says Papa. "I knew." His frown is knotted tight between his eyes. He won't look at me.

"I don't get what the problem is," I push. "Why shouldn't a king be magical?"

"A king is supposed to exemplify the standard," says Papa softly.

"So?"

He meets my eye with a small smile. "I'd have thought in the whole two days you've been here, you'd know what they think about different."

I grind my teeth until my jaw aches. "But I don't get *why*."

"Helston is in a very unstable position," says Papa. "That attack on the moors? That's just a taste of what's stalking Helston."

"You mean the witch?"

Papa nods. "It's easy to underestimate a fairy tale, but she's real as anything, and she wants Helston to fall."

"Then what's she waiting for? Why doesn't she just strike?"

"What do you think is scarier?" says Papa. "A battle where one side wins and one side loses, or being held on the cusp of one without any idea when the attack will fall? She is playing with us, kiddo, and it's got everyone badly on edge."

"Who is she, Papa? You wouldn't tell me on the moors, so tell me now. Why's she got it in for Helston?"

Papa sighs and shifts uncomfortably. "It's an old grievance, rooted in everyone's mistakes and left to grow wild. She was a princess once, the king's sister. I remember her well, and she was perfectly fine until one day she wasn't. She lost control of her magic, of herself. She nearly burned the palace down and everyone in it. No one saw it coming, and no one knew why it had happened. Perhaps we could've helped her and avoided it if we had. She just . . . lost it."

I squirm, trying not to understand how that feels quite so much. Not magic, obviously, but that feeling when your body feels too small for everything inside you. I've exploded before, in rage and frustration. I've hurt people. Is that why the dragon targeted me? Because we're the same, me and the witch?

"What happened then?" I make myself ask.

"Princess Alis was banished across the bridge. The first to go. That set the precedent. And she's been bent on revenge ever since, determined to finish what she started. For the last few years, she's preyed on those who cross the bridge, either taking them down or kidnapping them for her army. We have no idea of the size of her force, only that it's growing. So you can understand the pressure Peran is under. He's just trying to get Helston stable before the strike. I know his methods seem harsh—believe me, I've had that same argument with him—but ultimately we have to trust that he knows what is best for the kingdom. Once we've got the prince sorted out and settled, I'm sure Peran will relax a little. Let's assume best intentions, okay?"

I can't imagine Lord Peran doing any kind of relaxing even if the whole world was at total peace. There's a big difference between being mean because of stress and being mean just because you're mean. Maybe I'm wrong, and Lord Peran's the first instead of the second, but I doubt it.

"Sorted out how?" I demand with more bite than I can help. "Elowen says Peran doesn't want *anyone* to have magic, even the girls, and if boys aren't supposed to have it—"

"Yes, unfortunately a significant part of the plan is to help the prince do away with his magic," says Papa softly. "Peran believes doing so will better focus His Highness on skills more useful in a leader."

My whole body coils tight with rage. I'm more aware than ever how much I dislike the magical part of myself, and how often I've wished it away. It doesn't work like that. If it's part of you, it's part of you. Whether you're a girl or a boy, or both or neither. You don't get to pick and choose, *especially* not for other people.

"I don't want you worrying about it," says Papa, tipping my chin. "Focus on *you* and staying out of trouble. I meant what I said—you are my priority, first and always. Let's get you through this mess first."

I stick my tongue out. "What's gonna happen?"

"Council meeting," says Papa. "Apologize, promise to be good, and we can all move forward." He gives me a significant look. "Even if you don't mean it."

Ugh.

I'm not sorry.

I tell myself so over and over again when the summons comes, when Papa and I walk the long way through the palace from the Queen's Quarters to the Council Chambers, where we stop before an ornate door flanked by two guards dressed in identical livery and identical glares.

I changed out of Elowen's ruined dress and into my own clothes, knotting my hair up in a messy tail. The worst of the blood's gone, but I'm still a disaster and glad of it.

If I'm going to face my doom, I'll face it as myself.

And I'm *not* sorry.

Papa squeezes my shoulder. "Ready, kid?"

I give one firm nod. "Ready."

It's like a Throne Room, cavernous and richly decorated—a place of ceremony and decisions—but instead of a throne, there's a table. Vast and polished so shiny, it's like a mirror laden with platters of picked-over pastries. All the seats are filled with men. Their heads swivel at the same time to me.

I stare right back, meeting each pair of eyes in turn and making sure they *know* I'm not scared of them. I look longest and hardest at Lord Peran, seated at the head of the table, all the way at the other end of the room, with Edwyn on his left.

Edwyn's gaze flicks up as we enter, looking at Papa, at me, at us together, and then he scowls down at the table. He's next to his dad, but it's like there's a gulf between them, wider than the one spanned by the bridge. I'm still angry at him—if he wants to be a knight, he'd better start acting like one—but

I get it. I don't know what I'd have done if it had all been switched round, and Papa had made me attack the prince.

The man who gives the orders is to blame when those orders are carried out.

We scuffed each other up pretty bad, but I didn't make that cut on Edwyn's cheek. Something sharp did that. Something sharp like the ring on Lord Peran's finger that flashes in the torchlight. All the damage I dealt has been cleared off his face like it was just dirt. That cut's deep, and it'll take more than a quick healing. I hope Elowen used her magic the way it's intended and pulled a good disappearing act. If she got hurt because of me . . . I take a deep breath and raise my chin to look Lord Peran in the eye.

His lips twitch into a smile. "Welcome, Lady Calliden. Gentlemen." He inclines his head to the thirteen indistinguishable men sitting on either side of the table. "This is the girl you have all heard so much about."

They stare at me with the kind of curiosity usually reserved for scientific specimens, and it's all I can do not to scowl. One of them—a man with a pointed gray beard and eyebrows bushier than Flo's mane—smiles at me.

"Welcome, child. How are you finding your time here with us?"

Like Lord Peran hasn't filled them in with all the gory details.

"It's been . . . educational. My lord," I add quickly at Papa's nudge in my back.

Be nice, behave, say sorry.

"Lady Calliden has had a difficult time adjusting to the way we do things," says Lord Peran softly, never taking his eyes off me. "Haven't you, girl?"

Be good, behave . . .

"Yessir." I bow my head and clasp my hands in what I hope at least looks like repentance, even if my blood is boiling so fast I can hardly think beyond the steady thud of *I hate him I hate him I hate him.* I don't care what kind of excuses he has, there is nothing in the whole world that can justify being a bully. And that's what he is, even if I'm the only one who can see it.

Anyone who doesn't isn't paying attention.

"I see that temper of yours has finally been quashed," Lord Peran notes, his voice little more than a murmur. I hate how pleased he sounds. "What do you have to say for yourself, girl?"

I'm not a girl and I'm not sorry, and I'd do it all again.

Somehow I don't think that'll help anyone.

Sometimes knights need to swallow their pride to achieve their goals, even if it means lying. "Sorry."

"For what?"

"For . . ." I falter. I kind of feel like he wants me to apologize for my whole existence, but that's not really specific enough. Every breath I've taken in his presence has been wrong so far. "For standing up for the prince. For fighting with Edwyn." I'm pretty sure those are my worst offenses, but judging by the stony silence that follows, maybe not.

"What else?" Lord Peran demands, all clipped like it's an inconvenience even to speak to me.

"Uh . . . sorry for . . . not listening?"

"Child," says the man with the pointed gray beard, "there are places for boys and places for girls, and you broke those barriers. We need to be assured that you understand your limitations and will abide by them in the future, should you be permitted to stay."

"Wait, *what?*" I laugh before I can stop myself. "You're mad because I left the Queen's Quarters? That's it?"

"That is by no means 'it,'" says Lord Peran curtly. "It is not an insignificant transgression, Lady Calliden. The other issues would not have occurred if you had remained in the appropriate location in the first place. Can you see and understand the cause and effect that took place?"

"And if you hadn't been making Edwyn bully the prince, it wouldn't've happened either! It's not *my* fault! It's not because I was in the wrong place, it's because *you* were doing the wrong thing!"

The council lords start muttering among themselves, and my face heats up. Even more when Papa sighs my name behind me.

"Callie—"

Apparently logic doesn't matter. Rules only get applied one way here.

And I *don't* like the way Lord Peran is looking at me, like he's swallowing a whole mouthful of anger, like that ring's going to rip into *my* face if I don't watch myself.

"As you can see," says Lord Peran softly, "the girl is entirely unrepentant. I suggest she be sent away with immediate effect before she does any lasting damage to the Crown."

"Now wait a second!" Papa pushes in front of me. "You asked Callie to apologize and they did. There is absolutely no need for such dramatics, Peran! Lasting damage to the Crown . . . I am surprised you see so much threat in one kid!"

"I'm surprised you do not," Peran snaps back. "Did we all not learn a valuable lesson in not underestimating"—he looks like the word tastes bitter in his mouth—*"females?"*

"This is *nothing* like Alis!"

My stomach jolts. As much as I want to be taken seriously, I definitely don't want to be compared to Helston's biggest threat. Suddenly this all feels very big and very real.

"I will not risk it, Nicholas," says Peran, standing up with both hands flat on the table. "Not with so much to lose. Helston cannot afford another internal attack."

"Callie is twelve years old—"

"Every villain has a beginning. I will not be undermined. I will not have all the work I have put into that boy be *ruined* by one obstinate little girl!"

Silence rings through the Council Chambers. Edwyn looks like he's trying his best to disappear completely, sinking back and down in his chair with a visible lump in his throat.

Even the lords shift in their seats, passing glances between them like platters of food.

I hold tight to the back of Papa's tunic and try to feel as brave as I know I can be.

"Callie stays with me," says Papa, low and calm in the voice he uses when I need to be talked down. The one he learned from Neal. "And if you want me to continue my work with His Highness, then Callie stays *here*. Otherwise, I wish you all the luck in the world in finding another man able to train him. We stay *together*."

Peran opens his mouth, eyes as hard as Satin's tempered steel, but one of the lords on his right speaks up. "Consider it, Peran. We all agreed that Sir Nicholas was His Highness's best and last chance, and there are only five weeks left until the tournament. If we are to keep to schedule—and I do not believe we are in a position to delay—then we *must* compromise."

Peran pulls a face like "compromise" is a dirty word. "If we make allowance for one," he says through gritted teeth, "then what follows? There *must* be consequences, at the very least as an example to anyone else who might take advantage of such leniency. And I will not have her running around unchecked." He glares at Papa. "You will be occupied with your duties and unable to supervise her, and I will not have my daughter exposed to such *corrupting* influence. What would you have done with her, my lords?"

There's a moment of polite mumbling between the men. It's like Papa and I aren't here at all. Edwyn's ignored too. He keeps himself small, glaring down at his lap with tightly knotted brows. Like he's only here for decoration.

At least I have Papa.

I lean against him, and he rests his hand on the top of my head. Whatever happens, we do it together. We can do anything together. We can beat anything together, whether it's a pack of wolves or a pack of lords, all baying for our blood.

"Very well." Lord Peran clears his throat and stands to face us like this is a formal trial. "You may have your compromise, Sir Nicholas. The girl may stay, only as a courtesy to you, the king's champion and His Highness's trainer. But the condition is this, Lady Calliden. You will be confined to your chamber until we, the council, are satisfied that you are appropriately repentant, that you understand and respect the rules here in Helston, and that you do not pose a threat to the fabric of the Crown. Do you understand?"

I hear the words. They go into my ears and buzz around like a headful of bees.

Confined.

I can feel Mama's hand pinching my arm, dragging me to my room, locking the door behind her. Promising I won't come out until I'm really, truly sorry. She never did that when Papa was home. When he wasn't, I was locked up more than I wasn't.

I don't want to be locked away again.

"Callie, you don't have to do this."

I have a choice. We could leave right now. Ride back across the moors, gallop all the way home, back to Neal. We could be there in two days.

I want it so bad, my chest hurts.

Not all battles are fought with swords, Callie. Not all enemies want you dead.

I came here to prove myself worthy of my shield, to fight for the same chance as everyone else. To prove myself a true knight.

And a knight does not run from people who need them.

I think of the prince cradling his bruised hand.

First duty to the Crown . . .

I know what I have to do.

I bow to Lord Peran, straight-backed and low. "I understand, my lord. I accept these terms."

The chancellor smiles. "Lovely." Then he snaps his fingers, and Captain Adan appears in the doorway.

"Escort Lady Calliden to her chambers," he says. "And ensure the door is *locked*."

I breathe through the urge to struggle when hands lock around my arms. I'm not afraid. This was my choice. *I'm in control.*

"Your daughter is a credit to you, Nicholas," Peran murmurs. "I hope you will accept your station as quickly. Let's talk about His Highness, shall we?"

"Richard would hate this," Papa growls. "You know he would."

"His Majesty isn't here, and whose fault is that?"

Lord Peran rises and steps around the long table, every footfall measured. "When I ordered the king's champion home, I expected the knight who had earned his reputation for instilling disciplined efficiency. Not"—he waves a disgusted hand in Papa's direction—"whatever your so-called 'retirement' has turned you into. I am disappointed, Nicholas."

"I am sorry to have disappointed you." I hate the way Papa's voice wavers. I hate the way he steps backward, like he's retreating. "Watching Prince Jowan fall, being unable to prevent it, seeing what it did to his family . . . Priorities change, Peran."

"Change them back," Peran growls. "Renew your pledge to the Crown."

The grip on my arm tightens, pinching, pulling me around just as Papa kneels before Peran. "Move."

"Papa—" It's not right that he's kneeling. It's not right that Peran's standing over him like he's won. *It's not right!*

"Go, Callie." His voice is soft and defeated and rings louder than if he'd shouted.

I flinch, stunned, and Adan jostles me away.

This isn't what winning is supposed to feel like.

CHAPTER
ELEVEN

They leave me alone with the knot of guilt in my chest and nothing to distract me from my last image of Papa, kneeling before Lord Peran.

If I'd just done what I was supposed to do in the first place, if I'd stayed good and still and quiet like I'd been told—

Five weeks.

I count time in plates of food I don't eat and visits from servants who don't speak to me. It's three days before I make myself get up and move. I clear as much floor space as possible, shoving everything into the crevice between the floor and the walls. It's not enough, but I make it enough. This is my training grounds, and it's the best I've got. Five weeks is dwindling into four, and I stayed for the tournament, to prove myself in front of everyone, and that's more important than ever now. I will not be beaten.

I'm a sweaty disaster, in the middle of a particularly

ruthless lunge at a bedpost with an invisible broadsword, when the lock clicks for the third time today. I jump back onto my bed and do my best impression of a listless, repentant child with nothing to do other than reflect on their crimes. It'll take the full five weeks just to perfect the act enough to convince the chancellor.

I keep my face turned away and wait for the sound of a plate on the dresser, for receding steps, for the door to shut.

Instead, I hear: "Good grief, what have you done to this place?"

I bolt up so hard my neck cracks. "Elowen!"

She smiles with an armful of books and a small plate balanced on top. *Biscuits!*

I lunge, for her, for them, because it's the chivalrous thing to do, to help a lady with a teetering armful. And it would be a real tragedy if we lost those biscuits.

Cinnamon. I could kiss her!

"What're you doing here?" I ask, doing my best not to visibly drool. "I figured your dad would be as keen to keep you away from me as he is to keep me away from, well, anyone."

Elowen deposits the books on the desk by the window. "Contrary to popular belief," she says softly, "the queen still outranks Father, and it's Her Majesty's wish that you continue with your studies. I offered my services."

"Why?" I ask, because if I don't, it'll bug me forever. "Your dad was pretty angry, and Edwyn looked really chewed out. Did you get in trouble too?"

"Well, he wasn't terribly pleased that I'd let you escape again, but I know how to stay out of Father's way until the storm passes. Fortunately, our paths do not cross often or for long, and Father doesn't care enough to really come looking for me." She starts picking up my mess of clothes, busying herself with carefully folding them on the bed. "I'm sorry that you had to face him like that. I know what he can be like."

"I'm fine." It's not as much of a lie as I thought it might be. "It definitely could've been worse, and at least I get to stay."

Elowen glances up, almost shy. "And you're happy to stay? I was certain you would choose to leave."

"Nah. I'm not scared off by a bunch of old men."

She laughs, and the sound is like tinkling bells. "Good! I'm glad. We have work to do."

I can't help my grimace. She sounds just like Neal when he's trying to get me to sit down and study with him. "I'm a terrible student, El—don't underestimate that."

Elowen smirks. "Luckily I'm an *excellent* teacher. But time for that later. First, eat. You earned them."

She does not have to tell me twice.

I devour three biscuits in four bites while Elowen nibbles carefully around the edges of her first. Sugar has never tasted so good.

Turns out the sugar isn't just a thank-you, it's a barefaced bribe.

Elowen is a strict teacher—way worse than Neal, who lets me wander off whenever I get frustrated and fed up. Not that there's anywhere to wander off to. Magic's never come easy to me, but under Elowen's instruction, it's as exhausting as the most difficult drills.

"Relax," she orders. "Breathe. We're starting from the beginning. You might not care about art or music or creating things, but your magic is still there, waiting to be used. Close your eyes and feel it. And stop fidgeting."

I make myself do as she says, even though it feels all kinds of wrong. It's hard to remember that I'm not in Clystwell with Mama, I'm in Helston with Elowen. And it's not the same as before. She's not going to hate me if I can't do it right the first time or the second time. She won't. Right?

"Most people think magic is invisibility and silence. But they're wrong. Others think it's just beauty and art. They're wrong too. Magic is power. It can be anything you need it to be, anything you want, if you learn to harness it. Watch."

A candle replaces the biscuits. Elowen brushes a hand over the wick, and a tiny flame spits to life. It flickers, silent and steady.

"Now, observe." She shifts, facing the hearth, then hurls something invisible into the logs.

They burst into flame, so hard and fast I stop breathing for a moment. The fire licks all the way up into the chimney, violent and ravenous, snapping like a hungry wolf.

Elowen smiles. "If you master control of your magic, you can do anything."

I shiver. Neal never explained it like that before. "I didn't know magic could be so . . . scary."

The smile switches, turning cool and sharp like her dad's. "Magic is power," she repeats. "And the secret is that no one wants you to know it." A ball of pure white light swells in her palm, and Elowen tips it casually from one hand to the other like a toy. "You think it's useless because that's what they want you to believe. They're scared of it. Of you. And why should your magic help you if you think it's worthless? It's an ally. A friend. You grow stronger *together*."

It's like she's holding a star; so bright, it hurts my eyes. But I can't look away. I feel like I'm being pulled right into it.

"And this is what . . . Her Majesty teaches the Queen's Daughters?"

"Not in so many words," says Elowen. "There would be outrage if anyone ever suspected she was teaching us how to really use our magic."

"Like the banished princess . . ."

Elowen extinguishes the flame in a fist. "What?"

"Yeah, Papa told me. The witch of the moors, the enemy of Helston, she was a princess, but apparently she lost control of her magic and she nearly killed everyone, so they kicked her out." I frown at her surprise. I figured Elowen knew everything about everything in Helston. "You didn't know?"

"I know about the witch," she says carefully. "Everyone does. No one ever told me she was a princess."

"Yeah, apparently it's all about revenge or something. I dunno. Sounds like a rubbish reason for war, but what do I know?"

Elowen doesn't say anything, just considers her hands, the soft crease of a frown between her eyes.

I nudge her. "What's up?"

"Nothing." She fixes her smile the way other people fix their hair and sits up straighter. "Come along," she says briskly. "By the time Father lets you out, I expect you to be a fearsome sorcerer, *just* like this princess."

I pull a face. "I think you'd be better at that, El."

Turns out it *is* a lot of work, and Elowen pushes me harder than Papa and Neal ever did.

I don't know what I'm lacking more, potential or peace, but either way my magic does *not* want to cooperate. No matter how hard I bully, beg, or bribe, it point-blank refuses to show its face.

I flop backward on the floor with a dramatic groan, flinging an arm over my face. "I'm no good at this. . . ."

"You'll get better," Elowen says. "With patience and practice. No one's good at anything straightaway, and you worked hard. Look, I have a reward for you."

I crack open my eyes, hoping for more biscuits. Elowen is on her feet. She goes to the wardrobe I still haven't used and starts feeling along the wall with her fingertips.

"I think all that magic has gone to your head."

Elowen keeps on with her search, tracing invisible lines into the stone until—

"*There* you are." She pushes and the wall clicks. *The wall clicks?* She turns back to me, grinning. "It's been a while," she says, like that explains anything, and the wall opens up.

Just a little. A space the size of a door.

"Whoa." I pick myself up and run. The corridor is unlit and endless.

Elowen claps her hands once, and light sparks into two lanterns. Their flickering beckons me on.

"Not yet," she says when I start to step inside. "Wait until it's nighttime. If you're caught, you won't get another chance."

I nod and make myself retreat. I don't know how I'm going to wait all those hours. "Where does it go?"

"Everywhere," says Elowen. "All across the palace and out. It was designed as an escape, if Helston was ever to be attacked, though I think it was only ever properly used as a way for servants to get around. Hardly anyone uses it anymore."

"Except you."

"Everyone needs an escape sometimes," says Elowen. "Listen, if you want a place to practice, remember that tiny bit of beach I showed you? I don't think anyone else knows about it. There certainly won't be anyone there at night. Just be mindful of ghosts."

It's not ghosts I'm worried about.

CHAPTER TWELVE

I t's agony to wait, but I make myself watch the sun go all the way down and hold out for the movement in the courtyard to stop. Elowen's right—I get one chance. I can't afford to waste it.

It's not like I'm scared of the chancellor, but if I'm caught, that would implicate Elowen *and* it would cause even more trouble for Papa *and* there's no way I'd get to stay, so all that humiliation would be for nothing.

I have to be cautious and sensible, and neither comes naturally.

Finally, when the shadows are the right shape and the lanterns have been lit for long enough, I sweep my cloak around my shoulders and make my move.

I copy the pattern of Elowen's fingertips on the wall, expecting nothing, half-certain I dreamed her and it, the girl and the door just figments of an imagination desperate for escape.

But the stone gives, and the door opens for me.

It feels much darker than when Elowen opened it, and it takes seven goes before I can light my way. It's frustrating, trying to keep my breathing and my heart calm enough to raise the flicker of light, and the frustration makes it harder.

I nearly give up and stomp my way through the darkness and hope for the best, but I'll never find my way back if I can't see.

So I try. I close my eyes and sink into myself, searching for the little fire inside me. It's tiny, next to useless, neglected for way too long. Elowen's right—no one's good at anything straightaway. You have to work at it. And I just haven't.

But I will. I want to be better. I will be better. And if it takes time, that's fine.

I coax my magic to life, bringing it up and out of my body, to my fingers like Elowen showed me; then I cast it into the darkness. There's no great explosion, no burst of bright light, just a tiny twinkling speck that catches in the lanterns and lights my way.

It's enough. I grin and follow it all the way through the palace on the other side of the walls, as close to the lives living in the rooms as possible without being seen. Like a ghost. I pass by bedrooms and living chambers, down narrowing winding staircases, and beside the kitchens that are still loud and bustling.

I feel like a mouse, scurrying and keen not to be seen,

hunting for scraps, and when I finally burst out the last door, it's like escaping a cage.

I suck in a lungful of sharp, fresh air. And another and another until I feel like myself again, and then I run, bee-lining straight for the training yard, the stables, *the armory*. It takes ages, trying to steer clear of the main paths just in case there's anyone still wandering around, but eventually I make it down the windy path toward the smell of horses.

The training yard is empty, peaceful. All mine.

This is where I'm supposed to be. This is what I came here to do. Not sit, cooped up, trying to make something out of nothing. I came here to run and fight and *train*.

I sprint laps. Round and round until my lungs burst, and then I push through and keep going. I don't stop until I'm sweating; then I go through my morning routine in the moon-light, practicing my forms and focusing on the balance of my body, reconnecting with myself in a way I can't indoors.

Four weeks, a handful of days, then home and free.

I can last four weeks if I can escape after dark. Most important, I can last six weeks unbroken. With a reprieve, there's no danger of me giving in and giving Peran what he wants. I can come out the other side with my pride intact.

I can last. I can survive. I can win.

I actually have a chance now that I can train properly.

Speaking of which . . .

The armory is opposite the stables. The familiar smell of leather and polish coaxes me inside.

I shiver.

Rows and rows of polished steel, lovingly cared for, waiting to be used. Waiting for *me*. We have a wide range at home, but nothing compared to this. It's endless, the choice vast. Every blade is polished and sharpened, ready to work. Even the practice weapons are kept and displayed as carefully as their steel counterparts—from light wooden starter swords to weighted weapons with blunt edges. Everything anyone would need from beginning to end; from kid to warrior.

If I had these resources available to me, I could do anything, *be* anything.

Boys don't know how lucky they are.

I search for Satin. There are hundreds of blades, but I know I'll be able to pick her out straightaway if she's here.

Voices accompany the crunch of gravel, and I freeze. I don't have time to look for Satin. I snatch a practice sword off the rack and run, keeping to the darkest shadows until I find the path Elowen showed me earlier.

The path down to the beach is narrow and winding, set flush to the cliff. It's made of nothing but gravel, and I half slip all the way down until I hit the sand. No one will find me here unless they're actively looking, and who's going to come looking for me?

The hush of waves welcomes me.

I stand in the foam and look at the moon on the rolling water.

Everyone needs an escape sometimes, said Elowen. And

this one's mine. This tiny scrap of beach, between the cliff and the ocean. Perfect.

Kicking off my boots, I fall into the pattern Neal taught me, starting slow and getting faster and faster until my blade is a blur and the sword becomes an extension of my arm. I am complete again.

Back in my room, I practiced in anger, throwing punches at an invisible chancellor and dueling him with an imaginary sword, longing for the day when I can challenge him for real. But out here, where I can breathe, I choose not to be angry.

True strength comes from conviction, not rage, Neal told me back in the early days, when my temper was sharp and untamable. Anger is a spark. Conviction stays burning.

Lord Peran isn't worth burning out over.

Instead, I will stay strong and certain and myself and—

A falling stone jerks me out of my thoughts, and my stance shifts from casual to defensive in a thudding heartbeat. There's movement on the cliff, no more distinct than a shadow. I don't believe in ghosts, so that means it's a living, breathing someone who can get me in trouble, and my ratio of allies to enemies is not ideal.

And that's not including everything on the other side of the bridge. Yeah, sure, those defenses are pretty tight, but don't tell me that dragon couldn't barrage right into them if they wanted to.

I sweep my sword in a tight circle. It's not as heavy as I'd like. The best it'll do, if it comes to it, is stun.

It'll have to be enough.

Keeping low, I speed back up the hill as quickly and quietly as I can. Running away is not in my nature, and if I'm going to fight, I'd rather face my enemy head-on and take the advantage. At the top, I crouch in the bushes at the fork in the path, hold my breath and my blade ready, and wait.

It's not long before the sound of footsteps skidding in the gravel pricks my ears. They're coming down the hill behind me; a soft light cradled to their chest.

Elowen, I think first. But it's not El. Whoever it is, they're wrapped up tight in a cloak, with the hood pulled up. Their shoulders are all hunched up, and they're scurrying like they're sorry for even existing.

I know who that is.

"Hey!"

The prince freezes, brown eyes wide and terrified. Even wider and more terrified when he sees the blade I have not lowered.

Oops.

I drop the point quickly to the ground. "Sorry," I tell him. "Instinct."

The prince says nothing. He doesn't move. I'm not even sure he's breathing. The light cupped in his palms flickers like a fragile candle.

"Sorry for scaring you," I tell him. "But you freaked me out too. I thought you were a beast or something. What were you doing up there? Spying on me?" I laugh to prove it's a joke, no big deal, but the prince flinches.

"N-no," he stammers. "I wasn't. At least . . . not exactly. Forgive me, I—" His gaze drops to the light like he's seeing it for the first time, and he jams his hands into his armpits, extinguishing the magic. The moon's bright, but it takes a long moment for my eyes to readjust. In the darkness, he whispers, "Please don't tell. It wasn't my intention to spy. I swear. I—I was up there anyway, and I saw you and— Please don't tell."

I give a laugh that lodges in my throat. "Tell what to who? It's not like you don't have ammunition against me too. Looks like we're both in the same boat, which could be pretty useful, if you ask me."

The prince's silence is thick and awkward, and, me being me, I start jamming it full of words. "Look, you didn't need to run away, you know. You could've come down and said hi. I wouldn't've minded. Unless you were gonna go tell on me, in which case I would've definitely minded, but—"

"I won't tell."

"I won't either."

We share a smile in the moonlight, and the prince's body relaxes a little.

"Did you mean it?" he asks. "You really wouldn't mind if I . . . watched?"

"I mean, don't be weird about it, but sure. Dunno why you'd want to, though. I bet princes have way more interesting things to do."

The prince's blush looks silver in the moonlight. "It . . . reminded me of my brother. The way you moved. Like you were dancing."

"I don't dance," I say tightly. "Not a bit."

"But you move as if you love it," the prince insists, taking one step closer. "As if you don't even have to think about it. Like it's as natural as dancing. And if I may—if you don't mind—and, of course, if you come back, I would very much like to watch. To study."

It's like he's holding back on actually begging and about to lose the battle. I don't get people wanting to spend time with me that badly, *especially* not princes. It feels like a trick.

"Why?"

"Oh . . ." The flush deepens. "Well, it makes sense to me, dancing, in a way that sword stuff doesn't, so if I can study it that way by watching you, then I might"—he takes a deep, shuddering breath—"not fail quite as spectacularly as everyone expects me to."

Ooft.

The prince looks so totally *miserable,* my chest hurts just looking at him, and if he's down to watching *me,* then it must be going bad. I guess he has a little under five weeks left before time runs out. If I were him—

"Forgive me," he mumbles, making me realize I haven't actually replied yet. "I won't tell anyone about you. I only ask that you do the same." He bows low, form perfect, expression dead. "I'll leave you to your practice, Lady Calliden." Bundled up tight like he's holding himself together, the hopeless prince starts back toward the palace.

"It's Callie."

Prince Will stops, glancing back as though hopeful and scared to hope all at once.

I know I shouldn't do it. It'd all be so much easier if I were left alone to get on with what I need to do by myself without complications. Princes are *certainly* complications. But I like this kid. And yeah, I'd have definitely treated him differently if I'd known who he was. And if I didn't know now, I don't know if I'd even be hesitating.

That proves something, doesn't it?

I stick out my swordless hand. "My name, my real name, it's Callie. No lady or anything. Just me."

He considers my hand the way Flo did when she was brand-new around people, like it's some kind of cruel trick he's fallen for before. Finally, he asks, "Don't you . . . care?"

"About what?"

"That I'm . . ." He sucks his lip, assessing me warily, like the word is forbidden and he'll get slapped if he says it out loud.

"Magical?"

He gives a tiny nod.

"Do you care that I want to be a knight?"

"Of course I don't!"

"Then why should I care that you're magical? I know a bunch of boys with magic. You're not so special, Prince Will."

Most people aren't too thrilled to hear they're not special, but a smile breaks across the prince's face, and he lights up with a laugh. It's like the shell he's crammed himself into cracks and he unfurls into himself, shaking out his wings.

"It's Willow, by the way," he says.

"What is?"

His face pinkens. "My name. My *real* name. And I figured, if we're to be . . . friends, then perhaps it would be okay for you to call me Willow. Just out here? When it's just us?"

There's a whole bunch of questions that I should reply to, but my head is pinpoint focused on one thing and one thing only. . . .

"They took away your name?"

There's no point even trying to temper my fury. Taking away someone's name is like taking away someone's identity. It *is* taking someone's identity—the very part of them that makes them *them*. I know what that's like. "So let me get this straight. You lost your brother, your dad left, you're not allowed to see your mum, and they took your name too? Did they let you keep anything of yourself?"

Prince Willow recoils slightly, slipping back into that clamped-up shell. "They're just trying to help me," he whispers. "It isn't exactly a kingly name—"

"But it is *yours!*"

"The fight isn't worth it."

The bleak statement of fact makes me stop, my anger turning into plain sadness.

A knight's first duty is to the Crown.

And this Crown doesn't need a knight or a war, he needs a friend and a hug.

I can do both.

"I'd love to be friends, Willow."

The prince lights up like a star, and he finally grabs my hand in both of his. "Really for real?"

I laugh. "Really for real."

CHAPTER
THIRTEEN

Willow looks almost surprised to see me when I meet him the next night at the cross paths—the agreed-upon place at (roughly) the agreed-upon time. Specifics get fuzzy when you're sneaking around after dark.

"I—I wasn't sure you were coming," he admits. "And then I wasn't sure I hadn't imagined you. And *then* I wasn't sure it hadn't all been a big trick and you'd tell on me." He winces. "It's been a bit of a day."

"With all those worries, I'm not surprised." Nothing worse than when a worry builds and builds, and there's nothing you can do but wait it out. That makes anyone pretty useless. "Everyone has bad days, though—don't worry about it."

We start down the narrow trail leading to the beach. Willow creeps behind me, cloak pulled tight around himself like it isn't a balmy spring night.

"Every day is a bad day," he mumbles. "Today just happened to be one of the worst. I'm afraid your father isn't very happy with me."

"Yeah?" I'm about to turn around and go backward so we can have a proper conversation, but one bad step would send me over the cliff, and knowing my luck, I'd take the prince with me. Not a good start to a friendship! "How is Papa?"

"Doing his best," says Willow bleakly. "Which isn't saying much. I can tell he's trying to be patient with me. And I can tell it's hard."

"If Papa can put up with me, you'll be no problem. Just give it time."

"We don't have time."

I wish that wasn't as true as it is.

"Callie, may I ask you something?"

"Course."

It's a long time before the prince manages to put words to his question, and by the time he's ready, we've hit the sand and my boots are off. Nothing worse than sand in your boots.

"You said yesterday . . . you said you knew plenty of boys with magic. Is that true?"

"Why would I lie?" I throw off my cloak and draw my sword, relishing the sing of steel. It feels so good to be out after an endless day cramped up in my room.

Willow stands statue stiff, one step away from the sand and sucking his lip so hard he won't have anything left by the time we head back to the palace. "I've . . . never met anyone like me before. What're they like?"

I shrug. "Fine. Same as anyone else. Except Neal."

"Neal?"

"Yeah. He's the best." I give my sword an experimental swing, then another and another until I fall into the right pattern to loosen up my muscles. "He used to be here, actually. Ages ago. He was gonna be a knight."

Willow makes a sound like the breath got knocked out of him. "A magical knight? What happened?"

"He quit." I imagine the giant wolf in the middle of the beach, and I circle it with my sword pointed at its shaggy throat, then lunge, getting it in the jugular and spraying the sand with imaginary blood. "He said they don't like different here."

"Did they know he was . . . you know?"

"No. They could just tell something was weird about him." I wheel on a whole pack of imaginary beasts with fangs the length of my arm, my own blood hot and racing like the fight is real. It feels real.

"Weird," the prince echoes bleakly. He sighs and starts carefully across the tiny scrap of beach to the shelter of the cliff's overhang. There he settles on a rock, drawing his legs up like he's folding himself in half.

He's nothing like Prince Jowan. I can't help seeing all the differences between them. They've got kinda the same face,

145

dark hair and brown eyes, but Jowan was all life and energy, and this kid is . . . half-dead.

My blade whistles a tune in the air while my feet keep a steady beat. I guess it is a bit like dancing, though the moment my head thinks it, my body stumbles like the inelegant thing it knows it is. Anyone else, and I would've assumed they were mocking me, telling me I look like I'm dancing. But I don't think Prince Willow has an insincere bone in his body.

I glance back at the prince. He's got himself settled comfortably, and there's a book lying open on his knees. That must be what he's been hiding in his cloak. He's more than half-hunched over it, but even so I can see that it's not a reading book at all. There's a stick of something black between his fingers, making deft lines across the page.

He falls so deep into his work, he doesn't notice me creeping up on him, and his soul just about leaves his body when my shadow falls over him.

"Whatcha doing?"

"Nothing!" The book snaps shut, and his eyes go as wide and guilty as they did with the magic. Seems like everything he enjoys is a punishable offense. "Studying." Willow relents. "I—I told you—the way you move, it makes sense to me. And I have to . . . I have to work this out." His voice goes tight and brittle. "I know it's unusual—*different*—and I . . . I know it wouldn't be considered appropriate, but if it works and I can prove to them that I'm . . . that I'm not h-hopeless, then the means don't matter, right?" He looks at me fearfully, desperate for my confirmation.

And I'm desperate to give it him. But I can't make my mouth move. All my words are stuck in the back of my throat, and I just feel *sad*. That deep, heavy kind of sadness that settles in your chest like wet clay. I don't think Peran would want a dancing prince any more than he wants a magical one.

"I just need . . . *someone* to tell me it's going to be fine," Willow says stiltedly. "Even if it's a lie. Because no one thinks it will be. No one believes I can do it. And they're all just waiting for me t-to— So they can pick someone else. Someone better. Someone who was born to lead."

"That's *you*," I say fiercely, finding my voice. I plop down in the sand in front of the prince and glare up into his face. "You were *literally* born to do this."

But Willow only shakes his head, the waves of his hair falling about his face. "No. I wasn't. That was my brother. That was Jowan. That was *Father*. It wasn't supposed to be me. It was never supposed to be *me*."

"But it *is*. Whether anyone likes it or not." *Even Lord Peran.*

"You don't understand," Willow whispers. "Perhaps that would've been enough in another time. A peaceful time, when it didn't really matter. But we're about to . . ." His eyes fill with tears. "It's coming. War's coming. And they need a leader, and it's supposed to be me, and I can't do it, and they all know it, and I can't expect them t-to just ... *d-die*, just because they're stuck with me. That's not right. And I'd give it up. I would! I'd give it all up in a moment, but ..." Tears spill, and Willow squeezes his eyes tight shut. "I—I can't let them down, Callie."

"Who? The council?"

"No. Jowan. Father."

Oh.

I reach for him instinctively, to comfort with a hug the way that works for me. "They're not here, Willow."

But the prince pulls away with a brittle "You think I don't know that? You think I'm not reminded of that every single second of every single day, every time someone looks at me, wishing they were here instead of me? I *know* they're not here! But I wish they were. I wish they were here instead of me, just like everyone else wishes it."

"I bet no one really thinks that—"

"They do." Willow's voice is high and breathless. "They wish it'd been me instead of Jowan. He would've been the king everyone wants. And—" He laughs suddenly, a weird, crazed sound. "The really funny thing is, if it'd been that way around, he wouldn't've even needed to. Because Father would still be here. Everything would be as it's supposed to be. But I'm the only one left because my brother is dead, and Father would rather have nothing at all than just me, and Mother won't ... Mother can't ..." He shudders and lets his head fall heavy into his hands.

We have to be very careful with her, Elowen said of Queen Ewella, afraid that she could disappear too if reminded of her elder son.

But what about her younger one?

Did the king give any thought to Willow, or was he so consumed by grief for Jowan, Willow disappeared from his mind? King Richard was Papa's best friend for forever. Papa wouldn't be friends with someone who could just forget about his kid.

"Hey." I tug Willow up by both hands, letting the book fall into the sand. "I didn't know your dad, but I definitely knew Jowan, and I know for a hundred-percent *fact* that he'd be totally proud of you, and he'd say—" I scrabble for the bits of wisdom that always seemed to come from nowhere out of the prince's mouth. "He'd say your best is always enough, no matter what."

Willow laughs softly, scrubbing his face on his arm. "I haven't heard that for a long time."

"Yeah, I can't imagine Lord Peran giving that kind of pep talk."

The prince's fingers spasm and tighten in mine. "He'd . . . he'd say that sort of thing didn't work then, so why should it work now? He'd say that's what r-ruined me. That if Jowan and Mother and Father hadn't spoiled me, h-he wouldn't have such an impossible time fixing me."

My frown dips so deep, my brows ache. "He says that to you?"

"Only on the worst days."

"And how many of those are there?"

Willow's shoulders rise. "It isn't his fault. He's frustrated. It's difficult for him. I understand it."

"I don't," I snarl through my teeth. "You lost your brother *and* your dad, and then he took your name too. What did he lose? His bad feelings aren't the important ones here!"

The prince pulls away from me, hugging his middle. "He's doing his best, Callie. Helston would fall apart without him. We have to be grateful."

I can't roll my eyes back far enough. "Sure. By taking your name and taking your magic, and trying to turn you into something else."

"By trying to turn me into a king," Willow insists.

"You *are* a king, whether you're magical Willow or non-magical Will. It doesn't matter if Lord Peran doesn't like it—he doesn't get to decide."

The bleak smile Willow gives me cracks my heart down the middle. "You haven't been here long enough to understand. Lord Peran decides everything."

I breathe through my anger using the method Neal taught me to bring me back from the edge when I'm about to lose it. *In two three . . . Out two three . . .*

It doesn't work.

"That's *stupid*! Just because someone says they're right, doesn't mean they are! And it's not working, is it? Forcing you to be someone you're not? It's just making everyone

150

miserable! Sorry," I add when Willow shrinks back. "Look, I know I'm new and I haven't been around long enough to understand, but maybe that's not a bad thing. It's like ... it's like there's a crack in your bedroom wall, and you look at it every single day without seeing it. And then someone new comes along and points it out, and they're like, 'Oh, there's a crack! Let's fix it!' Or something." It's clunky, but it gets the message across. At least I hope it does.

"How?" Willow asks.

"How what?"

"How can we fix it?"

"Uh..." I lunge for something—*anything*—'cause I have no idea how to fix something so broken. It's not just a cracked wall, it's a whole crumbling palace, with Willow right in its heart.

A knight's first duty is to the Crown.

"I'm gonna help you. I'm gonna teach you."

Willow does not look convinced. "Sir Nicholas is my seventh teacher," he whispers. "Every single one is the best of the best, and they've all given up on me."

"Well, Papa doesn't give up on anyone," I say fiercely. "And neither do I. Besides, I'm not bound by whatever silly rules Peran's pushing on Papa, and you said yourself that the way I move makes sense to you. So we're gonna make it make sense, and you're gonna prove to everyone that you're just as good as anyone else. Magic or not."

"You really think ... I can?"

"I *know* so."

"Four weeks and five days . . ."

"Plenty of time!" The more confidently I say it, the truer it feels.

Even if it isn't.

When I return to my drills, I'm not stabbing at fighting wolves anymore. I'm fighting imaginary chancellors.

CHAPTER
FOURTEEN

But it's harder than I thought it would be. Even away from the judging eyes of the court, Willow can hardly bear to touch a weapon, let alone wield one.

The first night we get serious, we sneak into the armory. I guess the sneaking around a potentially populated area, especially the site of Willow's worst experiences, makes things harder than they should be, and by the time we actually reach the racks of swords, the prince is a shrinking mess.

"Which do you normally use?"

"I—I don't know."

I laugh before I can stop myself. "What d'you mean you don't know? How do you not know what sword you use?" To my eye, every single blade is distinct and different, not interchangeable.

But the prince just gives a reluctant half shrug and refuses to step close enough to examine the swords.

So I pick for him.

"I'm surprised you don't have your own," I chatter on as I carefully examine the blades. "A sword is a warrior's partner, not just a tool. It's your ally. Your best friend. I bet if you had your own sword, you'd find it easier to connect with them. Here." I pick a semiweighted long sword the right size for Willow, who's just about the same height as I am (short), and offer it to him, hilt first.

He flinches away like I've taken a swipe at him.

"It's not gonna bite you," I insist. "Unless you grab the pointy end, but I reckon even you know which end to hold."

Willow doesn't laugh. It's like he doesn't even see me. His eyes have gone glazed, and his chest heaves with the effort of breathing.

I prop the sword up against the wall and go to him. "Hey, Willow, it's okay. It's just us. Just you and me. And we're gonna head down to the beach, and no one'll see us, and it's all gonna be fine, right? We're just . . . we're gonna dance. With swords. It'll be fun!" I don't really know what I'm saying, but I'll say pretty much anything to bring the prince back to reality.

And the sooner the better, 'cause I doubt our luck is infinite, and I don't like the idea of explaining to the council why I've broken confinement and why I'm hanging out with the crown prince in the armory.

I end up somehow carrying both swords *and* holding

Willow's hand all the way down to the beach. To his credit, he doesn't run away, but every step forward is reluctant and dragged out, as though he's forcing each individual muscle in his body to obey.

The mean part of me understands Peran's frustration.

I kick that part of me away.

Everyone learns differently, Papa says. And a good teacher adapts to their student's needs, not the other way round.

So we take it slow.

Painfully slow.

And we start at the beginning.

I place Willow's fingers in the correct position on the hilt. His knuckles are bruised, and his fingers are as callused as a seasoned warrior's. The calluses are good. The bruises are bad.

"You should get that looked at," I suggest gently. "I know the best healers in the kingdom are here."

"Lord Peran says it's proof that I put the work in," Willow responds dully, touching a dark scab on one knuckle. "I might not've made any progress, but at least I can prove I tried."

"That's—" I swallow my curse. "Ridiculous. Even knights don't have to put up with injuries unless they have to. Fighting in pain is just gonna make you fight worse. Here." I stab both swords into the sand and take Willow's hand.

I don't have much magic, but I give Willow what I have. Touching the damage lightly, I breathe, digging down deep to pull out the little scrap of magic lingering somewhere in my blood and press it into the prince's bruises.

Willow clenches his teeth, tears rolling down his nose to splash in the sand.

You're not supposed to feel healing at all. You wouldn't even notice a good healer. I'm not a good healer. "Sorry," I tell him. "I'm really bad at magic."

"No, it's . . ." Willow swipes at his face and touches his knuckles gingerly. They're still scabbed up and bruised, but the angry swelling has definitely gone down at least a little. "It's better. Thank you. I don't believe you're as bad as you think you are." He offers a wobbly smile. "And everyone improves with practice, don't they?"

I doubt Elowen, my long-suffering teacher, would agree, but sure, I guess.

Still, even with Willow's hands fixed up a bit, we're starting way back from where I thought we would. Even if he's not a natural, the prince has still been training rigorously for years. I at least figured he'd have some kind of muscle memory, but it's like we're starting from scratch. Like he's never touched a sword in his life, much less swung one.

Four and a half weeks is nowhere *near* enough time.

Willow never complains, not even once, but the toll the lesson takes on him is painfully visible. He thinks too hard and doesn't trust himself at all. Worst of all, he doesn't trust me. Whoever his six other trainers were, they weren't good ones, no matter what Lord Peran has the prince believing.

Teachers aren't supposed to scare their students. That's not teaching; that's bullying. Big difference.

I stop the lesson when his breathing starts to go.

"All right!" I stab my sword back into the sand and grin. "Good job, pupil! You are dismissed for the day! Excellent work!"

The prince stares at me like I've just sprouted a second head and two extra sets of legs. He doesn't lower his sword, even though his arm is visibly shaking. "But we're not . . . But I haven't—"

"You did *good*," I tell him bluntly. "Let's leave it on a high point and pick up tomorrow." That's what Papa always does when he's training—stops before exhaustion makes everyone feel like a failure even if they've achieved something. And the prince *has* achieved something tonight. "Look at where you started and look at where you've finished. *That's* progress, Willow!"

The prince looks doubtfully down at his sword with a deep frown dipped between his eyes. I don't reckon anyone's ever said anything like that to him before. Not even Papa. That particular thought twists my gut.

"Go rest," I tell Willow. "You've earned it. I'm gonna go through my drills for a bit."

He settles in what has become his usual spot beneath the cliff, and I sink into my rhythm and my thoughts.

Papa is the best of the best—not just in skill and experience as a legendary warrior, but in patience as a teacher. He knows how to coax out the most from everyone, from soldiers who're flinchy from the battlefield to kids who've never touched a stick before, much less a sword. He knows how to turn lessons into games and make them feel like fun instead of work. He *knows* how to make even the most hopeless student feel good about themselves.

So why hasn't it worked on the prince?

If *I* can do it, Papa certainly can.

I don't get it.

I wish I could talk to Papa.

I swipe viciously at my imaginary enemy. If I was just allowed to do what I came here to do, and assist Papa like a proper squire, between us we could totally get Willow ready for the tournament.

Every new night is its own battle, and whatever's going on during the day sets him nearly the whole way backward by the time we meet up. It's a dance to get him to even touch the sword. I have to show him where to place his fingers and how to hold it. Every night, I hear "Sorry, Callie" more than anything else, and I have to literally bite my tongue not to snap at him to stop apologizing.

It's not his fault, and it's not him I'm angry at. It's the whole situation, and it feels way too much like he's just being set up for inevitable failure.

Five days in, and nothing's changed.

Willow flinches, withdraws, apologizes just the same as last night and the night before and the night before that, like we're stuck in some kind of time spell. I curse under my breath and stab my blade deep into the sand, stalking a few paces away and tearing out my ponytail to retie it tighter.

"Are you angry with me, Callie?" Willow creeps forward, staying well out of reach.

"Yes, I'm angry," I tell him, because there's no point lying. "But not at you. I don't know what to do. I don't know how to fix this."

The prince gives a sloping apologetic shrug. "I did tell you I was hopeless. It isn't your fault."

"You're not the one who should be comforting me," I snap, then immediately feel like the worst person in the world. "Sorry. It's true, though. I don't get it. I don't *get* what we're doing wrong."

"Not everyone can be good at everything," says Willow softly.

I hiss through my teeth. "You've got that right."

Willow raises a dark eyebrow. "I can't imagine you're not good at *anything*."

I don't think I could ever get bored with Willow's starry-eyed faith in me. "Well, I'm really bad at magic stuff. Like, *really* bad. I always have been, and I thought I always would be, but someone's actually starting to explain it in a way that makes sense, so—"

"I could—" Willow goes bright red. "We're ... we're friends, aren't we?"

"Of course."

"But I mean . . . really. I mean . . ." He sucks his lip. "If I told you a secret, you wouldn't tell anyone, would you? Not anyone at all?"

"I swear it." I drop to one knee, head bowed. "Knight's honor."

"What about friend's honor?"

"Is that stronger?"

Willow nods and offers his hand. More specifically, he offers his little finger.

I laugh. "What does that do?"

"It's the most serious oath you can take," says Willow. "We link fingers and you give your solemn vow as a friend. It's unbreakable."

Little fingers are very breakable, but I guess that's not the point. "Do we have to spit or bleed or anything?"

Willow looks horrified. "That's disgusting. No! Just . . . link fingers with me."

We arrange ourselves opposite each other in the sand, and I solemnly link my finger to his. He squeezes with surprising strength.

"Do you, Callie, swear on our friendship not to reveal what you see here tonight to anyone?"

"I, Callie, swear on our friendship not to reveal anything I see here tonight."

I half expect bright sparks to leap out of our entwined fingers and bind us together with unbreakable magic. But there is no spell. It's just us.

And that seems to be enough.

"All right." The prince resettles, breathing deeply. He sets his book in the sand between us and flips it open. The cover is black leather, used so much it's worn soft, and the pages inside are yellow and loose. Willow treats it gently, like an ancient artifact or a beloved pet on its last legs.

My heart jumps. "Hey! That's me!"

I'm splayed across the page in deft black lines. The sketches are rough, almost messy, but I recognize myself in the forms as though they were drawn in meticulous detail. That's the way *I* move. I flip through the book, turning page after page. They're all me. All practically moving right there on the paper.

"This is the one you drew that first night?" The sketch is clumsier than the others, and I remember feeling clumsier in my body, trying to remember how to move after days of being cooped up.

Willow nods. "Up on the cliff."

"Wow!"

"But this isn't . . . this isn't what I wanted to show you. Not entirely, anyway." The crease between his eyes is deep and anxious, and he looks like he'd rather dash all the way back to the palace than tell me his secret. But I guess friendship oaths go both ways.

Prince Willow takes a deep, steadying breath, then brushes a hand across the page.

I knew he was magical, but I had no idea he could do this.

The sketches rise and stand beneath his hand. Willow looks like a puppet master, invisible strings tying his fingers to the pictures, making them move exactly the way *I* move.

My form *is* pretty impressive. Not to boast or anything.

"Willow, that's amazing." I mean it, with every bit of myself. "*You're* amazing!"

But the prince's face stays somber. "I know it's wrong to entertain this part of myself. I tried not to. I tried to forget about it and pretend as though I didn't have it. The way they want."

"The way *who* wants?" I demand, as though I don't know.

"Lord Peran says my magic is more corrupted than anyone else's. It's wrong in everyone, but my magical line is evil. He says that's why I have it. It's so unnatural in boys, so it must be stronger. Wronger." His head goes down and his shoulders hunch up. "A curse to be broken. He says."

My stomach hurts. Looking at Willow—*knowing* Willow, even after just a few days—I don't need many guesses to work out how Lord Peran's going about breaking this "curse." But I do my best to keep my face and my voice still.

"Why does he think that?"

Willow worries his lip with his teeth, fingers absently tracing over his sketches. "My aunt."

"The banished princess."

He nods miserably. "I don't remember it. I wasn't even a year old, but everyone who was there remembers. She tried to burn Helston, and when they stopped her, she settled on

162

cursing me. That's why I'm magical, Lord Peran says. That's why I'm corrupted."

"Willow, you're not—"

"Magic in boys is unnatural," he says bitterly. "Everyone knows that. It's a sign of corruption, and mine is . . ." He swallows, turning his face away. "Mine's even worse. Lord Peran says that's why it's so hard to get rid of it. Why it's fighting so hard to stay. It's the last part of my aunt trying to take over Helston. And that's why I can't be king if I don't get rid of it. But I—I—I don't understand. I mean, I do. I know what magic can do and why it's bad, but it doesn't *feel* bad. It feels . . ."

"Beautiful?"

He nods, sending tears spilling into the sand. "Yes! Exactly! I don't understand how something that can create such beautiful things can be bad. And I know that's where my problem lies. I don't *want* to get rid of it. Not deep down. And I know that's wrong. I know it's my own fault, that I'm not trying hard enough, and I understand why everyone's so frustrated with me, why everyone g-gives up and . . . l-leaves. And I want to be better. I want to be good enough. I want to want to be what they want me to be."

Through the desperate tangle of words, the heart of Willow's fears hits me. Because they could be mine. They *were* mine once. Calliden's.

Wanting to want, and failing in that along with everything else. Certain there was something unfixably wrong with me on the inside. Hating myself just as much as Mama did.

I haven't thought about that time or those feelings since we rode away. I left them all back in my bedroom in Clystwell, along with the dresses and ribbons and everything that was Calliden's, not Callie's. And the old hurt throbs through me like a fresh bruise on my heart.

Willow gives a half-wild laugh and scrubs his eyes with both palms. "It's like there are two people inside me, and they're fighting so hard I can't think, and I don't know what to do. I don't know how to fix myself."

"I get it."

Willow eyes are wide through his fingers. "Really?"

I nod, pushing through the ache in my throat warning me away from talking about it. But I want to. I *have* to. I have to put this feeling into words for myself and for Willow, just to prove that neither of us is as alone as we've been made to believe.

"I get it so hard, my stomach's all twisted up in knots," I tell the prince. "My mama . . . she wanted me a way I knew I'd never be. I thought for the longest time that it was like a deal. If I could just turn myself into the daughter she wanted, it would fix everything. But it didn't. And trying just made things worse because I *didn't* want it. Not all the way through. Like I was fighting myself *all the time*." My body remembers the exhaustion and the ache from those days.

Willow unfolds a little. "What did you do? How did you . . . win?"

I push my fingers deep into the sand and lean back. "Papa noticed. He helped me. We left and he took me somewhere I could *just* be myself. No conditions."

The prince's shoulders sag with a whispered, "Lucky. No one's coming to save me."

I shuffle closer in the sand and lock Willow's bony body up tight in my arms and hold on. He might not have a Papa to take him away from this place, or a Neal to help him heal, but *I'm* here, and I'm the sum of both of them. I can pass all that good on. "You've got me, haven't you?"

The prince quakes. I can feel his teeth grind with his head against mine.

And then he breaks.

All the big complicated feelings come rushing out in a wind that whips up the sand around us, and I hold on to Willow as he sobs; crying for the loss of his brother, his father, his mother. Himself.

I hold Willow the way Neal held me, and I repeat Neal's words like a trusted spell. "It's okay to have complicated feelings about complicated things."

The prince leans heavily in my arms, his tears deep and silent, like they come from inside his heart, each one a crashing wave.

"Crying's like puking," I offer helpfully. "Once it's out, you'll feel a whole lot better. Holding it in just makes you sicker."

Willow makes a sputtering sound that I realize is a laugh.

He rubs his eyes with the arm not holding on to me, taking huge gulps of air. "That's what my magic's like," I just about hear. "That's why I come out here. I tried not to for the longest time. I tried to do what they told me to, to forget I have it and snuff it out. But it's not . . . it's not so easy as that. It made me so ill, and eventually I could tell—it was a choice between letting it out or d-dying. The first time, I wished I'd made the other choice. It sent me all the way backward, and the . . . and the way they looked at me, Callie." Willow buries his face in his hands. "That's why I come out here at night. So no one'll see. No one'll know. Just so I can function during the day. Even if that doesn't mean anything."

"You shouldn't have to," I whisper.

"But I do," Willow returns simply.

Yeah, he does.

It's weird to feel luckier than a prince.

Willow's head bumps gently against mine as he sighs. "Will you stay with me, Callie?"

I don't know if he means for right now, for the weeks until the tournament, or for forever after. It doesn't matter.

I squeeze him tight around the shoulders. "Yeah, I'll stay. And you know what? We'll make you the best king there ever was. You're not just gonna pass their ridiculous tests, you're gonna flourish, and then no one—even Peran—will be able to deny that you are who you're supposed to be, and once that's all solid and final, you can have your magic out in the open."

Willow wipes his face and looks up at me all hopeful. "You really think that'd work?"

"Sure!" My voice goes way too high to be convincing, but Willow doesn't seem to notice, and that's fine with me. "Once you're king, no one gets to tell you who you can and can't be!"

It's just a matter of getting him to that place.

CHAPTER FIFTEEN

The problem with partnering up with the prince and making it mutual is that I get homework too. As he says, it's only fair. It's my job to imagine the monsters and creatures I'm going to set on him down on the beach.

It's harder than I expected.

First of all, every day has to be different and has to push him a bit harder, but not hard enough to freak him out. Second of all (and most important), my imagination is crap.

My pictures are terrible. Like, really terrible. Like, worse than stick-figure terrible.

It's embarrassing.

I don't try for realism the way Willow does, or for painting pretty scenes that make you feel something, like Neal's. My mirages are just monsters whose primary goal is to have big teeth and be intimidating enough to fight. I picture the wolf who came for us on the moors—all ragged gray fur, and hungry yellow eyes, and teeth sharper than the keenest blade. I pull my fears and push them into the image, and they come out—

Well, the first time I tried, Willow burst out laughing. He laughed so hard he got a stitch and had to lie in the sand as tears rolled down his cheeks.

"You're not supposed to laugh," I grumbled, kicking sand at him. "You're supposed to be fighting for your life! This is what's out there, you know. *I've* faced them, and they're not funny."

But it's the good nights when he can laugh, and those are few and far between. Most days, he comes to me beaten down and miserable, and the patching up of the prince takes longer than the actual training.

To Willow's credit, though, he always tries. He always does his best, whatever that means day to day. And he *does* improve. It's a rush to notice it, even if it's just the lightness of his feet or the slight confidence in his grip. I am making a difference, and he isn't hopeless.

I just wish we had more time to see it through.

We don't talk about the deadline.

It hangs over Helston like a storm cloud biding its time.

Four weeks, four days . . .

And I resent every moment Willow and I can't spend together.

Don't get me wrong—I love spending time with Elowen. It's really cool having a friend, especially one who brings me biscuits and actually seems to *want* to spend time with me, and in a perfect world I would spend every moment of every day with her. But my lessons feel pointless. I don't need to learn, at least not so urgently. It doesn't matter if I don't master my magic before the tournament, and all the energy I'm compelled to put into my own learning *should* be put into teaching Willow.

Every day I resent my captivity a little more.

I should be out there, helping. Not just with the prince, but with everything else. There's a war coming, and I *should* be a part of it. Not stuck in here, useless.

I glare down at my truly rubbish sketch of the beast I'm going to throw at Willow tonight. I won't attempt to draw the dragon, when even a simple wolf is beyond my capability. I hate it. I hate everything. My stomach hurts and my head aches, and I'm so tired, I just want to call it quits and sleep for a week.

"Callie?"

I jerk up and slash a line through the middle of my monster.

I glare at Elowen. "I thought it was good manners to announce yourself when entering a person's bedroom."

"I did," Elowen retorts. "It's your own fault you weren't paying attention." She peers over my shoulder, long fingers curled over the back of my chair. "What're you working on? That's . . . interesting."

"Shut up." I flip the page and lean on it with my whole

body, glaring even harder when Elowen smirks. "I'm practicing imagining, all right? Just like you ordered."

She sets her daily offering of biscuits by my elbow. "Take a break. You look exhausted. You must've been studying since dawn."

"Ha ha." But I feel it too. Must be something in the weather. I yawn and don't bother shutting my mouth again before stuffing a whole biscuit in. Lemon. Score. Or maybe it's all those late nights finally catching up with me. Either way—

A cool palm pushes back my hair and presses to my forehead. "Well, you're not feverish," says Elowen. "But you do look pale."

"Rude." Usually I hate being fussed over, but apparently I mind it a whole lot less when it's Elowen.

"Well, it's true. I'm not going to lie to you. Friends tell each other harsh truths."

"Wish you'd tell me nice lies instead."

Elowen smiles sweetly. "Find someone else."

"Don't you have needlework to stab?"

"I'm a prodigy. I can leave my lessons whenever I like."

"To come and bother me?"

"To bestow upon you the company you so desperately crave." She dips into an elegant curtsy. "Man cannot live by a sword's companionship alone."

"I have too many responses to that and I'm too tired for any of them." I leave my sorry excuse for a lesson plan safely in the desk drawer and drag myself over to fall on my bed.

All I want to do is lie down and sleep, but I guess I quite like having Elowen here and—

"Ugh." My stomach curdles, and I curl in on myself. "El, I think this is the end. I'm pretty sure my insides are coming out and—"

Any concern Elowen might've had evaporates. "Ohh."

I glare at her as best I can without moving. "What do you mean, 'oh'?"

"Are you bleeding?" she asks.

"No? I'm pretty sure I'd notice if I was— Oh."

Oh indeed . . .

Okay, so it's not like this is the first time. I've been going through this dance with my body for about a year pretty regularly. Every month, to be exact. And every month I get mad because I should be used to it by now. But every month I forget, and every month it catches me off guard like the sneakiest, most underhanded opponent, and it's just not fair!

"Did you bring supplies?" Elowen asks.

"What supplies?"

"Callie."

"What?" I snip back. "Usually I just lie in a pool of my own guts for three days. It's fine."

Elowen makes a strange hissing sound that is more disapproving than any noise Mama ever made.

The first time I got my period, I really thought I was dying. It hurt worse than anything else I'd ever experienced, and inside pain is always scarier than outside pain you can see. It was the first time I'd cried at the camp. Papa hadn't the first clue what was happening and was all ready to ride out and fetch a healer, or take me somewhere, or anything.

Neal talked him down.

He didn't know much, but he did have sisters, and he knew vaguely what was going on. That vague explanation is all I have. Something about uteruses and pregnancy and monthly, and realizing I'd have to go through this over and over was even worse than the slimy chunks of blood coming out of me.

"Well," says Elowen briskly, "then it's lucky you're here, isn't it?"

I groan long and loud into my pillow.

"Stay there," she orders, and the bed bounces as she jumps off. "I'm bringing supplies."

I do as I'm told, grateful for the softness of my bed that catches and keeps me. I think Elowen likes bossing me around. I think I like being bossed around by her.

⊷

Supplies means tea, more biscuits, and weird bandage-like pads that stop me from looking like I've cut an artery.

"Drink," Elowen orders, pushing a fragile teacup into my hands. "It tastes disgusting, but it'll make all the difference."

I sniff cautiously, wincing when the sharp herbs tickle my nose. "What is it?"

"Chamomile"—which is already my least favorite tea—"fennel, and ginger."

Vomit.

"It'll help," Elowen repeats in a voice that invites less than zero argument. "I suggest just downing it before you can taste it. Come on, oh brave Sir Callie, I believe in you."

I realize a little too abruptly that I would probably do anything anyone said if they called me "brave Sir Callie." I down the tea and come up choking.

"Poison?"

"Of course."

"Knew it." I curl deeper into my bed. The tea, despite its deadliness, *does* make me feel better. More tired, but in a soft, comfy way. "Sneaky."

Elowen settles beside me with a sheaf of papers. "Want to hear about your heroic escapades told in verse? You're a popular subject for our composition lessons lately. Emmeline composed a particularly elaborate story in which you single-handedly take down a whole pirate fleet. Very realistic."

"I am pretty heroic," I mumble. It feels good to let my eyes close for a moment. Just for a moment. There's plenty of time before I meet Willow.

CHAPTER SIXTEEN

"Callie!" Elowen's whisper is urgent, and soft though it is, it startles me out of the best sleep I've had in ages.

I grope automatically for the sword I don't have, assuming a siege. "Whassit?"

Elowen's eyes are wide, staring at the place in the wall where the secret door is. "I think there's someone there," she breathes. "I think there's someone trying to get in."

First, I'm nervous about intruders, then I'm nervous about spies. Fear knocks through me when I realize what's really happening.

"Hey, shut your eyes and block your ears for a moment, okay?"

Elowen blinks. "Huh?"

"Please?" It's a terrible plan, but I'm desperate. There are too many secrets, and they're slipping between my fingers like sand.

Elowen takes too long.

The secret door clicks softly open and Willow blinks in the light. "Callie?" The second he sees Elowen, he retreats back into the dark.

"Hey, wait!" I leap up and shove my way through the door the moment before it shuts. I leave it open just a sliver, to let just enough light through to illuminate the prince's pale face. "Look," I start. "I'm really sorry—"

Willow withdraws. "No, it's . . . I—I shouldn't've come. It was stupid. The agreement was to meet outside. I . . . I'll leave. I just— I needed you to have this." Willow pushes a heavy something into my hands.

It's too dim to see, but my thumb finds the familiar shape of my name stamped into new leather. *Callie.*

I swallow hard, my throat thick. "Where'd you find her?"

"Sir Nicholas's chambers," Willow admits. "He and Lord Peran were having their daily meeting. I—I know how much she means to you, and I wanted to . . . I wanted to thank you. For everything." He dips in an awkward bow, then quickly backs away. "Forgive me for intruding and assuming, and—"

The door opens wide and bathes us with light.

Willow freezes up like Elowen's about to attack him.

But she just says softly, "Hi, Willow." No "Prince," no "Highness," just "Willow."

It feels pretty ridiculous to ask, "You guys know each other?" when everyone knows everyone here, but I don't mean it like that. I mean it the way me and El know each other, and me and Willow know each other, and it's weird to think they know each other like that without me.

Willow hesitates between needing to flee and wanting to stay. "I—I shouldn't be here—"

"Yes," says Elowen firmly, "you should." She grabs us both by the sleeves and drags us into my room.

Willow catches my eye. He looks like he's going to throw up.

Elowen works quickly, with an expert's eye, painting a seal of light around both the secret door and the main one.

"What's that do?"

"It'll warn us before anyone comes, and it'll stop sound getting out. I promise it works."

Between Elowen's seal and having Satin finally—*finally*—in my hands, I feel untouchable. I can't stop running my fingers over her scabbard, counting the stitches as if to make sure she's all there. It's the hardest thing not to draw her right here and now, but I'm not sure that would be good manners.

Not that Elowen would care. Looks like she's got bigger things on her mind right now.

When Elowen turns back to us, her mouth is set tight and her eyes are wet and fierce.

"I'm so glad you found each other. I hoped, but I couldn't—"

"You set this up," I breathe, clarity knocking me on the

back of the head. "When you sent me down to the beach . . . you wanted me to meet Willow."

The prince laughs softly, shaking his head like he's just found the answer to a complicated problem that wasn't so complicated in the first place.

I still don't get it.

"Of course I did." Elowen meets my eye, almost challenging and wholly without guilt. She sits by the hearth and arranges her skirts neatly around herself, waiting for me and Willow to join her. "I understand if you're angry with me," she says. "But I'm not sorry. I did what I had to, and I'm glad I did."

It's hard to be annoyed when those are my words.

"You are proof," Elowen continues, as close to angry as I've ever seen her, "that the rules are wrong. I've known it for forever, but you . . . you're the only person brave enough to say it out loud and make people hear. We *need* that. We *need* a hero."

A hero. I swallow as Willow nods like it's some kind of fact. I should be elated. I should be all puffed up and thrilled that anyone thinks I'm any kind of hero. Why do I feel . . . disappointed?

"Well, great for you." I drag my legs up and tuck my knees under my chin. My cramps are cramping even harder, despite Elowen's tea. "Glad to've helped, I guess."

"Callie." Willow scooches closer, and my scowl is useless against his smile. "You know you're stuck with us, don't you?"

"Why?" I growl half-heartedly. "You don't need me any-more. You've got each other."

"It's not over," says Elowen. "Not even nearly. And want is better than need."

Willow nods. "Friends are better than heroes."

I stare between them, a laugh bubbling up and about to burst. This feels like a game, but they're both dead serious. Elowen, the most personable person I've ever met, and Willow, the crown prince. The two people who, by all rights, should be surrounded by heroes *and* friends.

Should be.

Aren't.

I stop and look at the two of them properly.

Elowen was friendly when I met her, playing her part, doing her duty, but it wasn't until we spent real time together that she actually let me see her. In the Queen's Quarters, among all those girls, she is the Chancellor's Daughter—quiet and accomplished, the perfect host. With me, she is Elowen—sharp, astute, and *powerful*.

And Willow . . . the prince who flinched when I made the mistake of trying to touch him, who stumbles over his words and doesn't believe he's worthy of being loved, much less worthy of being a king. He is the boy who can bring draw-ings to life, who adores dance and beautiful things, who loves so deeply it hurts him.

They have both been taught the only way they are

acceptable is by being something other than themselves. They have heard it so often, it became true.

Then I came along and proved it doesn't have to be that way.

Friends are better than heroes.

CHAPTER
SEVENTEEN

F our weeks and four days.

Four weeks and three days.

Two days.

One . . .

Suddenly time that felt too long feels too short.

Elowen joins us on our nightly sneak-outs, our two groups of two becoming one group of three, and it's different but it's better. They are more themselves together than alone, getting more comfortable with old familiarity. For a while I stay scared that I'll get left out because of all their history, but that doesn't happen. There's no going backward. Only forward.

I have to leave them with that momentum. I have to make a difference that'll last. Even if it's just a legacy for two people.

I'm not going to make any kind of difference to anyone holed up in my room, pretending to be good, and it's not like anyone's coming to ask without me saying anything first.

Willow shrieks as Elowen splashes him with salt water, bounding along the shore and getting even wetter in an effort to escape. Her dress is knotted up out of reach of the shallow tide, shoes left discarded on the shore. She laughs, loud and unbridled, her grin so wide that the confines of the palace can barely contain it. The thought of her getting crammed down and shut in hurts my chest.

Elowen's right—the battle on the other side of the bridge isn't the only one that needs fighting, the enemy not just a dragon watching from the shadows. It's right here, living in the palace, waging its own war unchecked because no one's willing or brave enough to pay attention and do the tough job of calling it out.

But *I'm* brave. *I'm* willing.

Helston's best can go out and save the world or whatever, but my fight is just as important.

And I'm not going to win locked up and sneaking around.

"I'm gonna apologize." I don't even know I'm thinking it until the statement exists in the air.

Willow and Elowen freeze in their game to stare back at me with identical expressions—all confused and a little bit scared.

Yeah, me too.

This little world we've made where we can be ourselves is

wonderful, but it isn't real. We still have to go back and wake up tomorrow in the real world where we pretend we're something else. Even me. Out here in the middle of the night, I can pretend I'm brave and fierce, worthy of my friends.

I have to prove it for real. I have to try to be the hero my friends have decided I am. Can't do that locked up.

"To Lord Peran?" Willow asks, joining me on the sand. His expression flicks between relieved and terrified. "Do you mean it?"

"I mean I'm gonna say it. I don't mean I'm actually sorry. But I can't stay stuck in there, and if the way out means apologizing, then fine." I look up at Elowen, whose arms are crossed tight over her chest, her lips pressed in a hard frown. "Will you help me? You know your dad. What do I need to do to convince him?"

"I do," El agrees slowly. "You need to be perfect. Anything less, anything that even *hints* you are insincere—" She takes a deep breath. "If you are going to play the game, you'll need to play it properly."

Willow nods, fingers an anxious flutter at his sleeve. "Yes, you must learn. Lord Peran is . . . well, he's—"

A bully.

"Particular. And if you've already found yourself on his less-than-good side, it's going to take even more work." Willow bites his lip, gaze roving over me like he can see all the bits the chancellor will find lacking. So—everything then. He grimaces. "Callie, I—I don't think you should do it. Just stay

183

put. It's only three weeks. It's safer that way, and if you get into any more trouble, he'll— I—I can't lose you."

I pull a face. "I'm not gonna let myself get sent across the bridge. I'm not careless."

Elowen and Willow exchange looks. "It isn't about careless," says Elowen. "Father has not forgotten you."

I squirm at the thought of Peran thinking about me at all. "What does *that* mean?"

"It means he will take a fraction of an excuse to send you away and turn it into ten. He already has people afraid of you, Callie."

My stomach twists. "Afraid of *me*? Why?"

Her lip goes guiltily between her teeth. "Rumors have been . . . circulating in your absence. I only know what has reached the Queen's Daughters. I can tell you that the girls, most of them anyway, do not believe it for a moment. But they got it from their mothers, who got it from their husbands, many of whom are on the council. They think you're a witch's weapon."

I burst out laughing. "Seriously?"

But neither Elowen nor Willow finds it funny.

"They say there's only one place that accepts people like you, one home for peculiarities. He says you must've been recruited by Dumoor, and you're one of the witch's weapons being used to infiltrate Helston."

The laugh dies on my lips. "And people *actually* believe that?" I push back the little niggle of knowing that I nearly fell for the dragon's false promise of *There is a place for you with us*, because I didn't. I wouldn't. I never would!

"They don't know you," says Elowen. "And maybe that's what you need to do—prove you're not a threat."

I bite my tongue and keep my words in. I'm not any kind of witch's weapon, but that doesn't mean I'm not a threat.

"We'll teach you," says Willow. "We both know exactly what Lord Peran wants, and how to navigate his, ah, particularities."

"But you will need to master the act *perfectly*," says Elowen. "And when I say 'perfectly,' I *mean* 'perfectly.' Etiquette, penmanship, keeping your mouth shut and your thoughts inside. Invisibility . . ."

I think I've just fallen straight into a fiery pit of doom. There's no way I—

"But I believe you can do it."

My whole face burns beneath Elowen's certainty. It doesn't even sound like a compliment, just a cool fact.

She raises her chin. "It's going to be hard, and it's going to take work, but I believe it is worth doing. And I believe if you try, you will win."

She makes me believe it too.

Once upon a time—that is, yesterday—I was young and foolish and thought magic lessons would be the most obnoxious thing I would ever have to suffer. Young, foolish Callie had no idea what fresh torture awaited them in the guise of Etiquette Lessons.

My teachers are ruthless, demanding nothing less than utter perfection and withholding the very possibility of biscuits until said perfection has been achieved. The smell of cinnamon sugar mocks me from where the platter sits on the dresser.

"Stop holding on to your skirts like they're the only thing saving you from drowning," Willow says, adjusting my hands for the umpteenth time.

I scowl but do as he says, even though they basically are the only thing that's going to save me. El picks me out a new gown, an enormous pink confection with more layers of skirts than I can count. It poofs out three times my width, and if I move, I fall. I don't know how I'll walk to the Council Chambers, let alone perform a curtsy good enough for Lord Peran. But that's the deal, the price of freedom *and* biscuits.

"Bowing's easier," I mutter, shuffling back into position, one ankle twisted impossibly around the other. "I can do a really good bow."

The moment I move, I and all my skirts land in an inelegant heap on the ground.

Willow drags me up without even a moment to catch my breath. "Again," he orders.

From the desk by the window, Elowen smothers a smirk. She spends the countless hours of my reeducation composing a letter to her father with my name on the bottom, searching for the perfect balance of appropriately contrite without being obviously fake. There's no way I'd ever be able to do it myself. It's gonna suck hard enough having to perform in person.

Ugh.

I don't know if freedom's even worth it.

Biscuits are, though. Do it for the biscuits.

It takes three long nights before my teachers are satisfied. My final test is performing ten curtsies in a row without falling on my butt, and when I finally manage it, I jump on my bed with a yell of triumph.

"Can I have my biscuits now?"

Willow and Elowen exchange glances. The prince shrugs. "I think you've earned them."

But Elowen has one more challenge for me. She presents her pen with ink-stained fingers. "Sign the letter—*then* you can eat."

The plate is empty in two minutes flat, crumbs and all.

Elowen seals the letter neatly. "Give it to the servant tomorrow morning when she brings you breakfast. Tell her it's for the council; that way Father will have to open it in front of the others and acknowledge it."

I can totally see Peran casting one eye over the letter, then shredding it into the fireplace and pretending it never existed, but Willow's eyes go wide with concern.

"But this is what he asked for, isn't it? These were the conditions. Surely he *wants* Callie to apologize and go free?"

Elowen forces a smile. "Of course he does. We just want to make sure everything's perfect, so there can be no misunderstandings."

The prince nods, reassured. He doesn't see the breath Elowen releases. She knows her dad well enough not to assume best intentions, even if Willow doesn't. Part of me wants to shake him and tell him to wake up and see Lord Peran for what he is. Part of me hopes Willow will never have to know.

"And, finally, smile." Elowen demonstrates with the most perfect smile, which lights up her whole face.

I bare my teeth.

Willow winces. "Try just with your eyes so you're not so—"

"Demonic?" Elowen supplies.

"Precisely."

I scowl instead, but when Elowen laughs, I grin for real. I want to bottle that sound.

"Perfect," she says. "You're ready to face Father."

CHAPTER EIGHTEEN

The response comes swiftly and without warning. Luckily, I'm more than ready. My hair's done up nice with the pink ribbon Willow gave me for luck. My face is smudge-free, and when I catch my own eye in my mirror, I see what everyone else will see: girl.

I take a deep breath and keep my focus on my mission.

Not all wars are fought on the battlefield, not all fights are with blades. Some are fought with pretty ribbons and pleasant smiles in Council Chambers. Doesn't make them any less important. Doesn't make me any less brave.

Oh brave Sir Callie.

I focus on my friends.

I'm passed off to Captain Adan at the entrance to the Queen's Quarters, and he escorts me to my doom. I breathe deep and steady. *I* am in control and *I* am going to win.

The whole council stares at me with the same mild

interest, all sitting in the same chairs with the same kinds of pastries as I stand before them.

Only Lord Peran is different. It's tiny, just the faintest twitch of a muscle when he looks at me, but I read him like a scroll. He's learned the same lesson I have in these last few weeks: *Do not underestimate me.*

I take a deep breath, drop my gaze, and make the perfect, sweeping curtsy Elowen made me practice a million times last night. *Play to win.*

"Thank you so much for agreeing to see me, my lords."

Said lords murmur approvingly at my new meekness. They see exactly what I want them to see—*just* a girl. I work to keep my triumph off my face.

I'm going to use that to my advantage.

"It has taken you over two weeks to reach a conclusion that ought to have come quickly, Lady Calliden," says Peran crisply. "What inspired this sudden revelation?"

I twist my hands fretfully the way Willow does, all repentant. "You deserve no less than a fullhearted apology, my lord. I needed this time to truly and fully reflect on my crimes. Not simply the disrespect I showed toward you but throughout my entire life." I'm definitely going overboard, but they eat it up like dessert.

Lord Peran is the only one without sugar on his fingers.

"I see no harm in releasing her from her confinement, Peran," says one of the lords, a miscellaneous old man sitting closest to where I stand. "The girl is truly contrite, and a sincere apology *was* the condition of her release."

"Yes," says Peran slowly. "It is *precisely* what is required of her."

He doesn't believe me, not for half a second, and judging by the flex of the hand resting on the table, he's itching to shake the truth out of me.

Good. Try it. Grab the girl in the pretty dress and call her a liar, I dare you.

He has to play by his own rules.

"Peran, you did give your word—"

I hide my smile.

Check, my lord.

"Thank you, I am aware," Peran says curtly. "I would be remiss in my duties to the Crown and His Highness if I did not ensure that Lady Calliden's intentions were true."

I keep my eyes down so they don't see my glare. "I have also had time to reflect, not only on myself but on the unnatural power that dwells inside me. I understand that it must be controlled and regulated, and that will be possible only if I myself am"—I try not to puke—"controlled and regulated. I understand that I do not need the power I clung to, when it is the job of so many to protect me. I don't need weapons. Of any kind. It is not appropriate for me to think I can fight."

Peran sits back and assesses me carefully, trying to fish out the lie he *knows* is there.

"What do you intend to do with your liberty were it granted, my lady?"

Take you down from the inside out.

I smile just the way Willow and Elowen taught me—sweet and sincere, trying not to show too much tooth. "It would be a privilege to be permitted to rejoin the Queen's Daughters and learn, once and for all, proper control and discipline." I dip into a curtsy that makes my ankles hurt. "I hope you will grant me the education I lack so that I may leave Helston a better person and not fall back into unacceptable habits."

The delivery comes out *exactly* as I've practiced and hits its mark squarely—right in the bleeding heart of every councilman present. As straight and true as an arrow. *Bull's-eye.*

"A better *what*, Lady Calliden?"

My tongue dries up. "Pardon?"

Lord Peran's head tilts and his eyes flash with victory. "You will leave here a better *what*?" *Say it*, he dares me without words. *Go the whole way and forfeit yourself.*

It's not like I wasn't expecting this.

I dig my nails hard into the soft part of my wrist. This isn't about me. Play the game to win. It doesn't matter. *It doesn't matter.*

Except it does.

Other people calling me "lady" feels like being bashed in the shoulder because they don't see me. Calling myself "lady" feels like agreeing I don't deserve to be seen, that I don't matter, that I don't exist.

My eyes, my face, my blood *burn*. I'm taking too long, I *know* that. Taking so long, Peran's already sitting back like he's won.

Not all battles are fought with swords.

I fix my stance, look my opponent in the eye, and strike. "I want to leave here a better lady, Lord Peran. Please permit me that opportunity."

Peran grits his teeth. "Very well," he says because he's got no choice. "You are . . . *free*, henceforth, to rejoin the court as appropriate. Do not abuse this gesture of good faith. You will not receive another. Do we have an understanding?"

We do, but it's not the one he's willing to say out loud, not the one that says *I see you and I know what you're doing and I will expose you at the first opportunity.*

Right back at you, sir.

I bow my head. "Thank you *so* much, Lord Chancellor. I am forever indebted to you, and I look forward to proving I am worth taking a chance on."

A lord with a silly hat smiles at me kindly. "We are sure you will be a credit to us, Lady Calliden. We appreciate your change of attitude. Your daughter's been tutoring her, hasn't she, Peran? Elowen always was a good girl. Clearly her influence has been effective."

I freeze. So does Peran. He catches my eye, and I don't have time to lie before his hands slam down on the table and his chair screeches back.

The other lords watch him, confused.

"Peran, we have other business—"

"It can wait." He storms past them, past me, on his way out of the Council Chambers.

"Wait!" I trip over my skirts, but I don't care if I'm a stumbling mess. "It's not Elowen's fault! The queen told her to. Don't—"

Lord Peran rounds on me so fast my back hits the wall. "Stop."

One word. One syllable. That's all it takes to force my body to obey. I stop breathing. I stop moving. I stop.

With a sweep of his cloak, Peran's gone, leaving behind nothing but a breeze and a pain in my chest.

CHAPTER
NINETEEN

E lowen's waiting for me at the entrance to the Queen's Quarters. Her eyes are bright; she's excited to hear how it went, relieved to see me.

"How did it—" I grab her in a fierce hug, and there's only one beat of hesitation before she returns it with a laugh. "You did it. I'm *so* glad."

Every drip of joy makes me feel worse and worse, and I'm so shaken up, my legs hardly hold me. I don't get spooked easily. I don't let myself get intimidated, especially not by men just throwing their weight around. But Lord Peran's something different.

"I—I messed up, El."

"What do you mean?" She draws back with her hands still on my shoulders, smiling like everything's great. "You're here, aren't you? You're free."

"Yeah, but . . . your dad. He knows you've been visiting

me. Helping me. One of the councilmen knew and blabbed. I couldn't lie in time and he's angry, El. I-I'm sorry."

She rests a hand on my shoulder. "It's okay, Callie." If I didn't know for a fact that that wasn't true, I'd believe her. Elowen's face is smooth and calm, like I've just told her that her dad was drinking coffee instead of tea. "Did the council adjourn?"

"Yeah. It wasn't supposed to, but your dad just stormed out. I figured he was coming for you."

Elowen laughs. "There's no need for dramatics," she says, like the last few days of extensive training *just* to persuade Lord Peran to let me out of my room haven't happened. "Father's very busy, and the council has a habit of running meetings too long. Still, I should go and speak to him. Make sure everything's fine. You go in. I'll find you later."

Everything in my body screams this is a *bad idea*. "Elowen—"

"It's fine," she says brightly, stepping across the threshold into the main palace. "I'm fine. You don't need to worry about me."

Elowen is the best liar I've ever met.

───◆───

I'm greeted like a hero the moment I step into the Queen's Quarters, surrounded by a whirl of cheering and clamoring bodies, hands all grabbing at me like they have to prove I'm real.

Elowen should be here. I should've gone with her. I should've insisted she stay, hide. I should've protected her even if she doesn't want me to.

The queen steps through her girls and smiles down at me. "Welcome back, Lady Callie. You have been missed."

There is absolutely nothing to smile about.

"Your Majesty, please, I think Elowen's in danger—"

Her dark brows dip. "What do you mean, child?"

I fight to pull myself together. She's listening. That's more than I expected. I can't lose this chance.

"Lord Peran," I say breathlessly. "Her dad. He's angry she's been spending time with me. *Helping* me. Because you told her to—"

"I did not instruct Elowen to keep secrets from her family," says Queen Ewella. "And Lord Peran is well within his rights to be displeased if she has."

"He's gonna hurt her!"

Silence falls in the crowded chamber apart from my own panting. The dress is tight and itchy, and I just want it *off.*

"Come, Callie. Teatime, I think."

I'm seething hard as Her Majesty leads me into a small, quiet room furnished with just two comfortable chairs and a tiny round table. She takes one chair, and I perch on the other. A tea set waits for us, the same blue floral pattern as the cups Elowen brings to my room. Queen Ewella heats the pot with a delicate wave of a hand, pours, and passes me a cup without ever touching the porcelain.

I sip tentatively. The tea is the perfect temperature to drink; the taste, delicately bitter.

"Milk?"

"Yeah. Please."

Tea doesn't fix everything, but there's not much it doesn't help.

"Elowen's loyalties have always been complex," Queen Ewella begins once we're on our second cup. "She isn't like the others, who live and sleep as a collective. She comes and she goes, splitting her time between here and the Chancellor's Chambers. Elowen knows she has a home here if she wanted it. It is her choice, Callie, to stay with her family."

This china is tougher than it looks. I'm surprised it doesn't crack in my hands. "You think he gives her any kind of choice?" I grind out. "You think Peran would let El go if she just asked?"

"You should give your friend more credit, Callie," says the queen. "Elowen is sharp. She knows what she's doing."

"That doesn't mean she doesn't need help!"

"I know you have had your disagreements with *Lord* Peran." The queen's voice takes on the slightest warning edge, and I squirm. "But let me make it clear—I trust him implicitly. There is a difference between strictness and cruelty, and he must be strict in order to bear the responsibility he has taken upon himself. You might not agree with it, and you are not required to. This kingdom would be lost without Lord Peran. *I* would be lost without him, and I would not charge him with the responsibility of my son if I did not fully believe in him. I ask you to understand that and, if that is not possible, to accept it anyway."

One of the delicate blue flowers has one fading petal from too many fingerprints. I wonder if anyone else has noticed. I wonder what she'd say if she knew how miserable her son is in the chancellor's care. I remember what happened last time I mentioned Willow and I keep my mouth shut.

"He hates magic," I mumble. "And everyone who has it. He'd wipe it out if he could, El says."

"But he cannot," the queen reminds me gently. "He is only one man, Callie, no matter how it may feel. I know it is difficult, for you and Elowen both. It feels personal. But it isn't. Lord Peran doesn't hate magic—he fears it. And justifiably so. He is only doing what he believes right to protect Helston."

"By hurting people?" I snap. "Just because he's scared of magic?"

"His fear is justified—"

"But his meanness isn't!" I shout. "If people were allowed to be the worst just because they're scared, then everyone would be mean to everyone. He's made loads of people scared of him—does that make it okay if they go bully other people?"

Queen Ewella sets her cup down and folds her hands in her lap. "It does not," she says carefully. "However, I would ask you to weigh this fear you believe Lord Peran has instilled against the good he is doing for Helston."

"What *good*?" I know she wants me to nod and agree and shut up, and honestly, I'd love to. I wish I could summon even a fraction of faith, enough to stop worrying and stop being angry, and trust the grown-ups. But I can't. "Helston's not just a city and a palace. It's not just grown-ups, Your Majesty—it's kids too. It's every person here, and maybe he's doing good for some but not all, and that's not *right*! He shouldn't get to . . . to pick on magical folks just 'cause some *princess* went and got banished—"

Queen Ewella goes ashen. "What do you know of Princess Alis?" she asks sharply.

What do you *know?* I want to ask right back, because that's not any kind of reaction I was expecting. Instead, I shrug up to my ears. "Nothing much. Only that she lost control of her magic and she got kicked out of Helston for it."

The queen relaxes a little, fingers loosening around her teacup. "I'm afraid it's more complicated than that, child, and Lord Peran is right to be wary. We have taken so many steps to ensure we do not fall into that situation again, but . . ." She sighs. "Magic is power, and power used poorly is *very* dangerous."

"Yeah! It is!" I'm half out of my seat and trying really hard not to slop tea all over myself. "And that's exactly what Lord Peran is—"

"Enough." The command is softly spoken, but it's a

command nonetheless, and I lower myself back into my seat, mouth shut. "The line between good and bad, right and wrong, is clear when you are young. As you grow, you will come to learn that line is not so straight. Go on," she says. "Join the others. They've been longing for ballads of your brave deeds."

My heart heavy in my stomach, I make myself rise, bow, and leave. I keep my face blank and my mouth shut, and my rage *in*.

Like a *good, obedient* knight.

I've never felt less heroic.

CHAPTER TWENTY

In the evening, I drift down to the Great Hall with the girls. It beats loud and alive, packed with so many people, it feels like a whole city in this one room.

I balk in the doorway, the heat hitting my face. It was bad enough being attacked by the mass of the Queen's Daughters, but this is them times a hundred. I don't do people. Not in these quantities. Maybe it would be easier if Elowen was here. She would know what to say and how to push me forward and make me feel like I could do this.

The girls drag me in, weaving between the rows and rows of benches and long tables.

It's impossible not to gawk.

Helston truly is a royal palace, and if I didn't know better, I'd call it a haven.

Everything is rich and beautiful and bright, from the stained-glass windows to the gold adornments detailing the architecture. It is an ancient place, a sacred place, perched on the edge of the sea. The window at the end of the hall is vast and looks out on the ocean, affording a perfect vision of the setting sun, which bathes the hall in deep orange light. The high table sits upon a dais before the window, seating all the councilmen who stared at me and judged me just a few hours ago. It's like they're one unit, can only exist together in a pack. In the very middle, like some kind of king, is Peran. El's not with him, but neither is Edwyn nor anyone I can peg as their family.

The queen's words thud through me at the sight of him. *I trust him,* she said. How can anyone look at that man and trust him? He surveys the hall, as complacent as a cat, lazily holding a crystal goblet of something red.

The prince is small beside him, dressed in a clean black tunic, shoulders hunched and eyes dead. It's like he's willing himself away and trying not to exist. No wonder people think he's not strong enough to be king. I *know* Willow. He is as bright and as brilliant as a star when it's just us, down on our little scrap of beach, but in the chancellor's presence, he's snuffed out.

That's what Peran does.

That's what he's doing.

I *hate* him.

If the queen would just step outside her bubble and see for herself, just for a moment, then I'm sure—

"Hey, kiddo."

I whip around, all thoughts of Helston and the chancellor, and even Elowen, shoved out of my head.

It's him. It's really him. Standing right there with his head tilted and a crooked smile on his mouth, hesitating.

Papa.

I hesitate too.

It feels like forever since we were parted, like everything has changed and me most of all. All the memories of the last time we were together slam through me: Papa kneeling. Papa giving up. Peran winning.

Go, Callie.

My fault.

Then he closes the last space between us and wraps me tightly in his arms, one hand warm on the back of my head.

"I'm so sorry, Callie."

I cling.

I don't care that we're in the middle of everyone and neither does Papa. No one else matters but us. Just the way it's supposed to be. He feels the same and smells the same, and if anything has changed, it isn't us.

It isn't us.

I'm so relieved, it catches me in the throat. I bury my face in Papa's shoulder.

"I missed you."

"I missed *you*," he says. "I wanted to come for you. I tried. I swear. But they stopped me and I was afraid if I—"

"It's fine, Papa." I don't want him to say it. I don't want to think about my dad being scared.

"It's not." He pulls back, touching my face, his eyes sweeping over me like he's trying to memorize every detail. There are lines on his face that weren't there three weeks ago. "It's not okay, and I'm sorry. I should've fought for you. I should've just taken you home. I should've put you first." He drops to his knees right there in the middle of dinner and bows his head. "I failed you. Forgive me, Callie."

My laugh bubbles, all relief and tears, and I scrub my face with my sleeve. "I'm pretty sure I'm the one who needs forgiveness." I bite my lip as he looks up at me all confused. "I got you in trouble. I made everything worse. I—"

"Darling." Papa wipes away the rest of my tears and kisses the top of my head. "I am responsible for myself and I am responsible for you. You have nothing at all to apologize for, and I'm sorry you were left believing otherwise."

"It's okay—I got some good distractions."

Papa's face brightens and he looks more like himself again. "Yeah? You've been keeping busy?"

I grin. "You have no idea."

"Tell me about it," Papa begs, tugging me onto the nearest bench, where the Queen's Daughters are staring at us. They scrabble to make room, Papa sticking out like a sore thumb, a grown knight in the middle of a sea of girls. He doesn't mind. I don't think he even notices. Papa's as comfortable among kids as he is around soldiers or nobility. Always has been.

The girls, on the other hand, treat Papa like he's some kind of mythological creature.

I revel in their wide-eyed wonder, feeling exactly like I did on the ride into Helston, watching my disaster-dad get heralded as a great hero. Papa chats with them and indulges the girls' hero-worshipping tendencies, and then he's mine again.

I can't tell him everything, not here, and I can't shake the knowledge that Willow is still afraid of him, but Elowen is a safe topic, so I tell him all about her.

"And I'm getting good," I say. "It's making sense like it never did before. And magic . . . Papa, did you know what you can do with it? *Actually* do with it? Anything! Anything you want! It can be soft and quiet, but it can be huge and loud too. I didn't know that. No one ever showed me that. Not even Neal. I can't wait to show him what I'm learning."

Papa laughs. "He'll be so proud of you, Callie. I hope it's soon."

"Me too." Neal being here would make everything perfect. Well, nearly perfect. I wish El was here to take her credit. I've no right to be here, having a good time, with Papa and my freedom, and everything I want, when she's I don't know where. Doing nothing isn't anything other than doing nothing, no matter what the queen says. I should be doing *something*. I should be—

Movement catches my eye. Lady Anita enters the hall, as graceful as a queen, with Edwyn at her heels.

One twin without the other.

"'Scuse me."

"Callie?"

I'm on my feet before I can think about it. I have to reach them before they get closer to Lord Peran. There's enough clamor between them and him to hide a conversation, and if El's in trouble, then their mum'll tell me or want to know or *something*.

I don't have much of a handle on Lady Anita apart from our brief meeting on the first day and a bit from Elowen, but even if it's not great, then at least she's not like Lord Peran? I don't think? Anyway, better to try than not, and hope for the best.

"Hey!" I practically have to climb over people to get to them fast enough. "Hey, Edwyn!"

He turns at the sound of his name, and when he sees it's me, his face twists in automatic dislike. I couldn't care less if he doesn't like me. Elowen is more important than any of that.

"Where's El?"

He looks me up and down like I'm some undesirable apparition. "They let you out, did they?"

I draw myself up tall. Given the whole head's difference between us, that doesn't mean much. "Yeah, they did. Where's Elowen?"

"Stay away from her," he snaps at once. "If she doesn't want to be near you, I'm not going to encourage her otherwise. Leave her alone. And me."

He turns to rejoin his mother, who is waiting for him a little way off, but I grab his wrist before he takes a step. "Just . . . tell me she's okay. Please."

Edwyn flinches, and there's the sharpest flash of fear before he turns it into a snarl and whips his arm away. "Don't touch me!"

"Sorry." I hold up my hands. "I'm just worried about her, all right? Tell me she's fine, and I'll leave you alone."

I expect a terse "She's fine," but Edwyn actually hesitates, casting a quick eye around the hall for his sister. Not finding her.

A hand falls on his shoulder, and their mother looks down at me with the same sweet smile she gave me those first few moments in Helston. "We appreciate your concern for Elowen," she says in a voice that sounds like a broken bottle of perfume—all sharp glass and cloying sweetness. "I'm afraid she has taken ill and will be staying in bed for the next few days. We will tell her you were asking after her."

This is, quite clearly, the first Edwyn knows of this, and the look he gives me before he can stop himself spells out in plain letters: *She's lying.*

"No, wait! Please!" I'm too loud. I know I'm too loud, but my head is too dizzy and thick with worry to care. "If she's in trouble, you gotta help her. You gotta—"

"It is good to have you back with us, Lady Calliden," Lady Anita says sharply. "I hope you will not find yourself incarcerated a second time. Do not take your liberty for granted." She turns to continue her way toward Lord Peran, steering Edwyn with her, but there's no way I'm letting her go so easily.

"Hey! Look, I know you hate me, and that's fine, but this is about El—"

"My daughter is *ill*," says Lady Anita icily. "No doubt from the stress of all that"—she lowers her voice to a dangerous hiss—"*sneaking around.* I strongly suggest you do not make her worse."

My whole body seizes up tight as she stalks away to join her husband. I hardly even notice that Edwyn lingers behind until he grabs my arm and leans in.

"What did you do?"

I break his grip with a quick twist. "*I* didn't do anything—"

"Elowen defied Father for *you*. I told her it wasn't worth it. I *told* her it was only a matter of time before she was caught." He glares at me with more hatred than anyone's ever thrown at me before. And that's saying something. "She was never thoughtless before you showed up. I don't know what kind of curse you put on her—"

"I didn't!"

"But if you have any semblance of decency at all, you will leave her alone for good. Just because your family is broken doesn't mean you're allowed to break ours."

Hot angers flares through my blood. "Yeah, well, at least my dad *likes* me."

Edwyn's whole body bunches up, but I don't wait around to get into a fight with him. My dad's waiting for me. I stomp back to him.

Papa looks at me all concerned when I slide back onto the bench next to him. "What was all that about?"

I hunch down, staring down at the meal I've lost my appetite for. "We're a family, right? You and me and Neal?"

"Of course we are." Papa squeezes me close, and it feels like home. "Where's this coming from?"

I open my mouth to tell him, to ask "Are we broken?" but my throat feels too thick, and I can hardly breathe, let alone speak.

Papa reads me easily. "All right." He rises, squeezing my shoulder. "Let's go catch a breath outside."

CHAPTER
TWENTY-ONE

I t feels weird, being out in the open. It feels wrong, but I walk with Papa out the main doors and onto gravel. It's getting dark fast, but there are still plenty of people out finishing up their day. I'm used to waiting until they're all gone and hiding on the rare occasions I ever nearly cross paths with another human.

It's hard to suppress that instinct now.

Papa perches on the wall of the fountain and pats the space beside him. I hop up, legs dangling; the gentle sound of water grants an ounce of privacy.

"What's going on? Why're you getting into it with Peran's boy?"

It's weird having someone ask. Good weird. I missed him.

I pull my legs to my chest and lean against him. "Elowen— his sister—she's in trouble. I figured he'd want to help her, even if he didn't want to help me. And I know it's 'cause of me, but it's not *my* fault, and even if it is—" I suck in a deep breath and take a second to unknot all the thoughts tangled up in my head. "He called us broken."

Papa is quiet for a long moment. Then he bumps his shoulder to mine. "What do you think? Do you think we're broken?"

I give a shrug that nearly touches my ears. "Dunno. It's not like we're normal."

"And what's normal?"

I shrug again, and my shoulders really do hit my ears. "A mum and a dad. Living in a house."

"Is that what you want?" Papa asks. "To go back to Clystwell?"

Even the question sends a lump down my throat. I shake my head hard. "No."

"Normal doesn't exist, kiddo." He rests his chin on top of my head and squeezes me. "Not when it comes to people. Every person is different, every family is different, every normal is different. Do you like ours?"

I think about Papa and Neal, and Eyrewood and everyone all together, easy and happy and *liking* each other. When I think of "family," I see the whole of Eyrewood—Josh, Rowena, Faolan, Pasco . . . everyone who welcomed Papa and me in like we'd been there the whole time; who loved me through my worst tempers and biggest confusions, who made me feel like I belonged even when I felt most alone. "I love ours."

"Good. Family's the people who love you exactly as you

are. That's it. Whether you share blood with them or not. And pay no mind to Edwyn. It's tough to see someone else with the thing you want most in the world."

I twist round. "You think he's jealous?"

"Wouldn't you be?" Papa counters.

I roll my eyes. "Bit vain, aren't you?"

Papa laughs. "I mean, anyone *should* be jealous of your dad, but—" The grin drops into something more serious. "For real, kiddo, how would you feel if you had Lord Peran for a father? Whatever else we are or we're not, I think we're pretty lucky, aren't we?"

The people who love you exactly as you are.

"Yeah, we're lucky."

The luckiest. I've never really gotten to notice that before, and I don't tend to put much stock in luck when most of the time luck is shorthand for hard work, but in this case it's true. I didn't choose Papa, and I didn't choose Neal. But I would've, every time. Elowen and Willow, they didn't land so lucky. And I guess Edwyn didn't either.

"You know," Papa continues softly, hardly audible against the noise of the fountain at our backs, "it's really hard for people who aren't allowed to be themselves to see people who are. Imagine if we'd stayed with your mama. You and I, we had a choice. Most people don't get that. Most *kids* don't get that. They have to make the best of what they've got. Be a little patient with Edwyn. There's not much room here to stretch your wings and see things from a different angle."

"It's not what I imagined," I mumble. "It's not what you made me picture."

Papa sighs and rests his chin on the top of my head. "I know. And I'm sorry. It's . . . not what I remember, either."

"You think it's changed?"

"I think *I've* changed."

"How so?"

Papa takes his own time before replying. "When I used to come here before, I was at the top of the pile. I was a champion, the king's right-hand man. I didn't need anything to change. I didn't *want* anything to change. Everything was as it should be because it suited me for it to be so. If there were cracks, they were easy to ignore. They didn't affect me. They didn't matter. As far as I was concerned, everything was perfect."

He looks around, face lit by the lamps and the lights in the stained-glass windows, and his expression is bleak.

"Now I see this place as Neal would've seen it, how the prince sees it. And you, Callie. This should be a place for you to grow and be your best, as it was for me, but I see the way they squash anything that doesn't conform to their image of what is acceptable. They pick and choose between people, and that isn't right. That's not how it should be. And I'm trying to make things better, but I don't know how. I don't know if I can."

I hug my knees tighter. My dad's the best knight in

the whole realm—he can fight off dragons single-handedly and save whole towns in an afternoon. Navigating Helston shouldn't be a problem. And as far as I can tell, the place to start is obvious.

And he steps out of the palace, shadowed by the prince.

CHAPTER TWENTY-TWO

"*Please!*" My voice rings through the evening air.

Papa casts an anxious eye around, but I don't care if anyone else hears. I hope they do. I hope everyone comes out and sees and hears for the first time in their sheltered lives.

"It's not *fair*! We're going to leave and we're going to go home and we're gonna be fine, but what about everyone left behind? It's all going to just stay stuck and it's not fair. You're supposed to be here to help Willow, so help him! Help *us*."

Papa catches my hands in his, steadying me through my rage. "Callie, how do you know about the prince?"

I chew my tongue. I promised Willow I wouldn't tell, but me and Papa, we don't keep secrets from each other.

Choosing is easy.

"He's my friend," I confess, going as fast as I can because there's no time. "Elowen showed me how to get out of my room, so I've been training at night, and I met Willow because he sneaks out too because it's the only time he can be himself. We've been helping each other. But it's not enough. It's not enough if we're just going to leave everything to stay the same. He's scared of you, you know? He thinks you're just like all the others Peran's brought in to break him. He's amazing and brave, and every bit as good as he needs to be, but he's so scared and it's not fair and you have to *help!*"

Papa recoils, devastation written in every line in his face. "He's scared of me?" He curses bitterly under his breath. "Callie, that's . . . I swear to you, that's not what I wanted—"

"Then *fix* it."

Papa's gaze is where mine is, seeing what I see: Lord Peran and the prince in his shadow.

Then Papa's expression shifts and hardens. "Tell me how."

"Call him by his name. Call him Willow."

The chancellor and the prince take the steps down from the door and make their way in the direction of the barracks, not seeing us.

Papa rises. "Your Highness! A moment, please."

Willow cringes as Papa strides toward him.

Peran turns too. "Good evening," he says, cool with impatience. "If you'll excuse us, it is late, and His Highness has a great deal to cover before we retire."

"Bookwork in the evening?" Papa laughs like they're having a totally casual conversation, but the edge in his voice is impossible to miss. "Give the kid a break, Peran. He worked himself to death today."

"Be that as it may, time is fast running out, as well you know, and a king's job isn't only hitting things with swords. Come, Prince Will."

Willow drags himself reluctantly toward Lord Peran's waiting hand, but Papa gets to him first.

"You did good today," he says, squeezing the prince's bony shoulders. "Really good. You are truly making progress, and I am so proud of you. I know your dad would be too."

Willow's lip trembles, and even concealed by the fountain, I can see the tears in his eyes. "Really?"

"Really." Papa smiles the same warm smile that always chases away my coldest feelings. "You will make a great king, Willow. I am certain of it."

The prince's eyes go shield wide, flicking fearfully to the chancellor, who looks like he's about to bust a vein.

"*Nicholas.*"

Papa raises his face to Peran, keeping a hold on Willow's thin shoulders. Tension crackles like a storm's first lightning between them.

"A word," says Peran through clenched teeth. "*Now.*"

"No," says Papa coolly. "I have nothing to say to you. I have three weeks' worth of lesson plans to rebuild from scratch. Good night, Lord Chancellor." He pulls Willow around, away from Peran, and stoops so it's just them. "It's going to get better, kid. On my honor as the king's champion and your father's friend, I swear it to you." He kisses the top of the prince's head, just like he does mine, and straightens up. "Get some rest. Tomorrow's a new day, and we're gonna have some fun."

Apparently the word "fun" is Peran's snapping point. "Have you lost all sense? There is no time for *fun*—"

But Papa's right at his too. "Enough," he says in the thundering growl that makes tenured soldiers freeze. "You have been allowed to mistreat Willow for far too long. Children need to rest, they need to *play*—"

"Not when the child in question bears the responsibility of the realm," Peran snaps. If he was a statue, the cracks would be getting wider and wider. "And he has been indulged too long by too many. If he hadn't been left to rest and play unchecked for so long, then maybe I wouldn't need to work him so hard now. Maybe he would have some hope. Maybe this wouldn't be such a worthless task!"

Only I see Willow flinch.

If Peran's cracking, the prince is breaking.

"Be careful," Papa warns. "That is your future king you are talking about. You might have forgotten your place, but I know mine. A knight's first duty is to the Crown, and you are walking dangerously close to treason, Peran."

"Treason is intentionally sabotaging Helston's only hope for stability. I knew there was something wrong with you the moment you stepped across the bridge with that *girl*. You have changed, Nicholas."

Papa chuckles like they're having an easy conversation. "You're right. I have. My time away from this place *has* changed me. I see the cruelty and the disparity, well hidden behind duty and necessity. I see the twisted logic you and your precious council use to control and condemn. I see the benefits you give those who fit your perfect little mold, and I see the methods you use to break apart those who do not. And I see you." Papa's head tilts as he looks the chancellor up and down. "You want to talk treason, my lord? Let's have that conversation. Shall we include Her Majesty, or would you prefer she remain in the ignorance *you* have placed her in?"

Peran's face twists, and he makes a violent motion, and Willow flinches. "How *dare* you. Her Majesty has been subjected to intolerable grief. You want the boy to lose his mother as well? The whole family is corrupted with weakness. They are lucky they have had as many chances as we have granted, when it is clear the boy is the weakest of them all."

Whoever said that words don't bruise has never been around someone like Lord Peran. Every syllable batters Willow, and if I don't get him away from this fight, he's going to shatter into unsalvageable pieces.

I gather my courage and dash for him, grabbing his hand, pulling him away, but another hand locks around my wrist and yanks.

The chancellor's eyes are metal. "I warned you, girl—"

Papa's sword sings, but my magic is faster.

It's nothing that Elowen's taught me, nothing I've practiced, just a raw defense that snaps through my blood and sparks straight into Peran's fingers. *"Get off me!"* It feels good. It feels natural. It feels *me*.

Peran lets go with a yelp, staring at me like I've turned into something wild and dangerous. "I knew it," he hisses. "I knew it from the first moment I laid eyes on you. Your kind has been set on poisoning Helston for years. I don't know how she got her hands on you, but the mark of Dumoor is all over you."

"You've lost your senses," Papa growls. "All your reason and all your judgment. . . . You're the one who has been corrupted, Peran." He keeps one arm around me and the other shielding Willow. "The kids are staying with me tonight, and tomorrow we're changing things. You're out of line, Peran."

"Oh, it will change," Peran calls as Papa guides us away. "I promise you that, Nicholas."

CHAPTER
TWENTY-THREE

Papa's rooms are a predictable disaster. Clothes are strewn across the floor and draped over the chair at the desk among half-finished plates of food and papers that look like fallen leaves.

Some people were not made to live alone.

He clears off the sofa in front of the fireplace and gently guides the prince down. Willow lets him. He hasn't said a word since the courtyard. I don't think he even notices the state of the room. His breath comes out in little hitches, all sharp like it hurts to breathe. His face is ashy pale and his eyes are dead.

A knight's first duty is to the Crown, and right now what the Crown needs most is a friend.

"Throw a fire in, would you, Callie?"

Any other day, I'd argue and complain. Today's different. With my magic still fresh on my fingers, I kneel by the hearth and take a moment to steady myself, gathering the power in my blood and drawing it out into my fingers the way Elowen taught me. It takes three goes, three sparks, but eventually the fireplace is blazing. I sit back and admire my work, the heat sharp and comforting on my face.

I made that.

"Your Highness?" Papa says softly. "Willow? Pay no attention to anything that man has told you. He is bitter and jealous and hungry for a power he will never possess. It isn't you."

"Yes, it is." Willow's voice is high and muffled by his hands. "It is me. It's not just him. It's everyone. Everyone knows how worthless I am, even if they don't say it out loud. Helston doesn't want me, Mother doesn't want me, and Father—"

"Your father's leaving had *nothing* to do with you." Papa's voice is almost fierce as he grips Willow's hands and forces the prince to look at him. "Grief messes people up. But your dad loved you *so much*. Both your parents do, Willow."

Willow glares at him, firelight dancing across his tear-stained face. "Then why aren't they here?" he demands. "Why don't they want me?"

"Your mum does." I perch on the sofa's arm, cross-legged. "She's scared, but I know she misses you. No one's allowed to talk about you because it'll make her too sad, because she misses you so bad."

"Lord Peran said . . . he said I remind her of everything she's lost. Just like Father. They'd rather have no one instead of me."

"He lied," Papa says firmly. "If you believe anything, please believe this. You are worthy and you are loved, exactly as you are. Peran removed you from everyone who believed it and surrounded you with those who didn't. He did so to control you, and to control the Crown. I am so sorry I didn't see it sooner. I am sorry I didn't fight for you. I'm sorry I haven't been here for you, Willow. I should've been. From the beginning. I'm sorry."

Most times when grown-ups say they're sorry, they do it to shut you up and make you move forward. When Papa says it, he means it. I don't think anyone's said "sorry" to Willow in a very long time.

He scrubs his palms deep into his eyes and clenches his teeth. Even just sitting next to him, I can feel his whole body rigid as a rock, like it's defending against all the things he's stopped letting himself feel because they're too big and too scary, and what's the point when nothing will change anyway?

Papa draws Willow gently into the kind of hug that makes the world stop spinning out of control for one precious moment. The prince accepts it like it's the first bread offered to a starving person, and clings.

"What's gonna happen tomorrow?" I ask.

Papa looks at me over Willow's shoulder, face set grim. "Tomorrow we fight, kiddo."

The sofa's long enough and deep enough for both of us. Willow lies at one end and I take the other, and Papa tucks a thick woolen blanket tight around us both.

The fire stays blazing long after Papa disappears into his bedroom, but I'm as far away from tired as it's possible to be. I want to move. I want to help. I want to do *something*! It's not like trouble's halted just because we're hiding from it. Peran's out there right now, angry as anything, and there's no way he's not planning something horrible in revenge, whether it's against me or Papa or Willow or all of us together. And Elowen's stuck with him. The only thing I can do is trust Papa and wait. Nothing can happen till tomorrow.

The hardest thing is to do nothing.

Willow's cold toes nudge up into my armpit. He's trembling all the way through the sofa.

I shift to sit up, leaning to touch the prince's shoulder. "You okay? I mean, obviously not, but—"

"You were right," he breathes, tears rolling down to pool in his ears. "You were right and I didn't listen to you and I should've."

"Right about what?"

"About—" The trembles turn into whole-body quakes. "He h-hates me. He hates me, Callie."

The prince is deadweight, but I pull him up by the wrists and hug him fiercely. Willow holds on to me just as tight, burying his face in my shoulder.

"It's not *you*," I tell him firmly. "Just like Papa says: Peran hates everyone who's any kind of different. It's just, you and me, we're not much good at pretending to be anything else. And why should we? I like what I am, and if anyone doesn't, that's their problem, not mine. Willow, you're amazing exactly as you are, and it's Peran's loss if he can't see that."

"I tried," says Willow, raising his head from my shoulder. "I tried so hard to be something else. Something better. I tried to be what they wanted, and I tried so hard it made me sick. He . . . he told me my magic was shameful, that I should hate it and that I should hate myself for having it, just like everyone else hated me. I did. I did hate myself. I tried to get rid of it!" Willow cries. "I loved it so much, but I wanted it gone, if only to stop people looking at me the way they did. My magic cried like I was hurting it, like it was a living part of me. So I decided to pretend instead. I thought, even if I can't pretend to be a good-enough knight, at least I can pretend not to be magical."

Willow's head hangs heavy, palms pressed to his eyes and shivering like there isn't a fieplace blazing just a few feet away.

"You shouldn't have to," I say, sweeping our blanket around his shoulders like an enormous cloak and bundling him up. "No one should. It's not a choice. No one should be punished just for being."

Willow clutches the blanket with white fingers. "That's not how it feels, Callie."

A bitter laugh catches in my throat. "Yeah, I know that."

We lean against each other, head to head.

"What do you really think will happen tomorrow?" Willow asks.

All I can see of the future is soldiers and Helston disappearing as we ride away, Lord Peran watching with one hand on Willow's shoulder and the other on Elowen's.

"We'll fight. And we'll win." That outcome feels a thousand leagues out of reach, but there's no other option worth believing in.

Willow shivers and huddles closer. "Sir Nicholas can't win against Lord Peran."

"Maybe not on his own, but *I'm* not gonna give up, and neither should you. I didn't say it was gonna be an easy fight. Nothing worth doing is ever easy."

"I'm tired of fighting," Willow whispers. "I feel like I've been fighting forever just to keep going. I'm tired. I don't want to do it anymore."

"Then let me do it for you. You *can't* give up now. You have to make it worth it. You have to be brave and keep fighting. For you and me, and El, and all the kids we don't even know about who're too scared to be themselves, because if a prince can be treated like that, what hope is there for anyone else?"

Willow scrubs his nose with his sleeve. "You really think there're others?"

"I know so," I say. "And they keep getting shoved down

and pushed out because people like Peran keep winning, and it's not fair and it's not right."

"Not fair, not right . . . ," the prince echoes. He takes a deep, shuddering breath and pulls himself up a little straighter. "I don't want anyone else to feel like this. Not ever."

"Then we need to fight."

He nods, twice, and each second he becomes a little stronger, even when he admits, "I'm scared, Callie."

"It's okay to be scared," I tell him. "It doesn't mean you can't be brave too."

Willow gulps down a breath, then another, each one steadier than the last. He's still shaking pretty badly, but he's regaining control on the inside, and that's what matters. Then he looks at me and he's both at once—scared *and* brave, and the sum of the two is *determined*.

"And you'll stay with me?" he asks.

"You know I will." I jump up and give my best bow. "Knight's honor."

A smile creeps across the prince's lips, and he slips off the sofa.

"What're you doing?" I ask when he picks out the pointiest poker from next to the fire.

Willow stands tall, chin up, cloaked in our blanket, and points with the poker. "Kneel, Sir Callie."

My face flushes hot. "Huh?"

Willow taps the rug, which is only a little bit burned. "Kneel."

I played this game a million times with the boys at Clyst-well, but Willow's not playing. He's dead serious. This is real.

In an ideal world, I'd have done my hair nicer and put on clean clothes, and we'd be in a fancy room in the middle of the day with a crowd of impressed people all there to watch me. But I guess the point is this isn't an ideal world.

Well, maybe this is the first step to making one.

I drop to one knee and bow my head, closing my eyes so all that exists are the words in my heart.

"I, Callie, do hereby swear my sword, my loyalty, and my life to you, Prince Willow of Helston. I will protect and defend you, and fight for a world you can be proud to rule. I will not leave your side or betray your trust. Win or lose, live or die, we're in this together."

They're not the proper words, but they're mine, and I mean them with every bit of myself.

The tap of the poker is gentle, one shoulder, then the other.

"I, Willow, Crown Prince of Helston, accept your oath, your sword, and your friendship, and promise too that I will not leave your side or betray your trust. Win or lose, live or die, we're in this together." He taps the top of my head. "Arise, Sir Callie, prince's champion."

The words catch me in the chest, like a blow that leaves me stunned.

I stare up at Willow, and his smile is soft and warm. "You mean it?"

"Of course." He offers his hand, and I let him help me up. "It doesn't change anything. It's just what you are. Now and always."

My lip gives an embarrassing wobble.

Willow laughs and hugs me hard. "Knights aren't supposed to cry."

"Knights cry all the time," I sniffle. "They just pretend it's allergies."

"Do you have allergies?"

I screw up my face. "Is it a breach of my oath if I lie and say yes?"

"Absolutely," Willow says gravely. "But it's okay. Princes don't tell secrets."

CHAPTER
TWENTY-FOUR

We sleep too long and too well. I don't even dream, I'm so tired. It takes an urgent shake before my head clears enough to even open my eyes.

"Whassit?"

Willow's eyes are huge, and his face is ghost white, like the good of last night never happened at all. He flinches at a fist to the door and a harsh voice calling, "Your Highness?"

"They're here," he rasps. "They've come for me. Callie . . . I—I don't want to go!"

I grind the sleep out of my eyes, forcing my body awake. "Who's come for you?"

But even in my semiconscious state, I know.

"Look, you don't have to do anything you don't want to. You're the prince." It doesn't matter—we both know that's irrelevant. Willow has got about as much power as Flo does, and a whole lot less freedom.

The knock comes again, harder this time, and the prince starts to tremble. "Callie—"

"Hey." I squeeze Willow's hands hard. "You and me, we've got this, right? The prince and the champion. We're unbeatable. *Right?*" I need him to believe it, even if it isn't true. I hold on to Willow until he manages to nod; then I pull the blankets back around his shoulders and bundle him up. "You stay put. I'll sort this out."

"How?" he asks, already nestling back into the corner of the sofa.

Good question.

I hop up and go to Papa's room. He could literally sleep through a whole battle, so it's not totally surprising he's not out here. But when I shoulder my way in, his bed is empty. It must be really late if he's up and at it already.

That's fine. No big deal. I can handle this myself.

I yank open the door, doing my best champion's glare up at Captain Adan. Again. We're practically best friends by this point, him and me. He's in Helston livery, obviously, but if Peran had his own colors, this man would be wearing them. And they'd totally be vomit green.

I flash my best grin and inform him sweetly, "The prince is having a break today. Come back later."

A boot jammed in the door is the only thing stopping me from slamming it on his nose.

His pasty face hardens, and my heartbeat spikes. I wish

I had Satin. My fists won't make much of a dent in this guy. Some prince's champion I am, totally unarmed.

"Lady Calliden, you are required to accompany His Highness to the courtyard immediately."

I look back at Willow, who's shifting reluctantly from the sofa. "Why?" he asks. "What's going on?"

"You will receive your instructions from the lord chancellor." Adan steps back, ushering us out. "Do not keep him waiting."

Willow moves in automatic obedience, but I plant myself in his way. "No. Not without my dad." If this is some kind of evil trap—which I'm pretty sure it is—there's no way we're walking into it alone.

"Sir Nicholas is waiting for you along with everyone else," Adan responds coolly. "These orders are not optional, and I suggest you do not wait to see the alternative, should you refuse to follow them."

I open my mouth to do just that, but Willow gently pushes his way past. "It's all right," he says softly. "We're coming."

I guess that's technically a royal decree.

Our fingers stay locked tight together all the way through the palace grounds. Helston feels different in the daylight. Bigger, filled with more people looking at me weird. I miss the cloak of nighttime. It's not that I care what people think of me, but there's nothing I can do about it right now, and I do hate that. We're in big trouble, and I'm not about to make that harder for Willow. At the end of the day, if worse comes to the worst, I can leave. He can't. This is his whole world, past, present, and future.

And they all stare at him like he's a dangerous stranger as we round the corner into the courtyard. His grip on my fingers turns bone crushing.

Horses snort, pawing the ground impatiently. Armor clinks and jingles. And the sea of voices is so vast, it nearly knocks me over.

"Callie." Papa cuts clean through the crowd and comes straight up to hug me first, then the prince. I don't like the look on his face, all tight and angry.

"What's going on?" I whisper.

Papa casts one quick eye around, then lowers his head so it's just us. "Lord Peran called a council meeting at dawn this morning. I didn't find out about it until hours after it had commenced. The decision had already been made."

"To do what?" I demand. Willow's eyes have gone glassy, and the way his breath's hitching, he's in no position to ask for himself.

"To bring the deadline forward." Papa reaches out and smooths Willow's black hair from his face. Willow lets him. "You can do this," he says. "I believe it. I need you to believe it too."

"Do what?" I don't get it. I thought Willow's test is supposed to be the tournament. A game. A tough one, but still, there's nothing set up that's even pretending to be a game.

With all the horses and the soldiers ready, it looks like a troop about to ride to battle.

"Ah, Prince Will, so good of you to finally join us."

Just the slick sound of Lord Peran's voice floods every drop of my blood with fury.

He smiles down at Willow, all easy like this is just another day and he's king of the world. The rest of the council lords linger close by, with Lady Anita and a pack of other ladies dressed up just like her. All here to watch the day's entertainment.

I don't get it.

I don't understand how they can just stand there and not say anything. I don't understand how they can pretend this is right, even to themselves.

"I'm glad you are properly rested, Your Highness," says Peran. "Even if we are running late."

"Late like you didn't just schedule—" But my biting sentence ends in *Mmph* as Papa claps a hand over my mouth.

Lord Peran looks down his nose at me. "I see your father is finally parenting you properly, Lady Calliden."

If he was in reach, I'd kick him in the crotch. I could probably land a good one if I just stretched—

Papa hustles me back. I wish he couldn't read me quite as well as he can.

"You will be pleased to know, Lady Calliden, that I took your critiques to heart and realized that I *had* misjudged His Highness's capability. So I thought, 'Why wait? Why not give him the chance to prove himself right now?'" Lord Peran gestures to the cloudless sky. "It is a beautiful day, after all, and His Majesty's tournament was only ever an arbitrary deadline. We are all of us keen to see you succeed, Prince Will, and prove you can be the protector of Helston."

Willow stares helplessly around at the watching faces of Helston nobility. None of them friendly. None of them even sympathetic. There is neutral apathy at best and hunger at worst; grown-ups all keen to watch Willow try and fail. I don't get it. If they have any belief at all that Willow's going to be okay out there on his own, then they have *no* idea what's waiting on the other side of the bridge. Me and Papa, we barely made it through Dumoor, and we're the best of the best. The thought of Willow up against that dragon, surrounded by a pack of yellow-eyed wolves . . . it doesn't end well.

And none of them care. They're doing what Helston does best: pretending that everything is squeaky-clean and absolutely fine.

Lying.

The one noticeable exception is Edwyn.

He's the only other kid here—a small figure lost in a sea of adults—and he's not fine at all. With his gaze fixed on the ground beneath a troubled scowl, he stands crooked, like he's trying not to put weight on his left leg. His skin is deathly white, broken only by a feverish flush in his cheeks. He looks like he's about to fall over.

When Lord Peran summons him with a snap of the

fingers, Edwyn's limp is pronounced as he moves to stand stiffly beside his father.

"You will not be going alone," Peran informs Willow. "After all, a king is expected to lead his men to victory. It is a simple task, though appropriately challenging, and you are responsible for the lives of your company. Find and slay the beast plaguing the neighboring farms. It has most recently been located on the edge of Dumoor Forest, so you will need to be very careful. But as I said, if Lady Calliden and Sir Nicholas are so certain of your capability, I am sure you will be just fine."

"Edwyn looks like he should be in bed, not riding out into battle—" I blurt out before Papa muffles me again.

Edwyn's eyes flick up to glare at me with a face full of shadows. "I'm *fine.*" The rasp in his voice gives him away as a liar.

"My son has been keen for a chance to prove himself," says Peran. "This is not an opportunity to be missed. He will be your second-in-command, Your Highness. Work together, and I have no doubt you will return triumphant."

Neither boy speaks. Willow looks like he'll throw up if he opens his mouth.

I don't like this. I don't like *any* of this.

"I'm going too!" I tell them, *all* of them. "I know what's out there. I've faced it before. I can help—"

"You are not going," Peran snaps at me. "You will stand here like a good girl and wait for your prince to come home."

I open my mouth, ready with a whole string of seriously unladylike words, but Papa squeezes my shoulders.

"Willow will be safe, Callie," he says as Peran escorts Willow and Edwyn to the rest of the party. "Even Peran wouldn't send the last chance Helston has for a king off to his death."

I don't know how he can say that so certainly. Edwyn looks like he's been through a week's worth of brutal drills without a single night's sleep, and the soldiers who are to accompany them give me such a bad feeling, I want to grab Willow and run a hundred miles in the other direction.

But even if I don't trust them, even if I don't trust Peran, I do trust Papa.

If Papa has agreed to this . . .

A squire twice Willow's size straps a sword to the prince's waist and helps him mount up. The horse is too big for him. No one helps Edwyn. He barely makes it into the saddle.

Neither of them should be riding into any kind of battle.

Helston's great and powerful mingle like it's some kind of social event, like they aren't sending two beaten-down boys off to conquer an unconquerable beast. I watch Lady Anita, trying to understand how she can laugh while her daughter is locked away somewhere and her son is just being sent off on a knight's mission that he's six years too young for.

Even my mother wasn't that cruel.

Lady Anita is head to head with a group of ladies in bright dresses, murmuring like they're at a garden picnic while

Peran chats to the cluster of lords gathered around him. They really do believe they're royalty.

Is that the plan?

My head hurts.

With Papa's arms wrapped around my shoulders and his chin resting on my head, I can only stand there and watch uselessly as Willow gives me one last desperate look before the company of five moves out toward the bridge and out of Helston.

"This isn't *right*," I hiss. "Let me go with them!"

"Callie, you have already been targeted by a dragon—"

"I'm not afraid!"

"But I *am*." Papa tips my chin, forcing me to look into his face and see his fear for myself. "I will not risk you."

I step back and away, my hands in fists, and glare at my dad. "It's not your risk to take."

And then I turn and run.

CHAPTER
TWENTY-FIVE

I don't have a plan. I don't even want one. My feet are driven by rage, and I'm happy to let them carry me wherever. I'm not about to pretend I'm not scared of dragons and wolves, but I'm more scared of what will happen if Willow doesn't make it home.

I end up in my room, shoving back my hair and tying it tight; changing out of the nice clothes that aren't mine into the comfortable weather-worn tunic that is, and buckling Satin's scabbard securely to my waist.

I don't have a plan, but at least I'll be ready when I do.

If I do.

Some prince's champion I am.

I stare at the Callie in the mirror, and I'm not the kid in Clystwell getting her hair yanked by her mum's brush. My freckles are the same, the color of my eyes is still hazel, my chin is still stubborn. But my scowl is different. Less petulant, more determined. I'm not a sulky child, reluctantly dragged through life. I am capable of making my own decisions and doing what *I* believe to be right.

I'm not Calliden.

I am Callie, the prince's champion.

And I won't sit by and wait.

Better to beg forgiveness than to ask for permission I know I'll never get.

But I can't do this alone.

I creep through the palace slower than I'd like, given that every moment wasted is another in which Willow could be eaten by wolves. But dressed up like I am, I'm about as conspicuous as it's possible to be, and there's no way I'm risking *anyone* trying to stop me. Not Peran, not Papa, no one.

There's only one person I trust enough to be on my side, and unfortunately, she's trapped on the other side of the palace and I'm nowhere near confident enough in my navigational abilities to make it through the secret passages.

Luckily—I guess—most people are down in the courtyard, waiting for Willow to return (or not) and I only have to deal with a few near misses. Still, the closer I get to the Chancellor's Chambers, the more my nerves make themselves known.

I hate the way Lord Peran can get to me without even being here. He's just one man, one human; he shouldn't have this much hold over *anyone*. I *have* to pull myself together. He's down there, and so is Lady Anita, and Edwyn's over the bridge, so no one will sneak up on me.

I take a deep breath and let myself into the chancellor's apartments.

It's a palace inside a palace, meticulously clean and wholly uncluttered. All the doors are closed except one, which leads into a richly furnished sitting room, filled with towering bookshelves and lit with bright windows. And no Elowen.

Not that I expected her to just be *out* here. If they're not even bothering to lock the door to the apartment, there's no way she's not secured somewhere.

I start tapping softly on each door. After no response, I try the handle.

One door goes to a dark, windowless room filled with a vast desk, and I shut it again quickly.

Another goes to a neat, sparsely furnished bedroom that looks like it's barely lived in. Honestly, that's a feeling the whole place gives. As dead as a graveyard.

I keep tapping, keep opening doors, keep trying to keep my hopes up.

They're almost at rock bottom when someone taps back.

My heart *leaps*. "El?"

"Callie?"

"El!" I tug on the handle. Nothing. I dunno why I expected anything else. "Are you okay?"

"I'm okay." Her voice is wispy, and I'm hoping that's more

a product of the door between us than whatever state she's in. "Callie, I can't get out. I tried to, and I nearly managed but Mother caught me. She put wards on my door. My magic doesn't work."

"That's all right." I keep my voice steady and free of the fear in my chest. "I'm gonna get you out. Stand back, okay?"

"What're you going to do?"

Good question.

"Uh . . . bash down the door?"

"You don't sound very certain."

"Do you have a better plan?"

A long beat of silence; then Elowen admits, "No."

"Well then. Stand back."

It's a *heavy* door. Only the best for the lord chancellor and family. But luckily it wasn't designed to withstand any kind of attack. It doesn't give on the first bash, or even the second, but once my shoulder starts to ache, I feel the give in the latch.

"Pull," I tell El. "I'll push, you pull, and maybe it'll be enough. Ready?"

"Ready."

I go back as far as the walls will let me, and I charge the door. I'm not big by any stretch, but I am strong. I close my eyes and brace for impact . . . and end up flat on my face on the other side.

"You broke Mother's wards," says Elowen, looking down at me. "Good job."

"Couldn't've told me that before I turned into a siege weapon?"

"I thought this would be more fun."

I groan.

"My hero." Elowen stoops to help me back up, and I can't quite tell if she's serious or joking. She traces the doorframe, inspecting for damage, like it's the door we need to be worried about.

"Hey, El, you all right?"

"You asked me that already."

"Yeah, well . . . you kinda disappeared on me." I brush door guts off my tunic. "What happened, El? After the council meeting."

But Elowen focuses on the bent lock, carefully undoing all the damage I did, making it look like it never happened in the first place. She's good. Really good.

And then I notice the tears gathered stubbornly in her eyes. "Elowen—"

"I thought Father was going to kill him."

"Who? Willow?"

"Edwyn."

My skin prickles with too much understanding too quickly. *Oh.*

Elowen swipes at her eyes with a brisk palm. "He came looking for me when he found out Father had caught me in the lie. He was scared for me. Scared of what Father would do, even though Father's never . . . He's never hurt me. Not like that. The worst he was going to do was forbid me from attending lessons with Her Majesty, and I could find my way around that. I could bear it until Father forgot about me again. But Edwyn wouldn't listen, and when Father came home last night—" No amount of swiping can keep her tears at bay now. "He was already angry. And when Edwyn begged him to forgive me . . . Father said he was done being ordered around by children."

I can feel my heart in my ears, beating so hard it hurts. No wonder Edwyn looked like death today. And it's my fault.

My fault Willow was sent out onto the moor, my fault Elowen was locked up, my fault Edwyn's limping.

"I'm sorry, El—"

"But that's not the worst of it. Callie, I . . . I wanted to tell you, but I couldn't get out. Father . . . the only reason he spared Edwyn—" She's gabbling now, the anxious line between her eyes as deep as the most seasoned soldier's. "He's sending Willow out, and Edwyn's to go with him . . . to make sure Willow doesn't make it back. And he said . . . he said . . ." She hides her face in her hands. "If Edwyn fails, he's not to come home. And I don't know what to do."

"They're already gone." My voice doesn't feel like my own. It sounds like someone else's, far away and underwater, and when Elowen looks at me, she looks like she's drowning.

"Callie—"

"But I'm going after them. I knew it was messed up. That something wasn't right. I came to get you. To go after them.

I figured it was just an impossible mission. I didn't think—" I swear under my breath. "You think he'll do it? You think he could—" *Kill Willow.* I can't even say it.

"I don't know," says Elowen. "Father's got him all tied up. He can make Edwyn do anything he wants. Especially if he thinks I'm in danger."

My heart's thumping so hard, it feels like a horse galloping in my chest. "Think we can stop him?"

"I don't know," Elowen whispers. "I don't know. But we have to try."

It already feels too late. I don't even know how long they've been out there, but people do desperate things in desperate circumstances, and Edwyn's had plenty of time to do away with Willow.

I don't want to think about it.

I can't think about it.

Don't think, just act.

"You coming with me?"

Elowen takes a deep breath, and her expression turns fierce. "Just try to go without me."

I could kiss her. I do. Right on the cheek. Then I grab her hand and run before I can see the look on her face.

⊣———

We sneak round the back of the stables, and I saddle Flo the fastest I've ever saddled her, my fingers moving automatically over the buckles and straps; and when I'm mounted, Elowen settles behind me like she grew up in the saddle.

There's no way we can get to the single path heading down toward the bridge without being seen. It's like the whole of Helston is gathered in one place to watch their prince succeed or fail. But there's no point worrying about being caught.

"Hold on tight," I murmur, and El's arms squeeze my middle.

I urge Flo into a gallop, and we're off—charging straight through the middle of the gathering, and trying not to hit anyone, as much as I would like to. Honestly, a stampede would probably wipe out half our problems in less than a minute, but that's not exactly the chivalrous route.

There's no time to look back, but I swear I see Papa grin as Peran yells his fury after us. But not a single person there expected it, and not a single person is ready to come after us. We thunder through the palace, down through the streets toward the sea, the bridge, and I feel Elowen hold her breath the moment Flo's hooves hit the wood.

I swallow my own nerves. It's not like the dragon's just going to rise up out of nowhere the second we're on the other side of the bridge.

Still, it's a heady relief when unoccupied moorland stays unoccupied.

Elowen's fingers pinch my back as she twists to look behind us. "I thought it would be harder than that."

"It's just a bridge. Nothing special."

"They always made it sound like you'd turn to dust the moment you set foot over it."

"Grown-ups lie," I say grimly, squeezing Flo's sides with my knees.

Elowen buries her face in my shoulder. "I'm sick of it."

"Yeah, I bet." The path from the bridge out to the moors is one option only, but I'm keenly aware that stops the moment we hit open countryside. "What're your tracking skills like, El?"

I expect her to say "Less than zero," or something to that effect, but instead she says, "I can always find Edwyn."

"Yeah? A twin thing?"

"Something like that." She fishes into her collar and pulls out a thin chain. It's nothing fancy, more like it was reconditioned from something else, and it holds a ragged loop made out of threads that clearly once were colorful. There are tiny knots at various intervals, and Elowen starts touching them in a pattern that feels intentional.

"What's that?"

"We made them forever ago. Willow had one too." Elowen's fingers move deftly across the thread. "They used to be bracelets, but it's safer this way. Easier to hide. Sometimes it's the only way we can talk to each other for days at a time. Weeks, occasionally."

"But you live together?"

"Father doesn't like us mixing," says Elowen. "Girls and boys are supposed to stay separate, otherwise there is cross-contamination, he says. Even in families. We have ways around it, but oftentimes it isn't worth the risk. Edwyn's not as willing to defy Father as I am."

"Yeah, I can see that," I mutter. "I dunno how someone can think they'll be a good knight if they just let themselves be bullied into being a bully. At some point, he's got to've realized that your dad's wrong?"

Elowen sighs. "It's more complicated than that. Father's got him all twisted around and tangled up. That's what I mean when I say I'm lucky. I have somewhere to escape to, with the Queen's Daughters, and different people to talk to. My brother doesn't have that. And he would do anything if he thought Father would forgive him."

"Forgive him for what? Being a jerk? I thought that's what your dad wanted?"

"No," says Elowen. "For being magical."

An arrow in the neck would've been less of a shock.

My laugh comes out weird. "No he's not."

"Yes he is. Despite Father's very best efforts, my brother is magical."

I swear under my breath, then again because what else is there to say? If that's the way Peran treats princes, what hope is there for anyone else?

"Precisely," says Elowen.

"I . . . didn't know."

"Of course you didn't. No one does. Just the family. And Prince Willow."

"Seriously? Willow knows?"

"Why does that surprise you?" Elowen asks.

"I dunno. . . . It's not exactly like they're on friendly terms, and that's a pretty big secret to let an enemy have." Not that Willow's the sort to do anything malicious, even to someone who makes his life miserable.

But Elowen laughs softly. "They were friends once. Best friends. And he knew before I did. It was Willow who persuaded Edwyn it would be okay to tell our parents. It had gone well enough for him when he presented. He . . . didn't know what Father was like back then. And Edwyn was still hopeful. Father was strict, but he wasn't . . ." She swallows around the word "cruel." "Edwyn thought—he hoped—that if he was honest, if he could prove that magic wasn't as bad as Father thought it was, if it could be useful, then it would be okay. He and Willow practiced together."

"I can't imagine it," I admit. I can't see Edwyn as anything other than the angry, hate-filled kid he is now, who spits at Willow's feet and calls him "princess" like it's an insult. I can't imagine him being friendly with anyone, least of all Willow.

"He was different back then," says Elowen. "They both were. Willow loved magic more than anything, and his love was infectious. He made Edwyn love it too, and see it as something beautiful and precious, to be nurtured instead of reviled."

"It is," I whisper.

"Yes," Elowen agrees, her voice bleak. "And precious things are the most easily broken. No matter how often they prove him wrong, Edwyn has always been determined to believe the best of our parents. I knew it couldn't go well. Not from the way Father always spoke of Willow in private. Edwyn was a fool to think otherwise."

"What happened?" I make myself ask because I have to know, even though my chest hurts and my stomach feels bottomless.

"Father caught him, long before he was ready. And then everything changed. We were separated. He was forbidden to spend time with Willow. There was no more playing, no more dreaming. Father designed a new training regimen just for him that left Edwyn with no time and no energy for anything other than eating and sleeping. Father thought—*thinks*—the method will purge Edwyn of his magic."

I flinch. "That's not the way it works."

"No," says Elowen bleakly. "It isn't. And the worst of it is Edwyn still believes in Father. He thinks it should work, that it's his failing that it hasn't, that Father will forgive him if it ever does. He thinks he deserves it."

My fingers are numb. I can't feel Flo's reins. My throat has gone so thick, every breath is hard as Elowen's words pull me back into the past I fled from. I know, better than anyone, that you can't just wish or work your magic away. It's part of you, whether you like it or not, even if the road to acceptance is long and tangled and feels impossible. I barely made it myself, and there's no way I could've done it alone.

We're lucky, aren't we? Papa said.

The luckiest.

"I try to help him as best I can," says Elowen through the haze in my head as Flo splashes through the first trickle of river winding its way in-between the hills. "Sometimes he lets me, but most of the time he doesn't. He's so afraid of magic now, he can hardly stand being healed. He certainly won't let anyone try but me."

I think of Willow's hands, bruised and bleeding when there are palace healers on standby. "This regimen your dad made for Edwyn ... that's what he's got Willow doing, isn't it?"

I feel her nod, and anger thrums through every muscle in my body. The thought of Willow, who still loves and hopes and dreams, being turned into someone like Edwyn makes me want to grab Satin and confront Lord Peran and—

"I hate him, Callie," Elowen mumbles into my back; the confession safe with Helston disappearing behind us. "I hate him so much, and no one else ... no one else sees it. No one else knows him the way we do. They think he'll save Helston, and no one cares how he does it."

"They're starting to see," I try. "Papa says he's changed.

They'll notice, El. We'll make them notice, and they won't stand for it."

I don't know who this disembodied "they" are. Certainly not anyone gleefully watching their precious chancellor send Willow and Edwyn across the bridge.

"He hasn't changed," says Elowen bitterly. "He's just gotten brave enough to be himself outside our apartment."

"He won't win, El," I promise recklessly. "We'll save Willow and Edwyn, and then we're going home and we're fixing things."

Elowen says nothing.

We ride in heavy silence toward the unknown monster, which is somehow far less intimidating than the one waiting for us in Helston.

Flo follows the bubbling stream cutting through the bracken. The ground is lumpy, and I'm not confident enough to urge her faster than a walk. Behind me, Elowen keeps touching the frayed thread, fingers darting from knot to knot.

"Anything?"

She shakes her head. "Not directly. But I can feel them closer. At least he has his with him. We're going in the right direction."

I don't remind her that that could kinda mean anything at this point, but the clear sky is getting decidedly less so with every minute, so I'll take what we can get.

I swear, if it starts storming . . .

But the first thunder doesn't come from the weather. It comes from over the hill on the backs of warhorses.

I draw Satin and brace myself, ready to get Flo moving if we have to run.

Helston scarlet charges down the hill toward us, and hope comes so fast and unexpected, I nearly throw up.

Except there are three instead of five. Soldiers and no kids. No Willow. No Edwyn. And they're grinning like they're in the middle of some kind of great joke, not like they're fleeing a dragon. My hope evaporates as fast as it came. I urge Flo into a canter right in front of them, so they've no choice but to stop and acknowledge us.

One of them frowns. He's not that old. None of them are. "You're Sir Nick's girl—"

"Not a girl," I snap back. "Where's the prince?"

The other two exchange looks, and I know guilt when I see it.

The first one sits up straighter in his saddle, raising his chin like he's delivering a rehearsed speech. "His Highness wandered off into the forest. Peran's boy went after him. We searched for hours, but there's nothing we can do."

"You haven't been gone hours," I snap. "And if you searched for them at all, you must've lost them straight after leaving Helston. So—what? You're just gonna leave them out here? Are those the orders Lord Peran gave you?"

Elowen tugs on the back of my tunic. "Callie—"

But I'm *way* beyond being capable of caution. "You are

soldiers of Helston!" I snarl. "Your first duty is to the Crown, and you just *left* him out there! What is wrong with you? Do you know what's in that forest? This is treason!"

In less than a moment, all their expressions shift and turn cold. Flo paws the ground as the trio surrounds us; bigger than her, bigger than us, their swords longer and heavier than Satin. I'm not scared of them, but we don't have time for this. Not if Edwyn's got Willow alone.

"If you go in there," says the first soldier quietly, "you'll get lost too. Everyone does. Dumoor Forest eats wandering kids. Didn't your father tell you that? I suggest you let us escort you back to the palace before you get into trouble."

I'd rather get eaten by the forest than give in and go back with my tail between my legs, and I open my mouth to say so when Elowen tugs on me again, more urgently this time.

"What?"

"Edwyn responded."

I forget the men around us immediately. "Yeah?"

"I couldn't make out the message, but they're close, Callie."

"Okay." That decides it, then. I stick my tongue out at the soldier, and Flo flies into a gallop past him and up the hill. I don't care what kind of message they take back to the chancellor. We've got a prince to save.

CHAPTER
TWENTY-SIX

D umoor Forest swallows us whole.

That's what it feels like—like the trees sucked us into the dark belly of the moors. All the light, all the sky, vanishes, like the darkness is too dense to touch.

Elowen lights a fire in her palm, but even that enables us to see only a few steps ahead. If those soldiers hadn't been so obviously shady, I would've totally believed Willow and Edwyn were truly lost.

"Left," Elowen murmurs, though even the softest voice booms in the stillness. There is no wind in the leaves, no rustle of creatures, just . . . nothing.

This is what I imagine death to feel like.

And it's taking way too long. We could be riding in circles for all I can tell, with no way of knowing for sure. The darkness presses down on us like a blanket tucked in too tight.

Every breath is an effort, and it takes conscious thought not to panic.

I don't like closed spaces.

"He's saying go back," Elowen whispers. "He's telling us to turn around."

"Tell him to be quiet if he's not going to be helpful." I want to be sympathetic, and I do feel sorry for Edwyn, but that doesn't mean I'm not annoyed at the position we're in or worried about Willow or wishing that none of this had happened in the first place. And the fact of the matter is that it *has* happened, it *is* happening, and we can only do our best.

It's a long while of trudging onward, and then the ground gets too perilous to even ride. Flo's ears twitch constantly, and I wonder if she can hear more than I can. I wish she would tell me.

"Are we close?" I ask El.

"I think so. . . ." Then she gasps as a light bursts through the tops of the trees, small and sparking, but bright as a star. Elowen picks up her skirts and runs, leaping over roots twisting up like they're trying to trip her.

"El—" But she's gone. I quickly tell Flo to stay put but run if she needs to, and I take off after Elowen.

Without Elowen's flame, I fall flat on my face twice before I find her. Even though it's just a few feet, there's a nasty second when I'm sure I'm lost for real. This forest is magical or cursed or something. But the sight when I finally find my way into the small clearing is worth it all.

Willow, alive and in one piece. Scratched up and scared, but alive. I hug him so hard his spine cracks. It's only then I realize how scared I was for him.

"I didn't think you'd be able to find us," he mumbles into my shoulder.

"Yeah, same. You guys didn't make it easy."

Willow clings a little bit tighter, and we stay like that for a long while. I get it. It's been a rubbish day, and it can't be much past midday yet. Over Willow's shoulder, I watch Elowen approach her brother.

Edwyn is sitting on the ground, and he doesn't look up from where his head is buried in his arms. Assassin's guilt, maybe?

"You okay?" I ask Willow. "No one hurt you, right? We passed those— Your soldiers. They didn't seem too concerned about your disappearance."

Hearing that, Willow doesn't seem super concerned either.

"No, I'm . . ." He lets out a long, juddering breath. "I'm okay. Better now that you've found us. I've never been on this side of the bridge before. It's bigger than I expected."

"Yeah, Helston's pretty tiny. There's a whole world out here. What about him?" I nod at Edwyn, who is not reacting to Elowen's attempt at coaxing him up.

Willow glances at the twins, mouth twisted down.

"Callie, if I tell you something, you have to promise not to be angry."

"I told them," says Elowen, glancing up. "I overheard Father's plan. We both know."

"Never mind me not being angry! What about you?" I don't care how complicated the circumstances are, if my ex-best friend had tried to kill me, I'd be pretty furious.

But the prince simply gives a hopeless shrug. "It's not his fault."

"He could've refused!" But even I know that's not fair.

"And then what?" Willow asks simply, like his life wasn't just in imminent peril. I don't know if I admire his willingness to forgive so easily or fear it. Both. Equally. But I don't have an answer for him. Bravery is always easier said than done, and when it comes to standing up against someone you love, someone who can and will hurt you . . . yeah, I get it.

Side by side, we look at the twins.

Elowen's magic is soft and warm in her palm, and she presses it gently into Edwyn's calf. Even in the low light, it's swollen visibly.

"You need to get this set properly," she murmurs. "As soon as we get home—"

"I can't go home." Edwyn's voice is cracked, muffled by his knees. "I told you not to come, El. You should've turned back."

"As if we were going to do that," Elowen scoffs, but there's no bite to her words.

"He's going to kill you."

"No, he won't."

Edwyn curls tighter and says again, "I can't go home."

"Then what's the plan?"

But Edwyn can't answer.

"This is what we've been trying to work out," says Willow softly. "If there's even any point going back to Helston."

"How can you say that so easily?" I demand, glaring from one Helston kid to the next. "You're all just going along and falling into place, just the way he wants. Don't you care? Don't you want to fight? If the conditions for going home are impossible, then the conditions are *wrong*! I don't understand how you can all just—"

"You don't get to say." Edwyn staggers to his feet, wincing as he puts weight on his injured leg. But the pain doesn't numb his anger. He hobbles over to us, glaring just as hard as ever. "You don't get to judge. You don't know *anything*, Calliden!"

"That's not true—"

"After all this is over, you'll just leave with your perfect father and your perfect life, all sanctimonious and smug that you'll always have it better than us. But you don't know what you'd do in our shoes. You don't know what it's like! So until you do, just *shut up*!"

And I do.

All my words stick in the back of my throat, and I can't speak. Because he's right. I *don't* know. Not really. I only know what I would do in this moment, but that's with a whole other life to fall back on and escape to, and a dad who will always help me, and another who will always love me.

The Helston kids aren't so lucky.

Edwyn's fists are balled up tight, ready to throw a punch. I was ready to get into it too. I expected to. But he's not the enemy. Not in any sense.

So I drop my defenses. "You're right. I'm sorry."

Edwyn falters like this is some kind of weird trick, narrowed eyes darting to Willow as though he's in on it too.

I put my hands up in surrender. "Tell me how I can help you."

The response comes in an automatic bite: "I don't need help."

"Yeah, you do. So stop being so damn proud and tell me how."

Edwyn's sword hisses as it's drawn. "Leave!" he snarls, pointing it at my throat. "If you want to help us, *leave!* Stop interfering! Stop making things *worse!*"

My hand goes to Satin, but I don't draw her in retaliation. I don't want to fight, but I will defend myself if I have to. Edwyn grips his sword in two trembling hands, his stance messy and desperate. Desperate people are the most dangerous.

"Let's go home," I tell him gently and firmly, doing my best impression of Papa. "We'll ride back, and we'll go straight to Papa. We'll help you. We'll protect you—"

"I don't need help!" I barely get Satin up in time to block the blow. "And I don't need protection! Your precious father's not as perfect as you think he is. He's the same as the others—you're just too *dazzled* to see it!"

The collision of steel rattles my body, but I don't fight, just block.

"What others?"

But Edwyn's not listening. The conversation he's having, it's not with me. "Father picked him for a reason. And they're all the same. Even if they don't start out that way. Even if they pretend otherwise. And they always do. And the ones who pretend the best . . . they're the worst of them all!"

One more blow, but it's weak, and my deflection sends the tip of his sword into the ground.

Edwyn leans on it like it's a crutch, head bowed, shoulders shaking.

I reach for him awkwardly. "Hey—"

He flinches away from me. "Don't."

So I don't. "Failing would be giving up and giving in to your dad," I tell him. "Winning doesn't always feel like winning. Sometimes it feels like losing, and twice as scary."

"My father loves me," Edwyn mumbles, scrubbing at his eyes with the hand not holding on to his sword. "I just . . . I just have to . . ."

"No, you don't." Willow steps tentatively closer and gives the hug that Edwyn would never accept from me. "There's nothing you need to prove. Even to him. Brave is being scared and doing it anyway, so let's do it. All of us together. Let's go home and show them we're brave."

"And what then?" Elowen asks. She stands a little way apart, arms crossed in a hard line. "Bravery is all very well in the moment, but Edwyn's right—you two can escape. We can't."

"Do you want to?"

The twins exchange glances like I just broke the fabric of reality.

"And go where?" Elowen asks.

"I dunno. Anywhere."

Edwyn rolls his eyes, looking a little more like his usual self. "*You* might be privileged to have those options—"

"Tell Mother," says Willow.

We all stare at him. Queen Ewella is one person none of us have considered.

"I . . . I think we should tell her," he continues. "I think she should know everything. And maybe nothing will come of it. Maybe she already knows. But maybe she doesn't. And if anyone can help—"

"Yes!" I say. "Let's do it. Let's go back and tell the queen. Tell everyone! Even if they try to ignore everything else, they can't ignore that he tried to get rid of the crown prince. That's plain old treason. Something's gotta happen. We've gotta *make* it happen."

Elowen and Willow nod their agreement.

Edwyn has gone deathly gray. "He'll never forgive me."

"He was never going to," Elowen says.

Edwyn recoils harder than if she'd hit him. "That's not true—"

But Elowen persists. "If everything had gone according to plan, if you'd done everything he asked, there would only be something more. Another impossible condition. There always is. You aren't supposed to succeed."

"That's not true," Edwyn repeats as Willow nods in agreement, but there's nothing but doubt in his voice. "I just haven't . . . I've never done enough. I've never proven myself. I've never shown him that I can be . . . that I'm not—"

"Yourself?" I ask.

And Edwyn breaks. All the hurt and the bitter hopelessness finally come crashing down, and Edwyn cries. It's Willow who holds him and promises it'll be better. The prince and his assassin. It makes a strange kind of sense, seeing them together. A friendship that persists despite the universe's best efforts.

Elowen's fingers curl through mine. When I look at her, her face is soft and neutral. "I'm glad we came," she murmurs. "I'm glad this happened."

In a weird way, I am too.

"We should start back, though," I say. "There's no way of knowing how long it'll take to find our way out. Let's get out of here before it really gets dark."

I don't think so, a voice oozes out of the darkness and into my head.

Every ounce of blood in my body freezes.

And why bother, anyway, when you know nothing will ever change? Why fight for a chance at the barest minimum, the voice murmurs, *when you know your lords will never even grant you that? Why spend that effort on those who will never accept you as you are? Why break your backs to fit someone else's idea of what you should be?*

The voice gets louder, closer, and I don't think any of us are breathing.

But I'm not the only one who hears them this time.

Willow and Edwyn spring apart, as startled as snagged rabbits. Elowen draws her magic, alert and ready to fight.

"You hear it too?" I whisper, and they each look at me with confirmation.

Somehow that quells the worst of my fear. It's easier to face monsters when the battle's shared.

The shadows gather and manifest, solidifying into a single figure who looks at us, head cocked, yellow eyes flashing, and when they speak again, their voice comes through their mouth, like anyone else's. "Why go through all that heartache when your people are right here, waiting for you?"

The dragon.

Except they don't look like a dragon this time.

CHAPTER
TWENTY-SEVEN

The dragon's human form doesn't quite fit them, like a shirt they laced up wrong. In one clawed hand they hold a fire that illuminates their red-scaled face and bright yellow eyes, catching on their pointed teeth when they smile. Curling horns grow out of snow-white hair, and they stand regarding us with a cocked head and an amused expression.

"Don't listen to anything they say," I whisper to the others, grappling for Papa's advice. "Dragons lie. That's how they catch you."

"So suspicious," the dragon drawls with a mock pout. "I would've thought that you of all people, Callie, would've realized I am right by now. You have witnessed Helston for yourself. That is why you are here, is it not?"

"We're going back," I growl. "We're going to fight and we're going to change things."

The dragon chuckles. "Of course you are. You think you are the first to have such dreams? Do you know what they do to dreamers in Helston?" Their yellow eyes flick to Edwyn. "*You* know, child. You know all too well. They have crushed your dreams and made you fear them. Why would you wish to return to that? And you, princeling—that crown will never fit you, but they will break you to make it fit. They will crush you to dust and blow you away, and only then will you be enough. As for you, sorcerer." The smile stretches wide as their attention settles on Elowen. "You could raze Helston to the ground with a snap of your fingers, given the room to grow. Isn't that what you want? A chance to stretch your wings and fly? These things you desire, Helston pups, they are not beyond the scope of reason or possibility, and there are those not so far away who are willing and wanting to give them all to you. And, Callie . . ."

They sidle up to me, as tall as Neal and with an expression just as warm, making me homesick. They tilt my chin up with one curved claw, their face so close I can smell the blood on their breath. I don't move away, and I tell myself it's bravery.

It isn't.

"You wish to be a warrior," says the dragon, "to make the difference you wish to see in the world and save the ones you love from those who wish them harm."

I feel myself nodding.

"You are not alone, little knight. You are one out of a thousand just like you, each one fierce and dedicated and hungry. Would you like to meet them?"

I swallow. Others like me. A whole community. Somewhere I wouldn't feel different. All fighting for the same purpose, to the same ends. . . .

I want it.

"I—"

"Stop!"

It feels like a broken spell, the voice jarring me back to my senses. My head still feels hazy, but I can see again, and what I see is—

"Neal!"

He shoves between us and the dragon's teeth, arms spread wide to protect us. He doesn't look around. There is magic in one hand and a sword in the other. "Stay back, Callie."

The dragon chuckles, and their eyes glow brighter. "Long time no see, friend. You look different."

"I am different, and you can't have these kids." Neal's voice is lower and darker than I've ever heard it. He doesn't sound like himself. "Walk away, Kensa."

Kensa. Neal knows the dragon's name, and the dragon called him "friend." And I'm hyperaware of the others staring at me like *I* have the answer to the dragon's bizarre question when really my head is filled with *only* questions.

"Shouldn't you ask them what they want?" Kensa returns.

"I seem to remember a young boy denied his autonomy who grew up into a very righteous young man. Or was that just for yourself? I hope adulthood hasn't turned you selfish."

"I grew up," says Neal firmly. "And I learned to see you for what you are."

Kensa's scaly face twists, becoming more dragon and less human. "And what's that, then?"

"No better than Helston. Just as corrupt. Just as twisted. I know you prey on the desperate and the vulnerable. You offer an army to the defenseless and a choice to the choiceless. I know the debt incurred can never be paid. And I won't let you take my kid!"

"Yours?" Kensa darts to get a good look at me before Neal can bar the way. "I see no resemblance." They hiss and retreat as Neal slashes at them.

"My kid," he repeats. "In all the ways that matter, and if you touch them, I'll kill you."

My heart warms and swells, filling me with certainty despite the danger.

Then the wind picks up in a howl.

Beside me, Willow whimpers and grips my arm, and the twins hold tight to each other as yellow eyes flicker and flash all around us.

We're surrounded.

Kensa's wings sprout and spread as their face lengthens into the fanged snout I recognize from the moor. *What authority do you think you possess, traitor?* they demand of Neal. *She never forgets, you know. None of us do. We have been waiting for you.*

Neal lowers his sword a fraction and raises his chin as Kensa slithers so close, their faces nearly touch. "Let the kids go," he says, voice perfectly neutral, "and I will return willingly to fight by her side."

My whole body sparks with shock. Even Satin falters. "Neal, what—"

Kensa grins, showing rows and rows of pointed teeth. *What makes you think she would have you back?*

"Because I was the best." He speaks bleakly, like it's nothing to be proud of, and my heart twists. We're not supposed to have secrets, me and Neal and Papa. That's what makes us different. Special. And I don't know the man standing here talking to the dragon. He's wearing Neal's face, but I don't know anything about him.

I wonder if Papa knows.

Kensa curls around us like a python about to swallow us whole, and I jump when Neal squeezes my shoulder.

"Get ready to run," he whispers. "Take your friends back to the bridge. Don't stop until you're the whole way across."

"What about you?" My head tells me I shouldn't trust him, not if he's familiar with the witch and the dragon. But my heart tells me this is still Neal.

Neal flashes a quick wink, and he looks like himself again. "I've got this, kiddo."

"I'm not leaving you!"

"Callie, I'm serious. Get your friends out of here."

If it was just me, I'd stay and I'd fight. But I'm responsible for more than myself.

I nod.

Kensa twists around, face as long as Neal is tall. *If I had my way, I would strike you down on the spot,* they hiss in Neal's ear. *You broke your oath.*

"Just because I had the courage to leave and you didn't."

The wind whips up as Kensa swells with fury, giant claws clenching the ground like they're about to rip the world to pieces.

If this is Neal's plan, it doesn't feel like a sensible one.

The bracken whistles, and the trees bend and bow in deference as Kensa rises up, mouth wide open to strike, leaving a gap between body and ground big enough for us to duck beneath.

"Go!" Neal yells, and shoves me in the back.

I grab all the hands I can and run, dragging and sprinting and stumbling, following the light that Willow conjures with a snap of his fingers, tiny but bright as a star as he hurls it into the sky to light our way home.

Edwyn's face is set in hard concentration against the pain in his leg. I've his hand and Willow's, but not Elowen's, and when I look back she's not there.

"Wait!"

The boys both halt immediately, realizing the same thing at the same time.

"Where's El?" Edwyn demands, looking desperately around, then glaring at me. "I thought you had her!"

"I thought *you* had her!" I snap back, guilt bringing out the worst in both of us.

"I'm going back—"

"Wait!" I grab his sleeve. "You're not going alone. I'm coming with you."

"No. You get His Highness home. Leave Elowen to me."

Indignation sparks and flares. "Why? Because I'm the *girl*? You take Willow back!"

Edwyn looks like he wants to get into this with fists. "No, you *dolt*, it's because that's a giant dragon and she's *my* sister, and *someone* has to go back with the prince."

I open my mouth, ready to fight this out, but Willow gets in between us. "Um . . . I don't want to go back either. Not without El. I want to fight too."

"No!" Edwyn and I say together, earning a mutual glare.

I cross my arms. "If you go and get killed by an angry dragon, guess who's gonna be sitting on that throne within a day!"

"You are too important," Edwyn adds begrudgingly.

"Says the one sent on a murder mission—"

Edwyn rounds on me with a snarl. "I didn't do it, did I?"

I hold up my hands in concession. "All right—"

"No! Not all right! You think you've got me all worked out, don't you? I'm the villain who can't be trusted. And maybe that's true, but I don't *want* to be. And I'm trying . . . I'm trying not to be. So *please*. Don't."

His voice is weird and stilted, like the words don't fit right on his tongue, like he's not used to speaking so candidly. There's no defensiveness, just a genuine plea for me to, well, stop.

So I do.

"Sorry," I tell Edwyn, trying to make sure I match his sincerity. "That wasn't fair and I know it. You're right—I thought I had worked you out, but that's not true. I apologize."

Edwyn blinks in the darkness, expecting an apology just about as much as I was expecting his confession.

"Not to interrupt," says Willow, "but there isn't really time to stand and chat."

"Fine," says Edwyn curtly. "You go back to Helston. Callie and I will go back for El."

I nod my agreement. "Find Papa. And your mum. Tell them the truth about everything."

Willow closes his eyes and takes a deep, steadying breath, summoning every ounce of courage he possesses. "I'll do my best."

The prince opens his palm and tosses another star-bright light high into the sky, illuminating the darkness. Then he hesitates one more moment, kisses us both on the cheek, and runs.

"What if he can't find them?" Edwyn whispers as Willow disappears into the dark. "What if Father finds him first?"

"They're not gonna turn him out before we get back," I say, hoping it's true. "I think the banishment of a prince will take longer than a couple of hours."

Edwyn rolls his eyes. "How long precisely do you think it'll take to slay the beast? Providing, of course, it doesn't slay us first."

"Your negativity is unhelpful."

"Well, at least the Crown is safe." He looks at me, and for the first time it feels like we might be on the same side. "You really think we'll survive this?"

I punch him lightly(ish) on the arm. "We're the best in Helston. If anyone's got a shot, it's us." I offer my hand. "Anyway, I don't see that we have much choice."

Edwyn sighs and accepts it like he's accepting an unpleasant yet inevitable sentence. His hand is as worn as a seasoned soldier's. "Anything to put off going home, I suppose."

"That's the spirit!"

CHAPTER
TWENTY-EIGHT

We charge back to the clearing as Kensa roars, calling on their army of beasts to surround Elowen and Neal. They stand braced in the middle of the monsters, unflinching and unfearful, fierce magic blazing in their hands.

But as amazing as they both are, there are too many beasts to face alone.

The beasts aren't attacking, though. Instead, they prowl forward, creating a dense wall preventing Elowen and Neal from running as Kensa bears down on them with fire and fangs.

Edwyn cries out and tries to rush forward, but I hold him back. "Wait!"

He rips away furiously. "What are you *doing*? They're going to kill her!"

But Elowen is more than holding her own. Her power is matched with Neal's as they stand side by side and throw up an immense ward around themselves, deflecting Kensa's attack. Through the haze of magic and smoke, her face is set with determined focus.

"We have time to be smart," I hiss at Edwyn. "And if we want to get out all together, we need to be smart. Got it?"

Eyes on his sister, Edwyn forces a nod.

Fire slams again against the force field, and Neal's feet skid on the ground. He grits his teeth, face smoke-singed. It's the hardest thing in the world to follow my own command and not rush to his side.

I motion to Edwyn to take one side, and I take the other. Together we circle round Kensa's writhing back and *strike* right into their body with a yell.

Satin pings off the dragon's scales like she's a kid's toy made of tin. The horror on Edwyn's face tells me the same happened to him.

Kensa doesn't even acknowledge us. We might as well not be here.

"What do we do?" Edwyn calls to me above the rush of fire. The whole clearing is blazing. If we don't get eaten, we'll burn.

I sheathe Satin, afraid she'll melt, and try to think through the heat.

And then I turn to Edwyn. "Use your magic."

Edwyn recoils with his whole body. "I don't know what—"

"Yes. You do. Elowen told me."

"She had no right!"

"Do you want to save her or not?"

Edwyn looks hopelessly through the smoke at his sister, caught fast between two horrors.

I don't have time to wait out his moral dilemma. I build up my own fire, using all my focus and all my energy and every lesson Neal and El have ever given me.

"What do you think's gonna happen?" I ask Edwyn. "You think your dad'll manifest out of nowhere?"

"I can't do it," Edwyn whispers, staring at the fire like I'm about to throw it at him. "I—I can't—"

"You have to! I can't do this alone! *Please!* For Elowen!"

His lips repeat *For Elowen* like it's a spell for courage.

It works.

Edwyn opens his palms and closes his eyes and breathes. His hair is sweat-sticky, and tears roll halfway down his face before they evaporate in the heat, but the thought of Elowen holds him steady.

Brave is being scared and doing it anyway.

Edwyn's magic spits and sparks like an angry cat disturbed in its sleep; bright and green and ready to burn. He glances to me for instruction, and I grin. My lips and my tongue are bone-dry, but the thrill of the fight pushes me forward.

"On three?"

Edwyn nods.

We hurl what little power we have at the back of Kensa's head between their great curling horns.

The dragon howls, more in surprise than pain, and wheels on us, wings beating a gale.

"Again!" Edwyn yells, already recrafting his magic.

Again.

And again and again, as fast and as hard as we can. There is no finesse in the attack, no skill. Just two people doing their best to stay alive, knowing there's only so long they can last.

It's enough.

Behind Kensa, Neal and Elowen recover and regroup, using the distraction to craft a real weapon strong enough to slay a dragon.

Teeth bear down on us, and Kensa's breath is almost as hot as their fire.

Edwyn looks how I feel—like he's out of energy and close to collapse, but he doesn't stop, not for one moment. He'll fight until it's over one way or another. Peran's training was good for one thing.

Then Kensa screams.

Not a roar or a howl; an actual scream of agony with their mouth open so wide I can see down their throat. Then Kensa's dragon body spasms and twists like a dying fish, shrinking and shrinking, down and down, until all that's left is their human body.

Elowen rushes through the dissipating smoke, and the twins cling to each other while Neal finds me.

"You reckless fool," he chides, kissing the top of my head.

"For once you are right," Kensa pants from the ground on

their hands and knees. "You fight for the wrong side, against your family. You let them clip your wings. Go back to your cage and tell your masters what is coming."

Neal turns on them with his sword drawn. "You do the same," he says in a cold voice that doesn't sound like his own. "Tell her you were beaten by three Helston kids and the deserter. And tell her she can't have them."

Kensa's yellow eyes flash with fury. "Tell her yourself. I *dare* you." But the moment Neal advances with a raised sword, they vanish with a hiss, leaving the clearing cold and dark and silent.

"Why didn't you kill it?" Edwyn asks, voice hoarse. He and Elowen hold on to one another like each is the only thing keeping the other from falling. "You should've taken its head and brought it back to Helston."

"Taking a life would have solved nothing," Neal responds. "You defeated them. That is enough."

"What're you doing here?" I ask. "How'd you find us?"

Neal smooths back my sticky hair and smiles down at me. "You think you can get yourself into dire trouble and I won't hear about it?"

On a different day, that would've been sweet and filled me with warmth. But today it's something else. Something that makes me step back, away from him, and ask, "Who are you?"

Neal flinches. "Callie—"

"No, for real. You know the dragon. They called you family. Why?"

Neal's gaze flicks to the twins. "Not here, kiddo, please. I promise—I *swear*—I will explain everything later. We need to get you three back and checked out."

"I'm not going," says Elowen immediately. "I don't want to."

Edwyn stares at her. "What're you talking about?"

She glares back. "There is a whole world out here," she says fiercely. "For people like me. People like *us*. And I want to be a part of it."

"Kensa was *lying*, El!" I shout. "They were lying to trick and trap you. Right, Neal?"

I need him to confirm what Papa told me way back on the moors. I need him to prove he's on our side, still the Neal I thought I knew. I need everything to go back to being nice and straightforward, with an easy line between right and wrong.

But Neal hesitates and my heart drops. "I know it sounds tempting," he tells Elowen carefully. "But they offer nothing without conditions. Believe me, trust me—I was in your shoes. It isn't worth it."

Elowen grinds her teeth furiously, tears bright in her eyes. "I don't want to go home. I don't want to go back to normal."

"That doesn't mean you can just run away and join the other side—"

"Why not?" Elowen demands of her brother. "Why shouldn't I? Don't you want to too?"

"Of course I don't!"

"You don't have to go back to normal," I tell El before the

280

twins can really get into it. "Willow went on ahead. He's gone to tell the queen everything. Things are gonna change. You don't have to go home. You can choose for yourself."

Elowen stays glaring at Edwyn. "I'm not going back to Father, no matter what you do. I'm done. And I'm going to tell him so."

Forget magic and dragons, I've never seen someone look so scared as Edwyn does now.

"One step at a time," says Neal. "I know we all have a lot we need to talk about, but here is not the place. Kensa is gone, but that gives us a moment's grace, if that. Callie, did you ride out here?"

I nod, feeling instantly guilty that this is the first time I've thought about Flo since we found the boys. "Yeah, I left her back there, but I dunno if she'll still be there." I wouldn't blame her if she wasn't. No sensible horse would stand near a furious dragon.

But she is *my* horse, so . . .

She's not where I left her, but as soon as I whistle, she whinnies in response and picks her way over to us, nudging Neal in delighted welcome.

He rubs between her ears, touching his nose to hers.

"What about yours?" I ask Edwyn. "Where did you leave them?"

But he only shakes his head. "He wasn't mine. He had no loyalty to me. I expect he went after the soldiers when they fled."

"We saw the company riding back to Helston," says Elowen. "What happened?"

Edwyn's mouth presses in a bitter line, two pink spots of humiliation pricking his cheeks. "I don't know. The moment we stepped into Dumoor Forest, they ran away. Cowards."

"More like traitors," I mutter.

Edwyn looks away miserably as Neal bustles him onto Flo's back behind Elowen. I'm glad he's distracted enough not to be stubborn about riding. I stay on the ground. Three riders would be too many, and the twins need a break far more than I do.

I take Flo's reins and lead her through the trees, and Neal walks close without quite touching. He knows what's in my head. He always does. This is the first time I wish he didn't.

I have no idea how far away we are from Helston. The ride here took ages, but there's no way we went the most efficient route. None of us talk. There's too much to think about and not enough sense to be made of any of it. And there will be no relief when we get home.

The darkness dissipates the closer we get to Helston, sunshine gleaming off the palace's spire. It should be a relief, the first sign of home. Of safety. But the bridge is just another pathway to danger.

Neal hesitates.

I hand Elowen the reins to let them go ahead, and I wait back with Neal. He might be a mystery, and that mystery might not be a good one, but he's still Neal.

282

"I didn't think I'd ever come back here," he murmurs, staring at the glittering spire in the near distance.

"Why'd you come?"

He gives me a sideways glance and a crooked smile. "Your dad and I have ways of talking even if we're not together. It sounded like you needed me. I told you I'd come if you needed me, Callie."

"Helston's not how I imagined." The confession falls heavy with no one else close enough to hear it.

Neal pauses, then kisses the top of my head like everything's regular and fine. "Big things rarely are. But different doesn't mean bad, either."

I nod. But it doesn't feel as easy as that. Half of me wants to give in to the comfort I always feel when Neal's with me, but the other half is screaming a warning I can't ignore.

One thing's true, though: Now isn't the time to think about it.

There are Helston guards waiting for us on the other side. I don't see Papa.

The wards are like a douse of icy water, and the twins cry out the second before it hits us. By the time we reach the other side, one enemy is left behind and the other surrounds us.

It's like before—cold expressions and sharp arrows all pointed at our hearts. Except this time there's no Papa to speak on my behalf.

I shove down my fear and do my best entitled snarl. "Put down your weapons—you know who we are."

The weapons stay up like they were expecting us. Like they've been prepped. And I imagine Willow arriving home to this welcome alone.

Captain Adan steps forward, ice-cold and twice as rigid. "Lady Calliden, you and your friends are to be brought before his lordship to stand trial immediately."

I try to laugh but it comes out more as a cough. "For what?"

At a glance, two soldiers step forward and flank Neal, gripping his arms like he's something dangerous. My hand goes automatically to Satin, but Neal gives a tiny shake of his head and I stop. It doesn't matter. She's wrestled from my grip, just like she was way back on that first day. Edwyn loses his sword too, though he doesn't fight. He doesn't do anything but allow himself to be wrestled into unforgiving hands. El as well.

Adan takes my arm, pressing bruises through my sleeve. "Treason, Lady Calliden."

CHAPTER TWENTY-NINE

Helston gawks at us. It's nothing like the first time I passed through these streets, when the stares were awed and welcoming. Now they are narrow-eyed and wary, looking at us like we're invading monsters ourselves. Peran's done his job well—sowing suspicion all across Helston. I'm sure it was easy as anything, far as I was concerned, but the fact that Elowen and Edwyn are being treated the same after living every moment in these streets with these people is impressive in the most twisted way.

The guards handle them just the same as me and Neal, hustling them roughly along, indifferent to Edwyn's stumbling like his bad leg isn't obvious, like Elowen's not covered in dirt and soot and scratches. Like they're not the lord chancellor's kids and the next thing to royalty.

I twist to face my captor, and we both nearly go over in a tangle of legs.

Adan growls a curse at me. "*Move* it!"

"Did Prince Willow get back?" I demand, half tripping backward. "Is he okay?"

He ignores me like I don't exist, like I'm just some kind of shadow at his side. I assume I'd be able to tell if Willow was missing. Surely there'd be some kind of sign. But it's not like anyone worried about him going off on his mission. I don't trust anyone here to care about him.

Dragged into the palace, we aren't taken left toward the Council Chambers when we go through the front doors, but instead straight ahead to a room I've never seen before.

The Throne Room.

In better circumstances, it could be beautiful, peaceful; bathed in rainbow light streaming through the enormous stained-glass windows behind the throne, which sits high on an elevated dais. The throne is made of a wood so rich and polished, it gleams gold in the sunlight. The wonder of it catches me in the throat. I could stand in here for hours, and the awe would never fade.

In better circumstances.

But here and now, the Throne Room is as perilous as the deepest depths of Dumoor Forest, Helston's great and powerful as hungry for our blood as any witch's beast. Anyone who's anyone is here, from the council lords and the captains to the ladies decked out in all their finery.

Lady Anita's cool gaze follows her children, not just silent neutral, but stony with anger, and I wonder if she knows that her husband sent their son out to his death. *Their magical son.* She knows about that, at least, and knows the way Lord Peran punishes him for something he never asked for. She knows. She's complicit. And she's just as culpable.

Not that that seems to matter to Edwyn. The moment he sees her in the front of the crowd, he reaches for her. "Mother—"

Lady Anita turns her face away, and the flash of pain on Edwyn's face is nothing compared to the bleak acceptance that follows.

Elowen, on the other hand, ignores her mother just as coldly as Lady Anita ignores her. Despite the hand locked on her arm, she takes the length of the room with a proud stride, chin raised, daring anyone to try to cow her.

Even beneath the sharp contempt of Lord Peran.

He sits elevated on the throne as easily as if he belongs there, and the queen's presence has never been more noticeably absent. No Queen Ewella, no Prince Willow. No Papa. And the last threads of hope slip through my fingers.

This is it, I think. *This is the end.* Willow didn't make it back. The queen has been dethroned, and Papa's been arrested already.

We're lined up at the foot of the granite steps and shoved to our knees.

I glare up into his face. "Where's Prince Willow? He should be here."

I don't like the smile that slides across his face. "You are correct, Lady Calliden. His Highness *should* be here. As should their majesties both. And yet"—he gestures a hand to the assembly—"where are they? Where have any of them been these past few years while the threat to our home and our lives has grown? What have any of them done other than prove their unreliability over and over again?" He looks down on me with a thin curl of a smile. "I am not obliged to grant you an audience, *girl*. Regardless of your continuous blatant disregard for Helston's rules and traditions, ignoring for the moment your sabotage of His Highness and your manipulation of my children, you have now brought a witch's traitor into our midst."

I hold myself still and physically bite my tongue, absorbing every accusation into my skin and reminding myself that none of them are true. It's hard when shards of truth are embedded deep in Lord Peran's lies, and they're so tiny and so many that it's all you can see when you look at them. I didn't sabotage Willow, I didn't manipulate Elowen and Edwyn, and Neal is not the enemy. But even as I remind myself of what I know for certain, I prick myself on those shards, and doubt seeps into my blood.

"Your poison is so insidious," Peran tells me, "and you administer it so expertly, I reluctantly find the need to prove myself before I do away with you. To make Helston see what I have seen from the first moment I laid eyes on you. That you are nothing but a witch's weapon."

Beside me, Edwyn shifts, rising on his knees. "Father, that isn't—"

"Be silent," Peran snaps at him, sending him back down again. "You lost your right to a voice the moment you defied me in the enemy's favor."

"Callie is not the enemy," says Elowen, her voice stronger and more level than her brother's, unflinching when she raises her head to Peran. "*You* are."

Peran laughs softly like it's an obvious joke Elowen should understand. "And you think I don't know who put that ugly thought into your head? Elowen, you are my daughter. I know you. You never showed such dissent before that girl arrived. The connection is plain, even if you cannot see it."

Ignoring Edwyn's desperate attempts to keep her on the ground, Elowen gathers her skirts and stands to face her father. "If you didn't see my dissent, it's because *you* were never looking. *You* never thought me capable. *You* underestimated *me*. But it was there long before Callie."

Edwyn stumbles up, pulling on her arm. "El, stop—"

But he shuts his mouth when Lord Peran raises a hand. "Your sister wishes to be heard. Let her speak. Go on, Elowen," he says when Edwyn drops back to his knees. "I am looking now. Speak your mind."

As much as I enjoy watching Elowen tell her dad exactly how she feels, I watch the faces of the crowd, of the council lords, of Lady Anita, watching the girl whose silence they most value as she finally opens her mouth to speak.

Watching her dig her own grave and hungry to see her fall into it.

"You only see what you wish to see," Elowen tells Peran. "And the moment you see something you don't like, you seek to destroy them. That's why we're here, isn't it? That's why you sent Prince Willow into Dumoor. That's why you've always treated Edwyn—"

"I seek only to maintain the high standards of morality and conduct that make Helston *great*," Peran cuts her off. "Prince *Will*, by right of his birth, was due a fair chance, which I gave him. He failed of his own volition. As for you and your brother—" His face twists in dislike. "It is a sad moment when a father can no longer trust his own children, and I take no pleasure in what must be done. But Helston comes first, and I cannot be seen to show partiality."

A short nod and the guards close in on us. Edwyn whimpers when they grab him. Even Elowen's icy bravado cracks. As for me . . . I'm numb. Willow should be here. Papa should be here. We can't do this alone.

"The price of treason is banishment, but I fear that will suit you too well. You will be locked belowground, where you can do no harm, until we decide what is to become of you. It saddens me to do this, especially to you, Lady Calliden, as you have barely had time to taste freedom, but I'm afraid it's time to finally face the consequences of your actions."

"Leave my kid alone!" Neal snarls. "What kind of an adult

are you? Proving your power by bullying children." He looks at the silent crowd surrounding us. "Is this really the sort of person you want leading you? What is wrong with you all?"

The soft start of a mumble is like the palest light in the darkest night.

But Lord Peran's smile snuffs it out.

"Ah," he says, "now I know how I remember you. Welcome home, Neal. You have changed since we last saw each other."

"And you have not," says Neal, and I've never heard him *hate* before. "People like you never do."

"Yet it is people like me who win while people like you . . . Well, just look at you. See how well you have turned out. And you're connected to this one, are you?" He nods to me. "No wonder she and her father are so *broken*."

Something inside me snaps. "Don't speak to him like that!" I shout, pulling against the restraining hands. "Neal's the best, goodest person in the whole world, and everything you *wish* you were!"

"Oh, child," says Peran sweetly. "I have warned you about corrupting influence, and now I can finally show you the evidence."

A snap of his fingers and a waiting guard grabs Neal. In one vicious motion, Neal's tunic rips from his neck to his waist.

Outraged fear floods the Throne Room, sweeping me along with it.

"See for yourselves," Peran says, and even his voice is disembodied, like I'm hearing him through a mile of water. "The mark of a liar, a traitor. An *enemy*."

Tattooed on the left side of Neal's torso is the same mark Papa showed me on the beast we killed. *The Witch's Kiss.* It's clearer on him, stark like a new bruise on his skin. More intentional.

I feel sick.

That mark's not supposed to be on the person I love most in the world next to Papa.

"Once you succumb to corruption, you are tainted for life," Peran tells Neal, cold and flat. "If you had repented, if you had submitted, we could've helped you find redemption. But there is no redemption for those who do not seek it. Rot must be cut away to prevent the spread of disease. And to that end—"

The guard pulls at me. I can't breathe.

Neal struggles furiously against the guards locking his arms behind his back. "And who are you to decide who is worthy of redemption?"

Lord Peran draws himself up tall. "I am—"

"*Enough.*"

The whole court shifts and turns in shock. Even Lord Peran freezes. I can't enjoy the look on his face. I'm stuck so hard in believing that the end is imminent, to have hope striding down the center of the Throne Room toward me feels like a dream I cannot believe in.

Queen Ewella. Willow.

Papa.

Relief comes so hard and fast, it *hurts*. He catches me before anyone sees my tears, forcing the guard's hand off with a warning growl.

"I'm sorry it took so long to get to you," Papa murmurs into my hair once the guards back away. "Are you okay, love?"

I snuffle and nod. I don't really understand why I'm crying. Everything just feels like a whole lot too much.

A warm hand slips into mine and squeezes. It's Willow, worn down and weary but smiling, dressed for the first time as a prince, in vibrant scarlet and gold.

"Hey," he whispers.

I scrub my eyes and give a wet laugh. "I didn't think you'd made it back."

Willow's gaze flicks to the wary eyes of the court. "I nearly didn't."

"What happened?"

But the prince just shakes his head with a murmur of "I'll tell you later."

We stand shoulder to shoulder, hand in hand, as Papa drapes his cloak around Neal's shoulders and holds him close, and Queen Ewella ascends the dais. Her crimson velvet skirts sweep the steps, darker yet somehow more vibrant than the usual Helston scarlet, and the gold brocade glitters in the rainbow-dappled light that makes the crown in her black hair sparkle like stars.

She towers over the seated chancellor. "Explain yourself, my lord."

Peran gapes at her without moving. "Your Majesty—"

But Queen Ewella's anger eclipses her patience. "Explain," she repeats, sharp and dangerous, "why *precisely* you think it appropriate to treat three *children* like convicted criminals. Three children, I might add, who saved my son, the future king, from peril *you* are responsible for placing him in."

She doesn't shout. She doesn't need to.

The court squirms like little kids caught with crumbs on their mouths.

Peran scrambles up and bows low. "We weren't expecting you."

"You should have been," Queen Ewella responds flatly. "I should have been involved the first moment the idea that my son needed *testing* was raised in council." She sweeps past him like he's no more corporeal than wind and takes her place upon the throne. "Step down, Lord Peran, and tell me why I should spare you any mercy."

Peran flushes furiously. "If Your Majesty would grant me the time for a private—"

"No. You sought to humiliate these children publicly; why should you be permitted any more grace?"

"I'm afraid there has been a terrible misunderstanding. Whatever information led you to believe I would ever wish harm to His Highness is certainly false. And as for these children—" He glances back and catches my eye. "Lady

Calliden has done nothing but undermine me and the laws of Helston since the moment she arrived. She has turned my own children against me and now brings a witch's traitor into our midst. It would be imprudent to underestimate her, Your Majesty, and treat her any less than the infiltrator she is."

"None of that is true." Willow's voice is clear and unwavering, though I can feel the tremble in his hand through my own. "Callie's the only person who's done anything to try to make things better, even if it's made things worse for them. They're not an infiltrator—they're a hero."

"I'm inclined to agree," says Queen Ewella smoothly, drawing Peran's attention away from me and Willow. "Whatever misunderstanding there is, I believe it is yours, Lord Peran."

"I have done *nothing* but act in the best interests of Helston!" Peran snarls, making Willow's hand spasm in mine and Edwyn flinch. "I have single-handedly held this kingdom together for *two years*, doing whatever I can to ensure its protection and sustainability. With all due respect, Your Majesty, you have no idea the obstacles placed intentionally in my way. I will not be condemned for doing my duty!"

Silence rings through the Throne Room, the whole court holding their breath, looking anxiously between the queen and the chancellor.

Us too. Because surely by this point, she knows what he is. He's not pretending to be anything else anymore. She has to do *something*.

Queen Ewella sighs and inclines her head. "You are right,

my lord. The task placed upon your shoulders was no small one, and you took it on without question or complaint. It is my shortsightedness that failed to recognize the toll that inevitably took on you, and I accept the damage done as my own."

Wait, what?

Papa moves, thinking the same as me at the same time. "Your Majesty—"

But she silences him with a raised hand. "I appreciate your bringing this trouble to my attention, Nick. And be assured I will do everything in my power to make amends for my neglect. Starting with the most important." She smiles gently down at us. "Rise, children. Willow has been singing ballads of your bravery. We cannot have champions on their knees."

Elowen picks herself up first, then helps Edwyn to his feet. He's shaking so badly, Elowen keeps a tight hold on him. There is no comfort for him in the queen's intervention.

Willow takes his hand in the one that's not holding on to mine and leads all of us past Lord Peran and up the steps to stand by his mother's side.

Elowen curtsies, and I follow her lead with a bow. The queen looks different away from the tiny rooms of the Queen's Quarters. Bigger. Undeniably regal. And beside her, Willow looks like a true prince, with a delicate gold crown nestled in his hair. More certain than I've ever seen him.

"Thank you," says Queen Ewella, taking the time to

address us. "Thank you for saving my son, and for everything you have done for Helston." She touches my cheek with cool fingers, and my singed skin tingles as she presses her magic gently into the damage. "We will get you all fixed up properly, and then you must rest." Her eyes sparkle with a smile. "Especially those who have ambitions of competing in the tournament."

I can do nothing but stare, trying to force my head to stop spinning. Five minutes ago I thought we were all facing certain execution, and now I get to rest and compete?

"It is the court's job not only to maintain standards and discipline," Queen Ewella continues, her voice taking on the slightest edge as she addresses everyone else, "but to recognize and reward excellence. To encourage and protect. To make those who choose to be a part of Helston know they are valued. Without exception." She dips her chin and looks directly down at Lord Peran, lingering uncomfortably at the foot of the dais. "I thank you, truly, for your commitment to Helston. You have been a stable pillar, and I apologize that you have been left to hold up the kingdom without support for so long. The children are not the only ones who have earned their rest, my lord."

Lord Peran's jaw twitches. "I assure you, Your Majesty, that rest is the last thing I can afford. Helston is in the midst of infiltration, and it is my duty—"

"No," Queen Ewella says firmly, "it isn't. Helston nearly faced yet more tragedy today because exhaustion overcame sense. I will not take that risk again. From here on, you are excused of all duties not directly pertaining to those of chancellor. Sir Nick has kindly offered to oversee the training and education of our future knights, and I myself will be assuming the throne, as I should've done the moment His Majesty left us.

"I apologize," she tells the crowd, raising her voice to fend off the first mutterings. "I apologize that my grief caused my neglect, and it took almost losing the last of my family to realize that my focus should be on what remains and not what is lost. I pledge to make it up to you. To *all* of you. And to guide Helston, finally, into the future. I know there is a great deal of work to be done with regard to our friends across the bridge, but our focus has to be on solving the conflicts within Helston's walls. The last few years have been, understandably, unsettling, but fear is not an excuse for abuse."

Queen Ewella lets the words settle in the air, and her people sit in their discomfort. Elevated, I've got a good view of every single face here, and there's guilt on nearly all of them.

Nearly.

Lady Anita's expression is as still as a pool on a warm day, and Lord Peran's is the storm about to come crashing down.

"Over the next few weeks, I expect to be in lengthy consultation with the council as we determine the best ways to move forward and make amends for the damages done," the queen continues. "New laws will be made as old ones are revisited. Archaic ideals will be laid to rest. I ask for your patience, and that you extend that patience outward. None of us here are without mistakes, and none of us here are undeserving of redemption. Do I make myself clear? Lord Peran, you look like you have something to say."

Peran looks like his mouth is crammed full of all kinds of things he wants to say, none of them nice. Finally, he jabs a finger in Neal's direction, safe in the circle of Papa's arms, and spits, "That man is a proven traitor to Helston. What-ever else, you cannot expect to accept a witch's *dog* into our midst and expose our children to his malice."

Papa makes a furious move toward Peran, but Neal stills him with a murmur in his ear and he settles with the deepest glare I've ever seen on his face.

"My lord," says Queen Ewella coolly, "you will apologize to Captain Neal. He is here as our guest, and a valued one at that. Not only has he returned to Helston to volunteer his time, but he also saved the lives of our children. That you would treat him with such *malice* for a choice made years ago is unacceptable. On that note, there are many to whom you owe apologies, but I think it best if you take the break I suggest and come back with a fresh perspective."

Lord Peran puffs up, then explodes with a furious "I will not be treated like a wayward child!"

"Then stop behaving like one," the queen snaps back. "Do not underestimate the courtesy I am doing you by stalling the rightful consequences of your behavior, my lord. I do believe you have always had Helston's best interest at heart, but that does not mitigate the way you have treated certain members of Helston's community. It is time you step back, reconsider your position, and prove to me that you are as worthy of forgiveness as I hope you are. My mercy is certainly not without condition."

Lord Peran sucks in a breath and holds it, glaring from Queen Ewella to Prince Willow to me. I glare back, daring him to say something. Wishing he would. *Show the world who you are.*

Then he releases it with a hiss and snaps his fingers at the twins. "Come." As if he didn't just try to have them arrested like actual dangerous criminals.

Elowen goes rigid, gripping Edwyn's arm, and I don't know if it's to keep him from obeying their father's command or for support for herself. I adjust my own stance, ready to fight for them both.

Willow turns urgently to the throne. "Mother—"

She acknowledges him with a nod. "A moment, Lord Peran, Lady Anita. Along the lines of rest and redemption, I would like to strongly suggest that your children are also permitted some time away. A vacation, if you will. It gives me no pleasure to break up a family, but I have a vested interest in Elowen, having spent a great deal of time with her, and in that interest, I think it best if the children are temporarily homed elsewhere."

Lord Peran gives a stifled laugh as Lady Anita joins him. "You cannot be serious?"

"I assure you, I am," says Queen Ewella firmly. "Even before I witnessed this bizarre display of control, the conversation had already been had and Sir Nicholas had already offered his home to your children until you are able approach your parenting with appropriate compassion."

Peran gives a disgusted hiss, as though sickened by the concept.

"It is temporary, Peran." Lady Anita steps forward and touches her husband's arm. "And, perhaps, for the best."

But Peran pulls free of her. "You said it was a suggestion," he throws at Queen Ewella. "I refuse this suggestion. They are mine. They belong with me! What kind of precedent are you setting when you can take children away from their parents?"

"A precedent that gives children the protection they deserve and parents the assistance they need," says Queen Ewella frankly. "A father who sends his son into the heart of Dumoor Forest on a near-impossible mission is a father who needs time to reconsider the value he places on his children."

Edwyn's face blazes, even as he stares down at his shoes, more than aware of exactly how much value he has in his father's eyes.

"Ask them, then," Peran demands, jabbing a finger at the twins. "If you place so much value on their heads, ask them what they want!"

"Very well." Ewella turns to the twins. "Elowen, Edwyn, it is your lives that are being discussed. You have the right to a say. Would you like to go home with your parents or take some time away? Elowen, you know you have always had a home in the Queen's Quarters, and Sir Nick is also offering you and your brother a family for however long you need it. It's your choice."

That's a really big choice for kids who've never had one before, and it doesn't feel fair that they've got to do this in front of everyone.

Elowen takes it all in stride, though; expression as placid as her mother's as she looks down on her father and addresses him directly with all the hatred that's been bubbling up spilling over into a single sentence: "I am never going back with you."

Only Papa moving swiftly to block him stops Peran from lunging up the dais to grab her.

"You heard the kid," he says softly, one hand locked on Peran's arm. "Walk away."

Peran throws him off with a hiss. "You have turned Helston backward, and they will all see you for what you are before long." He looks back to the twins. "You will soon learn how easy you have had it. No one but your parents would ever tolerate either of you."

He turns on his heel and starts to stalk out, but Edwyn breaks free of Elowen and half trips down the steps after him before anyone can stop him. "Father, wait! I'm coming home—" He freezes when Peran pauses to look back at him, and the desperate, faltering hope on Edwyn's face hurts. Because it doesn't matter what his dad does, or how worthless Peran makes him believe he is: Love is a hard dream to put down.

And Lord Peran snatches it out of Edwyn's hands. "There is no home for you."

Edwyn's legs buckle, and I leap from the dais to help. He doesn't resist me as I pull him up, like nothing else exists in the world but his dad's words—the longest-lasting, most lingering bruise.

"Hey," I murmur. "It doesn't matter. He doesn't matter."

It's as effective as striking dragon scales with a blade.

Edwyn lets me guide him back to the others, all willing and wanting to love him, but only because I'm pulling a statue. Edwyn's body is present, but his soul stays where his father left it. I know those feelings, from way back when Papa would ride away and leave me waiting for him at the gate.

It will take all our best efforts to stitch him back together again.

"I'm sorry, child," the queen tells Edwyn as Willow enfolds him, and to Papa, "Give me an hour, and you will be reaccommodated appropriately. You should have been in the palace from the start. You and Callie should not have been parted. I apologize. Whatever you need, it is yours."

With Papa's arms around me, I take in our newly grown family—bruised on the outside and the inside. The best way to heal those kinds of injuries is with time and space and safety, and with Lord Peran still here, I don't reckon we'll get much of any.

CHAPTER THIRTY

P apa gets moved out of his dingy rooms, I haul my stuff out of the Queen's Quarters, and along with Neal and the twins, we set up our new home in the fanciest, coziest suite I've ever seen.

It feels permanent.

It feels like home.

My head struggles to keep up with it all, from fighting a dragon to facing treason charges to being *safe*. And I'm not the only one. Elowen is dazed and exhausted, and Edwyn doesn't say a word. Neither brought anything with them, though Papa offered to collect their things from the Chancellor's Chambers.

"I want to leave it all behind me," says Elowen with a bitter bite. "I don't want anything from them."

And Edwyn barely exists at all, just allows Elowen to pull him along with her.

They stay locked together, and Elowen is like she's gone all the way back to when I first met her, sweet and polite and not quite herself. She calls Papa "Sir Nicholas" and Neal "Captain Neal" and barely even takes a step without permission. Edwyn is silent.

Finally, Papa ushers them into the biggest room, which they're going to share, to set them up with their own space where they (hopefully) won't feel like they have to stand on ceremony, leaving me in the living room with Neal.

For the first time since Dumoor.

Since I realized he was familiar with a dragon.

Since I saw the mark on his skin.

I don't know how I feel around him, and I hate it. Neal's supposed to be the person I trust most in the whole world alongside Papa, and it feels like there's something missing. I don't know how to bridge the gap and get back to where we're supposed to be, and every time I look at him, all I see is the Witch's Kiss like a bruise on his side.

I want to ask about it, to know what it feels like, to know what he thinks of it.

But I'm scared.

I'm scared of Neal.

In the peace and safety of our new home, my head is free to think. I hate it. I don't want the questions prodding at my mind and twisting my thoughts up into knots, sounding like the mean little voice I thought I'd left at Clystwell.

Because what about Papa?

Papa knows. The way he covered him up, loving him like nothing had changed. Because nothing had. Because Papa knew. And Papa kept the secret. And Papa—

Papa lied to me too.

The dark feelings pull me down like I've fallen into a peat bog, sucking me in, trying to drown me. And the more I struggle, the harder it is to pull myself out.

"You know you can ask me anything, Callie, right?"

I raise my head. Neal watches me from the other side of the sofa, legs drawn up beneath him. The few feet between us feel like a thousand miles.

He looks like himself, the Neal I know and trust, who loves me.

I chew my lip, then make myself ask, "Who are you?"

Neal sighs and takes his time with his answer, just like he always does. "The person who took this mark is not the same person I am now—that's the first thing I need you to understand. People change, day to day, moment to moment. I'm not making excuses. I made mistakes, and I did things I believed were right. It felt like a small price to pay for what they were offering in return."

"Which was what?"

Neal gives a grim smile. "Acceptance."

Kensa's words murmur in the back of my mind, sweet and luring. Offering me and Willow, Elowen and Edwyn, everything we've ever dreamed of and everything we shouldn't have to fight for. I know how much I wanted it in that moment,

307

and thoughts of what I might've done if Neal hadn't arrived make my stomach squirm.

"I left Helston the year I became a squire," says Neal. "It had been a hard ride. I wasn't as gifted as most of the others—combat arts didn't come as naturally to me. I was different. Magical."

I sit up a bit. "And you didn't tell anyone?"

Neal shakes his head. "Certainly not. The way the other boys talked about magic . . . They knew I was different already. Most of my energy was spent making sure it never came out. It was exhausting and left me with no energy for anything else. Every moment was spent terrified that I'd reveal myself. When the time came that I was supposed to enter into an apprenticeship with a knight and leave Helston, no one wanted me. I didn't know how to talk to people or make connections, and I spent all my page years keeping my head down and hoping no one noticed me, so by the time I was a squire, I couldn't stop."

He laughs softly. "All this is to say I was lost long before I ever found myself in Dumoor."

I shift two inches closer. "So why'd you leave Helston in the end?" Because there was no way it was just because he didn't get picked up by a knight. That sucks, but it's not unheard-of, and there're plenty of other opportunities for squires, even if they're not as exciting as riding off with a knight.

Neal's expression goes dark, and he looks just the way he did back in Dumoor Forest. Himself but not himself. "Someone found out about me."

"About your magic?"

He nods. "I was exhausted. The longer I went repressing my magic, the weaker I became. I started to give in and find a private place to let it out. Just a little. Just enough. But I was caught."

"Who by?" I ask, like I don't already know.

"Peran," says Neal. "He was a new knight with big ambitions. He didn't want to go out in the field and fight—he wanted to work at home, to make Helston the best it could be. Most people change, Callie, but some people don't. He had the ear of the royal family, the court, and everyone with any authority in Helston. He blackmailed me, threatening to tell everyone my secret if I didn't work for him."

"As a squire?"

Neal gives a dark chuckle. "That was the word on the official document, but the purpose of my duties was less to educate and more to degrade. To ensure I was under no illusion about my place in this world."

I gnaw the tip of my thumb, the nail long chewed down. Knowing how Peran treats Willow and Edwyn, I don't need much imagination to work out how he treated Neal. "I guess some people really don't change."

"I stayed longer than I should've, hoping, in a way, that

I could earn my place here. I didn't want to give up. I had worked hard, and my parents had pinned all their hopes on me. But it became clear that if I stayed, this was the life I was accepting for myself. So I left. I slipped across the bridge in the middle of the night and never looked back."

"And that's when Kensa found you?" I ask, imagining kid-Neal wandering, lost amid the same trees he found us in less than twelve hours ago.

Neal nods. "Kensa was different too. Everything was new, better intentioned. The plan was to create a realm for all those without a place to go. A home. A *family*. And when I was invited to be a part of it, there was nothing I wanted more. For the first time, I was around people like me, peo-ple who *liked* me, where I was useful and wanted. I didn't have to hide, I didn't have to pretend to be somebody else, I had the space to grow and learn who I was in a way I never thought I needed."

It could be me talking. Because that's exactly how Neal made me feel after years of Mama trying to recraft me into someone I wasn't. The camp was home and Neal was family, all cobbled together and mismatched but realer than real.

"So what happened?" I ask, shuffling closer.

Neal's lips press tight, brows dipped like it hurts to re-member. "Dreams come with conditions, and peace comes with a price, and—in the end—Dumoor was little better than Helston. I made promises I shouldn't have. Commitments to their army."

"Against Helston?"

Neal nods. "I made a deal. I could leave as long as I promised to keep recruiting for Dumoor, spreading the net wider than before. The problem isn't just within Helston's walls, Callie, you know that. Magical folk—*different* folk—are persecuted wherever there is power. I promised to find them, as I had been found, and offer them everything they'd never had in exchange for—"

"Their lives."

"Their love," Neal amends. "It was easy. Painfully easy. The lost, the angry . . . whether they craved shelter, or retribution, or the home they'd been denied, I could tell them where to find it. There were few who refused. And *I* was free."

I shuffle back to the other side of the sofa and pull my knees up. "Didn't you feel bad?"

"I did," says Neal earnestly. "I never lied, but I didn't give the whole truth either. And I knew how *I* felt. I hated myself a little more with every day, every person. I had escaped, but I was still trapped. The freedom I thought I had was false. And then you and your dad came along."

I rest my chin on my knees, hugging my legs.

"You would've been the perfect recruits," says Neal softly. "I knew it, soon as he rode into camp with you on his saddle. I recognized your dad immediately, the legendary hero, the king's champion, as lost and hurt as the best of Dumoor's recruits and with a very real grudge against a world that wished his kid harm. And you . . . I knew from the moment you glared at me that you had the fire Dumoor valued most."

I don't say anything. I remember it so well, it could've been yesterday, Papa and me riding into that little forest clearing. Neal welcoming us like we'd belonged there our whole lives. Or maybe we were just so desperate, we only saw what we wanted to see.

"So why didn't you?" I demand through gritted teeth. My whole body is hot and rigid, and my throat's thick with something I don't want to feel. "If we were so easy, why did you let us go?" I hate this. I hate feeling this way, and all the sweetest memories of the clouds of Clystwell clearing as we found our new life are being plunged into gray. I wish I didn't know. If he was going to lie to me, I wish the lie had been kept and preserved, like the fossils of ancient creatures washed up on the beach.

"I knew I had to be careful," Neal murmurs, head bent with shame. "That I had to do it right. So I watched and waited, and I—I used you, Callie. I'm sorry. You were the route to your dad. But the more time I spent with you, watching you grow, helping you heal, the more I realized I couldn't send you off to that life. You were not made to be indentured to anyone, on either side of the bridge. And your dad—he wasn't the man I'd known in Helston. He had changed too. For you. I had no idea that was even possible. Helston says people don't change. Alis's court says people do not change. But here you both were. The proof that they were wrong.

312

"I felt my purpose slip away, and it scared me. I pulled away. I planned to leave again, before I hurt you any more than you'd already been. And your dad—" A smile slips across Neal's lips and his face softens. "Your dad stopped me. He said if I was going to run, the least I could do was say a proper goodbye to you. You would be heartbroken if I didn't. So I agreed to wait until morning.

"We stayed up all night. We hadn't spoken much before, and I'm sure he didn't know me from Helston. But he treated me as though we'd been friends forever. Most of all he talked about you and the future he wanted for you, how desperately he wanted the world to change so you could have the life you deserved. I wanted that too. I wanted to be there, to watch you grow. I wanted to stay, and I wanted change."

I squirm. Papa hasn't ever said any of those things to me. But then again, he's never—not for one moment—made my dreams feel anything less than possible. He's never let me doubt that I can be a knight, even if I have to take a more roundabout path than the others.

"Why didn't you tell me?" The question comes out wobbly. "I thought we trusted each other?"

"I was scared," Neal confesses, the words a tiny whisper. "You were growing so well, so strong. I was terrified I would send you backward. I was terrified I would lose you and your dad."

"And Papa . . . he knows all this?"

Neal nods. "Yes. Nick knows everything. When we first

realized that our friendship was changing into something different, I confessed. I showed him my mark. I gave him the out he deserved. He told me that people are not the sum of their mistakes, but of the steps they take to grow. He said it looked like our step count was pretty similar and we should take the rest of the journey together."

He laughs, a weird, wet sound, and I realize he's crying. He wipes his tears away. "No one had ever said that to me before. No one had even told me it would be possible for someone like me. I thought if I wanted love—real love—then it would be at the expense of myself. But here was this man who knew all the worst parts of me and loved me anyway."

"Your worst parts aren't so bad."

Neal and I both look up as Papa drifts in, his expression as soft and warm as the flames in the hearth. He walks over to Neal and kisses away his tears, then turns to me.

"I'm sorry," he tells me. "You have every right to be upset. I chose not to tell you because, well, you were happy, and I didn't want to risk that for something I believed didn't matter."

"But it did. It *does*." I hunch up with a huff. It's hard to explain, even just in my own head. Even if it's over, left in the past, it still happened, and it *does* matter. And I don't know how I would've reacted if they'd told me then. It would be different, that's for sure.

I side-eye them—my two dads; Papa squeezing Neal's

shoulder, both of them watching me anxiously, caring about what I think and feel. Letting me decide for myself.

"I dunno," I mutter eventually, honestly. "I don't like that you didn't tell me before I found out. You should've. You should've *trusted* me, and I'm angry you didn't. But—" And the "but" is so big, it just about eclipses everything else. "But I still love you. You're still my dads. I can be angry and love you at the same time. Okay?" Papa starts to smile until I glare it right back off his face. "I'm not joking, Papa."

Neal, on the other hand, is stone somber. "Thank you," he says, bowing his head. "I know I have a lot of work to do to earn back your trust. Thank you for the chance to do so."

I give a rough shrug. It's complicated, and it's going to stay complicated, but whatever he used to be—good or bad or whatever in between—the one thing I do know is that the Neal I love, who loves me as much as Papa does, is the one who's sitting right here, right now. Just the same as ever.

I shuffle-fall into a tangled hug and *squeeze*. He feels the same. He smells the same. Like home.

"You're staying, right?"

"Seeing all the trouble you two get into without me?" Neal chuckles. "I'm never leaving you alone again!"

Good. Except—

"What about your garden? Your flowers will miss you!"

"Josh will take care of them. He's much better at growing than cooking. And Rowena is taking charge of the camp. She'll keep things going. They miss you both, you know. They told me to send their love."

"I miss them too."

We stay like this for a long while, all bundled up on the sofa, reconnecting with our kind of normal. It's a relief to know it can exist anywhere, even somewhere like Helston.

"How's El and Edwyn?" I ask.

Papa rests his cheek on the top of my head with a whole-body sigh. "Probably about as good as you'd expect."

"So not great then."

"No. Not great," says Papa grimly. "The boy's determined Peran will change his mind before morning. He won't hear a word otherwise. And Elowen . . . she thinks she's taking it in stride, but that anger is something to behold."

"It's the first day of the rest of their lives," Neal reminds him. "And that's a hard day for anyone. You said it yourself, Nick—they need time and patience, and a whole lot of love."

"Well, we have an abundance of two and very little of the third," says Papa. "Would it be bad manners to send a message out to Dumoor saying something like 'Sorry, let's put a pin in that war we were about to wage; we've got some messed-up kids who need our full attention'?" He swears under his breath, keeping his voice low so there's no chance it carries through to the twins. "I dunno what Ewella was thinking, letting Peran stay after what he did to those kids."

"You told her, right?" I ask. "You and Willow. You told her what he was doing?"

"Oh, yes," says Papa grimly. "And she was ready to draw blood. Or I thought she was." He curses again, a furious hiss through gritted teeth. "Those kids deserve *better.*"

"I get it," says Neal softly. "I wouldn't want to be in Ewella's position, and she couldn't exactly pardon me and not her chancellor. There would've been a coup."

"Let there be a coup," Papa growls. "All those vultures, hungry for blood. . . . Helston's better off without them."

"Those vultures outnumber the rest."

"For now."

"You can't expect her to fight two battles at the same time, love."

"Why shouldn't I?" Papa demands exactly when I think the same. "Choice is a luxury few have, and she cannot afford to lose either."

CHAPTER THIRTY-ONE

U nfortunately, I'm not allowed to get involved with either.

"*Your* orders," Papa tells me after the twentieth time I've complained about it in three days, "is to be a kid, and teach your friends how to be kids too. Go. Play! Let the grown-ups worry about the big things."

Neal's no better.

"No one's saying you're not capable," he assures me. "You have already proven yourself tenfold. And that's the problem. You're *twelve*, Callie. Go and be twelve."

Which is way easier said than done, when *none* of us have ever been treated like kids.

Me and Willow, and Elowen and Edwyn, we all struggle beneath the abrupt changes.

All lessons, for the Queen's Daughters *and* the pages, have been put on pause while the grown-ups restructure the whole fabric of Helston. They're calling it a vacation, but there's nothing relaxing about it for those who have spent their lives beneath the rigid discipline of the old administration. Asking kids who have never been kids to play is like asking a Westmoor pony to be a warhorse. A bad time all round.

Things might be better on paper, but it's going to take a lot of hard work before anything settles down.

And no one struggles more than my friends.

Everyone says it's just a matter of time, but we don't *have* time, and the grown-ups are taking so long discussing the changes that need to be made and arguing about them and making compromises that mean nothing actually happens, and *not talking to us*. . . .

"It's not fair," I mutter, kicking up sand on the beach three nights into Queen Ewella's regency. Even though we don't have to hide anymore, it still feels like the only place we can relax and just be ourselves. Helston has turned stifling, with all the whispered arguments going around the court. "If it wasn't for us, none of this would've happened in the first place. We've a right to be involved."

"Mother says it's too delicate," says Willow, pushing his fingers deep into the cool sand. "She says one inch wrong, and everything could come crashing down."

I roll my eyes. "Not like you're gonna be king or anything."

"I'm not going to be king of anything if Helston implodes," Willow points out. "Anyway, I don't need to worry about any of that for years, now Mother's taken charge as queen regent." He lifts a hand, letting fine silver sand trickle between his fingers. "It's a relief. I suppose."

"Only suppose?"

"I've been moving so fast in one direction for so long, made to believe it's all that matters. Now that I've stopped, it's like . . . it didn't matter at all, did it? He was just doing it to be cruel. I feel like I've gone backward, to how it used to be, except I'm different now. And it's good, it is, but it's strange too. It's strange being back with Mother, strange not having to hide my magic, strange not being punished for it. It's going to be a long time before I'm used to it, and right now it doesn't feel like I ever will be." Willow turns his face up to the sky, the stars bright and unfiltered by clouds. "I'm trying to practice being okay with not knowing how I feel."

"Easier said than done?"

"Easier said than done."

We sit side by side and watch Elowen and Edwyn walk the length of the shore and back again. El's the only person Edwyn will let go near his leg, no matter how many times Papa suggests the palace healers, and the one time Neal offered his own magic, you'd have thought he'd come at Edwyn with a handful of fire. El's good, for sure, but that wound runs deep.

"Heard anything about Peran?"

Willow shrugs. "Far as I know, he's doing as ordered and resting."

"Like that's gonna make a difference," I mutter.

"Mother believes it will."

Good people can make bad choices is what *I've* come to learn, and this feels like one of them. Sure, people can change, but not as fast as that. If Peran's stepping back, it's not out of obedience or a change of heart. He's stubborn as they come. Takes one to know one, and not being able to see what he's up to makes my head ache. Believing in redemption, hoping for the best in people, it's all well and good, but I am certain—with every single last bit of me—that it's a mistake to keep Peran around.

Away from her parents, Elowen is breathing life back into herself, teaching herself how to relax like it's a lesson she's catching up on. She's dead set on never going back to the Chancellor's Chambers, but I don't believe for half a second that Peran couldn't force her to go back one way or another. Edwyn refuses to settle in, determined that Lord Peran will call him home at any moment. With every day that passes and that summons fails to come, he sinks deeper and deeper into himself.

He hasn't spoken a word to anyone but Elowen since the moment his parents walked away. He avoids Papa and Neal, never even giving them the chance to get close enough to try to reach him. A shadow on a sunny day, disappearing the moment the light touches him.

"I don't get it," I mutter. "Peran treated him like rubbish. *Worse* than rubbish. Why would he miss that?"

Willow gives a sloping shrug. "I was lucky. I had years and years before Lord Peran got me, and a whole family who let me be exactly how I am. Even El has the Queen's Daughters to escape to, to remind her that his world isn't the whole world. But Edwyn's never had anything else. He doesn't know anything else."

"He has *us*!"

"And if Lord Peran does enough to get them back, that ends." Willow fiddles with a stray golden thread. "That's how I feel too," he confesses. "Like it's all going to come crumbling down and we'll be back to where we were. Getting comfortable will only make it harder when real life starts again."

"That's not gonna happen!"

"You don't know that—"

"Yes I do!" My stubborn fire stoked and blazing, I stomp to my feet, grabbing Satin and the sword Willow brought to practice with. "And it's about time you lot start putting the work in. *Hey!*"

I dash across the beach to the twins and thrust the spare sword into Edwyn's hands (hilt first). "You owe me a rematch, remember? Let's fight!"

"Fight?" Edwyn echoes suspiciously, like it's gotta be some kind of trick. "Why?"

I shrug and hop backward, swinging Satin in a satisfying circle. "For fun, obviously!"

I knew from the first moment I saw him on the training grounds that we're the same—dedicated to our craft, most comfortable with a sword in our hands and a challenge to defeat. Yeah, our friendship is super new, if it can even be called that yet, but Edwyn is hands down one of the most skilled knights-to-be in Helston.

And I've been *itching* to go another round with him for weeks.

Maybe fighting is the route to teaching him how to play, just like dancing was the way through for Willow. Everyone learns differently.

I skip around him as Elowen drifts away to sit with Willow as a spectator. "You scared?" I taunt without malice. "Scared to be beaten by a *girl*?"

A slow smile slips through the shadows on his face, and Edwyn adjusts his grip on the hilt. "Thought you weren't a girl, Sir Callie?"

The first clash of blades lights something inside me. This is what I was made for. These moments are when I'm most alive. Moving and breathing and *challenged*.

Edwyn meets me, blow for blow, face set in hard concentration. I notice it now, the slight shift to accommodate his injury, and though it affects him, it doesn't put him at a disadvantage. He's learned to win *with* it.

Edwyn shoves his blade against mine. "Don't underestimate me," he warns with a smirk, like he can tell where my head's at.

I push back. "Only if you don't underestimate me."

We're a collision of two equal forces, as evenly matched

as it's possible to be, despite the differences between us. All the little things that don't or shouldn't matter drop away from us, like rain sliding off oilskin. Magic or no magic; boy or girl, neither or both. What difference does any of it make in the end?

We're just here, two people, doing what we love and doing it well.

Edwyn fights better when he's not angry, as light on his feet as Willow is when dancing, even with his bad leg. I guess that's what this is. Dancing with swords. And this is how it was always meant to be: We should be playing and practicing, not trying to kill each other. Not being used as weapons by grown-ups who won't even fight their own battles.

This is what I dreamed of when I dreamed of Helston.

My muscles burn in the best kind of way, and I adjust my breathing to conserve energy. Edwyn does the same, and the focused peace on his face is a relief to see. He needed this: a moment to forget, a moment to just be the best of himself and shut out the little voice in his head convincing him otherwise.

For the first time in my life, I think, *I wish Peran was here.*

I wish he could see us and everything that we are without his poison seeping into our skin. I wish he could see Willow and Elowen head to head, happy together. I wish he could see how skilled his son is. I wish he could see how capable I am.

I know, of course, that even if he was standing right here, right now, looking straight at us, he wouldn't see any of it.

Men like him never do.

We pick up the pace, the beat getting harder and faster until Edwyn's sword is a blur and I meet every blow with my own, dancing, dancing, *one, two, three.* . . . It's fun and it's good, and—

And Edwyn starts glowing.

His magic is green—pale, like sea glass—and it starts soft and small, and if this were daytime, it would be lost in the sunlight. But beneath the moon reflected on the sea, he is bright.

Elowen and Willow notice it too. They stop talking, and Willow sits up with wide eyes.

The last person to notice is Edwyn, and when he does, his smile dies.

He freezes like his whole body's just stopped working, and the magic that was incandescent a moment ago shrinks and dims as though apologizing for its existence.

"It's okay," I start.

"It's not."

Willow picks himself up and comes toward us, his own magic a pale pink wisp in his palm. It rises, curling up like smoke, and twines around Edwyn, gently nudging the pale remnants of his green magic. Elowen's blue joins his pink, and I follow their lead, urging my magic out into the air to dance with the others and coax Edwyn's back into life, promising,

This is okay. Elowen's looks like drifting flower blossoms, Willow's is a flitting butterfly, mine is as shapeless and darting as a fish underwater.

Magic is weird and senseless and whatever you want it to be. And it's *okay.*

Edwyn recoils, barely even breathing, but his magic—almost like it's a separate entity—is hungry for companionship.

Little by little, it rises, brightens; and green threads—as thin and as tentative as vines—join the colors circling Edwyn. Our magic tumbles and dances like young creatures, careless and ignorant of the dangers of the real world because none of it matters right here and now.

That's how we should be is my first thought.

But we're not is my second. And we're never going to be, no matter how much Papa or Queen Ewella or anyone wants it.

If we ever were at all.

We tumble into a heap on the sand; breathless and giggling, and our magic dissipates in fading stars. Hair mussed, face pink, Edwyn reaches up to catch them, and they melt around his fingers like snowflakes.

"This is what I wanted," he breathes. "All the way back in the beginning. This is what I wished for."

Willow rolls over and props his head up on a hand, looking down at Edwyn like there has never been a bad word between them. "What do you wish for now?"

Elowen rests her head against mine, her long hair tickling my nose, our breathing matched.

I expect Edwyn to say, "I wish I could go home," or "I wish Father would love me." But as much as he might long for those things, even he knows they are little more than wasted wishes.

"I wish . . ." The lump in his throat looks nearly too big to swallow. "I wish I could move forward."

"What's stopping you?" I ask.

"Me." A little of the old fury casts a shadow in his eye. "I don't know how to change. I don't think I can. I don't think I'll . . . fit anywhere else. I think I'm too—"

"You're not," says Elowen fiercely. "So don't you even say it."

"What?" I ask, because unlike some, I don't have telepathic abilities.

Elowen stays glaring at her brother and spits the word like snake venom, *"Broken."*

Willow's eyes go wide and devastated. "That's not really what you think, is it?"

"Everyone doing their best to help me," Edwyn says stiltedly, "everyone bending over backward to show me kindness I *know* I have not earned, they're all going to be bitterly disappointed when they fail."

"First of all," I say loudly, holding up a finger, "you don't *earn* kindness. Second, no one is bending anything for you—

they're just trying to give you what you should've been getting already. And third, fail what, exactly?"

Edwyn flushes heavily and looks away. "Making me . . . *normal.*"

"Pfft. Normal doesn't exist. You're fine. Relax."

It's a gamble, dismissing his very real, very valid fears like that, and I wouldn't blame him too hard if he grabbed his sword again. That's probably what I would do.

"I just mean . . . normal's just the word they give you to make you fit, or feel bad about not fitting," I push on. "Everyone is different, even if they're pretending not to be. No one who matters wants to help you be anything other than what *you* want to be. Papa's not gonna be frustrated or give up on you, no matter how long it takes or what you choose. Neither's Neal. They just want to help. We all do. Whatever that means for you."

It's a hot mess of an explanation, but it's the best I can do.

Luckily Willow backs me up with an enthusiastic nod, and Elowen says, a little smugly, "I told you so."

"And it's okay if it's easier said than done," I continue. "Because I know it is. And that's okay. Neal says that progress doesn't go in a straight line, and I reckon that's true. Just . . . keep moving forward, okay?"

"Even if it's scary," Willow adds.

Edwyn looks at each of us like he's searching for the trick or the lie, afraid to trust, to hope, to dream.

I get it.

I remember being right there.

Then he lets out a deep breath and stands up, spraying Willow with sand. Edwyn's face is set in hard determination, and his fist clenches around his magic, the green light seeping out between his fingers to wrap around his knuckles like a gauntlet.

"I'm going to do it," he says, wavering and fierce, and I don't know if he's speaking to us or his magic or both. "I'm going to be brave, and I'm going to fight for myself. I'm going to move forward." He catches my eye and smiles. "Even if it's scary. That is my wish."

<hr/>

At the top of the palace's grand staircase, Willow kisses each of us good night and goes left toward the Queen's Quarters, and we go to Papa's apartments.

The lamps are still lit when we step into the foyer, the soft sound of conversation drifting beneath the closed door into the sitting room. Papa and Neal are both still up. Waiting for us.

Edwyn sees the light beneath the door and shrinks back, all the new determination dwindling down into old fear. It's one thing to be brave in theory. It's something else entirely putting it straight into practice. Even Elowen hesitates, mouth set firm like she's holding in an escape plan.

"It's fine," I promise them both. "It's not like we were even sneaking. They're probably just waiting up to make sure we're okay."

To prove it, I push the door open and head inside.

Papa and Neal are on the sofa before a crackling hearth; Neal lying lengthways, reading a book, his feet on Papa's lap. Papa, in return, is using Neal's legs as a table while he works something out on parchment.

They look up at the same time, and all the warmth from the fire is in their eyes.

Papa rises and greets me with a kiss to the top of my head, then Elowen.

Edwyn lingers behind, wanting and wary all at once.

Bravery is easier said than done; it's harder to fight dragons than give in and trust.

Papa cocks his head with a smile, keeping a respectful distance, and opens his arms wide. "Welcome home, kid."

CHAPTER
THIRTY-TWO

L ittle by little, Helston turns into festival grounds. I guess
this is what Helston does best—pretend that any problems on the other side of the bridge don't exist at all. Or on
this side, for that matter.

The palace, the grounds, the whole town is decked out
in millions of tiny rainbow flags strung up from building to
building; the training grounds get transformed into an awesome tournament ring, complete with spectator stands and
scoreboards, and every spare scrap of space gets filled with
brightly colored tents ready for the competitors.

I spend all my free moments wandering longingly between them, inhaling the smells of fresh paint and new
sawdust and imagining myself preparing for battle, polish-
ing up Satin, changing into my best tunic, going through my
stretches while listening to the crowd waiting for me. Chant-
ing my name. My *real* name.

Sir Callie.

A champion may choose their prize, and I've always known what I'd ask for.

Nothing has changed, even though everything has changed.

"What are you going to go in for?" Elowen asks as we drift together through the tournament grounds.

"Everything!" And she laughs.

Every time Elowen laughs, the sun gets a little brighter and my face starts to burn.

"I suppose beating every single knight in every single game is a sure way to win favor." She threads her arm around mine and laces her hands together. "Then no one can ever question your right to your shield."

"I dunno—if defeating a dragon and rescuing a prince aren't enough to prove it, I have no idea what is."

Elowen rolls her eyes with a thin smile. "You know people are more ready to pay attention to silly games than great deeds."

I certainly do know that.

The only evidence that there's anything serious going on is the hushed conversations and abrupt silences from the adults whenever any of us goes near them.

We're all getting sick of it.

We continue the grumble at lunchtime, roping Willow into it too. The prince is more than happy to join in after spending a fruitless morning trying to eavesdrop on the day's council meeting.

"It isn't like this doesn't affect us," Willow mutters, stabbing an innocent potato. It's probably the first time I've ever heard him complain about anything. "We were the first people to go into Dumoor Forest and come back alive. We could *help* if only they'd let us."

"But they won't," says Elowen. "They'll keep us inside and call it protection."

"Not when the battle actually comes. Then it'll be all hands on deck, including ours. Well—" He dips his head to El. "Not yours."

"What's the point of this grand new world if they're *still* not going to let girls fight?" Elowen growls. "It's ridiculous. . . . Swords were nothing against that dragon—do they not realize that? They *need* magic."

The absolute horror when Satin just bounced off those scales is still raw. We were lucky, and we all know it. It doesn't matter how awesome Helston's army is; a million swords wouldn't've made a difference.

El's right—they *need* magic. There's no way around that. It's almost laughable, all those years I spent, stubbornly determined that the ounce of magic in my blood was the one thing holding me back from being the warrior I knew I was supposed to be, and now it might be the only thing that makes me useful.

"It'll never happen," says Willow softly. "The council will never agree to it, and even Mother is hesitant. They're still afraid of what magic can do if it isn't carefully controlled, and I suppose I can understand that, but—"

"So—what?" I demand, throwing up my hands in frustration. "What's it gonna take for them to realize that magic's the only thing that'll save Helston? Total annihilation?"

I can see it perfectly—the last stone of Helston crumbling into the sea, and Peran on the edge of the cliff going, *Mmm, yes, should've listened to those kids.*

Even then, he would *still* never admit it out loud.

Grown-ups hate admitting they're wrong.

"Let them fail," says Elowen bitterly. "Let them learn."

Willow and I stare at her.

"Yikes, El."

"Well—" She sniffs and pushes her hair back. "If they're going to be stubborn, maybe it's the only way. Maybe Helston *should* fall. Maybe it's for the best."

"Helston can change," Willow offers, more hopeful than certain. "It's just going to take time—"

"Time no one has," Elowen snaps back at him. Two pink spots brighten her cheeks, and she drops her gaze with a sigh. "I'm sorry. I know it takes time. And I'm grateful for the progress that's been made. I just . . . I can't stop thinking about the dragon's offer."

My chest tightens. "It wasn't real. You know that, right?"

"Of course."

But I know a lie when I hear one.

I reach for her hand and squeeze. "It'll get better, I promise. Helston's gonna turn into a haven for everyone. Hang tight, okay? We'll make this a world worth sticking around for. Right, Willow?"

The prince nods quickly. "Absolutely! Look at how much has changed already!" He makes a wild gesture that sends a potato flying, and he slouches down before anyone can blame him. "It's only going to keep getting better," he continues in a whisper. "And once Mother's gotten through to the council, it'll be easy."

"You just said they'll never let girls fight," says Elowen. Her hand stays in mine, but her nails dig furiously into my knuckles. "You told us that they'll make all the allowances in the world for boys, but when it comes to girls—"

"Why do you want to fight?" I blurt out before I can stop myself.

Elowen stares at me like I've just struck her, then snatches her hand back with a cool "Why do *you*? Why aren't you content, sitting back and letting everyone else do the work for you? You're not the only one with something to prove and someone to save, Callie."

I wince, feeling like ten kinds of fool. "Sorry, El. I get it. And it's not fair. But just because it's that way now, doesn't mean it's always gonna be."

"And how long are we expected to wait?" Elowen asks. "How long are we expected to suffer the disparity on the promise that it's temporary if we're not even allowed to fight for our own equality?"

"I dunno, El."

"No." She sits back with crossed arms and a glare. "You don't."

We pick at the rest of our meal, none of us hungry, none of us willing to be the first to break the silence.

The fact of the matter is, Elowen's right, and her anger is more than reasonable. I felt exactly like that all the way up to a few days ago. There's no point pretending I didn't. And this war is far from won. All around us, mingled into the crowd, are enemies bent on maintaining the old order and sabotaging any of the queen's attempts to move Helston forward. It's not enough to take it one step at a time when each step takes a whole battle.

Fair is fair, and right now it's not.

The meal's almost over when Edwyn finally joins us, sweating and tired but bright-eyed and more at ease than I've ever seen him. With Papa stuck in Big Important Council Meetings day in and day out, Neal's found his own ways to stay occupied, and he's managed to rope Edwyn into assisting with construction for the tournament. It's a sneaky bonding method he used on me way back when, working closely and separately, with the chance but not expectation to talk. Progress is slow but forward, and that's all that matters.

He slides in beside Willow, reaching for bread before he even says hello.

I grin. "Neal really got you working, huh?"

Edwyn nods with his mouth full, and it takes several tries before he can swallow. "The construction's nearly finished. I didn't want to leave, but Captain Neal insisted I take a break. I'm going back in a few minutes."

"Don't make it too short, else he'll just send you back. Neal's dead serious about self-care."

I bask in this moment, surrounded by my friends, free and laughing and *happy*. Yeah, we've got a thousand miles to go, but we've started out on this journey *strong* and we know where we're going. Helston was the center of my dreams for as long as I can remember, the basis of all my games, the focus of my ambition. I always knew I would end up here, one way or another, but I never ever let myself hope for *this*.

In my dreams, I was alone. A solitary knight who didn't need anyone else. And that was just fine. My sword was all I needed. But that's not real life, and I don't want it to be. People are scary; they're unpredictable and uncontrollable, and maybe they won't stick around forever, but maybe that's okay. A knight needs something worth fighting for, worth living for, worth dying for.

It's scary to need something as fragile as love, but scary doesn't always mean bad.

Elowen laughs, open and bright, and I know I'm staring

but I can't help it. I want to make this world better for her. I want her to have everything she wants. I want—

Then her expression darkens as a shadow falls over the remnants of our meal.

"Mother."

Lady Anita smiles down at us. She nods respectfully to Willow, then addresses her children, ignoring me completely. "You both look well—"

"We are," Elowen bites. "Want to know why?"

Edwyn reaches for his sister. "El, don't."

But Elowen ignores him, glaring up at Lady Anita. "We're doing more than fine, and you can go and tell Father that. That's why you're here, isn't it?"

"I'm here because I missed you, Elowen. The apartment feels very empty without you both."

"Funny, that, seeing as when we were there, we had to be silent and invisible."

Lady Anita sighs, and if I didn't know better, I would think she's truly upset. "You exaggerate, Elowen, you know you do. All of this . . . dissonance, you have to know it isn't real. I know it's easy to take all the bad and overblow it, but enough is enough. Your father and I love you—"

I squirm. Love has never sounded like such a threat.

"Tell that to Edwyn," Elowen demands. "Go on! Tell him he's imagining it all. Tell him Father loves him."

Beside her, Edwyn fades. He doesn't need to use his magic

to become invisible, just the dip down of his chin and the rise of his shoulders, keeping his gaze carefully at a neutral midpoint. Going backward.

But when Lady Anita laughs, a bright tinkling sound that sounds too much like Elowen at her best, and says, "Of course he does," he looks up in surprise.

Willow catches my eye, confirming what I know in my gut: *This is not a good thing.*

"Edwyn." Lady Anita crouches so they're eye to eye, her expression soft and sincere.

"Leave him alone, Mother."

But Lady Anita ignores Elowen, reaching with long, delicate fingers to touch Edwyn's cheek. He flinches. She either doesn't notice or doesn't care.

"Darling," she murmurs, "I know things have not been easy. For any of us. We have all made mistakes, and no one knows that more than your father. He knows he has not treated you fairly. Either of you. Her Majesty understands the pressure he has been under and forgives him. Can you do the same? Please, give us the chance to apologize—"

"So apologize."

Lady Anita's eyes snap to meet mine from the other side of the table.

Elowen hides a smirk behind her hand, and Willow looks like he wishes he was just about anywhere else. Maybe this isn't the best time or place, but I don't care.

I give my most petulant shrug, the one that always got Mama yelling the loudest. "What's stopping you from apologizing right now?"

Lady Anita's face twists just the way Mama's did. Score. "It is a private matter, Lady Calliden. A *family* matter. Not something I would expect you to understand, given your . . . unfortunate circumstances."

I dig my nails into my palms and breathe deeply. Don't rise to it, don't rise to it. . . .

"Regardless." She stands, fingertips grazing Edwyn's cheek again, and smiles down at her children as though nothing is complicated between them. "Home will always be open to you when you are ready. I hope it is sooner rather than later. We both do."

"Unbelievable," I growl, glaring at her back as she drifts away. "The audacity."

"I hate her," Elowen mutters, shredding a roll beyond edibility. Her voice shakes. "Just as much as I hate Father. She thinks she knows exactly how to wind us back in."

Willow reaches across the table and taps gently to get the attention of Edwyn, whose body is still twisted in his mother's direction. "Hey, are you all right?"

"Yes, I'm—" He stands up like he's in a daze, like there's some siren song whistling to him, and when he looks back at us, we already know what he's going to say. The apology sits deep in the crease between his eyes. "I—I have to go. You don't, El—that's your choice—but I do."

"*No.*"

"If Father wants to talk—"

"He shouldn't be talking—he should be listening," I say. "Look, I get it, I do, but can't you sit on it for a day or two? See how you feel tomorrow?" It's hard work to keep my voice level, but my heart is thuddering so hard it hurts. *Come on,* I want to say, *don't undo all that progress just for one false wish.*

"At least let one of us come with you," Willow says softly. "Don't go alone."

"No. I need to speak for myself. On my own." Edwyn nods as though confirming to himself. "I know what I want now, and I need Father and Mother to hear it from me."

"Do you at least have your bracelet?" Willow asks, voice tight like he's trying to keep the fear out of it.

Edwyn touches his chest, where the bracelet lies against his heart beneath his tunic. "Of course. I'll stay in touch. Don't worry about me."

Elowen's head sinks down into her hands once Edwyn hobbles out of the hall. "He isn't coming back."

"He will," says Willow, but there isn't a speck of certainty in the words.

CHAPTER
THIRTY-THREE

Hitting things with sticks might not help us take down a dragon, but it goes a long way to making us feel better and not go wild with worry as we wait to hear anything from Edwyn. Elowen's bracelet stays miserably silent, and we all agree it's safest to let him make first contact with us. Peran's the kind of enemy you need total focus to face.

Papa joins us on the training grounds, fed up to the back teeth with being stuck in the Council Chambers listening to the tangled knots the queen and the council are twisting themselves into. He wasn't designed for desk work; he's like me—he needs to be moving.

"Keep your elbow up," he instructs Elowen, helping her position her bow. "And draw back with the lightest touch. It's all about your breathing."

Elowen's focus is needle sharp, her breath steady, and her determination fierce. She releases her breath and her arrow in the same moment, and the arrow flies straight and true, stabbing into the middle of the target.

Papa whistles, impressed. "Nice," he says approvingly. "Took me a whole year into squiredom before I stopped being a menace to society every time I picked up a bow. You're a natural, kid."

The look Elowen turns on him is piercing. "I know."

Neal and I fence lightly, focusing more on form than strength. Working with Willow, I really notice the similarities between dancing and fighting, especially in the grace of my arms and the placement of my feet.

Neal notices too, and his eyes sparkle with pride. "You've improved! If this is what you can do in six weeks, Callie, you're going to be formidable by the time you get your shield in six years."

I grin. Papa and Neal have always talked about my future in certain terms, but I knew they were just being kind. Now it's *real*.

Another *thunk*, and Elowen's split the first arrow straight down the middle with the second.

Neal glances her way with a soft chuckle. "Speaking of formidable . . ."

"She's angry that boys are getting a whole magical program but girls still aren't allowed to fight," I tell him. "I agree. It's not fair. And when the war comes, Helston's gonna need *everyone*. Especially people like El."

"I know," Neal murmurs as we pick up the pace with our

blades. "I've been trying to tell your dad to tell the queen to tell the council, but . . . well, you can imagine."

Tap tap tap, go our swords.

"Can't you tell 'em yourself?"

Neal laughs. "They can barely tolerate my presence this side of the bridge—they're not going to let me into their hallowed Council Chambers."

Tap tap, one two . . .

"You should be on the council."

Neal grimaces. "No thank you."

"You'd get stuff done."

"I would make a mess," says Neal flatly. "I can't do any of that negotiation, compromise stuff. Not about things that are important. And I don't have the standing to get away with it like your dad does."

"I dunno if Papa can get away with it either." He might be tight with the queen, but openly defying Peran in favor of an apparent traitor has not done his reputation any favors. As far as votes go, he and Queen Ewella are pretty outnumbered. "Hey . . . if I ask a question, will you give me a truthful answer?"

Neal's sword pauses, and he frowns. "You know I will, kiddo. What is it?"

I take my time to work out the wording, because right now it's just a bad feeling in my gut. Edwyn should be back by now, but it's not even just about him. It's the whole interaction with Lady Anita, and how niceness can sometimes feel a whole bunch worse than meanness, and the certainty that it means something *more*, something *bigger,* something dangerous—

"What if Peran wins?"

Neal hesitates. Unlike Papa, he's not pretending that this war is over. People like Peran regenerate like beheaded snakes.

"Why're you worrying about that, Callie?"

I give a sloping shrug, but my head's not in the game enough to lie properly. I grimace as I confess, "He's getting Edwyn back on his side."

Neal's sword point hits the ground, his whole being tense with worry. "What happened?"

So I tell him all about Lady Anita at lunch, how Edwyn went after her, allegedly to cut ties; but the feeling in my stomach says that something bad is happening. I tell him because I want him to say, "Let's go right now," and we'll march into the Chancellor's Chambers and rescue Edwyn.

But he doesn't. The worry doesn't harden into determination. If anything, it softens into grief, and my heart sinks into my boots.

"If Edwyn feels like he needs to talk to his parents, then we need to let him," says Neal softly. "He's allowed his choice just as much as anyone else."

"Yeah, but—"

"We can only trust that he will come back to us," says Neal. "And I do trust that. But if he doesn't . . . we have to respect that too. I'm sorry," he adds at my glowering disappointment. "But we will be here for him when he comes back to us. That has to be enough."

Except it's not enough.

Not even nearly.

Willow somehow manages to stay optimistic all the way through to dinner, but my mood and Elowen's plummets through the flagstones into the dirt below. It doesn't help that Peran's in the hall, as casual and comfortable as if nothing's changed, and Edwyn still hasn't returned.

"I'm sure it's a lot to process," Willow offers. "He probably just wants to be by himself for a while. You know what he's like. Right, El?"

"I do," she mutters, playing with the frayed threads of her bracelet. "I know exactly what he's like." She bites her lip in one final moment of self-control; then she gives in and her fingers start moving in a deft pattern across the knots.

Willow and I hold our breath, waiting and hoping.

Nothing.

El tries again, her frown getting deeper and darker.

Nothing.

She lets Willow snatch it from her and try it himself, and when he has no more success than she did, his throat flickers in a hard swallow.

"He doesn't have it," Willow breathes, fingers stilling on the knots.

"Doesn't have what?" I ask.

"His bracelet. Even when it isn't being used, you can feel when the other has it with them. Edwyn's is cold."

"What does that mean?"

"It means he was caught," says Elowen, face blank of all emotion. "It means they took it away from him."

Willow reaches cautiously to comfort her. "Don't lose hope, El—"

But Elowen shifts away. "You cannot lose something you never had."

None of us do more than play with our food, getting ready to face the hard fact that we let Edwyn go and he isn't coming back, when suddenly Willow's face lights up like a beacon. "There he is!" He jumps up and waves enthusiastically with both arms.

El and I twist around, the hope on her face unconcealed.

My own relief sparks hard when I find him in the crowd, picking his way between the rows of benches, and I have never been so glad to be wrong! But there's something not quite right about him. He doesn't look any different. He's not bleeding or limping worse than before; he's just . . . not quite right.

Danger. I don't have Satin. I wish I did.

"Callie." Elowen's fingers brush my arm, and she nods in

the direction of where the council is sitting. They're all chatting around their goblets, unaware of what's going on. All except one. Except Peran.

The sight of him, of the smile tugging one corner of his mouth, sends my pulse spiking. He's kept himself to himself ever since the Throne Room, and I like it that way. If he has to be here, at least I haven't had to see him or that awful smile.

Whatever's making him smirk like that cannot be good.

Willow doesn't notice any of the warning signs. He hops around the table and latches onto Edwyn's arm, beaming. "How'd it go? Tell us everything! Congrat—"

Edwyn throws him off with a hiss and a shove. "Don't touch me, *princess!*" His voice is loud and wavering, like it's meant for someone else's benefit. A performance. An *act*.

Willow recoils.

I step forward between them. "Hey—"

Edwyn pulls himself up as tall as he can. His shoulders look like they're not supposed to go that straight, and he addresses me in his old, cold monotone.

"Lady Calliden, I challenge you to a duel to take place one week from today, at the opening of the tournament that commemorates the twentieth anniversary of King Richard's coronation. You have brought shame and corruption into Helston. You have turned good people against each other and bewitched our royal family. You have—" His voice cracks, and he tries to hide it with a cough. "You have turned my sister against her family and tried to do the same to me. I

348

am not so weak and will not fall so easily. Enough is enough, and I will prove once and for all that . . . that m-magic—" He swallows hard, gripping his hands so hard to keep them from twisting, he's gouging visible marks into his skin. "I—I will prove that magic is nothing more than a vessel for the weak, and all those who possess it and seek to use it are corrupt and should be turned away like the traitors they are. If you refuse my challenge, you will prove yourself what I know you to be—a coward."

I make myself breathe through my fury.

My first instinct is to accept. To fight him right here, right now, in front of everyone. But these are not Edwyn's words, and he is not my enemy.

Just some scared kid caught between two impossible choices and taught he doesn't deserve one.

I make myself speak softly, the same way I comfort Flo when she's spooked. "You don't have to do this. We said we would help you. We meant it. Let's go home, right now. Just walk away with us. Away from him. Don't look back."

Other people are noticing, pausing in their meal and their chatter to turn and stare with open curiosity. The audience Peran counted on to crush his kid to dust beneath the pressure of their attention.

"Hey," I whisper, trying to pull Edwyn's attention away from everyone who doesn't matter and back to those who do. "Don't worry about them. Keep going forward, right? Come on, let's go home. It's safe there. He won't be able to get to you."

Edwyn's gaze meets mine, and all the light he gained is gone. "I can't."

It makes no difference, I realize with a pang. None of it does. Edwyn can wish a thousand wishes and fight as hard as he can; we can offer all the love in the world, everything he's never let himself hope for; but ultimately there is still a rope around Edwyn's wrist, and when it's yanked, he goes sprawling.

Lord Peran.

Just sitting there, watching, letting kids fight battles that aren't even theirs, pitting us against each other when there is nothing to fight about.

Just because he's scared.

Well, scared isn't an excuse anymore.

"Callie—"

I ignore my name in Willow's anxious voice. I ignore Edwyn, who's cracking at the sight of my fury.

I ignore Papa, who's moving fast to get to us, with Neal following close behind.

I ignore all of them and jump over the table, sending plates crashing and people scattering.

I don't care.

"You *coward!*"

Anyone in my way staggers back out of my path. Spit flies, but I don't care. I'm seething and kind of crying and definitely sweating, and the stupid chancellor with his stupid *face* is just sitting there with one stupid eyebrow raised like *I'm* the unreasonable one. "Challenge me yourself. Go on! Let everyone watch me take you down!"

Lord Peran's head tilts, chalice halfway to his lips. "My dear girl," he says, "you are not worth a single moment of my time."

I lunge with a snarl, but arms catch me from behind and lock around my chest.

"This isn't the way, Callie," Papa murmurs. "Come on. Step away."

"*No!* This isn't right and it isn't fair, and I'm not just gonna sit here and let him ruin *everything good in this place.* Challenge me yourself," I snarl in Peran's face. "Stop using your kid to fight your battles, and fight me yourself. Right now. No magic, no tricks. Just you and me and two swords." I'm panting hard and I've stopped struggling, but I mean it with every bit of myself. I've never meant anything more. I search for the queen and wriggle free to make a clumsy bow to her. "Your Majesty. With your permission, I challenge the lord chancellor to a duel. If he wins, fine, I'll leave and he can wreck Helston all he likes; but if *I* win, he goes and he leaves Edwyn and Elowen and Prince Willow and all of us alone forever."

That's how it's supposed to be done. This is what I should've done right in the beginning, the moment Willow told me what a pile of horse droppings Peran was, or at that first council meeting. From the first awful interaction we had, when he called me "girl" and took Satin away, I knew what he was, and I should've fought harder then. Compromising and smiling nicely doesn't get you anywhere good; it just makes people like *him* believe they can stomp all over you.

Moderation doesn't work.

"Please," I beg when she glances toward Papa and Neal, clearly not wanting to authorize this. "Give me leave to protect the Crown *and* my friends. Let me do this."

"Callie, no!" Papa says. "No *way*! I won't risk you. I won't *lose* you. It isn't worth it—"

"Yes it is," I snap back, glaring up into Papa's face. "It is worth it, and I'm not asking, I'm telling!"

Papa turns desperately to the queen. "Ewella," he pleads, voice cracking. "As a parent, I beg you, do not allow this."

"I don't care if I get permission or not—"

The queen raises a silencing hand. "Nick, Callie has every right to claim satisfaction, and Lord Peran has the right to accept. However, I do believe a compromise should be reached." Her dark eyes meet mine, then Peran's, where they stay. "There will be no fatalities. The winner will be determined by who draws first blood by sword point. Lord Peran, do you accept? If you refuse, you forfeit and therefore will be compelled to leave Helston by the conditions of the challenge."

Peran snorts. "I have more honor than to stoop low enough to fight a child."

"You never held back before," I spit. "Or do you only hit people too scared to hit back?"

Peran makes a motion that has Papa grabbing me back and Neal stepping between us with one hand warningly on his sword. I smile. I'm not scared. Let Helston see their precious chancellor for what he really is.

"I accept," he murmurs, his face so close to mine that I can see the flecks of steel in his irises. "*Gladly*. No tricks, no magic, and we'll see just how far that reckless courage takes you."

I grin. "Oh, you have no idea."

"Very well," says Queen Ewella. "It is set. One week—"

"No," I interrupt. "Tomorrow. The sooner the better."

Papa groans. "Callie, please be sensible."

"Bit late for that, isn't it?" I mutter back.

I'm pretty sure a smile twitches in the corners of Queen Ewella's lips, but she smooths them before it breaks free. "Very well. We will convene on the training grounds tomorrow morning."

"Perfect," I say grimly. And, to Peran, "Better get some practice in, my lord."

Peran looks down on me with every bit of hatred in his soul. "It will be my greatest pleasure to make you pay for every misstep you've ever made," he hisses back.

I give my best eye roll, the kind even Papa disapproves of, and turn on my heel.

The air is too hot and too close, and there are too many people staring at me.

I've got to get out.

"Callie!"

Elowen catches my arm just as I pass the fountain.

"Don't tell me I shouldn't've done that," I warn her.

Her face is flushed, probably from the chase. "I wasn't going to," she says breathlessly. "Only that . . . you didn't have to."

"Yeah I did."

Elowen sucks her lip, and it's impossible to tell if she's upset or angry or—

She darts in and kisses me on the cheek, so fast I'm convinced I imagined it until she says, "Thank you."

"Yeah sure whatever no problem" is my very eloquent response.

Willow and Edwyn catch up to us while El and I are still looking weird at each other, stuck in the middle of wanting to totally do that again and pretending it never happened. Edwyn's still deathly pale and shaken bad, and Willow's got his hand locked tight in his own. He'd better not let go until Peran's a hundred miles on the other side of the bridge.

"I'm sorry," says Edwyn breathlessly. "I'm so sorry. I thought I was strong enough. I thought I knew what I wanted, but as soon as I saw him . . ."

I squeeze his shoulder. "It's not about being strong enough. Parents, they're . . . they know how to take root in your head. *I'm* sorry, about your dad. I know what it's like, and I know how hard it is to get free. It sucks. But you know what? The best fix to get the worst of people like that out of your head is distance, and this time tomorrow you'll be free."

But Edwyn shakes his head hopelessly. "He's going to kill you, Callie." And when I start to say "nah": "I know my father. He doesn't care about any rule he didn't make himself, and if you think he'll hold back just because Her Majesty ordered it—"

"I'm not afraid of your dad, Edwyn."

"You should be." Papa marches up to me with a face full of thunder and grabs my shoulders, but up close he's not angry, just devastated. And scared.

I glare. "I'm not sorry."

"No, of course you're not," Papa growls. "You never are, are you?"

"Not when I'm right."

Papa turns away with a curse, shoving his fingers through his hair. "Talk some sense into them," he mutters at Neal.

I set my feet shoulder's width apart and brace myself, ready to fight. I don't want to argue with Papa, and I don't want to argue with Neal, but if I have to—

"You've made up your mind, haven't you?"

"Yeah. I have."

"No one would think any less of you if you let your dad or me fight in your place."

"*I* would."

Neal smiles with reluctant acceptance and nods. "I know."

"So . . . what? You gonna try and stop me?"

He looks back at Papa, still glowering at me, and sighs. "I think that energy could be better spent on getting you set up so you have less chance of getting yourself killed."

"At least *one* of my dads supports me."

"Sorry that I'm not terribly eager to see my only kid go up against a grown man who has proven he possesses less than a drop of mercy in his body," Papa returns, meeting my glare point for point.

"Yeah, well, the queen already changed the rules—"

"I don't give a damn about the rules, Callie! She could change them to first contact only and I still wouldn't like it. No one puts their hands on my kid! *What?*" he demands when Neal's mouth twitches into a smile. "This isn't *funny!*"

"Love," says Neal in the voice he uses when Papa is being his most ridiculous, "do you really think either of us is going to sit back and let Peran break the rules? The moment he steps out of line, so do we. But Callie has earned the chance to fight. We can't deny them that, no matter how much we want to protect them."

Papa glares between us like this is some kind of conspiracy, then deflates with a furious breath. "Fine. I concede. You're right." Then, more softly, with a hand on my head. "Of course you're right. You have more than earned your chance to fight. I can be afraid *and* support you."

Then he picks me up, easy as if I was six years old, and holds me high so we're face to face. "Go out there, Callie, and show Helston what a real knight is. Your family will be all around you to watch you win."

Just like they're here now, with Papa's other arm around Elowen, and Willow and Edwyn safe by Neal's side. All the people I love the most. Who love me.

Exactly as I am.

CHAPTER
THIRTY-FOUR

S *how Helston what a real knight is.*

I pull a brush through my hair, staring at the kid in the looking glass, all freckles and big hazel-green eyes. I used to see someone else whenever I looked in the mirror, some girl I didn't recognize, all scowly and snarling. She's not there anymore. It's just me. Exactly as I am.

Callie.

I tie my hair secure—I'm not about to lose the most important fight of my life just because I get hair in my eyes. I smooth nonexistent creases from my emerald-green tunic. It's perfect. The copper trim glitters in the sunshine dappling through the small window. It's a beautiful day. A perfect day. With a breeze in the air. Not too hot, not too cold. The sounds of the tournament preparation already underway drift through my open window. Helston is loud and alive, brightly painted in rainbows.

I should be excited.

I know I can win.

But I can't breathe.

A soft tap on the door, and Willow slips in.

I smile. "You look like a king."

He tugs self-consciously on the glittering hem of his scarlet tunic, the gold matching the crown nestled in his black hair. "And you look like a knight."

"I don't feel like one. I feel sick."

Willow closes the door softly behind him. "Knights can feel sick. They're human too, you know?"

I pull a face. Not going to lie—I wish there was some kind of super-strength invincibility that came with knighthood. "I figured you'd be down at the battleground already," I say. "Get a good seat and all that."

"I told Mother I wanted to see you first." Willow sits on my bed and pulls his legs up. The crown and the gold and the scarlet don't matter in here. Prince or not, we're both just kids. "Are you nervous?"

"Nah." I grimace, then admit, "Yeah. A bit. Don't tell, though."

Willow presents his little finger solemnly. "On my honor." And when I link mine to his, he grins. "You will win, though. I believe in you. We all do."

"Great." I don't mean it to come out as bleak as it does, but it's easier to shine when people have no expectation of you. "I hope I don't let you all down."

"Impossible!" Willow jumps up and pulls me with him. "Come on. Everyone's waiting."

———⊶———

Helston is a festival ground. Tomorrow I will be able to enjoy it; today I am surviving. The streets are crammed to bursting with what feels like every single person who lives on this rock, all eager for the tournament to start a whole day early.

Even the sun is present, dressed up in its best and making all the tiny flags glitter like real rainbows and the cobblestones sparkle silver.

Everything is so beautiful.

Willow's arm links with mine, our fingers twined, all the way down the hill to the battlegrounds and the bright tents that have popped up like mushrooms in damp soil. There's one whose flaps are wide open, and Willow leads me straight into it.

The moment we step inside, the collective cheer nearly knocks me over. The tent is full of sparkling flowers and the people I love the most, all cheering for me, cheering me on. I don't even know what to say as Willow tugs me closer. Neal drapes a new cloak around my shoulders, my favorite shade of green with a shiny copper clasp, and Papa puts Satin into my hands. Her scabbard's been cleaned up, and her blade is bright and sharp.

Queen Ewella pins a shiny crest to my cloak. For a

moment, I think it's the Helston crest that all the pages wear, but this one is different. I recognize from the carving on the door into the Queen's Quarters: Her Majesty's own crest.

She looks down at me with a warm smile. "Are you ready, Champion?"

I can already hear people making their way to the stands, eager to watch this showdown. I wonder if they know how important it is.

"Yeah." I nod. "I'm ready."

The queen kisses my cheek. "Good luck, Sir Callie."

Willow hugs me fiercely. "Don't die, all right?"

I laugh and hug him back. "I'll do my best."

He follows his mother out.

Papa ruffles my hair. "You die, I'll be mad at you. Got it? But seriously—you've got this, kid. Keep your head, stay smart. . . ." The smile flickers and he swallows, pressing a fierce kiss to my forehead. "I love you."

"Love you too."

Neal touches his forehead to mine, where Papa's kiss was. "I'm glad I'm here to watch you win. I'm so proud of you, Callie." His hug is fierce and final, and I don't want to let him go.

"I'm scared," I whisper, the confession muffled in his tunic. I don't want anyone else to know, not even Papa. Neal's arms tighten.

"I'd be more concerned if you weren't. You still sure you want to do this?"

In the safe circle of Neal's arms, I think it through for real.

361

I could walk away, right out of Helston. I could say I'm just a kid, and everyone waiting for the spectacle would get it. I could.

But I'm not going to.

I pull back with a hard nod. "Yeah, I'm sure."

The pride on Neal's face fills me up full to bursting.

"See you on the other side," says Papa as his fingers link with Neal's. "Do it fast—we want to celebrate!"

"You're lucky," says Edwyn, watching my dads leave the tent. "I've never seen anyone love their children that much." He looks at me with a flickering smile. "I'm sorry. For everything. I didn't know it would end this way."

I punch him lightly on the arm. "Calm down—nothing's ended yet."

"One day I'm going to punch you back, and you're going to feel it," Edwyn mutters. Then, after a beat, "Make sure you survive my father long enough that I'll get my chance, all right?"

I give a laugh that comes out more jagged than I'd like. "Any tips?"

"Yes," Elowen interrupts. "Do not hold back. He won't, so you mustn't either. No mercy, no heroics."

I fake gasp. "Me? Heroics? Never."

Edwyn rolls his eyes and follows my dads out of the tent, leaving me alone with El.

"So," she says.

"So . . ." My pulse trips and tumbles, and I can't get enough breath in my lungs, and I think it has something to do with the way she's looking at me.

"It's tradition for the lady to give her knight a token before they fight for her." She opens her hands, and a bud appears in her palm. With a brush of magic, it grows and bursts into bloom; bright white petals with a soft, buttery center.

"Captain Neal's been teaching me. I'm afraid I'm still not very good." Elowen reaches around and fixes it in my hair, her breath warm on my cheek. "It's not perfect, but I hope it will bring you luck."

My lips part to say . . . something, but the kiss comes before the words, faster than a heartbeat and lighter than a butterfly, and stays lingering like the warmth of a fire on a frozen day.

"Win for me," she says, and then she's gone too.

Alone, I sit and I breathe and I wait. I'm as ready as I'll ever be, and maybe that's neither too much nor enough, but there's no point worrying about that now. I've done my best.

It'll have to be enough.

CHAPTER
THIRTY-FIVE

The call goes up—a single blast of a horn—and I step out onto the field.

The stands are full, and my family's in the front. I make myself see only them, ignoring the council lords murmuring together and Lady Anita sitting with her friends, certain of the outcome and hungry for my blood.

Every person in Helston who's ever had an opinion of me is here to watch me win or lose, live or die.

I'm not afraid.

I am Callie, the prince's champion, and I will not fall.

A herald in Helston scarlet approaches. "Are you ready, Callie, Lord Peran?"

Just the sound of his name lights my blood on fire. I turn at the crunch of boots in the gravel, and it's Peran like I've never seen him.

Divested of his chancellor's robes, he looks somehow bigger. He wears a knight's tunic, and it's clear he keeps himself in peak physical condition as well as demanding it of everyone else.

I swallow. Not gonna lie—I've sort of made myself believe that Peran's the kind of guy who's never picked up a sword in his life.

That is certainly not true.

This is a trained warrior, just like Papa, and twice my size, who has proven over and over that he has no qualms about hurting kids.

But I'm not afraid. *I'm not afraid.*

I've fought dragons and wolves. I've saved my friends. I've saved myself.

I will not fall now.

The crowd is silent and staring as Lord Peran accepts his sword from a wide-eyed squire, the teenager tiny beside the chancellor. Peran takes his time, adjusting his grip until it's comfortable, shedding his cloak, testing the balance of the blade with a few good practice swings.

Satin has never felt so light in my hands. Never seemed so much like a toy.

I am not afraid.

"The rules are these: As this is a formal duel to determine the honor of the participants, victory will be awarded to the last man standing. A victory will be determined either by the other participant verbally yielding, and therefore forfeiting the match, or when first blood is drawn by sword point. Is that clear?"

Peran gives a curt nod. Standing in front of me—over me—Lord Peran is huge, and I guess I get why everyone's scared of him. He's like a wall, unbreachable and unyielding. There's not even a sardonic smile this time. He's stone serious, and we're not playing. He means to win. He means to crush me to dust in front of all the people depending on me.

I'm not—

"Callie?"

"Yeah, it's clear."

The herald nods and steps clear.

"Prepare."

I take a deep breath and ground myself, gripping Satin in both hands.

We're ready.

Every wall can be broken down.

The call goes up and Peran hits me first; a brutal blow that rattles every bone in my body. It's a miracle Satin doesn't break on impact. He hits me again before my senses clear from the first blow, and I stagger backward.

I don't know if the crowd's just gravely silent, or if the ringing in my ears is blocking everything out.

Wish it blocked out Peran's whiny voice.

"This will be the shortest fight you've ever had," he says,

forcing me farther back. "And the last. When I am finished with you, you will know your place, *girl*."

Girl.

I don't respond. It's not that I don't have a million witty retorts just waiting to spill, more that I cannot—I will not—let myself be distracted. I focus on Satin, on my breathing, on where my feet connect to the ground. On myself. He is wrong. Every word he spits is wrong, and that knowledge strengthens me.

When he hits me again, I don't move.

Lord Peran doesn't like that, like it's a personal insult.

There's a flash in his eyes I don't understand until it's too late; I'm expecting a sword, not the back of his hand. The crack across my temple sends sparks across my vision and I fall. Hard.

I skid, gravel ripping into my cheek and my elbow and my whole left side.

I groan on the ground, winded from the fall and dazed from the blow.

A shadow falls across my face.

Lord Peran smirks down at me. "Are we done here, Lady Calliden?"

I open my mouth to tell him exactly where he can shove it but cry out instead at a fiery pain in my leg.

His boot is on my ankle, and he's stepping on me, slowly applying pressure, and I believe without any doubt at all that he intends to break it if I don't agree to everything he says.

No way.

I grit my teeth and breathe through my nose.

"I'm doing you a favor," he murmurs, for my ears only. "You would never be happy here. Even if you get everything your little heart desires, surely you see the way people look at you? You're astute, not like that foolish prince. You know what people are whispering about you, about Willow, about your father." My bone crunches and I nearly pass out. "Your poor mother. No wonder she gave up on you."

That's not what happened, I think dizzily, clutching Satin to my chest in both hands. It wasn't like that.

"You think you have friends here, but they'll know soon enough how you have ruined their lives. Just like your mother. You broke her heart, you know? You and your worthless father. And they'll be glad you're gone, just like she was."

I remember what it felt like. The hole that opened up inside me when we left, that took years of careful tending to close over even if it never healed. It felt like my leg feels now.

But I'm not scared of pain.

If it happens, I will heal again. I've done it before. I'll be okay. Just like my bruises will fade and my bones will mend. It'll stop hurting eventually.

I can't live my life scared of maybe getting hurt when giving up and giving in will mean definitely getting hurt. That's faulty logic, even if I get how easy it is to fall for it.

Not me.

Not the prince's champion.

"Yield, Lady Calliden."

That's not my name.

I swallow a mouthful of blood and smile up at the chancellor. "You've already lost. You lost the moment I arrived in Helston. Do what you like to me, but they're looking at you now, and they see you for what you are."

The words are stronger and braver than I feel, just one last reckless act before it ends and I have to face Willow and El and Edwyn defeated. I don't know how I'll do that. I don't think I can. I wish I could just close my eyes and not open them until I'm thrown out onto the moors so I don't have to see the looks on their faces when I let them down.

But Peran falters.

The foot on my leg remains, pinning me down, but his attention is elsewhere, looking around at the stands, at the whole of Helston watching him crush me. Seeing him for what he is. Then he looks down at me, and I'm certain he's going to break the rules and this is it, and I brace for the blow that will finish me.

He snatches up Satin before I think fast enough to hold on to her.

"Little girls shouldn't play with swords."

And he snaps her across his knee.

The jagged edges catch the sunlight, sparkling as he tosses them into the dirt, her name split in two.

I barely notice the pressure lifting from my leg, the pain in my bone lost beneath the shock and the refusal to exist in a reality where my sword could just be . . . broken. Like she's nothing but a child's toy. The two pieces fit together but they don't stick. Of course they don't. He broke her.

He broke her.

Gravel crunches and I look up at his back. He is turned toward the crowd, to the queen, ready to claim his victory.

A victory he hasn't yet earned. It doesn't count, the blow, the blood. Victory by sword point. And I will make him play by the rules.

I wipe my mouth, smearing blood across the back of my hand, and stagger up. My leg screams in protest. I ignore it. Healing can wait. Resting can wait. The battle isn't done.

Gathering my strength, I slam my body into Peran's, kicking his legs right out from underneath him. He falls hard, unprepared. He groans in the gravel. Good.

I snatch up Satin's hilt, the broken shard of her blade more vicious than her sharpened point, and graze Peran's bearded chin, freeing a thin dribble of blood. First blood.

"I win," I whisper.

The crowd explodes, but I barely hear them. Everything sounds like it's underwater. Even the crunch of gravel and Papa's voice in my ear. Even Willow's cheer. Elowen's.

Winning doesn't always feel like winning.

My eyes blur, my throat closes up, and I bury my face in Papa's chest, clutching Satin's hilt like holding her close to my heart will fix her. Suddenly I'm exhausted, and all my feelings are too big for my body.

It's done.

It's over.

"Cheat!" Peran snarls, struggling to his feet and pointing a shaking finger up at me. "She cheated! I demand—"

"Enough!" Queen Ewella raises a hand. "The best you can do for yourself now, my lord, is leave with the remnants of your dignity. Callie bested you fair and square, and by the rules you agreed to, your time in Helston is done."

Lord Peran stares around at the crowd, looking for his supporters.

They do what they do best and stay silent. Even Lady Anita's expression has changed, like she's looking at a problem she has miscalculated.

But there's no time to figure her out before Queen Ewella calls me over.

She smiles down from the royal stands, soft and warm, just like Willow. "A champion may choose their prize," she reminds me.

I look around at the faces of Helston, all watching me, waiting for me to choose, ready to listen to what I have to say. I thought I knew what I wanted. It's been the same for as long as I can remember. Right up to a few weeks ago.

I know I can win on my own, with the Crown's blessing or not. I don't need to be treated like a boy to show what I can do. I can prove myself on my own. I already have.

Willow sits nestled into his mother's side, and the twins are together next to him.

The war is not won, not on either side of the bridge. The castle is still made of secrets and crafted from fear, and it'll all come crashing down before Dumoor even gets to us.

I know what I want.

I raise my face to the queen. "Make it fair. *Totally* fair. Girls can fight and boys can be magical; anyone can do both. . . . Pretending that everyone's split down the middle in two groups is ridiculous. It doesn't work like that. Helston will never win if you keep pretending it does. You'll just make more people miserable and turn them into enemies. Just like Princess Alis. Because that's what happened, isn't it? And that's what'll happen again if you don't change things." I draw myself up tall as I can. "So that's what I want."

Lord Peran gives a derisive scoff, and I wheel on him with my broken sword.

"You want to go again? I'm not tired, you know!"

"You are right, Sir Callie."

I turn, blinking, back to Queen Ewella. "I'm what?"

"You are right," she repeats gently. "Equality should not be up for negotiation, and it is my own failing for failing to make a stand."

To that end, she rises and addresses the whole of Helston in a voice so clear, she doesn't even need to shout to be heard.

"My friends," she begins. "The events we have all witnessed today stand as proof that the rules we have previously relied upon are *wrong* and that it is far beyond time we push Helston out of the past and into the future. I was afraid to push for the changes we need, believing it more sensible to take it one step, one person at a time. But that isn't enough, and it isn't *fair*."

I stand with my back to the royal stand, seeing what the queen sees—all eyes watching, all ears listening. Silence.

"The last two years have been greatly unsettling for all of us," Queen Ewella continues, playing absently with Willow's hair. "The fear of the uncontrollable and the unknown is understandable. It is not, however, an excuse to bully and abuse. We can only win against whatever and whoever is coming for us if we are *united*. No one should fear punishment or rejection for who they are. That is not a Helston worth fighting for."

She lets that statement settle, lets Helston's population sit in their discomfort for a long moment before continuing. "This tournament was originally planned to celebrate my husband's reign. I dreaded it, the funeral decked in rainbows. But that's not what this is. That's not what I want this time to be. This tournament is a celebration of everything good that Helston has to offer, to look forward instead of backward, and to start our new adventure together in a celebration of all our strengths. We need to prove to our children that we will fight for them. Not just on the battlefield but right here at home. And I have every faith that Helston will rise to the occasion and work hard to make us the best we can be. Change isn't coming—change is here, and it starts now."

Queen Ewella looks down on Peran, who's about to

explode, judging by the width of the vein in his forehead. "I'm sorry you won't be here to witness the new dawn, my lord. But there are so many who will shine that much brighter without you. Your children will be loved and looked after, and I have no doubt they will thrive."

Peran snaps out of his frozen fury. "No. If it is decided I am to leave, so be it, but my children are coming with me. You may have turned their heads with pretty promises and false futures, but they know who their family is."

"Yes." Edwyn struggles up, bracing himself on Elowen's shoulder. He wobbles slightly, but his face is still and determined as he looks down at his father. "Family's the people who love you."

"*Exactly* as you are," Elowen adds, as cold and as hard as Peran taught them. "And we're staying."

Papa takes Peran's arm before the chancellor can make a move. "Come on, Peran. There's nothing more to say. Let's go."

With one last filthy glance at his children, Peran's attention turns to his wife. "Anita, come."

But Lady Anita, surrounded by her friends, does not move. Her eyes are sharp and assessing, darting from her husband to her children to the queen as she makes her calculations and reaches her conclusion. When she moves, it's with the grace and certainty of a river flowing toward the sea. She sweeps past Peran and me and stands before Queen Ewella and Willow.

"Your Majesty." She drops in a deep curtsy. "I do not seek

to make excuses for myself, only to ask for a chance to do better, to make amends, to find my place in Helston once more."

Elowen makes a furious move, held back only by Edwyn's hand on her arm. "*No.* You are just as much to blame! If he is to go, so should you! We don't want you either! *Leave!*"

The crack in her voice hurts me, and even Willow looks startled by her uninhibited rage.

Lady Anita, however, does not flinch.

"I will not bother you," she promises. "On my word, I will leave you and Edwyn alone until the time comes when you want to see me. I only ask for the same chance for forgiveness as everyone else."

"You had it!" Elowen shouts with tears in her voice. "You had *every* chance to help, and you didn't!"

"I was afraid for myself," Lady Anita says, addressing the queen rather than Elowen. "And for my children. I felt I had no choice. Please, allow me to stay and grow. Give me the liberty you have granted my children."

"You hypocrite," Peran snarls. "We were a team. A *partnership!* You were a part of every decision I made!"

Lady Anita turns to face him and says simply, "Liar."

I don't know what's going on, what's real or isn't, but the look on Peran's face is the one I have dreamed of, and I never thought in a million years that it would be Lady Anita who put it there. He gapes, startled—finally—into silence.

He isn't the only one. Elowen stands rigid, with fists clenched and tears rolling down her face as Edwyn stands by her side. The crowd—the court—stares at the family like they're seeing them for the first time.

Whatever else is happening, Peran is losing.

I call that a win.

"You may stay," Queen Ewella informs Anita after a careful stretch of consideration. "But it is on the strict condition that you do not approach your children until they approach you, if they ever choose to do so. Also, if it becomes apparent that you have indeed lied and are seen to be sabotaging Helston's progress, your punishment will be the same as that of your husband and will be dealt without hesitation. Am I understood?"

Lady Anita's curtsy drops impossibly low, her skirts brushing the ground. "Of course, Your Majesty. Thank you. I am indebted to you."

"You are indebted to your children," Queen Ewella corrects. "Remember: You are not entitled to their forgiveness."

If Lady Anita is an actor, she's a convincing one.

Lord Peran's rage, on the other hand, is 100 percent real.

He turns on Queen Ewella as Lady Anita brushes past him like he doesn't exist. "You will fall," he vows, voice low and shaking, and points first to the queen and then to the prince. "And Helston will bury you both."

"Sir Nick, please escort Lord Peran to collect his belongings and then to the bridge. We've wasted enough time on this nonsense. We have a festival to begin."

Papa smiles grimly and strengthens his hold on Peran's arm. "It would truly be my pleasure."

He doesn't go quietly, but he does go, and I'll never have to look at him again.

I push back the sweat-slicked hair from my face and dip to retrieve Peran's fallen sword. It's enormous, and lifting it takes what little strength I have left. No wonder my legs feel like liquid, after being beaten by that thing.

I haul it over to the stands and pass it up to Edwyn. "Figure you should have this." And, to Elowen, "Your luck worked. Thanks for that."

Elowen leans down and touches her forehead to mine. "That was all you, Sir Callie."

"May I?" Willow takes the piece of Satin I've been holding, treating her gently as a bird with a broken wing, and traces the jagged edge with a finger.

My heart hurts all over again.

"She's fixable," says Willow. "I'm sure of it."

"But she won't be the same."

"No," the prince agrees. "She won't be. And you know what? It's okay to be different."

CHAPTER THIRTY-SIX

We don't see Lord Peran off across the bridge. I used up all my self-restraint by not stabbing him in the throat on the dueling grounds, and I don't trust myself any further.

Besides, I want to move forward. No more glancing back.

Satin's pieces are both taken away from me, and I don't believe for one moment that she'll come back whole. She broke too easily. She's too delicate. It feels silly to grieve a sword, but I don't have any other word for it. She should be with me. After all this, I never want to be disarmed again.

The festival blossoms around us, the party bright and loud, and it's as if Willow and Elowen and Edwyn and I stand out in the middle, the only ones to have taken any of the damage done by Lord Peran. A bruise in the middle of a flower.

But bruises heal, given time and patience, and we have more of both now.

Still, it feels odd to sit in the stands and watch fake battles and fights without consequences after everything that has happened and everything that still waits for us on the other side of the bridge.

Finally the noise and the clamor get to be too much, and I slip away by myself. I take it as slow as my bad leg requires—El says it'll need at least a month of regular attention to fix up right—along the path to the crossroads where Willow and I shook on our friendship, and go up instead of down.

Prince Jowan's statue looks out to the horizon.

He's looking the wrong way, I think, sitting in the daisies at his feet. Maybe if he'd been paying attention, none of this would've happened. All the dangers are behind him, in Helston and on the moors. The sea is safe.

Waves lap lazily at the shore, sending white foam spraying across the rocks. The bridge is tiny, fragile. When the banished princess and her dragon decide to make their move against it, they will not fail.

But, for now, the forest sits quiet and still beneath the sunshine; as inconspicuous as the moors surrounding it.

Dragons lie, but people do too. Helston's lying right now, pretending this was the plan all along and everything's fine. Everyone just lying to each other over and over, each person believing they're the only one telling the truth.

Trying to untangle it all makes my head hurt.

I close my eyes and rest against the statue's legs, breathing in the cool spring air. The breeze tickles my cheek, and gulls call to each other in the sky. I can hear the distant sounds of the tournament carrying on without me.

Everything's fine.

My friends are safe, and tomorrow they will still be safe.

"I told you they'd be up here," Willow chirps, muffled by the wind.

I open my eyes to see Edwyn hushing him and Willow not caring in the slightest as he bounds across the grass to plop down beside me.

"It was supposed to be a surprise," says Edwyn by way of apology, glaring at the prince. "You weren't supposed to notice us."

Willow sticks his tongue out. "It *is* a surprise." And to me, "You weren't expecting us, were you?"

"No?" I rub my forehead with a grimace. "I thought I'd been sneaky enough."

"You think anything gets past my sister?" Edwyn asks with a crooked smile.

I dip my head in acknowledgment. "Fair. Where is El? Or is it just you two disrupting my peace?"

"Champions aren't permitted peace," says Edwyn. "Get used to it."

Willow hops up as fast as he sat down and waves to the

figures making their way up the last of the slope, like there's any way we could be missed.

Elowen, Papa, and Neal.

I guess I can't be too annoyed about it.

"Did you bring snacks?" I ask Elowen as she settles on my other side. "That's the only way I will tolerate this invasion."

She produces a small package of something cinnamon scented and wrapped in a handkerchief. "Of course."

"My hero!" Though it comes out more like *"Mmmph!"* as I stuff two biscuits straight into my mouth.

"I'm retiring for real now," Papa grumbles, finally making it the rest of the way, braced on Neal's shoulder. "A knight shouldn't be done in by one hill."

Neal rolls his eyes. "I'm sorry, but what did you expect when you signed up for *every single tournament*?"

"I have a reputation to prove!"

"Moderation in all things—"

"Is advice not worth taking."

"Then stop complaining when you overdo it. Tell him, Callie."

"Stop overdoing it," I tell Papa obediently. "You're too old."

"Treacherous child!" I giggle as Papa wrestles me over, sending the Helston kids scattering.

"Nick, their leg—"

Papa blinks innocently up at Neal with me in a headlock. "I'm being careful of their leg, don't worry."

"I was having a nice quiet time," I say, squirming and trying to elbow my way free. "What do you lot want other than to bother me?"

"Ah!" Papa drops me unceremoniously and stands back next to Neal, Willow and the twins around them, all with very suspicious expressions. Even Edwyn's smiling, though he's obviously trying not to.

But none of them move, or say anything, or *do* anything.

My patience snaps. "*What?*"

Willow darts behind my dads and reappears with a package that sparks something in my heart. He crouches in the grass and places it in my lap with a soft "I told you she was fixable."

My first parcel came to me bound in twine and oilskin.

This package is tied with a velvet bow and wrapped in—

"Satin."

"The smith said they could hide the crack," says Elowen as I lift my sword gently from the wrappings.

"But we thought you would choose to keep it," says Edwyn.

They're right. I would.

She's heavier than she was. Sturdier. Stronger. Her scar is visible, cut across her name etched in the steel. More herself than she ever was.

Mine.

"It'll take some time to get used to the new weight," says Papa. "But I figured you wouldn't mind the challenge.

Besides"—he grins wickedly—"you've got a lot of work to do if you want to make squire by next year."

My heart jumps into my throat. "You mean I actually get to—"

"You think you get to skip a step and just get straight to knight?" Papa nudges me with an elbow. "Being a champion's really going to your head, isn't it?"

"Nick, leave them alone." Neal rolls his eyes, but he can't help his smile. Neither can I. Mine's so big it hurts. "You're really doing it, kiddo. You're going to be a real Helston knight."

A real Helston knight . . .

I punch the sky with a whoop!

And I'm going to do it as myself.

As Callie.

ACKNOWLEDGMENTS

It takes a village to raise a child, and book babies are certainly no different! I have always been amazed that writing is at once such a solitary endeavor and yet impossible without a whole army! Callie is dedicated to every single name on these pages. Thank you for making my greatest dreams become more real than I ever allowed myself to hope.

First of all, my dearest wife, Christine: We met through fan fiction, and I am so, so incredibly lucky to have you on my side. Thank you for your support and your love, and for listening to me complain under your mom's table when writing and publishing felt the most impossible. Thank you for always believing in me more than I ever could myself. And, of course, my fiendish fur babies, Lexie-Noodle and Delta Hilary, the best assistants a person could hope for!

Equally, Megan Manzano, my most wonderful agent: I knew you were the person I needed on my side long before you were even an agent, and I wasn't wrong. Thank you for loving my messy kids and championing us through the pandemic and beyond. I can't wait to go farther and higher with you. And thank you, Bob DiForio, for growing such an awesome agency and always being there with your expertise!

Equally equal, Liesa Abrams: I don't really have the words to tell you how thankful I am that your meeting was canceled that day in early March 2021. You have truly given me and Callie a loving home in Labyrinth Road, and it is my greatest honor to be part of this imprint. Thank you for elevating this story about Queer Kids and their battles, and saying "more, please."

To the whole team at Labyrinth Road and Random House that had a part in growing these pages from my computer to a book in the hands of readers: Thank you not just for making my dream a reality but for doing it with all the love and care I never let myself believe I would find. I never for a moment felt like my wings were being clipped; rather, you have enabled Callie and their friends to fly. Thank you, Kate Sheridan, for bringing Callie, Willow, and El to life exactly how I imagined them!

Thank you to Carrie DiRisio, Stephanie Allen, and Sarah Matulis for raising these kids from the first disaster draft and lovingly poking them all the way to publication. Your feedback and joy made the pandemic bearable. I can't wait to share shelves with you all!

To Cat Bakewell: I don't even have the words. Thank you for being my best friend, for making me a better human, and for walking this road with me. To Sarah Schultz, my

NaNo buddy and my sprint partner from the earliest days. To Princess Maria Overlady of the Universe Tureaud, thank you for your wisdom and for always lending an ear when I need it most. To Shannon Dybvig, who taught me the power of Stabby Queers—one day I'll get to read your words! To D. S. Rae, Sabrina Kleckner, Natalie Crown, J. J. Clapton, Caro Crisostomo, and Tommy Childress: Your talent and kindness inspire me every day. To Jamie Pacton, who took me under her wing and paved the way for a new generation of knights, thank you for your guidance.

To Simone Holland, my first reader and my dearest friend: Nearly twenty years and a whole ocean between us, but it feels like nothing has changed since you were reading fic on my bed. Thank you for helping me grow as a human and a writer. Your kids are so lucky to have you!

To Alder VanOtterloo, Em Dickson, Moll Kasperek, Nicole Meleby, and Elle Grenier, the genderqueer family of my heart: You are changing the world with your stories, and it is my privilege to be in your orbit.

To the Forge, Megan Verhalen, Keira Nelson, Laura Chilibeck, Ruth Singer, Christian Doucette, Amber Clement, Colin Dory, Kelly Ohlert, Mandy Nygren Daellenbach, Megan, Mary Gibbs, Sarah Mughal, Michael Colianna, Melissa Tyndal, Michael Nelmark, and Leira Lewis: I can't believe how far we've come since those first Pitch Wars days! Thank you for all the feedback and enthusiasm, and for being the best D&D a jaded paladin could hope for. And shout-out to the Forglings, Addie Singer and Maya Moon, the authors of the future!

To the Cool Kids: Eliz Anderson, Chelsea Abdullah, Erin Fulmer, S. J. Wood, Gates Palissery, Jen, Gabe Moses, Charlotte Hayward, Sara Kapdia, Ryan, Emma Gula, Amanda Tong, Catriona Page, Amanda Pierce, Ash Nouveau, Monica Bea, Mel Grebing, Isa Arsén, S. J. Whitby, Kyla Zhao, Miranda, Eris Mullins, Kamilah Cole, Tyla Kunkle, and Neha Das: Thank you for being the most supportive community on the Bird Site. You are truly the Cool Kids!

To the Dragon Hatchlings: Alexandra Overy, Tiffany Elmer, Tara Gilbert, and Briston Brooks, thank you for taking me under your wings! And the Writing Barn Level-Up Group: Kayla Cobbe, Brook Findley, Becky Mahoney, Dev Jannerson, Christie Anderson, Kiara, Katja, Laura Weymouth, and Lauren Spieler, for pulling me through the query process and being the writing family of my heart.

To my sub siblings: Leta Patton, Mary Averling, Shannon Ives, Lynn Jung, Joanne Machin, Kim Bea, Jackie Khalilieh, Gabi Burton, Brittany Evans, Gloria Huang, Susan Wallach, Jacy Sellera, Erin Madison, Lisa Matlin, Sarah Van Goethem, Melissa Bowers, Rachel Greenlaw, Trisha Kelly, Megan Lynch, S. J. Pounds, Lorelai Savaryn, Lillie Vale, and Mary Roach, for making the publishing road a little less scary.

To Deke Moulton, C. J. Listro, Alexandra Lazar, Ronnie Riley, Sierra Kemme, Hanley Brady, H. E. Edgmon, J. J. Clapton,

Amanda Woody, C. K. Malone, Laurie Lascos, M. J. Beasi, Jess Creaden, Emily Luedloff, Lucy Mason, Lynn Schmidt, Lou Willington, A. J. Sass, Peter Lopez, and everyone else in the Writing Twitter Family. This community has been the best school/club/workplace an author could hope for, all the way from drafting to querying, sub and beyond.

Thank you to the English Literature and Creature Writing faculty at Aberystwyth University, especially Katherine Stansfield and Tasha Alden. And thank you to Anwen Hayward, Beth Hayward, and Rhian Stevens for the best three years on the beach and drinking too much tea! Thank you to my English teachers throughout the years, who both encouraged and suffered the sheafs of angsty stories I shoved in their faces. Special shout-out to Miss Windsor, Miss Graham, Miss Pritchard, and Miss Carvill for being the kind of teachers every kid deserves.

To my grandparents, who believed in me from the beginning: Linda, who has read every word I've ever written; Rodney, who taught me how to fall into books; John, who introduced me to the magic of the moors; and Anne, who gifted me a wealth of stories. To Paul, Simon, Ruth, Caroline, David, Kit, Rory, Jessica, and James, thank you for always supporting me. I hope this makes you all proud.

To my American family, the Wingroves: Vanndelle, Ken, Anthony, Maria, Eric, Iris, Jennifer, Rob, Megan, Ella, Bella, Tori Brody, Sebastian, Santi, and Sienna, thank you for welcoming me and giving me a home in all the best ways.

And thank you to the Millmans—Amanda, Britney, and Courtney—for being the best found family and adopting us!

Thank you to all my work families for your support and indulgence, especially Mary-Anne, Debbie, Kevin, Andy, B-Lo, Amanda, Sam, Tristan, Emily, Katie, Max, Elise, Grace, Janet, Gina, Kelly, Lisa, Christy, Sam, Devon, Melissa, Nick, Makayla, and Alyssa. To my Starbucks regulars: Dee, Rose, Darren, Gabby, John, and Liz, thank you for always being excited for me. To my KinderCare kids, you inspire me every day and I am blessed to watch you grow.

Thank you to Josie Southam, Ilya Pitta-Bird, and Bal Jacques, and everyone else who let me hit them with wooden swords in the name of fun when we were kids!

Thank you to everyone who ever told me this was worth doing, on my fics, at school, in NaNoWriMo, and beyond. I can't believe this is my real-life grown-up job!

And, finally, thank you to everyone who picks up this book for giving me and Callie your time.

I can't wait to continue this adventure with you. See you in Book Two!

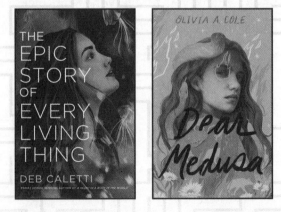